EGYPT GREEN

Other Books by **Christopher Hyde**

THE WAVE
THE ICARUS SEAL
STYX
THE TENTH CRUSADE
MAXWELL'S TRAIN
WHISPERLAND
LOCKSLEY (as Nicholas Chase)
JERICHO FALLS
CRESTWOOD HEIGHTS

CHRISTOPHER HYDE

EGYPT GREEN

SIMON & SCHUSTER

LONDON • SYDNEY • NEW YORK • TOKYO • TORONTO

First published in Great Britain by
Simon & Schuster Ltd in 1989

Simon & Schuster Ltd
West Garden Place
Kendal Street
London W2 2AQ

Simon & Schuster of Australia Pty Ltd
Sydney

British Library Cataloguing-in-Publication Data available
ISBN 0–671–69943–1

Typeset by Selectmove Ltd in Times 11/12.
Printed and bound in Great Britain by
Richard Clay Ltd, Bungay, Suffolk

To Jim & Cheryl
Who did make it to Vancouver after all.

PROLOGUE

Leukertal, Switzerland, 18 August 1968

The hunting lodge was huge and, to most people who saw it, an architectural monstrosity. Constructed of massive logs chinked with plaster, with soaring turrets, high-beamed halls and immense fireplaces, it seemed out of place perched high above the Leukertal Valley in the Graubunden Alps. Called Ravenshal, the lodge had been built in the early thirties by a high-ranking official of Hitler's Reichsbank. It had been intended as a summer getaway and winter pied-à-terre for ski vacations.

By 1943 the official, an intelligent man, was able to see the handwriting on the wall and decided that a final trip to Ravenshal was in order for himself and his family. With several large and extremely heavy suitcases, they made for the border crossing at Auberstaufen. Nothing more was ever heard from the official or his family, and the suitcases disappeared as well. What is known is that they never reached Ravenshal.

Without an owner, the lodge eventually reverted to the Swiss government in lieu of taxes and was kept as an out-of-the-way spot for large corporations and other organisations who occasionally required that their meetings be held in secret.

In June of 1968 the Swiss Department of Lands and Forest Resources received a request from a group calling itself the Phoenix Foundation, asking if Ravenshal was available to rent from August 17th to the 21st. The Foundation was assured that Ravenshal was indeed available and could be reserved on receipt of a deposit of US$5,000. The total amount for the four days would be $10,000, which would include staff and meals.

The Foundation wrote back that neither staff nor food would be required. The letter included a certified cheque drawn on the main office of the Bank National de Paris for the full $10,000.

Keys to the lodge as well as any necessary documentation were to be sent to the Hotel Le Richemond in care of M. le Docteur Chetwynd. The keys were to be at the front desk of the hotel no later than noon on 16 August.

On that day, by train, air and automobile, representatives of the United Kingdom, France, West Germany, the USSR, the USA and the People's Republic of China began arriving at the Richemond and several of the other prestigious hotels along the Lac Leman waterfront. They were an odd combination of military men, scientists, epidemiologists and mathematicians, but they had all come to Switzerland for the same purpose.

At nine a.m. on the 17th half a dozen unmarked mini-vans made the rounds of the hotels, picking up passengers for the trip south to Ravenshal. The mini-vans, in convoy, arrived at the small farming village of Leukertal shortly after one in the afternoon, then proceeded a dozen miles beyond the town to a narrow winding road leading up into the mountains. None of the passengers were surprised to see a parked automobile at the turn off, nor were they surprised when the vans were stopped and each passenger's documents checked.

This happened three more times before they reached the lodge. The security groups monitoring their passage were as odd a combination as the mini-van occupants, being made up of CIA (American), KGB (Soviet), MI6 (British), SDECE (French), BfV (West German) and ILD (Chinese). Each security group consisted of six people, one from each organisation. The perimeter and interior of the lodge were also under guard.

The passengers were assigned rooms in the lodge and given the rest of the day to relax and go over their notes for the opening meeting the following morning. They ate separately and there was very little social interaction between the delegates to the meeting except for those people who already knew each other.

The opening meeting began at 10.00 a.m. on the 18th and was held in the central dining area around a gigantic oak table easily capable of seating the thirty-five delegates. The meeting was chaired by Dr Nelson Baines Chetwynd. He was a tall, slightly stooped man, dark-haired and blue eyed, with a faintly military air that made him look as though he would have been more comfortable in a uniform than in the slightly rumpled blue suit he was now wearing. He looked briefly down at the inch-thick stack of paper in front of him, cleared his throat, and began.

'Good morning, gentlemen,' he said loudly, smiling without humour. 'At long last we are all together. I've been in correspondence with each of you over the past two or three years, and even met some of you face to face, but this is the first time we've all been together in the same place.' There were a few sighs from around the table at Chetwynd's stating of the obvious, but he ignored them.

'As you are aware, we have all independently come to the same conclusion. For the sake of simplicity I will use my own statistics initially, but we will pool resources later in the meeting. At this point I think we should be dealing in general terms rather than specific.' He gazed around the table, looking for objections, but there were none. He cleared his throat and went on.

'As a group we are undoubtedly a cross-section of the world's best minds; this isn't ego, this is simply a statement of fact. We represent the best our various nations have to offer in the disciplines of science, in medicine and in the art and practice of war. We have all recognised a basic fact of life: we have reached a point where no amount of education and no enactment of law will lower the population of the world in any material way. Quite the contrary – the world's population is increasing at a geometric rather than mathematical rate, and this is already having a marked effect on the economies of our home nations. Our leaders, by their very sponsorship of this meeting, have agreed that this state of affairs cannot, indeed, must not go on.'

Chetwynd paused and looked beyond the far end of the table. 'Lights, please.' Three security men pulled heavy drapes over the picture windows that faced the valley. The overhead chandeliers were dimmed and a bright beam of light appeared from the projection booth hidden behind the far wall, illuminating the screen slightly above the doctor's head. The first slide appeared. The doctor stepped to one side and picked up a pointer.

'This is a graph of projected population increase worldwide for the next twenty years. As you can see, it shows an increase from today's 3.693 billion to 5.246 billion by 1988. The projection for the year 2000 is in excess of 6 billion. This illustrates the basic conundrum we are faced with; although the population in

ix

terms of growth rate is declining, the total numbers of people are growing at 74 million per year. By 1990 that number will have increased to 84 million per year.' Chetwynd paused again. 'Next slide, please.

'This slide shows a projection of those people who will have fallen short of World Health Organisation malnutrition standards. That is to say, people who will be living at below starvation food intake. This year it was some 600 million people. By 1990 it will have grown to in excess of 800 million people. As you can see, almost half of those live on the Indian subcontinent, a quarter in sub-Sahara Africa and the remaining 200 million are spread between Central America, North Africa and the Middle East. Next slide.'

For almost an hour Chetwynd showed slides demonstrating statistical problems facing the world at large. In almost every case it was clear that the divergence between the major developed nations and the Third World was increasing at a devastating rate. At the same time, the supposedly 'developing' countries were borrowing money in larger and larger amounts, and as Chetwynd pointed out, it was unlikely that those loans would ever be paid back; statistically there was a very good chance that the borrowing nations would eventually be forced to default.

After the last slide, Chetwynd sat down and the lights went on again. The security men pulled back the drapes, revealing a dull, overcast sky. Acting as stewards, another group of security men appeared, bearing trays of tea and coffee. The delegates were served and then the stewards withdrew. Chetwynd sipped his coffee, staring over the rim of his cup at the serious-faced men around the table, wondering which of them would speak first. It turned out to be Vladimir Kulagrin, the Nobel laureate agronomist from the Soviet Union. Short, bull-necked and with a grizzled crew cut, he looked more like a wrestler than a scientist.

'You tell a very sad story, doctor,' the Russian said, his voice reflecting half a century of Balkan tobacco and vodka. 'In my country you would have been a poet able to bring tears to the people's eyes. Unfortunately what you have said is true. Our own information supports this. Within twenty-five years, thirty at most, we will begin to see the first real famines in the world – Africa, India, South America.'

x

'And plague will follow hard on famine's heels,' Roger Dussault said. Another Nobel winner, the Frenchman's expertise was epidemiology. Thin, balding and wearing thick spectacles, Dussault looked much more the scientist than Kulagrin. 'In France we have done a number of studies of this nature. As population increases, the per capita state of medical servicing declines. Increasing urban populations also support the establishment of plague sinks – environments where such things as cholera and bubonic plague will thrive. Calcutta, Cairo, even Mexico City are prime targets for this type of occurrence.

'With increasing air travel from one country to another, such diseases become increasingly difficult to contain. We can look forward to a number of new diseases as well, I'm afraid. Crossovers from the animal world to homo sapiens as man encroaches on their habitats.'

Han Tsu Lin spoke next. Presently deputy director of the Chinese Ministry for State Security, the elderly, white-haired man was known around the world as a master of military strategy and tactics. He was one of two military men invited to the Ravenshal meeting.

'I'm afraid we could go on like this for some time,' he said, his voice deceptively quiet. 'It is usually the way when one has a problem without a solution close at hand. We are all aware that the world is in a sorry state, and that, one way or another, the most powerful nations of the world must join forces, no matter what our personal or political differences.' Lin smiled, nodding briefly at Kulagrin on the far side of the table. The Russian smiled back and returned the nod. 'It is like the Chinese story of the forest fire. In the face of flames which will consume all creatures, great and small, the eagle must help the bear, the bear must help the lion, the lion must help the dragon . . . for if we stop to argue our differences, the flames will devour us in the midst of our debates.'

'Your point is well taken,' murmured Sir James Stephenson, the pinstriped British economics professor. 'But parables aren't answers. What we need is something to put out the forest fire.'

'At the present birth rate we're talking about 10,000 little flames being added to the conflagration every hour of the day,' Chetwynd said, a sour note in his voice.

The Chinese general nodded. 'The American brings us back to practical terms as always. As Dr Chetwynd suggests, the fire is made up of people. Logically we must assume that to quench the fire which threatens us we must . . .' He let the sentence dangle. There was a long silence.

'We must do away with the people,' Kulagrin said finally.

'Ugly thought,' Stephenson murmured. 'Unavoidable, though.'

'What we are speaking of then . . . is genocide?' Dussault queried slowly.

'I'm afraid that *is* the word.' Chetwynd nodded. 'The question is how?'

ONE

THE house at the end of South Morning Sun Avenue wasn't the grandest in Mill Valley, but the big Tudor split-level perched on the hill had an air of solidity and understated class that Lorne Hagen liked. It stood on a sloping lot set back from its neighbours, and from the patio and the pool at the back there was a great view all the way down to Richardson Bay.

Lorne kept a huge Tasco Junior Astronomer permanently mounted on the back deck, supposedly to use for star-gazing, but everyone knew he used the big telescope to spy on the HagenSpa store in the Strawberry Village shopping centre on the far side of the bay.

Lorne rarely made it into the store before eleven, but more than one junior employee had been docked pay because the boss had seen him arrive at the store a little late. In Lorne's book the laid-back philosophy of life in Mill Valley was the prerogative of management and he hadn't built HagenSpa into the multi-million-dollar chain it was by letting his people slack off.

Lorne's wife Jan had a sneaking suspicion that her husband occasionally used the telescope to do a little long-distance peeping at the pools lower down on Lowell Avenue and California Way, but she never mentioned it. If some reasonably innocent voyeurism kept him happy, that was just fine with her, and anyway, their son Toby really *did* like astronomy.

The average thirteen-and-a-half-year-old doesn't spend a lot of time looking through telescopes and if he does he is usually regarded as a nerd or geek by his peers. Toby Hagen hadn't been relegated to either group, perhaps because his astronomical interests were offset by the fact that he could use a skateboard the way Nijinsky could dance and even at a

1

relatively short five foot four he was the best quarterback the Tam High School junior team had ever drafted.

Instead of attending a regular elementary school Toby had been enrolled at the Mill Valley Center for Exceptional Children, which made him almost a full year younger than most of his classmates, but even that didn't seem to matter. It was accepted as a fact of life at Mount Tam High; Toby Hagen was one of those one-in-a-million kids who aced class and did well in sports, and he was as popular with the auto-mechanic types bussed in from Sausalito as he was with the kids whose moms were members of the Mill Valley Art Commission or the Bread and Roses Club.

On the morning of his last day in Mill Valley Toby woke early. The hours between dawn and leaving for school were precious to him and he usually set his alarm for six. If he kept to the kitchen and his own lower-level territory he could get away with two peaceful hours and then slip out before his parents came down for breakfast. Sometimes he used the time to read or finish his homework, but usually he spent it tinkering with whatever invention or project he had on the go.

And there was always something; the state of his room was proof of that. The short wall at the end of the room was covered in cork, the cork in turn covered with a layered mass of mechanical drawings, sketches and doodles. Under the cork tiles the wall-to-wall workbench was littered with half-finished electrical boards, the remains of several different motors, the gear hub from a trotting-horse sulky that he had transformed into an electric winder for the huge tetrahedron kite that hung from the ceiling, blobs of solder, lengths of wire and a one-twelfth-scale working model of a single-seat aeroplane he intended to build when he was old enough to get his licence.

The long wall opposite his bed was a madcap assortment of crammed bookcases, a cantilevered drawing board, a desk loaded with foot-high stacks of paper and a long table he had built himself to hold his Macintosh computer, hard disk, printer and the graphics plotter he used to generate the working drawings for his ideas. There were more drawings pinned up over the computer, and what wall space remained was covered with half a dozen old movie posters, a pegboard for his tools and a large, framed photograph of himself receiving first prize in the junior category at last year's national science fair.

The floor fared no better than the walls. The corner closest to the en suite bathroom held his football uniform and pads; half a dozen cardboard boxes piled at the foot of his bed held his collection of *Science, Discover, Omni* and *Scientific American* magazines; and a trail of socks, sneakers, jockey shorts and jeans stretched from the bed to the closet beside the bathroom, completing the slightly eccentric adolescent decor.

Ramona, the once-a-week cleaning lady, refused to have anything to do with it, so the chaos was constant, changing marginally only when he ran completely out of clothes or needed something that was embedded in a lower stratum of mess. For Toby it was a nearly perfect working environment and it had the added benefit of being completely at odds with the earth tones, *ficus Benjamina* trees in pots and all the rest of the hip, California chic bullshit upstairs.

Eyes open and instantly awake he pulled himself up against his pillows, slapped at the alarm clock on his bedside table and did a quick visual inventory of his domain. Everything was in order. He had a constant, nagging paranoia that one of these days his mother would get totally fed up and clean the room into sterility while he slept, but so far it hadn't happened.

Yawning, he kicked back the dark-grey duvet and stretched, painfully aware of the early-morning erection poking up the front of his shorts. He swung his legs over the edge of the bed, yawned again and stood up, letting a long, luxurious stretch ripple through his body. Picking his way through the litter and muttering under his breath, he crossed the floor and went through the doorway into the bathroom.

He stood over the toilet, letting his tongue test the level of fuzz on his teeth as he hooked his rigid, ceiling-pointed organ over the waistband of his jockeys. A prize-winning woodie, but it made taking a leak absolute hell in the morning. With a conscious effort he demanded action from his sphincters and after a few seconds mind won out over matter. Peeing done with he flushed, then tucked himself back into his shorts. Now the day could really start.

'Priapism,' he said, moving from the toilet to the sink and looking at himself critically in the mirror. The word had a nice medicinal feel to it. He checked himself out in the mirror, idly considering the nightmare of what it would be like to spend an entire day at school with a boner.

3

Standing up to answer a question in Miss Seebernaller's bio class as Andrea Hughes and her junior-miss friends giggled and stared at your crotch. Lusting leers from Fernie the Faggot in English. Nurse McCone's surgical-gloves fingers applying an ice pack to the end of your dick as she asked you how often you abused yourself. He grinned at his reflection. That thought alone would be enough to cure you of the problem.

The face smiling back at him wasn't half bad even if he said so himself. Slightly olive complexion that made him look permanently tanned, hair thick and so black it had an almost blue tint. Large, intelligent brown eyes, reasonable mouth full of teeth that were naturally straight, and a good strong nose.

He lifted a finger and rubbed the slight bump just below the bridge, souvenir of a break during last year's football season. Barely twelve and a broken nose during try-outs. His football career had almost ended right there. His mother went into a fit of hysterics and it had taken him the better part of a week to convince her that the game wasn't an act of suicide. She still muttered occasional threats about plastic surgery, but as far as he was concerned the slightly misshapen hooter gave his face character, offsetting features that he considered to verge on cuteness. His cheeks still had the last remnants of the baby fat maiden aunts like to tweak and he couldn't wait until the soft, dark down that ran along his jawline turned into real beard.

He checked his pits briefly, wrinkling his nose, and dug around in the medicine cabinet for deodorant. He washed, brushed, peed again and then left the bathroom, browsing through the wardrobe on his floor. It was still only late May and Mill Valley was always a little cooler than the Bay, so he picked out a reasonably clean T-shirt with a Carl Sagan decal, covered that with a comfortably worn, red-checked lumberman's shirt left unbuttoned, and finished off with fresh jockeys, faded jeans and a pair of Reeboks that looked as though they had run a half-dozen Boston marathons. If it got too hot later in the day he could dump the shirt in his locker and make do with the T alone.

Dressed, he went back towards the bathroom, turning right this time and climbing the stairs up to the kitchen. The big, airy room on the upper level was as trendy as the jet-black Merkur Scorpio parked in the driveway. The countertops were real granite, the cupboards were *faux* marble and the floor was quarry tile. The fridge was digital, the range was Thermador and most of the other appliances were either Braun or Kitchen-Aid.

Behind the Italian-hinged cabinetry was a huge assortment of health foods and the refrigerator was stocked with everything from home-made yogurt to fresh-pasta salad, but Toby opted for a couple of Eggo waffles, eaten dry, standing over the salad sink set into the food-preparation island in the middle of the room. He ran some water to flush away the crumbs, put the rest of the waffles back into the freezer, then went back down to the lower level and out into the garage.

He reached around the doorsill in the darkness and tapped the automatic door opener. There was a low, mechanical whine and the big door at the far end of the garage began to lift, letting in a grey-blue slab of early-morning light. Toby's mother drove a second-hand Rabbit as a political statement against the lavish, leather-upholstered Merkur and it took up less than a third of the wide, two-car garage. The rest of the space had long ago been taken over by Toby and his work on SHUPOV-3.

The garage door slid up onto the overhead rails and Toby walked around the Rabbit, letting his eyes caress the sleek silver-and-blue creation gleaming in the watery light. A full year of his life and every penny he had been able to scrape together were invested in SHUPOV and he was justifiably proud of his work.

SHUPOV stood for streamlined human-powered vehicle, and this third version was Toby's best hope for the competition being held later in the summer by the International Human Powered Vehicle Association at UCLA. He was already a member of the association, its youngest ever in fact, and SHUPOV-3 was entered in four of the six categories offered: Speed, Innovative Technology, Design and Practical Applications.

At first glance the vehicle looked like an outsize bowling pin on wheels. The front end was bulbous, the design based on the high-tech bow nodules on modern ocean vessels. Hidden under the teardrop-shaped nose were two ultra-thin carbon-polymer spokeless wheels and the tiny, Swiss-watch-styled universal gear Toby used for steering. Behind the flared nose the body shell narrowed over a featherweight aluminum chassis, then broadened, repeating the teardrop shape and covering the power mechanism, webbed seat and the high single drive wheel at the back.

Because of the high back wheel there was no way to install a rear-view mirror, and an outside mirror would have spoiled the aerodynamics. To overcome the problem Toby had raped the innards of a pair of Fisher-Price kiddie video cameras, mounting the view screen on the cockpit dashboard. He had also installed a small cooling fan, an Avocet liquid-crystal speedometer and odometer and a removable cassette deck/radio, all of them powered by four square feet of foil-thin solar cells bonded to the shell over the rear wheel. On overcast days the instruments could be connected to a six-volt motorcyle battery.

Stripped down into its racing configuration SHUPOV-3 weighed only twenty-three pounds – two pounds more than the most expensive racing bicycle on the market and ten pounds less than the average touring bike. On a flat track over a measured distance the vehicle was capable of reaching speeds hovering around the 60-mph mark. Over the past few weeks Toby had been making some modifications and hoped he could get it going even faster for the UCLA competitions.

He flipped the canopy open, and with one hand on the steering yoke he guided the machine out into the driveway. Once clear of the garage he eased himself down into the webbed seat harness and pulled the canopy down over his head.

He did a quick systems check, turned on the cooling fan, slipped a tape into the cassette deck and put on the little Walkman stereo headphones. He poked his feet into the piston grips, and with the strains of a Mozart concerto in his ears he moved off, heading downhill along South Morning Sun Avenue, speeding silently and alone past the sleeping houses.

By the time he reached Pine Hill Road he was completely at one with the machine, legs pumping steadily, hands gripping the yoke firmly as he sailed the SHUPOV into a sweeping turn, then straightened. His eyes were fixed on the road ahead and he was completely unaware of the dark-blue Econoline van as it pulled away from the kerb and took up a position a hundred yards behind him.

TWO

DEVON Talbot sat in the bottom row of bleacher seats in front of the Tam High track, reading an old issue of *Cinefantastique* and smoking a Schimmelpenninck little cigar. There was a bulging Adidas bag on the bench to her right and on her left, within easy reach, was her most prized possession a twenty-five-year-old Cinema Products 16-mm motion-picture camera with a 400-foot magazine. The camera was loaded with high-speed colour negative film and the gym bag contained a fully loaded spare mag, two lenses, and a backup Nicad battery.

Devon was fourteen, almost exactly a year older than Toby and two inches taller. She was solidly built, broad-shouldered and blonde, her hair cut shaggy and on the short side, her eyes a bright, flashing blue. She had the healthy, boyish good looks usually associated with athletes, which was odd since she abhorred physical exercise and lived on a steady diet of junk food.

Today she was wearing her standard working uniform: jeans, low-heeled cowboy boots, a well-worn blue Oxford-cloth man's shirt and a bleached-out Topsider sailing hat. A beat-up Spectra light meter on a shoelace hung from her neck and she was wearing a black nylon Lucasfilm windbreaker to keep off the morning chill.

Bored by reading about what everyone else was doing in the movie business while she rotted away at Tam High, Devon tossed the magazine down on the seat beside her and took a deep drag of the Schimmelpenninck. She pursed her lips into an O and tried to blow a series of smoke rings but the light breeze carried the smoke away in little ragged plumes. She glanced down towards the far end of the track and then checked her

7

watch. Still no sign of Toby. The idiot was late again and she was losing the soft early-morning light. Not that the Whizzer would care.

She grinned, thinking about the nickname. Every now and again she'd use the name in public, just to watch him squirm. Everyone else thought it was short for Wizard and had something to do with Toby being such a brain, but they both knew better.

They had known each other for as long as either one could remember and the nickname went away, way back. He had been five, she six, and at her insistence they had done a little bit of anatomical investigation in the scrubby brush behind her parents' place on Lowell Avenue.

She had an older sister but no brother, and it had been her first sight of a male organ. He had referred to it proudly as his whizzer and she still thought it was the funniest thing she had ever heard. She teased him with the name now, but it was more than just a way to get his goat. It was a private, special thing, a coded message between two people who didn't quite fit in.

Devon took a last drag on the little cigar, pinched out the end and slipped the butt into the pocket of her jacket for later. Devon Talbot and Toby Hagen. He had been there for her when her parents divorced and when her mother split for that stupid commune in Colorado. She had been there for Toby when Shazam, his cat, died, and when he broke his nose. Thick and thin, better or worse. More than a friendship, less than a marriage. She took a deep breath and let it out slowly.

Things had been changing for them over the past year or so, and they both knew why. Sex was rearing its ugly head. Her boobs were more than a joke now, and she couldn't borrow his jeans because her hips were flaring too much. They hadn't done anything about it or even talked about it much, but both of them knew they were at some kind of balance point and sooner or later the teeter-totter was going to teet or tot in one direction or the other. He was too popular and too good-looking formally to 'go out' with her, she knew that, but at the same time he hadn't found anyone else he liked better, male or female, or who understood him as well. Certainly not Andrea Hughes with her bruised little lips and her sweetie-pie friends. One step down from airheads. Vacuum brains maybe.

It was all pretty confusing, and sad too, which was probably why she had decided to get it all down on film. Her father, a production designer for Lucasfilm, had seen an ad for the CP-16 in the San Rafael headquarters of the film company and asked her if she wanted it for her birthday the year before. He didn't have to ask twice, and right from the first moment she held it in her hands she knew what her initial project was going to be: a documentary about her friendship with Toby. There wasn't the slightest doubt in her mind that Toby was going to be famous one of these days, and the documentary, done over a long period of time, would be a perfect promo to get her into the Berkeley film school.

So far she had almost seven hours of film, rough-cutting as she went along, using the facilities of the Mount Tam High School Film Club, which to her mind was the only really good reason for going there. Most of the other members were heavily into making rock videos of their friends' stupid bands, so she usually had the old-fashioned Moviola and the splicers to herself. A lot of the footage dealt with Toby and his work on SHUPOV, but there was some straight, head-on interview stuff as well as her talking to the camera.

Recently she had been gathering material for a 'day in the life' sequence and yesterday she had even managed to get her dad to work as a driver, following Toby from his house down to the school while she operated the camera. To finish that sequence off she wanted a shot of Toby in the SHUPOV driving onto the track, which was why she was waiting for him now.

It didn't look as if she was going to get the shot. In another five minutes the light would be too different to match yesterday's footage and the reversal shot from the bleachers would look contrived.

'Shit,' she muttered under her breath. She dug into her pocket, pulled out the Schimmelpenninck butt and lit it, using the clunky old Zippo Toby had given her. Clenching the wet-ended remains of the little cigar in her teeth, she squinted at the stainless-steel object, wondering if she shouldn't go for a shot of it. The lighter was another icon of their friendship.

Late last summer they had gone on a hike in Cascade Park, just north of town, cutting off the main trail to an ice-cold little pond they had discovered earlier in the season. They had gone swimming, respectably suited, but later, drying off on the rocks, side by side in the warm sun, some kind of current had passed between them and right then and there Devon would have happily offered up her virginity and his.

And not a damn thing had happened. Toby never made a move, even though she *knew* he wanted it as much as she did. After a while the feeling dried out along with their hair, leaving her with nothing but an odd, hollow feeling in the pit of her stomach. On the way back Toby found the old Zippo on the path and gave it to her, almost as though it was some kind of apology for not seizing the moment back at the pond.

'Shit,' she said again, sighing this time. Sometimes it was a total drag knowing what you wanted and not being able to get it, or wanting to be something and having to wait. It was almost enough to make her envy Andrea and her trendoid Esprit and Calvin Klein cronies. The most complex thought *they* ever had was trying to figure out what flavour to order at the Swensens on Blithedale and sex was letting your boyfriend feel you up in the back five rows at the Sequoia.

She looked at her watch and frowned. The light really *had* gone now. She stood up, stuffed the magazine into her sports bag and flicked away the last half inch of the Schimmelpenninck. Hefting the bag and the CP-16, she climbed down from the bleachers and headed for the gate. To hell with him. Just for that she was going to call her film *The Whizzer of Mill Valley* and when *American Cinematographer* came to do a feature story on it she'd tell them *exactly* what the title meant.

By the time he reached Median Way Toby knew he was in trouble. He had spotted the van at the foot of Pine Hill Road and watched anxiously on the view screen as it closed in, hanging no more than a few feet off the rear of the SHUPOV. It was crazy, but it looked as though the idiot was trying to ram him. He pumped harder, watching as the speedometer ticked up to forty, then forty-five, then fifty. Even with the fan full in his face he was sweating, hands clenched on the yoke as he kept the vehicle on course.

As he hit the intersection at Peralta he jerked the yoke to the right, going into a screaming turn that almost made him lose control. He leaned left, trying to counteract the tipping of the fragile machine, and managed to keep going, rocketing along Stanford and into the maze of switchback streets that cut down

10

the side of the hill, all of them named after universities. He took the S-curves along Princeton, praying for a cop, and watching as the van edged even closer, pulling up alongside him as they careened down the empty street.

He braked, the rear end slewing as he dropped into the Y intersection at Harvard and Yale. Without thinking he swung the yoke around again, choosing Yale. If he could get onto Stadium Avenue and then Almonte Boulevard he stood a chance of reaching the school. He took an eyeblink look in the view screen and yelled.

'Bastard! Leave me alone!' He went hard right onto Stadium Avenue and the van made its move. Suddenly accelerating into the turn it came up on the right, sideswiping the SHUPOV almost gently, barely nudging the back end. It was enough. The axle struts buckled under the impact and the drive wheel seized up, sending the vehicle into a long skid and tearing the yoke out of Toby's hands. Spinning around, the SHUPOV smacked hard into the trunk of a cedar, the entire rear portion of the shell splitting open. Toby lurched, restrained by the safety belt he always wore, but his head cracked into the side of the canopy as the machine finally came to a stop.

Marshall Bricklin, temporary director-in-residence at the Mountain Play Association and the only eyewitness to the attack, later estimated that the events following the crash couldn't have taken more than fifteen or twenty seconds.

Bricklin, nude, doing his morning exercises on the deck of his friend's house, watched open-mouthed as the van pulled up beside the shattered wreckage of the SHUPOV. The rear doors of the van crashed open and two men appeared, dressed in coveralls and wearing what Bricklin described as Aztec Gold ski masks pulled down over their faces.

One man pulled Toby out of the wreck while the second grasped the boy's wrist, 'stabbing at him with something shiny', presumably a hypodermic. The two men then carried Toby to the van, dumped him inside and followed, slamming the rear doors behind them. The van took off down Stadium Avenue and disappeared.

It took Bricklin almost three minutes to rouse his friend and another two minutes were lost as the two men discussed what should be done. By that time the van had already reached the 101 interchange at Manzanita Center and the Golden Gate

11

Freeway. Bricklin's friend eventually called the police, who arrived on the scene eight minutes later.

An advisory on the van was broadcast after Bricklin and his friend were questioned, by which time the van, travelling well below the speed limit, had crossed the Golden Gate Bridge and vanished among the streets of San Francisco.

The van was discovered fours hours later, parked on Clawiter Road at the foot of the San Mateo Bridge, not too far from Hayward Municipal Airport. Unceremoniously but very professionally, Toby Hagen, the Whizzer of Mill Valley, had been kidnapped.

THREE

MICHAEL Mark Robbins sat on his patio, sipping his third cup of coffee, reading the morning edition of the *Chronicle* and enjoying his waterfront view across the glittering reaches of San Francisco Bay.

Sort of.

The patio was part of the cracked slab of concrete his single-wide trailer home perched on, the coffee was instant, the waterfront was a breakwater built by the Alameda Department of Sanitation, and the only view he had was obscured by a low-lying bank of fog that stretched from Hunter's Point to the Embarcadero.

Then there was his name. Michael Mark Robbins was as phoney as the stories under his byline in the *Mirror* and the *National Enquirer*. He had been born Mischa Morris Rubinek and anyone who knew him called him Mickey or the Rube. His mother and father, rest their souls, had always called him Mouse.

The coffee mug on the plastic table beside his lawn chair began to rattle, and he groaned, knowing what was coming next. A few seconds later the air above Unit 16 of Brown's trailer camp filled with thunder as the 10.30 Continental shuttle for Los Angeles went into its noise-abatement routine directly over his head. Part of his regularly scheduled apocalypse.

He had once tried to log the number of flights over his trailer in a single day but he gave up when he reached sixty-three before it was time for lunch. Brown's trailer park was five miles north of Metro Oakland International, San Francisco International was less than fifteen miles away across the Bay and he was six miles south of the Alameda naval air station. According to the most recent statistics there were at least

13

fifty near collisions in the Bay area every year and deep in his heart Mickey Rubinek knew that inevitably there was going to be a full-scale head-on disaster between a couple of jumbos 800 feet over the trailer park and he'd wind up being crushed in his bed by the white-hot remains of a DC-10 tail section or, worse, incinerated by the flaming luggage of a bunch of Chinese millionaires sneaking their money out of Hong Kong.

The 737 shuttle stood on one wing as it screamed into a routine U-turn and then howled south along the Bay, heading for LA. The vibrating coffee cup settled down and Mickey picked up the paper again, scanning the personals, looking for some action.

He raked at his thick mat of black, curly hair with the fingers of one hand, frowning as he felt the niggling beginnings of a headache. He had less than five hundred in the bank, his insurance on the Mustang was coming up and Berwick, the freelancers' editor at the *Mirror*, had turned down his last two stories. It was time to do some fast hustling.

> **Andrea – from Bob, I want to
> tell you what I discovered while
> you were away. I love you.**

> **Janice: I apologise for my insincerity.
> Can we talk – please?
> TNP**

> **Recently widowed Caucasian male
> seeks single white female for
> companionship and dinner.**

'Shit,' he muttered. Barely half a column, and most of them were thanks to St Jude. There was only one item that was even mildly interesting.

> **VERA Bellamy, daughter of the late Amy
> Bellamy. Please contact your father Richard.**

The accompanying telephone number had a 604 area code. Mickey closed his eyes and let the wheels turn. What the hell was 604? It took a moment but then he had it. British Columbia. Canada. Probably Vancouver. The two-line ad told the tale. Daughter estranged from parents. Probably quite a while ago.

14

Mother dies and father is trying to get in touch. An inheritance, or just a funeral.

He took a felt pen out of his shirt pocket and circled the ad. If the father was placing an ad in the personal column it meant the daughter wasn't listed in the phone book, but a street directory would probably have her, and if not, he had a contact or two at Immigration and Naturalization. Two phone calls and a trip to the library would probably do it. He nodded to himself. He'd run her down, then call the old man in Vancouver. If he was in good form he could spin it out to a couple of days and maybe as much as a grand.

He sighed and folded the paper back into some kind of order before he dropped it onto the table beside him. On the other hand there was a pretty good chance that he'd find the daughter, call the old man and get jerked for the fee. Canada was a long way off and once the father had the information, why should he pay off? Mickey shook his head, wincing as a brace of F-14s from the naval air station whipsawed overhead, leaving multiple trails of vapour and bruised eardrums. He dug a cigarette out of the crumpled pack of Winstons on the table, lit up and leaned back in the lawn chair. Half a column and only one possible. It sure as hell wasn't like the old days.

At the age of eighteen, Mischa Rubinek had set out for the west, leaving his home port of Newark, New Jersey, standby student rate on American Airlines. Somewhere over Kansas he decided to change his first name to Mike and by the time he found his duffel bag at the airport in San Francisco he had decided to grow his hair and ditch the yarmulke his mother had carefully packed for him. After all, it was 1967, and the good-little-Jewish-boy image wasn't going to get him far with the girls in the school of journalism at Berkeley. Riding the bus across the bridge to Oakland he decided to grow a beard as well.

By the spring of 1968 he was failing every course, working as a reporter for the *Berkeley Barb*, and bore a vague and not particularly attractive resemblance to Leon Trotsky, but it didn't seem to matter. In 1968 almost anyone could get laid, especially if they had a bit of extra money for dope. By then everyone was calling him Mickey.

That summer removed the last tattered vestiges of Mischa Rubinek's relatively conservative past. It was the gathering of

15

the tribes, the Summer of Love, and they were giving guided bus tours of the Haight–Ashbury district. Mickey loved every minute of it, collecting venereal diseases the way he used to collect stamps, and writing occasional bits for the *Barb* and the fledgling *Rolling Stone* magazine.

He also discovered that he could make a fair bit of money finding other people's kids. Because he didn't dress too outrageously and could still put on the good-little-Jewish-boy routine, he managed to develop a few contacts with the cops. From time to time he fingered runaways for them, especially the really young ones.

Twice, and unsolicited, he received gifts of money from grateful parents and it didn't take him long to figure out that he was on to a good thing. It was easy enough to access the missing-persons files and by midsummer he was doing land-office business, tracing half a dozen kids a week. He branched out, using the personal columns, placing his own ads in out-of-town newspapers and following up leads in the San Francisco papers as well. In September he dropped out of school and devoted most of his time to tracking down runaways and keeping up his reporter cover by doing 'colour' pieces on the scene. To the straights he was an expert on hippies, and to the hippies he was a barely tolerated fink.

Of course, it was too good to last. By November the runaways were down to a trickle, and half the parents he talked to were perfectly content never to see their kids again. The Haight turned into a parody of itself and the word Vietnam was taking on a new meaning. Being near-sighted and too short kept him from being drafted, but even so, the joy of hippie life was fading. Mickey Rubinek had his bad points, but stupidity wasn't one of them. Long before most people he saw the handwriting on the wall; there wasn't going to be a revolution, nobody was about to legalise marijuana and he was pretty sure Richard Nixon was going to become president.

Then his parents died. Saul and Becky Rubinek always went to visit Becky's family in Detroit over Hanukah and they had the misfortune to book Christmas Eve tickets home on Allegheny Airlines flight 736. The plane, a twin-engined Convair, crashed into a Pennsylvania mountainside during a blizzard. After everything was settled Mickey wound up with a little over $10,000.

He went a little crazy after that and blew almost half of the money on a powder-blue 1966 Mustang convertible loaded with every conceivable option. Six months later he was in Vietnam covering the war for *Rolling Stone* and a year after that he was running for his life after getting involved in a dope-smuggling operation. Mexico seemed like a good place to wait out the heat.

Somehow he wound up married. To pay for her drug habit he came up with the Michael Robbins name and started working as a stringer for three or four US papers. Once again he found himself implicated in a drug-smuggling situation and this time it was the Mexicans who were on his ass, as well as some very nasty people who were in the illegal-immigrant business.

Hair cut short and wearing a business suit, he took himself and the Mustang across the border, returning to his Mickey Rubinek persona in the process. With almost no money and even less nerve, he made his way back to San Francisco, bought the trailer in Alameda and went back to finding strays. By that time he had blown whatever credibility he had ever had with the working press, so he started writing for the tabloids, pounding out 'Woman Raped by Bear Gives Birth to Grizzly Twins' stories on a second-hand IBM. And he was still doing it, hating every minute of it and waiting for the break that never seemed to come.

His social life was almost nonexistent, consisting of irregular trips to the editorial offices of the papers he wrote for and visits to the library. The closest thing he had to a friend was George, the guy who ran the coin laundry at the entrance to the trailer park; his only hobby was maintaining the enormous news-clipping file he kept in his trailer.

He flipped away the butt of his cigarette and reached down for another, the folded newspaper catching his eye. He had turned it to the front of the Metro section and a familiar name jumped out at him. The story ran under a straightforward headline:

MILL VALLEY KIDNAPPING
Ilagenspa Heir Abducted on Way to School

Mickey read through the story quickly, his interest quickening as he realised that the Lorne Hagen referred to in the story was the same one he had known briefly at Berkeley. Lorne had been

17

an ad salesman for the *Barb*, always coming up with ideas on how to make money out of the whole hip phenomenon.

According to the story, Hagen's son Toby had been kidnapped on his way to school and so far there hadn't been any request for ransom or any contact at all with his abductors. Mickey made a little snorting sound under his breath and poked his glasses back up on his nose. If there had been a note the story wouldn't have been running in the paper at all because good old Lorne would have been paying off the bad guys and keeping his mouth shut.

Mickey frowned, a distant bell ringing in the back of his head. A JAL 747 lumbered into the sky on the other side of the Bay and began blundering in his direction, but he ignored it, sitting blank-faced on the lawn chair as bits and pieces began to solidify in his mind.

If Mickey Rubinek had any real talent beyond the ability to write absurd stories for the kind of people who got their news off the magazine rack at the check-out counter, it was his memory. It wasn't so much photographic as cumulative, like a gigantic filing cabinet. He had gone out of his way to foster the skill, collecting shards of information like an archaeologist at a dig. Sometimes it took a while, but if he had any kind of clue he could usually come up with the information. Lorne Hagen's name was one of those clues.

Within five minutes he had put enough together to realise he had something potentially hot. He stood up, muttering to himself, and headed for his trailer. Half an hour later, seated at the card table in the kitchen section, he stared down at the collection of notes and clippings he had culled from the rats' nest of filing cabinets and cardboard boxes crammed into the trailer. He could feel the blood zipping through his veins as though he had just dropped an old-fashioned hit of Owsley blotter acid. This wasn't just hot, it was incendiary. Sitting there he felt something else too – fear – and he didn't like the feeling at all.

He lit another cigarette and pulled at his lip, looking down at the clippings again. He drummed his fingers on the table, trying to talk himself out of it. Then he thought about the car insurance and his bank account, the balance tipping. Wisdom told him to forget it and see what he could squeeze out of the father in British Columbia. Easy and safe. Greed told him to go for it.

18

'Aw, shit,' he whispered softly. He scooped the files up off the table, crammed them into the camera bag he used as a briefcase and dug into his pockets, looking for the keys to the Mustang. Mickey knew that given a choice between wisdom and greed, wisdom didn't stand a chance. He also knew that greed always got him into trouble.

FOUR

T HE man in the neatly tailored grey suit entered the anonymous office building behind the Wells Fargo Bank on
Market Street and rode the elevator up to the twenty-sixth
floor. The building had been put up during the $50-million
revitalisation of the area during the mid-sixties, one of a score
of nearly identical office towers that sprouted between the
Ferry Building and Powell Street. The first dozen floors of this
particular building housed the corporate offices of an insurance
company, but the rest of the floors were a glass-and-steel rabbit
warren of lawyers, accountants and small business offices.

The man stopped in front of suite 2601 and put a key in the
lock. The small brass plate on the door discreetly announced
that it was the office of Phoenix Holdings Ltd. The man entered
the office, shutting the door behind him and locking it.

The large room was carpeted in dark-green industrial poly-
ester, white-walled and empty except for a desk, chair, computer terminal and telephone. The man went to the desk and
put his attaché case down beside the computer terminal. He
opened the briefcase; within was a thin file folder, a portable
modem and three small black boxes, one fitted with a digital
VU meter, the other two with vacuum-clamping suction cups.

The man removed the suction-cup boxes and took them over
to the floor-to-ceiling windows that covered the far wall. From
where he stood he could see the park at Union Square on Geary
and beyond into Chinatown. It wasn't likely that anyone would
be using a laser surveillance device from that direction but he
had his orders.

He suckered the devices onto the glass, one on either side of
the window, flipping the microswitches as he did so. He heard
a faint humming and nodded to himself, satisfied that they were

both working. The high-speed vibrations would be transferred to the glass, disrupting any coherent light transmission of his activities.

He returned to the desk, turned on the third box and quickly swept the room. Once again it was unlikely that anyone would be eavesdropping, but he was a very careful man. The VU showed nothing. The room was clean. The man sat down in front of the terminal, attached the modem and plugged the phone into the jack under the desk. He turned on the terminal, dialled the phone and waited. There was a brief pause followed by a series of electronic tones and then he was on line. He tapped an access code into the terminal and turned his attention to the file folder.

It contained a dozen eight-by-ten colour photographs, all of the same man, all candids. The man in the pictures appeared to be in his late thirties or early forties, slim, brown-haired and bearded. The hair was full and thick, but there was grey in the beard. In half the photographs he was in a garden setting, an ultramodern glass-and-wood house behind him. The rest were assorted portraits taken from a variety of angles. The grainy texture of shots taken with a telephoto lens was obvious. All of them showed the man wearing a black patch over his right eye.

The last one in the pile was different. It was a formal, full-length publicity photograph of the man wearing a white pressure suit and carrying a helmet under his arm. The chest riband on the left said NASA, the one on the right said WOLFE. The man was a good deal younger, his hair cut short and there was no eye patch.

The man in the grey suit closed the folder and placed it to the right of the terminal. He pulled his chair closer to the screen and began to read:

NAME: PETER JAMES WOLFE
BORN: JUNE 18,1948
EDUCATION: BSC STRUCTURAL ENGINEERING MIT 1969
   MSC STRUCTURAL ENGINEERING CAL TECH 1973
   PHD ARCHITECTURAL ENGINEERING MIT 1979
SERVICE: NAVAL FLYING SCHOOL/QUANTICO
   VIETNAM/ONE TOUR/SILVER STAR/PURPLE HEART
   HON DISCHARGE AUGUST 17, 1972

21

EMPLOYMENT: NASA, SEPTEMBER 1973
    SHUTTLE PROGRAM 1975
    SHUTTLE FLIGHT 1982
    EMPLOYMENT TERMINATED VOLUNTARILY MARCH 11, 1983,
    AFTER ACCIDENT BLINDING SUBJECT IN RIGHT EYE
PUBLICATIONS: VARIOUS PAPERS, MIT PRESS, UC PRESS,
    SCIENTIFIC JOURNALS [SEE ADDENDUM 'A']
    'SEEING THE LIGHT, SCIENCE, THE STATE AND THE 21ST
    CENTURY'
    WILLIAM MORROW 1985
    'AVALON II, PLAN FOR A COLONY IN OUTER SPACE'
    MIT PRESS 1987
PRESENT EMPLOYMENT: SELF/AUTHOR, CONSULTANT
PRESENT ADDRESS: 'RED LOTUS' SLIP 26, SAUSALITO YACHT
    HARBOUR, BRIDGEWAY AVENUE, SAUSALITO, CALIFORNIA
COMMENTS: SUBJECT DIVORCED 1983, LAURA DEVORE
    WOLFE. NO CHILDREN.
    LITTLE IN THE WAY OF SOCIAL LIFE. CONFIRMED
    HETEROSEXUAL. NO PARTICULAR LIAISON UNDERWAY AT
    THIS TIME. NO KNOWN POLITICAL AFFILIATIONS. NON-
    VIOLENT
ACTION: IMMEDIATE REMOVAL. TO JOIN LOT 9012

The man in the grey suit took a pen and memo pad out of the inside pocket of his jacket and jotted down the address of Wolfe's boat. Replacing the pad in his jacket he spent the next five minutes retrieving his equipment and then stood at the window, looking out over the city again.

He had been with the FBI for almost twenty-five years, almost all of that time spent in California as a 'doorknocker', running security checks on various people. He had been re-cruited by Phoenix within a year of becoming an agent and for a long time he was fairly sure that Phoenix was a proprietary company of the CIA. Now he wasn't sure.

In the past his work for them involved keeping tabs on three hundred or so individuals living and working in the state, but in the past six months he had done almost twenty 'scoops', all of them children between the ages of twelve and eighteen. The Hagen kid yesterday had been the latest. Now it was Wolfe, an adult. The man lit a cigarette and shook his head, worried.

Two scoops within twenty-four hours and one of them an ex-astronaut and very high profile.

The fact that he had no idea why he was doing it was irrelevant, but snagging Wolfe was going to bring down a lot of heat. He had had a reasonable amount of time on the others, and most of the kids he had picked up had been put down as runaways or simply logged among the hundreds of children and adults who vanished every year, never to be seen again. The Hagen operation had been rushed, though, and doing Wolfe would be worse. People were going to ask questions and that was the beginning of the path that led straight to a witness chair at a Congressional hearing.

He took a deep drag on his cigarette and blew a series of neat little smoke rings against the glass, watching as they spread and thinned against the window like ripples in a pond. He had built a nice life for himself here, complete with a house, wife, two kids and vacations in Acapulco every second year. He had no desire to risk any of that.

On the other hand he had been in too deep for too long and he really didn't have much choice. He glanced at his watch and frowned. They wanted Wolfe to go out with the Hagen kid and that gave him less than eight hours to wrap things up and get the ex-flyboy to the staging base. He was going to have to hurry.

23

FIVE

MICKEY Rubinek sat in the Donut Deli beside the Mill Valley fire station, chewing on a glazed cruller and staring out through the window facing Hamilton Drive. A silent onshore breeze was ruffling the leaves on the trees in Bay Front Park, and beyond, out in the narrow reach of Richardson Bay, he could see a few small sailboats.

Mickey ate a lot of his meals in places like the Donut Deli, but even here he was feeling a bit uncomfortable. Mill Valley was distinctly foreign turf, especially when he had spent the last couple of hours skulking around while he bugged the Hagen residence on South Morning Sun Drive. He shook his head. Christ, what a name for a street!

But the phone cables had been buried, which was a blessing. He wasn't good with heights, and climbing up and down telephone poles in the middle of the day required all sorts of fancy bullshit like spike boots and a uniform. As it was he had simply located the branch feeder box closest to the house, popped the simple lock and connected his lineman's handset to the first set of lines he had seen.

He dialled the Hagens' number and then, with a spit-wetted finger, he had run down the line of terminal posts until he felt the mild jolt of current that told him which set of wires ran back to the house. With the line identified he clipped on a small induction tap, plugged it into a voice-activated memo-corder and closed the feeder box. The cassette in the recorder would log up to two hours of calls. He'd go back later in the day, retrieve the bug and the recorder and see what his fishing expedition had caught.

He lit a cigarette and watched as a kid on a Honda scooter pulled up in front of the donut shop. Shaggy blonde hair, a little

24

butchy, but cute, and the jean jacket looked as if it had aged naturally, which was a point in her favour. She unstrapped a bulky looking knapsack from the back of the bike and headed into the store. Mickey allowed himself a small, nostalgic smile. Probably coming in for a jelly donut after school, full of piss and vinegar, horny as a pistol. The kind of girl he had always craved in high school and never once managed to get.

The kid pushed through the door, padded down the length of the restaurant and dropped the knapsack onto the bench seat of Mickey's booth. She sat down, sliding the pack out of the way with her hip, and stared at him. Mickey stared back.

'Can I do something for you?' he asked after a long, silent moment.

The kid reached across the table, shook a cigarette out of his package and lit it. She took a long drag and let the smoke snort out through her nostrils. 'For a start you can tell me who the hell you are and what you're doing here.'

'I'm eating a cruller and minding my own business,' Mickey said, startled. 'Maybe you should do the same.'

'How come you put a tap on Toby Hagen's telephone line?'

'What are you talking about?' Jesus! Who *was* this kid?

'This.' She rummaged around in the knapsack on the seat and hauled out his tap, alligator clips, induction coil, memo-corder and all. She put the jumble of electronic equipment on the table and slid it across him.

'I've never seen that stuff before in my life,' stuttered Mickey, horrified.

The girl shook her head, reached out and dragged the equipment back. She returned it to the knapsack and took another drag on her cigarette.

'Bullshit,' she said succinctly. 'You drive a mint, dark-blue, 1966 Mustang, plated King Alpha X-Ray two nine nine. You drove by Toby's place a couple of times about two hours ago and then you went to the telephone junction box at the corner of South Morning Sun Drive and Pine Hill Drive. You installed the tap and then drove over here. And you're not a cop neither.'

'You're crazy, kid. Why don't you go away and quit bothering me?'

'In case you hadn't noticed, the Mill Valley police station is two doors down from here, right next to the fire hall. Maybe I should go talk to Captain Harris. He's been out to Toby's, so I guess he's handling the kidnapping. He might be interested in what I have to tell him.'

'You're a fucking space cadet, kid. Why would he believe you?' Mickey was frightened, but he was also angry. The girl was screwing up everything.

'And you're an incompetent boob. He doesn't have to believe me. He can watch it all on TV.' She reached into the bag and pulled out a very professional-looking 8-mm Sony Camcorder.

'Jesus!' whispered Mickey. 'You got all that on tape?'

'Bet your ass,' she said blandly. 'So talk to me, or talk to the cops.'

'Why are you so interested?' His brain was whirling. He needed time to figure this out. Stall.

'I'm a friend of Toby's.'

'You always hang around his house making videotapes?'

'No. Usually it's film,' she answered, seriously. 'I've been putting together a documentary on Toby for the past year.'

'You're kidding.' Mickey blinked. Christ, when he was her age it had all been drugs, sex and rock and roll, maybe a bit of political activism if you were really a serious type. But making documentaries about your friends?

'No, I'm not kidding. And you still haven't told me who you are.'

'Mike Robbins,' he said, the lie coming easily. 'I'm a reporter.' No way he was going to give her his real name. 'What about you?'

'Devon Talbot.' She took another drag on the Camel. 'You're investigating the kidnapping?'

'You might say that.'

'Pretty weird putting a tap on their phone.'

'The cops aren't talking.' He shrugged. He had to figure out some way of getting the tape away from her.

'I know.' Devon nodded. 'They won't tell me anything. Toby's mom and dad won't tell me anything either.'

'The FBI been around?'

'Most of yesterday. I found a little place on the hill across from the house and I've been taping everything that's been going on.'

'And you followed me?'

'Uh-huh. You want the rest of that cruller?'

'Help yourself,' Mickey said, still thinking hard. He watched her wolf down the pastry.

'So, you've got a tape of me putting a bug on the Hagen phone line. What are we going to do about it?'

'I dunno. I'd like to know why you're so interested.'

'It's news.'

'Bullshit. Kids get kidnapped all the time. What makes this one so special?'

'It's a sideline. I track down lost children.'

'For money? Like the ones you see on the milk cartons and the last thing before sign-off on TV?'

'For money. Sometimes.'

'You think you're going to get money out of Toby's father?'

'Maybe.'

'I don't believe you.'

'Why not?' asked Mickey. He was beginning to wish he had never picked up the paper; the girl was like a pit-bull terrier.

'Doesn't add up. The police are already involved. And Toby's not a runaway. You've got something else going.'

'Really?'

'Uh-huh.'

'Like what?'

She shrugged. I'm not sure. But this whole thing stinks.'

'What makes you say that?'

'You've probably figured most of it.'

'Indulge me.' A pain in the ass, thought Mickey, but a bright one, and close to the Hagen kid.

'OK.' She leaned forwards, eyes bright. 'In the first place, why Toby?'

'His old man is rich.'

'By your standards maybe, but there's lot richer around here.'

'Maybe the guys who snatched him were stupid.'

'I went and talked to the gay guy who saw it happening,' Devon, said, shaking her head. 'He said it went like clockwork. If he'd sneezed he would have missed the whole thing. Very professional.'

'So?' Mickey asked, curious. 'What are you getting at?'

'They didn't kidnap him for money. It has to be something else.'

Mickey tried to keep his features expressionless. The girl was

27

batting a thousand; it was the same train of thought he had followed.

'Like what?' he asked. 'His old man sells Jacuzzis and saunas. It's not like he was a nuclear physicist.'

'I thought maybe you could tell me,' she answered, watching him carefully.

'I'm a reporter. It's a story. There's been a lot of kids disappearing recently and I'm just trying to see if I can find some sort of connection.'

'That's it?' Devon frowned. Suddenly, it seemed as though all the intensity he had seen before simply washed away. She looked like what she was, a frightened, confused young girl.

'That's it. Sorry to disappoint you.' He paused. 'Uh, about my stuff . . .'

'Take it.' She pulled the tap and the recorder out of her bag and handed it across the table.

'What about the videotape?' he asked.

'There isn't one. I used up my last cassette watching Toby's house. You came along afterwards. I just followed you. I figured you wouldn't talk to me unless I had something besides the tapping stuff so I made it up.'

'You're pretty sharp,' Mickey said.

'Yeah, sure,' she muttered unhappily. 'That's not going to help Toby much. I . . . I'm worried about him, you know?'

'I know,' said Mickey softly. The girl was ready to cry, tears filling her eyes. 'The cops will find him.'

'Right.' Devon picked up her bag and slid out of the booth. 'Just like all the kids on the milk cartons.'

'I'm sorry I couldn't help you.'

'I'm sorry too.' She managed a weak smile. 'I hope I didn't scare you too much with that equipment and the video story.'

'You scared me shitless, as a matter of fact.' He smiled. 'But there's no harm done.'

'No, I guess not.' She held out her hand and he shook it. The grip was warm and firm. 'Thanks anyway.' She gave him a little wave and then left, climbing back onto the motor scooter and buzzing off, heading north towards Hauke Park and the road back into town.

Mickey let out a long breath, watching her go. He hadn't lied about being scared. A tape of him placing the tap and the equipment itself was enough to get him into a whole lot of trouble. At least a year in the Marin County correctional facility.

He frowned, thinking about what the girl had said. She had run it down pretty easily, and if a kid on a scooter could do it, so could the feds. He wondered if they had put it together yet. Because there *was* a connection, just as the girl thought, even if he didn't understand it. Yet.

On the face of it, the kidnapping of Toby Hagen was an isolated event, but the fact that Mickey had gone to school with Lorne Hagen had pushed a button somewhere. That morning he had gone to his file of recent child disappearances and come up with a list of seven, all in the past two months. Three of them stood out. Frank Churchill in Barstow on the 16th, Max Fujiwara in Riverside on the 17th and Theo Gallager in Ramona on the 18th. All three had been simple runaways, at least according to his information. But that wasn't what counted. It was the names of the parents. Jake Churchill, Tom Fujiwara, Bill 'Chunks' Gallager, and now Lorne Hagen. Four names out of the past. His past. Four men who had all gone to Berkeley at the same time, more than twenty years ago. And all four with missing kids, each of them vanished within a few days of each other. It was a pattern all right, but what the hell did it mean?

SIX

PETER Wolfe sat at the galley table in the midships cabin of the *Red Lotus* and stared at the blinking cursor on the screen of his IBM. The 36-foot motorsailer was anchored close to the shallows off Drake's Bay and the former astronaut tried to ignore the gentle motion of the boat as it bobbed in the light onshore wind. It was hot outside and the water would be warm; just right for a bit of scuba diving or maybe even some spearfishing.

He leaned back against the padded, dark-blue banquette and sighed. Scuba diving and spearfishing were fine, but they weren't going to get him any closer to finishing his new book. On the other hand he wasn't accomplishing much by sitting there staring at a blank screen. Frowning, he slid out from behind the table and made his way aft, ducking his head as he climbed the four steps up to the open cockpit in the stern.

Stripping off his T-shirt he settled back against the cushioned tiller seat and closed his good eye, letting the heat of the early afternoon sun beat down on his already tanned face. This way he could almost convince himself that he was at least *thinking* about work.

He made a small snorting sound under his breath, Work. It was a funny word and, for him, it had meant a lot of different things over the years. Back in the sixties he would have said he worked as a student, on his way to being an engineer. A few years later, he would have said he worked as a fighter pilot, his future as an engineer depending entirely on his ability to avoid ground fire from the Charlies as he ran low-level strikes in from the Gulf of Tonkin. After that, and by a process he still couldn't quite understand, he was back being a student, getting a PhD at Cal Tech and training to be an astronaut at the same

30

time. Then he was belting around the earth on the Columbia's first operational flight along with Brand, Overmyer and the other two. What were their names? Christ! He couldn't have forgotten. No. Joe Allen and Bill Lenoir. They had been slated for the first Shuttle EVA, but Lenoir had a bout of space sickness and neither his nor Allen's suit worked anyway.

Student, fighter pilot, astronaut and then bam! A steel splinter in his home workshop sliced into his right eye and it all came tumbling down. NASA offered to keep him on, working for the space-station programme, but his heart wasn't in it any more. Quitting NASA brought a few other problems home to roost, including too much booze and a lot of extracurricular screwing around. His marriage to Laura, always a bit on the shaky side, came tumbling down along with everything else.

Somehow, between then and now, he had shaken the alcohol habit and put out two books, on the possibility of founding space colonies, the second one successful enough to get him on national best seller lists and university lecture circuits. The eye patch and the rakish beard he had grown at his publisher's suggestion did wonders for a sagging sex life, but if he didn't get to work on the next one he wasn't going to be able to keep up the payments on *Red Lotus* and he'd be in the shit can once again.

All that and he was barely forty years old. He pulled himself up against the cushions and opened his eye, squinting. His gold NASA Dunhill and the three-inch stub of his morning cigar were still resting on the gunwale where he had left them. He was relighting the butt when he heard the faint growl of a boat somewhere in the distance.

He sat up, a shading hand across his forehead. The boat was a good size, forty feet or more. One of those chunky trawler-style coasting yachts with a top-heavy deck house. A party boat. As he watched, it turned in towards shore, heading directly for him. The engine noise deepened and the bow wave flattened as she slowed. Fifty yards away the boat's engines went into full reverse and it turned away to port, coming to a dead stop about fifteen feet off his stern. Whoever was at the wheel knew his business; barely a ripple slapped against *Red Lotus*.

Peter stood up, one hand still shading his eye, the other holding onto the transom rail. Good helmsman or not, he still resented the breach of privacy. A figure appeared on the pilot

31

deck, loud-hailer in hand. The man was dressed oddly; who wore a grey business suit cruising up the coast?

'*Mr Wolfe? Mr Peter Wolfe?*'

'That's right!' answered Peter, cupping a hand around his mouth. 'Who wants to know?'

'*Just a moment, please.*' A second figure appeared. The new man was dressed more casually in a dark-blue pullover and a pair of jeans. He was carrying a rectangular plastic case about three feet long. Squinting against the harsh light splintering off the water, Peter watched as the second man raised the case to his shoulder. Only then did he realise that the thing in the man's arms was a weapon of some kind. Before he had a chance to react, the man fired. The weapon, a Hechler and Koch caseless rifle, fired a 4.7-mm cartridge capable of pinpoint accuracy at up to 750 yards. Before Peter's ears picked up the sound of the round being fired, the bullet had travelled the dead-flat trajectory to its target, catching him in the upper chest. He fell, crumpling down into the tiller well, the stogie in his mouth dropping onto the polished teak decking. Peter had a brief, final moment of consciousness, and absurdly he found himself wondering if the burning end of the cigar would scar the deck.

And then the world came to an end.

SEVEN

OR most people, waking up inside a brightly lit, white
plastic coffin would cause a certain amount of anxiety.
Despite his extraordinarily high level of intelligence, Toby
Hagen was no exception. He screamed. Or tried to. His mouth
and throat were cottonball dry and all he actually managed was
a weak gagging noise.

He lay rigidly for a moment, blinking, trying to get his eyes
to work properly. The upper surface of the coffin was no more
than six inches above his head, but the seamless plastic gave
him no focal point. He closed his eyes and gritted his teeth,
trying to ignore his pounding headache by sheer force of will.
Opening his eyes again he took several long breaths. The air
was cool, with a faintly artificial taste that lingered in his nostrils. Air-conditioned?

It took him a few seconds but it eventually sank in that he
could feel the air over his entire body. He was naked. Lifting
his chin he peered down the length of his torso. Buck-naked
with his skin coloured a rusty-red. Here and there he could see
electrodes suckered onto his chest and limbs and from the looks
of it he had been shaved.

He let his head sink back down and bit his lip. The headache
was receding quickly, but it was being replaced by a rising tide
of panic and fear. The last thing he remembered was the crash
of the bike. Now this. What kind of people kidnapped you,
then shaved your entire body, painted you red and buried you
in an air-conditioned blister-pack?

Money. The old man was worth a few million, but not all that
much of it was liquid. People with the smarts to come up with
this kind of high-tech tomb wouldn't waste it on someone who
couldn't cough up a very hefty ransom. OK, so rule out a big

ransom, where did that leave you? The coffin had a medical feel to it, and the electrodes had to be attached to some sort of monitoring devices. Kidnapped by a new breed of white slavers so they could cut him up and use his body for organ transplants? No way.

The only logical answer was a looney. Some freak with a lot of money and a psychopathic urge of some kind. It didn't matter much when you got right down to it, because if he didn't get out of this place pretty soon he was going to go right out of his mind. His breath was coming in short gasps now and he could actually feel his heart smashing against his ribs.

He tried to move his arms and winced. Not only electrodes, but intravenous lines in his wrists. He gritted his teeth and shifted his arms again. There was a brief, tugging pain as the IV lines pulled out and then he was free. He slid his hands up and began tearing off the leechlike electrode suckers. Squirming, he managed to roll partway on his side and got his hands up over his head. He searched blindly with his fingers, pushing hard, but all he felt was smooth plastic. He swallowed, desperately trying to still his panic. What if he really was buried underground?

He froze, his ears picking up a faint whining sound, like a motor starting up. The coffin lurched, throwing him to one side, and he automatically pushed out to brace himself. The motor sound deepened and the coffin began to move smoothly, tilting up on its end. Jaw tight and both hands fisted close to his chest, Toby waited for the movement to stop, wondering what was going to happen next.

When it reached a fully upright position the coffin stopped moving and the motor sound snapped off abruptly. Toby had a split-second vision of himself climbing out of the coffin and finding himself in the presence of a bunch of little green men from the planet Zeenon, and he began to laugh, his fear transmuted into nerve-taut hysteria. The motor noise started up again and he saw the entire casing of the coffin slide around and out of sight behind him. There was a second casing beyond it and a few seconds later it slid around in the opposite direction. There were no little green men.

In fact there was no one at all. Toby stepped out of the upright coffin and found himself in a room as bright and white as the capsule behind him. The ceiling was made out of some sort of translucent material, a bank of hidden lights

34

erasing any shadows. There was a small oval hatchway on the wall opposite, fitted with a large wheel. Beside the hatchway there was a plastic-covered sheet of printed paper fitted into a metal holder.

Swallowing hard, Toby padded across the room to the hatchway. The floor was warm against his bare feet and he was immediately aware that the room was warmer than the capsule. He stopped in front of the printed sheet.

WELCOME

1. IF YOU FEEL ANY NAUSEA, VERTIGO OR DIZZINESS, PLEASE REMAIN IN THE ROOM UNTIL THE FEELING PASSES.
2. WHEN READY, PLEASE TURN HATCHWHEEL IN A CLOCK-WISE DIRECTION UNTIL THE BUZZER SOUNDS.
3. WHEN BUZZER SOUNDS TURN HATCHWHEEL ONE HALF TURN COUNTER-CLOCKWISE AND PULL TOWARDS YOU.
4. PROCEED TO LEVEL ONE AND FOLLOW INSTRUCTIONS.
5. NOTE: INSTRUCTIONS ARE FOR YOUR OWN HEALTH AND SAFETY. FAILURE TO COMPLY WITH ANY WRITTEN INSTRUC-TIONS PRESENTED TO YOU WILL RESULT IN NON-ACTIVA-TION OF LEVEL HATCHWAYS.

THANK YOU.

'Welcome to what?' Toby murmured. He shrugged. It could have been worse; at least the instructions were in English. He spun the hatchwheel in the proper sequence and pushed it open, noting the puffing hiss of air as he did so. He stepped through the hatch and it closed automatically behind him. The difference in air pressure was a clue. The room behind him had been at a slightly lower pressure than this one; air would escape back to the first chamber, not forwards to the second. He nodded to himself. This was some kind of decontamination procedure. The shaved body hair fit too, and the red paint job was probably some kind of disinfectant like Mercurochrome.

The second room was smaller than the first, painted a pale, surgical-suit green. Once again there was a small hatchway in the far wall and a set of instructions. The only furniture was a moulded plastic bench on the left. Looking up Toby noted a set of recessed nozzles in the ceiling. He crossed the room to read the sheet.

LEVEL ONE
1. PRESS BUTTON BESIDE INSTRUCTION SHEET.
2. SIT ON BENCH.
3. WHEN FOGGING PROCEDURE BEGINS, BREATHE DEEPLY AND REGULARLY.
4. END OF FOGGING PROCEDURE WILL BE FOLLOWED BY A SINGLE TONE.
5. AT END OF PROCEDURE OPEN HATCH BY TURNING WHEEL CLOCKWISE TWO FULL ROTATIONS.
6. PROCEED TO LEVEL TWO.

There was a small red button beside the laminated sheet. He pressed it and went to the bench.

Almost immediately the nozzles a few feet over his head begin to emit a thick, foggy cloud of moisture. Within less than a minute the entire room was filled with the gas. It was cool on his skin, and breathing it in he detected a faint peppermint odour. He relaxed slightly, telling himself that it was just another part of the decontamination process.

By his calculations the procedure took about five minutes, and by the time it was done he was soaking wet. He went to the hatchway after the tone sounded and went on into the next chamber. The third room was even smaller than the second, not much bigger than the average bathroom, and pale blue. This time there was no hatchway in the far wall. The only thing in the room was a rectangular, moulded plastic tub about four feet high. To the right there was something that looked like a sanitary-pad dispenser fitted onto the wall, and beside it, the regulation instruction sheet.

LEVEL TWO
1. PULL LEVER ON MASK DISPENSER.
2. REMOVE MASK FROM PROTECTIVE POUCH.
3. PULL MASK OVER HEAD, ROLLING DOWN OVER FACE AND NECK.
4. PULL SEAL-STRIP TAB AT NECK.
5. BREATHE IN ONCE, SHARPLY, THROUGH MOUTH TO ENSURE SEAL.
6. PEEL OFF MOUTH-SEAL AT TAB.
7. NOTE: 3 THROUGH 6 SHOULD BE DONE QUICKLY TO PREVENT SUFFOCATION.

8. ENTER POOL AND FIND HAND GRIPS.
9. WHEN TONE SOUNDS IMMERSE HEAD, HOLDING HAND GRIPS FIRMLY.
10. KEEP HEAD DOWN!
11. WHEN TONE SOUNDS AGAIN, RELEASE HAND GRIPS AND SURFACE.

Jesus. It was like something out of *Alice in Wonderland*. The next thing you knew he'd find a bottle saying 'Drink Me'. Shaking his head he pulled the lever on the dispenser and pulled out a long plastic packet. Opening it he discovered something that looked like a ludicrously huge condom. It was puberty education all over again except there was no Mr Megley the hygiene teacher to roll this sucker over a banana and show you how AIDS could be prevented. Toby felt a hot tug in his guts and tears welled up in his eyes. Shit, even Mr Megley would be a welcome sight right now.

Feeling like an idiot he rolled the mask down over his head and neck. It clung to him like a second skin, and after pulling the neck tab and breathing in he could feel it sealing itself completely except for the eyes. He reached up quickly and pulled the tab in front of the mouth section of the mask and took in a deep gasping breath. Very weird. The stuff the mask was made of was sealed around his lips, but there was enough play to open his mouth and somehow he could breathe. What did they call them in chemistry? Semi-permeable membranes? He had a brief flash of an old movie he had seen with Devon, *The Andromeda Strain*. Something about a gas going from one side of a box to another. A filter.

Following instructions he climbed into the pool. The fluid came within six inches of the edge. It was dark, slightly viscous and warm. Definitely not water. He found the hand grips and held on, waiting for the tone. When it came he closed his eyes, ducked his head and kept it down. He felt a pulling sensation and held the grips tightly. A few seconds later he was jerked forwards, completely submerged. He was dimly aware of the tone sounding again and he bobbed to the surface, sputtering against the mask. A trace of the fluid seemed to have leaked through the filter and it smelled like a thousand dentists' offices. Gagging, he stood up and clawed at the mask, peeling it up over his head and opening his eyes.

37

Level Three was even smaller than Two, about the size of a big telephone booth, and bright yellow. Another hatchway, another set of instructions. Dripping, Toby climbed out of the tub.

LEVEL THREE
1. PRESS RED BUTTON BESIDE INSTRUCTION SHEET.
2. CLOSE EYES TIGHTLY.
3. PROCEDURE BEGINS TEN SECONDS AFTER BUTTON IS PRESSED.
4. KEEP EYES CLOSED UNTIL BUZZER SOUNDS.
5. AFTER BUZZER SOUNDS OPEN EYES AND OPEN HATCH.
6. DRESS.

Toby did as he was told. Even with his eyes closed he could see the intense light and he could feel blasts of hot air coming from all directions. When the buzzer sounded a second time he opened his eyes, completely dry. He opened the hatch, stepping over the sill into a tiny closet-sized area. The only thing in it was a plastic-wrapped package of clothing. He dressed, slipping into the bright-yellow, one-piece zippered jump suit. It was tight, with elastic at the wrists, neck and ankles. The footwear was part of the suit, like a little kid's pyjamas, and had soft, padded soles.

Instead of a hatchway there was a door with a press-bar square. Toby tapped the square and watched as the door slid back into a recess with a faint pneumatic hiss. Beyond it was a three-foot-deep vestibule and a second press-bar door. He stepped into the enclosure and the door behind him slid shut. He pressed the bar on the second door and stepped through the opening.

The second door swished shut behind him and he looked around. No more levels. By the looks of it, this was the end of the line, at least for now. The first thing that occurred to him was that he had somehow stepped into the living quarters of a submarine. The room, capsule, or whatever it was had walls that curved up into the ceiling and a single, narrow corridor leading away from the small foyerlike room he had stepped into.

Going down the passage he saw that there were sliding doors

on either side. The walls were gunmetal grey and the lights were fluorescent, hidden behind recessed panels in the ceiling. The floor was covered in a dark-grey industrial carpeting material.

The passage opened up at the far end into a kitchen lounge area. There was a counter on the left, and behind it Toby could see a few built-in appliances, some storage cupboards and a sink. To the right was a built-in couch, a modern chair bolted to the floor and a large-screen TV built into the wall. As Toby came into the room a tall, dark-haired man with a beard and a black eye patch rose from the couch. He was dressed in exactly the same kind of jump suit as Toby, right down to the booties.

'Company at last!' the man said with a grin. He extended a hand, but Toby backed off.

'Who are you?' he asked. 'And where the hell am I?'

'My name is Wolfe. Peter Wolfe. What about you?'

'You don't know?'

'Hey,' the man said, 'I'm as much in the dark as you are, kid. I don't work here, I'm just visiting.'

'Oh,' said Toby, still wary.

'You haven't told me your name.'

'Toby Hagen.' He paused. 'I was kidnapped. I think.'

'They took me off a boat on the coast. You wake up in one of those sleep chambers?'

'If that's what you call them,' Toby said. 'How long have you been here?'

'Three or four hours.' Wolfe shrugged. He dropped down onto the couch and gestured towards the chair. Toby sat down. 'From the headache I had when I woke up I'd guess I was out for quite a while before that. A day, maybe even more.'

'You have any idea where we are?' Toby asked.

'Not the slightest,' said Wolfe. 'But we're sitting in a NASA space-station module, or something very close to it.'

'How do you know that?' Toby asked, frowning. The guy was wearing the same kind of jump suit, but he could easily be a plant from whoever had snatched him in the first place.

'I used to work for them,' Wolfe answered. He gestured to the ceiling a few feet over his head. 'And I've been doing a little snooping.' Toby looked up. Directly above Wolfe a chunk of the ceiling tile had been peeled away roughly.

'I took a kitchen knife to it,' Wolfe explained. 'Stuck my head up there for peek. There's about two feet of honeycomb steel baffle. Like the slosh baffles on the Shuttle LOX tanks.'

'Pardon?'

'Sorry. Baffles in the liquid oxygen tanks they use on the Shuttle.'

'How do you know that?'

'I used to fly it.' Wolfe smiled. 'And anyway, half the baffles have North American Rockwell stamped on them.'

'I don't get it,' Toby said. 'What kind of place is this, and why kidnap either one of us?'

'Beats me,' said Wolfe. 'I'm a half-blind ex-astronaut with a couple of degrees in engineering. What about you?'

'I'm a kid.'

'Anything special about you?'

'I guess I'm pretty smart,' he admitted. 'That's what they tell me anyway. I'm a decent computer hacker too.'

'But no Einstein, right?' The ex-astronaut grinned again.

'No Einstein. Thomas Edison maybe, but no Einstein.'

'Modest, too.' Wolfe laughed.

'What about getting out of here?'

'Not much chance. The door you came in doesn't have any hardware on the inside. There's another door this end, but it's the same.'

'The floor?'

'I doubt it.' Wolfe shook his head. 'If this really is a NASA module or even close to it, then it's built as a unit. The baffles will be under the floor as well.'

'So what do we do?'

'Wait,' said Wolfe. 'And see what happens next.'

EIGHT

IT was early evening by the time Mickey Rubinek slid the
Mustang into its spot behind his trailer and he was beat. He
was also more excited than he had been in years, and on top of
that he was petrified that he was getting in too deep. Psychologi-
cally and physically he was being pulled in half a dozen different
directions and what he craved more than anything was a stiff
belt of Scotch and ten hours' sleep.

He knew perfectly well he wasn't going to get either. He
didn't have enough money to buy Scotch and he still had to
sort through all the documentation he had gathered during
the day. Three hours in the morning spent at the main branch
of the library on Civic Square and another six hours skulking
around the Berkeley campus in the afternoon. Wearily, he
climbed out of the car; if he wasn't careful he was going to
be mistaken for a real journalist. He hadn't done this much
legwork in years.

Opening the trunk he pulled out the seven bulging manila
envelopes containing the day's booty and shuffled around to
the front of the trailer. He stopped dead, staring, and let out
a groan. Beside the steps, sitting primly on its kickstand, was
Devon Talbot's motor scooter.

'Shit.' Just what he needed – some wet-behind-the-ears kid
following him around, whimpering for her boyfriend. Then he
frowned. Maybe not so wet behind the ears after all. She was a
long way from Mill Valley and he hadn't given the kid his real
name, so how had she found him?

Swearing under his breath he climbed the three steps and
slammed open his front door. She was there all right, curled
up neat as you please on the old wreck of a couch he kept at
the back of what passed for his living room. The trailer was

41

dark except for the blue light coming from his old black-and-white set.

'Hi,' she said brightly, looking up as he came through the door. 'I came by and you weren't here, but the door was open, so I let myself in.'

'Bullshit,' he grunted, dropping his stack of envelopes on the Formica-topped table. 'I always keep the door locked. Where'd you learn how to B&E?'

'Probably the same place you learned how to tap phones,' she shot back. He cocked an eyebrow and couldn't help admiring her. The kid had style.

'OK, so we're even. Now what are you doing sitting in my trailer, and more to the point, how'd you find out where I live?'

'The police aren't doing anything to find Toby. The FBI says there's no evidence to prove that he was taken across a state line, so they've backed off, and it's not in the SFPD jurisdiction. The Mill Valley Police Department isn't going to find him on its own.'

'So?'

'So I'm going to find him, or at least get some evidence to get the FBI interested again.'

'And what does that have to do with me?'

'You want to find him too. You didn't put that tap on for no reason. You've got something going.'

'How did you find out where I live?'

'How did I find out where Michael Rubinek lives, you mean?'

'Mickey.'

'Mickey then. It wasn't too hard. I reran the tape I took of you and did a freeze frame of your car. I took down the licence-plate number and pulled a few strings at the police department. Friends of my dad. They got your address from DMV. Simple.'

'Jesus.' Rubinek winced. What did you tell them you wanted the address for?'

'I told them my dad was interested in your car as a prop and that he wanted to get in touch with the owner.'

Mickey sat down and stared at her. Neat and simple, and perfectly reasonable. The kid was dangerous. 'OK. So you know my name, and you know where I live. Now what?'

'We look for Toby.'

'I don't think so.'

'Why not?'

'Because you're getting back on your scooter and going home.'

'No. I'm not going home.'

'Go somewhere else then,' said Mickey. 'I don't give a shit where.'

'I need your help.'

'You're not going to get it, sweetheart. Give it up, OK? I've had a rough day.'

'I've got my tape of you putting on the tap,' said Devon.

'Yesterday you said you didn't.'

'I lied.'

'Maybe you're lying now.'

'Uh-uh.' She dug into the breast pocket of her shirt and brought out a crumpled-looking Polaroid. She tossed the photograph across the trailer and it landed on the table in front of Mickey. He picked it up and looked at the image. Blurry, but good enough. Mickey Rubinek fiddling with the innards of a telephone switch box. Je-sus! The kid didn't miss a trick.

'OK, you got me. We know you're a bright kid. But you can't just take off and go looking for your boyfriend. What about your parents?'

'It's just my dad, and I left him a note.'

'A note.'

'Sure. I told him I was going to look for Toby and that he shouldn't worry.'

'And you figure he's just going to sit still and take that? He's probably already worried.'

'I doubt it. He left for a location shoot today. Morocco. Six weeks.'

'And he left you without a baby-sitter?'

'I was supposed to stay with my aunt. She lives in Sausalito.'

'So what about her? Don't you think she'll be worried?'

'Nope.' Devon grinned. 'She's a real-estate agent. I phoned her office at lunchtime and told the receptionist I was my dad's secretary. I left a message saying that my dad had decided to take me along on the shoot. He's done it before. I'm in the clear.'

'You're nuts.'

43

'No I'm not, Mr Rubinek. I told you. I'm worried and I'm frightened. I've got to do something or . . .' The tears began welling up in her eyes and Mickey winced.

'Shit, don't start that again.' He took a deep breath and let it out. Digging around in the pocket of his jacket he found a packet of cigarettes and lit one. 'What about money?' he asked after a few moments. 'Investigations cost money.' A bit of cash-up-front reality might cool her off.

'I've got it covered.' She pulled a wallet out of her back pocket and opened it, revealing a concertina of credit cards.

'You're going to forge your old man's signature?'

'No,' Devon answered blandly. 'You are.'

'And if I don't want to?'

'Then I turn my tape over to the police,' she answered. 'They don't have any suspects in Toby's kidnapping. You'd be right on top of their list.'

'Could be,' Mickey nodded. She was right, of course, and it would only get worse when they found out he had been at Berkeley with Hagen. The kid had him boxed. The best thing was to go along with her, at least for the time being. She *was* the kid's girlfriend, so maybe she could help.

'What have you found out?' she asked, looking pointedly at the stack of envelopes.

'A connection.' Mickey shrugged. 'A slim one.'

'A connection to what?'

'About two months ago there were three disappearances. Kids. One in Barstow, one in Riverside and one in Ramona. Three kids, three days, three different towns, all within a hundred miles of each other.'

'I still don't see what that has to do with Toby.'

'Their parents.' Mickey began emptying the envelopes onto the already littered table. 'All three fathers went to Berkeley at the same time as Toby Hagen's father. I know that because I knew his dad back then.'

'I don't see what you're getting so excited about.' Devon shrugged. 'The parents are all about the same age and they all live in the San Francisco area. It's not that much of a coincidence that they went to Berkeley around the same time.'

'No, but it was enough to get me interested.' Rubinek began sifting through the pile of fresh photocopies on the table until he found a folded piece of yellow scratch paper with his list

44

scrawled on it. One sheet of paper with a bunch of names, and it represented a whole day's work. And maybe a lot more.

'I went back to the library today and dug a little deeper. Instead of just checking disappearances and unsolved kidnappings in the Bay area I checked the national clipping files. They're about six inches thick and that's just for this year. I went back two months and got a list of 350 runaways, all of them important enough to hit the papers. They go from New Hampshire to Florida.'

'And?'

'I checked them against the people in the same graduating year as Toby Hagen's dad.'

'OK, OK. What did you find?'

'Ten names, fourteen if you include Hagen and the three in California. All of them snatched or runaways within the last sixty days or so, all of them unsolved, and all of them with either mother or father from the same graduating year at Berkeley.'

'That's it?' Devon frowned.

'It's way too many to be a coincidence,' said Mickey.

'OK, so it's weird.' Devon nodded. 'But what does it mean?'

'Nothing . . . yet.' He grinned. 'But it's a place to start.'

'What's next?'

'Back to Berkeley tomorrow. With this.' He pulled an IBM floppy disk out of the pile of papers.

'Which is?'

'I went into the alumni office and asked for a print-out of my file. This is the disk with the command-code list on it. The secretary had to go into the next room to get me an envelope for the print-out, so I hooked the disk and put it under my shirt.'

'I still don't get it,' said Devon. 'What does this have to do with Toby?'

'He's part of a pattern,' Mickey explained. 'We have to find a way of connecting the parents to each other. That should take us a step further. If we can figure out what the pattern means we might have a line on Toby, not to mention the other thirteen. If I can get onto a terminal at the university tomorrow I can use this disk to access the files for all the parents involved and that might give us the link. It's a hell of a story.'

'That's all you care about, isn't it?' Devon asked sourly. 'The story. You don't give a damn about Toby or those other kids.'

'Hey! In case you hadn't noticed, this trailer park is fresh out

45

of bleeding hearts and knights in shining armour. Try Big Sur or Monterey, maybe they've got a few left up there.' Mickey stubbed out his cigarette in the saucer he used for an ashtray. 'I'm in this for what I can get out of it, sweetcakes, you're just along for the ride, and you wouldn't be doing that if you didn't have my ass in a sling, so let's not have any moral-ethical shit, OK? Speaking of which, I'll give you a sleeping bag and you can bed down in the back of the car. If you have to use the toilet, there're public washrooms in the snack bar up by the entrance to the park.'

Devon stood up and flicked off the television. She eyed Mickey Rubinek coldly. 'I get the picture,' she said quietly. 'I have to play by your rules. But remember that tape.'

'I don't respond well to threats,' he lied. 'And they have a tendency to backfire on the people who make them.'

'Just remember,' she warned.

NINE

'THIS whole thing is starting to get on my nerves,' said Peter Wolfe. The lights had come on a few minutes before, indicating that they were beginning yet another sleep-wake cycle. So far there had been three.

'Me too,' Toby agreed. The bunk beds in the module were comfortable enough, but neither one had been getting much sleep. It was Toby's turn to cook and he stood at the microwave, waiting for the prepackaged meals to heat up. The bell rang and he opened the door, taking out the foil servers with a pot holder. He sat down across the small galley table from Wolfe and peeled back the cover.

'Surprise, surprise,' muttered the bearded man, unwrapping his own plate. 'Chicken à la king yet again. There was a time when I used to get danger pay for eating this crap.' He shook his head and then dug in with his fork.

'If you hate it so much, why do you eat it?' Toby asked, staring at the pale-yellow mound in front of him.

'In our situation food is a privilege. Our captors, whoever they may be, can revoke that privilege any time they want. If they do I want to be working on a full stomach.'

'Why would they take away our food?'

'Why did they kidnap us in the first place? And why are they bothering with this bullshit with the lights?'

'I don't get you.'

'It's an old-fashioned disorientation technique. They alter the length of your sleep-wake cycles so you won't know how much time has passed.'

'You think they're doing that?' Toby asked sceptically.

'Do you shave yet, kid?'

'Uh, yeah,' said Toby, feeling himself redden.

'How often?'

'Maybe a couple of times a week.'

'Feel your cheeks,' Wolfe said. 'We just finished our third sleep cycle. Supposedly that means three days and nights.' Toby followed the older man's lead and rubbed a hand over his jaw and cheek. There was only the barest hint of stubble.

'A day and a half, two at the most,' he said.

'There you go.' Wolfe forked up another mouthful.

'Who *are* these people?'

'Beats me. But they aren't your basic crazed Libyan extremist type. Too much money spent for that. Not the Russians either, the equipment is too good.'

'Take your best shot.'

'Uncle Sam, or an agency thereof,' said Wolfe. 'Not that I can figure out one good reason for it.'

'It's crazy,' Toby said. He dropped his fork onto the foil plate and watched it sink into the congealing mess of chicken and pseudo-cream sauce. Two days, five days, ten days, it didn't matter; the walls were closing in on him and he knew he would go crazy if something didn't happen, and soon.

'Bit of cabin fever?' asked Wolfe.

'I guess so.' Toby shrugged. 'Does it show?'

'Just a tad.' Wolfe smiled. 'I'm pretty good at picking up the symptoms. Just hang on, though, Toby. Whoever brought us here isn't going to leave us in this cosmic trailer camp for too much longer. There's method in their madness. You can bet on it.'

'I hope so.'

Almost on cue the television set behind them on the wall suddenly snapped into life, putting out a set of colour bars and a humming tone. Frowning, Toby looked over his shoulder at the screen. The hum lasted for less than half a minute and was replaced by a drifting, Muzak-style melody. A few seconds later the music was replaced by a flat, uninflected male voice.

'This is a recorded announcement. My name is George Revik and I am senior administrative director of this compound. When you have completed your meal, please go to the module door, which has now been opened. Follow the blue line on the floor to the main reception area. Thank you and welcome to Egypt Green.'

The voice clicked off and the music returned. A moment

later the sound went off completely and the colour bars faded to black.

'Cute,' said Wolfe, staring at the now blank screen. He glanced at Toby, gesturing at the plate in front of him. 'Finished?'

'Absolutely.' Toby pushed the plate away and stood up; Wolfe did the same.

'Let's go find Mr Revik,' Wolfe said.

Toby followed his older companion down the narrow, L-shaped corridor to the end of the living module. As Wolfe approached the doorway it slid back soundlessly. Beyond it, Toby could see a tubular corridor curving off into the distance. There were recessed light panels in the ceiling and a thick blue line on the floor. Wolfe paused in the doorway.

'What are we waiting for?' asked Toby, joining him. Wolfe reached out and ran his hand over the wall of the corridor.

'Plastic panels.' He squatted down and tapped the floor with the knuckles of one hand. It rang metallically. 'Steel floor. The corridor is a tube, the flooring's probably been laid over a whole bunch of service cables. Electrical, water, waste, that kind of thing.'

'So?'

'It's interesting,' said Wolfe, standing again. 'I saw something like this a few years back at the Ames Research Center. Boeing and some of the other big aerospace companies had been working up modules for a lunar colony.'

'You're trying to tell me we're on the moon?' said Toby, laughing.

'No. But it's interesting.'

'There's something else that's interesting. Mr Revik or whatever he calls himself said it was a recorded announcement, didn't he?'

'That's right.'

'If it was recorded, how come he knew we were eating?'

'I guess the walls have ears,' Wolfe said.

'Eyes too, maybe,' said Toby. 'Now what?'

'Do as we're told,' Wolfe answered, pointing. 'We follow the blue line.'

The corridor went on for several hundred feet, curving slightly to the right but with no perceptible incline or slope. Looking back, Toby saw that the module entrance had gone from view. A few moments later the corridor curved sharply left, then straightened. Fifty feet ahead it widened into a hublike reception area. A man in a dark-green jump suit sat behind a scarred wooden desk that was totally at odds with the high-tech surroundings. Toby noticed the man's shoulder flashes immediately. A circular patch in blue, stitched with two capital Ps back to back in gold. Beneath the patch on the right arm there were sergeant's chevrons in red. A plastic name bar on his chest said BERKOWITZ.

Behind the sergeant was an electrical status panel with a confusing array of blinking green and orange lights and on the desk in front of him there was a telephone and a computer terminal. Apart from that the reception area was a sterile circle of gleaming white plastic. To the left and right Toby could see two more circular corridors stretching off into the distance. Directly in front of the desk the blue line on the floor split. To the left it turned yellow, following the corridor floor, and to the right it was the same dark green as Berkowitz's uniform.

'Wolfe and Hagen?' asked the uniformed man, tapping at the computer keyboard. The voice was bored.

'Colonel Wolfe, sergeant.'

'Not here you're not,' Berkowitz said briskly, without looking up. 'Follow the green line to the elevator at the end of the corridor. It's set for Green Three so don't try and hit any of the other buttons 'cause they won't work. Report to Corporal Newton. Got that?'

'Fuck you,' Wolfe said, smiling pleasantly.

Berkowitz looked up and Toby shivered. The man's eyes were cold and completely emotionless. 'You don't go and I'll call someone to get you. A big nasty someone.' Berkowitz reached down and came up with a handgun the size of a small cannon, pointing it at Wolfe. 'Take one step towards me and I'll turn your face into an elephant's asshole. Got that?'

'Got it. Just checking,' said Wolfe, maintaining the smile. The gun in Berkowitz's hand stayed where it was. Wolfe turned and shook Toby's hand. 'I'm glad we met,' he said, ignoring Berkowitz and the gun. 'We'll see each other again.'

'I hope so,' said Toby.

Wolfe nodded, turned, and went down the green-lined corridor.

'Hagen,' said Berkowitz.

'Yes.'

'Yellow line. You'll come to a bulkhead with a big red circle on it and a palm button on the wall. The button opens the bulkhead. Ten feet on there's another bulkhead and another button. Second button won't work until the first bulkhead is closed behind you. Got that?'

'Sure.' Toby nodded, trying to keep the equal parts of fear and anger from showing on his face. The gun was still in Berkowitz's hand.

'Buzz off,' said the sergeant. He picked up the telephone. 'I'll let them know you're on the way. Someone'll meet you.'

'Wonderful,' said Toby. He headed off down the yellow passage.

TEN

TOBY found the bulkhead doors without difficulty and went through the airlock-style enclosure. Like everything else he had seen so far, the passages all seemed to be one way only.

The second door slid open and he found himself in a short, grey-painted passage, this one rectangular, like a normal hallway. In keeping with its shape, the corridor ended with a plain metal door, complete with a knob. He reached it, turned the knob and pushed it open.

The room on the other side of the door was the size of an aeroplane hangar, the arched, high ceiling criss-crossed with girders and strung with industrial fluorescents. The floor was rough concrete, dull grey and surface-cracked, except for a black plastic runway that circled the perimeter. A giant high-school gym, complete with an indoor track. Beyond the track the floor was littered with long tables, almost a perfect match for the ones at his school.

There were half a dozen kids doing callisthenics at the far end of the massive chamber and twice that many scattered among the tables, most of them reading. All of them were dressed identically in jump suits exactly like the one Berkowitz had been wearing, except these were bright yellow.

As Toby looked around he spotted a short, dark-haired kid wearing glasses cutting across the room and coming in his direction. Seeing Toby standing by the door the figure waved and kept on chugging forwards, zigzagging between the tables. No one else in the room seemed to be paying any attention.

The boy pulled up in front of him, panting. The glasses were half the size of his face, balanced on a too small nose above a prim accountant's mouth. At close range Toby could

52

see that the jump suit was food-stained and the edges of the two hip pockets were grimy. The kid had shoulder flashes but they were diamond-shaped, a yellow capital S on a red ground. Dead centre in the middle of his chest was a large red square.

'Hagen?' the boy asked.

'Right.'

'Ivan Lumby. Everyone calls me the Lump.'

'Toby.' He looked over the Lump's head. 'I don't suppose you can tell me what any of this is about.'

'Not much.' Lump shrugged, frowning, the mouth getting even smaller. He spoke rapidly. 'They called up and told me a newb was coming in and I should show you around. You're booked into Kennedy House, Corey Shire's hut. That's green Level Three. I'm in Lincoln myself, red Five.' He touched the square of fabric sewn onto the chest of his jump suit. 'They usually ask one of the firsts to round up the newbs, though. Makes it easier.'

'You lost me back at the first newb,' said Toby.

'A newb is a new boy. A first is a kid who was brought here early on. Corey's about the earliest. He figures almost eighty days. I'm about seventy days in myself.'

'You were kidnapped?'

'I guess that's what you'd call it. The last thing I remember was going in to the clinic for my allergy shot.'

'San Francisco?'

'Philly. Philadelphia,' answered Lump. 'Corey's from New York.'

'Jesus,' Toby whispered. 'How many kids are here?'

'I don't really know. No one does. Three, four hundred maybe.' Lump took Toby by the elbow and starting leading him across the cavernous room. 'We have meetings all the time to talk about things like that. We've done as much snooping as we can. Tony Deetz and his friends. They're in Kennedy too. Most of the hard cases are in Kennedy, as a matter of fact. You must have given them some trouble coming in.'

'What's Kennedy?' Toby asked.

'There are five houses,' Lump said. 'Lincoln on the red levels, Kennedy on green, Owens on blue, Jefferson on black and Bell on silver.'

'Like a private school?'

'I guess. That's what Corey thinks anyway, and he went to one.'

They reached the far side of the room and ducked through an oval hatchway set into the rough concrete wall. Beyond it was a short hexagonal corridor that took them to a large, low-ceilinged chamber which was fitted out like a cafeteria, complete with display cases, steam tables and infra-red warming bins. The room was empty. Half a dozen corridors led off the hub, each marked with a different-coloured stripe along the floor.

'The main mess. Each hut has a stooge and he collects the meals for his group.'

'Stooge?' Toby asked, following Lump to the green-lined passage.

'Deetz came up with it. He says that's what they called them in prisoner-of-war camps. He says *The Great Escape* is his favourite movie. He can even quote from it.' Lump grinned. 'Deetz is a bit crazy.'

Toby was trying to keep some kind of feel for direction, but after half a dozen abrupt zigs and zags along the green corridor he was completely lost. The place was a labyrinth, and the only thing he was sure of was its size. Whatever else it was, the Egypt Green complex was enormous.

The corridor ended and Toby stepped through another hatchway. He stood frozen, eyes wide at what he saw but could barely believe. The rough, concrete-walled chamber beyond the hatch was big, but its exact size was obscured by the complicated structure built within it. The only thing Toby could think of to match it was a giant, multi-levelled beehive.

The framework was made of metal tubing rising seventy or eighty feet above the hatchway, its topmost levels lost in a faint, humid mist. There were angled stairs and catwalks running in all directions, bundled cables and colour-coded pipes, and spaced at regular intervals there were dozens of white enamelled containers, each one the size of a tank-lorry trailer. The tanks were bolted into niches within the framework, interlinked by the cables and pipes that snaked through the tubular framework. Toby tried to count the tanks and gave up at fifty. He could hear a faint electrical hum, and a hissing sound from the pipes. The place smelled a little dank, like a musty basement.

'Pretty bizarre, huh?' Lump said almost proudly. 'Those things like big Contac C capsules are the huts, eight guys in each. Most of them are empty, though. Corey figures there's room for two or three thousand people here. Lincoln and the others are about the same, so the whole place could probably hold about fifteen thousand.' The short boy tugged at Toby's sleeve. 'Come on. I'll take you to Corey and the others.'

Lump led Toby up the set of stairs nearest to them, climbing to the third level. Stepping off the open metal stairway they went down a grated catwalk. Two kids appeared from a side catwalk and came towards them. They were both wearing yellow coveralls like Lump's, except theirs had a green patch on the chest. They looked to be fourteen or fifteen, one blond, the other oriental. They ignored Lump but nodded to Toby as they passed.

'Jake Skelly and Russell Ching,' said Lump, after the two boys had gone by. 'They're both prefects on green Five. That's two levels up.'

'What does a prefect do?' Toby asked.

'Not much.' Lump grinned. 'Fancy name for a hut leader, like Corey.'

They followed the narrow walkway almost to the end and then Lump stopped in front of the closed hatch to one of the tanklike huts. 'This is where we part company,' said Lump. 'I'd go in with you but Corey and I aren't on the best of terms.'

'Why?' Toby asked.

'I run errands for the adults. He figures I'm some kind of traitor, I guess. It's not my fault, I mean, like it's not like I asked for the job.' He shrugged and smiled. 'It's like my dad used to say, we all have our crosses to bear.'

'I guess,' Toby said.

'Pull on that big lever and the hatch will open,' Lump instructed. He held out his hand and Toby shook it briefly. Then Lump turned away and headed back along the catwalk to the stairs. Toby dragged open the hatch and stepped through the opening, pulling the door closed behind him.

He found himself in a small, low-ceilinged room, lit from above by a single fluorescent tube. To the left there was a counter and sink with cupboards above, and to the right there were storage lockers. The angled walls and the ceiling were made out of some kind of plastic sheeting and the floor was metal mesh like the catwalk outside. In the centre of the room was a rectangular plastic table and eight folding chairs. Four boys were seated at the table, playing cards.

'The newb,' said the boy seated facing the hatch. He was thirteen or fourteen, red-haired and freckle-faced. Like everyone else Toby had seen, he was wearing a yellow coverall. The boy at the end of the table stood up, smiling. He looked older than the others, perhaps sixteen, his dark hair almost shoulder-length and parted in the middle.

'Corey Shire,' he said.

'Toby Hagen.'

'The redhead is the Dick. Richard Dubrofsky. The one with the zits and the glasses is Eric Lowery, he's the hut stooge, and the skinny one over there is Jason Sanchez, the only person from the Dominican Republic who can't throw a baseball worth shit.'

'Not only is Corey the boss, he's also the hut asshole.' Dubrofsky grinned. 'He says he's from New York but he's never been to F. A. O. Schwartz, so I figure he's from Jersey.'

'Anything's better than Baltimore,' said Corey. He motioned to Toby. 'Come on, I'll show you around, fix you up with a bunk, and then we can talk.' He tossed his cards into the middle of the table and Toby followed him through an open hatchway into the rear of the hut.

The middle compartment was fitted with eight bunks set high on the wall, separated from the one next to it by a narrow bulkhead. The bulkhead was slotted with openings to form a ladder. Below each bunk there was a built-in bookcase and desk shelf that extruded out of the plastic wall surface, a circular light set flush into the bulkhead and a folding chair. To the right of the chair was a narrow locker. Like the front section, the bunk area was lit by fluorescents in the ceiling. At the far end of the room was another bulkhead, and behind it there was a row of urinals, half a dozen sinks, three toilet cubicles and an open shower stall. The whole place smelled faintly of disinfectant.

The brief tour over, Corey took Toby back to the bunk section. 'Take six,' he said. 'I'm right across the way in seven. The Dick likes his privacy, so he's up front in one. Snatch is in three.'

'Snatch?'

'Snatchez. Sanchez. All he talks about is girls. He figures

they have to have girls here somewhere and he's starting to get desperate.' Corey climbed halfway up the bulkhead ladder and pulled a cord Toby hadn't noticed. A wide-vaned venetian blind rattled down, following a pair of wire guides. 'Privacy screen. There's also a fan switch and a light up here.'

Corey dropped down to the floor again and ducked under the bunk. He pulled open the locker, reached in and tossed Toby a bulky, plastic-wrapped package. 'Coveralls, toilet kit and underwear. Three pairs of briefs, three T-shirts. Gets replaced at the end of the week, so hang on to the bag. Coveralls get washed every two weeks, not that they ever seem to get dirty. Change, and then come out front. Eric's just going out for a snack. You hungry?'

'No, not really. Thirsty, though.'

'They've got something that passes for milk, some kind of fake Coke and coffee.'

'Coffee,' said Toby. 'Thanks.'

'No sweat. See you in a minute.'

Corey left the bunk section and Toby stripped open the zip-lock garment bag. He peeled off the one-piece jump suit he had been wearing and changed into the yellow coverall. So far he had been able to keep it all together, but it was wearing thin now. He bit his lip hard as he jammed his legs into the canary-yellow uniform, willing the tears not to come. For all the private-school jargon, this place was like some kind of science-fiction jailhouse, and one without windows. But if it was a jail, then what was his crime?

Dressed again, he padded back to the front room. It was empty now except for Corey Shire. The young man was seated at the table smoking a cigarette. The other three had disappeared.

'Snatch is out looking for girls and I sent the Dick off with Eric. I thought we could use a few minutes alone.' Corey gestured towards a chair and Toby sat down.

'They let you smoke?' he asked.

'Deetz gets them off the monitors. He's got a real sweet tooth, so we trade him chocolate bars. Deetz is in hut 19.'

'That Lump kid mentioned him,' Toby said. 'What's a monitor?'

'Security guard,' Corey answered. 'From what we can tell, most of the surveillance is done by remote cameras and other

57

sensors, but they have a few warm bodies wandering around just to keep us in line. You see them every now and again.' The young man paused, looking at Toby carefully. 'What did you think of the Lump?'

'He was all right.' Toby shrugged. 'He told me you thought he was some kind of traitor.'

'Ferret,' said Corey. 'A snoop. He asks too many questions, sticks his nose in too many places. I'm pretty sure he's reporting back to the adults.'

'What's to report? A bunch of kids can't do much.'

'Maybe not,' said Corey. 'You have any thoughts on what's going on here?'

'No. Not yet,' Toby said, shaking his head. 'I just want to get out.'

'You and everybody else in here,' grunted Corey. 'You come in alone?'

'I was alone when I woke up, but there was a man named Wolfe in that waiting-room place.'

'An adult?' Corey asked, sitting forward.

'In his forties, maybe late thirties. He said he was an astronaut. Or he had been.'

'Did you talk much?'

'Some. Why?'

'I'm not sure. Everyone else I talked to came in alone, or with another kid.'

'Lump said you were one of the first.'

'Tony Deetz and I came in together. Eighty-seven days ago.'

'You have any idea why they took you, or what this place is?'

'Not really. I was in school. I got called into the office for a phone call. It was the hospital. They said my mom had been in an accident and that a cop car was coming for me. I got into the car and someone stuck a needle in my arm. That was that. With Tony it was pretty much the same except they told him it was his dad. We've been rotting here ever since. No threats, no questions, no explanations, nothing.'

'I wonder if it's random,' Toby said, frowning thoughtfully.

'The kidnappings?' Corey said. 'I haven't figured that out either. I've talked to maybe seventy-five kids so far, usually right when they come in. I can't make any connections at all. We come from all over, even the Dominican Republic like

Snatch. Two or three of the kids come from rich families, but most of us don't have parents who could raise any kind of ransom. There doesn't seem to be anything to tie it together. My mom is a doctor, my dad is a university professor. Tony's old man is a journalist. The Dick's parents are both microbiologists. Eric's mom and dad own a health-food store.'

'And my old man sells hot tubs,' Toby said. 'It doesn't make any sense.

'It must make sense to someone,' answered Corey. 'At last count there were about seven hundred kids here, all guys. Snatch is sure there's a whole girls' school thing going on as well, and it's not just because he's horny either. He saw some supplies being trucked towards one of the service elevators and he was sure he saw a couple of big boxes of Tampax. If there's an equal number of girls, that makes fourteen or fifteen hundred altogether, and there's room for a whole lot more.'

'Wolfe, the guy I came in with thinks it's some kind of government thing. But he couldn't figure it out either.'

'I think he's right. The scale is too big for it to be private, but since when was the US government in the business of stealing kids and making human ant colonies?'

'Wolfe worked for NASA. He said the place we were in was identical to a prototype space-station module they were working on.'

'That was one of the theories we came up with,' Corey told Toby. 'Maybe we're some kind of experiment to see how people would react in that kind of environment. This guy you're talking about fits too, ex-astronaut and all. But why just kids, and why all the cloak-and-dagger shit? No matter how you figure it, whatever they're doing they sure as hell don't want anyone to know about it.'

'So what do we do?' asked Toby. 'Sit around and get experimented on?'

'Deetz figures this is just a high-tech version of a prisoner-of-war camp,' said Corey. 'He thinks that's how we should treat it.'

'What does that mean?'

'I was talking to him a little while ago. He thinks it's about time we formed some kind of official escape committee.'

'Well, count me in,' said Toby. 'I don't like the idea of being turned into a lab rat running around in some freako's maze.'

The hatch swung open and Eric and the Dick appeared. Eric was carrying a loaded food tray while his red-haired companion held a crumpled sheet of paper in one hand. Scowling, Dubrofsky sailed the single sheet down onto the table in front of Corey Shire.

'We've got our marching orders,' he said, slumping down into the chair across from Toby. Eric began unloading the tray. 'Tomorrow morning we get all our stuff together and report to the gym. They're moving us.'

ELEVEN

B Y noon the following day Mickey Rubinek's sour mood of
the previous evening had vanished. He and Devon had
had breakfast in a greasy spoon close to the trailer park and he
had been pleasantly surprised when she offered to pay. He was
even more surprised when she paid for a full tank of gas for the
Mustang. Apparently she had emptied out her savings account
before splitting from Mill Valley and although she wouldn't tell
him exactly how much, a few surreptitious peeks at her wallet
convinced him that she was carrying a healthy wad.

Things had gone smoothly at the university as well. The
school year was pretty much over so there weren't a lot of
people on campus, and the grey-haired librarian was easy prey
for the Rubinek charm. After a bit of patter and a flash of his
alumnus card the woman had set them up with a terminal in the
reference section and left them on their own. A few minutes
later he and Devon were merrily digging their way deeper and
deeper into the Berkeley mainframe, trying to put the pieces of
the puzzle together.

And came up empty.

'OK,' Devon said, checking her scratch-pad notes. 'Fourteen
names, and except for the fact they all went to Berkeley at the
same time, I can't see any connection. Jake Churchill was in
arts, Linda Kudelka was in honours English, Mike Foot was in
marine biology. And the graduating years are all different too.
Briane Weldon was class of '70, Joanna Yearwood '69, Tom
Fujiwara was '71. Freshmen, sophomores, even Jim Beattie,
the graduate student in anthropology.'

'But they all had their kids snatched within a few weeks of
each other, twenty years later,' muttered Rubinek. 'It's crazy.'

'The only other thing we've come up with is their IQs,' Devon

61

said, biting her lip thoughtfully as she leafed through her notes. 'Every one of them is over one-forty. That's a lot of bright people.' She shook her head. 'I still don't believe this, though – Toby's dad has an IQ of one fifty-four. It sure doesn't show.'

'Wait a second,' said Mickey. 'Who did the testing?'

'Hang on.' Devon began flipping through the pages. 'Here it is. PF Surveys Corporation.'

'Let's see who they are,' Mickey said. He began hitting keys and came up with the answer within two minutes. Devon read the information off the screen.

'PF Surveys Corporation, a wholly owned subsidiary of the Phoenix Foundation Inc. of Washington DC. PF Surveys conducted a survey for the Rand Corporation under government contract 62-30409/2237609. Full title of project was "An Assessment of Academic Standards in Fifty United States Universities as a Basis for Establishing Long Term Educational Goals". Rand contract terminated 1970, now being carried out on an ongoing basis by the Georgetown Institute for Strategic Studies in Washington DC as part of their "Best and Brightest" programme. See also Phoenix Foundation/American Health Standards Institute.'

'Interesting,' Mickey said. He turned to Devon. 'You get all that?'

She nodded, scribbling on a fresh sheet of paper.

'Let's dig a little deeper.' Mickey worked the keyboard again, ferreting out the file on the Phoenix Foundation.

'Campus Free Clinic Program,' Devon read as the screen filled again. CFCP funded by Phoenix Foundation as part of American Health Standards Institute Study on student health. Object was to ascertain a baseline level of information on the general health of students on an ongoing basis. See also Chetwynd Birth Control Study.'

'Chetwynd Birth Control Study,' Mickey repeated. A moment later the information appeared.

'Chetwynd Birth Control Study. Long-term study of physiological and psychological effects of a variety of different types of birth control on a cross-section of students. Students screened and chosen were paid a per-examination fee and agreed to continue their involvement for a period of at least five years after graduation. Chetwynd Study funded by Phoenix Foundation under the auspices of American Health

Standards Institute. Chetwynd Study directed by Dr Nelson Chetwynd. Study continued by Department of Sociology, UC Berkeley. See also Dr Nelson Chetwynd.' Devon tapped her pencil against her teeth. 'I wonder if they have a list of the people who were part of that study.'

'Probably,' Mickey said, tapping at the keyboard as he searched for the right menu. 'Jesus!' he whispered when the list appeared. 'They're all there.' He scrolled through the people who had taken part in the study.

'You're sure?'

'Check them yourself.'

> Atkins, Susanne P.
> Beattie, James W.
> Churchill, Jacob C.
> Foot, Michael J.
> Fletcher, Katherine V.
> Fujiwara, Thomas S.
> Gallager, William T.
> Hagen, Lorne D.
> Kudelka, Linda B.
> Kushner, Elena
> Pocock, Valerie W.
> Stewart, Jasmine R.
> Weldon, Brian G.

'What about this Chetwynd guy?' Devon asked. 'See what they have on him.'

A few moments later the information appeared:

Chetwynd, Dr Nelson Baines. Princeton, class of '58. 1959–61, Captain US Army Medical Corps, Walter Reed Hospital, Washington DC. 1962–64 Lt Colonel, Director, Dugway Proving Ground Hospital, Utah, Honorable Discharge, 1965. 1966, Associate Director, Medical Studies Programs, Phoenix Foundation, Washington DC 1967, Chetwynd Birth Control Study, UC Berkeley. 1979, Director, Medical Services, Earthlab Resources Inc., Oakville, California.

Mickey nodded thoughtfully. 'That's in Napa Valley.'

'OK.' Devon nodded. 'We've got a connection. All fourteen were part of this Dr Chetwynd's birth-control study during the sixties and seventies. So what? Somewhere along the line they all stopped using whatever he was giving them, because they all had kids.'

'I'm not sure yet,' Mickey said. He began shutting down the terminal. 'But it's more than just Chetwynd. What did that first thing say, an assessment of standards in fifty United States universities?'

'Something like that.'

'Think about it.' Mickey leaned back in his chair. 'I found fourteen kidnapped kids whose parents went to Berkeley, and all fourteen were associated with this Phoenix Foundation. If the study was being done at forty-nine other universities, how many other connections do you think I'd find? I'm willing to bet Berkeley's just the tip of the iceberg.'

'Not only does this sound like some crazy Dr Strangelove thing, I also don't see how it gets us any closer to finding Toby.'

Mickey Rubinek stared at the screen, frowning, his elation slowly evaporating, replaced by a sour feeling deep in his gut. For a while there he had actually been thinking like a journalist, bird-dogging towards a red-hot story. But he wasn't a journalist, not any more, if he ever really had been one at all. He was a hack, a joke, scuttling around on the fringes, not even a has-been, just a might-have-been. And he was way out of his league, that much he did know. He also knew he was scared; fear was one of his best-trained emotions.

'We should forget this whole thing,' he said quietly. 'Right now.'

'What?'

'Drop it. Forget it. You go home to Mill Valley and I'll go back to my trailer.'

'What's the matter?'

'This is very big time, that's what the matter is.' He realised he had gone for almost two hours without a cigarette, and he suddenly had a desperate craving for one. He wanted to get up, run out of the library, and light up.

'Explain,' Devon said coldly.

'OK, kid, I'll explain. The Rand Corporation. The people who came up with that original study. You know who they are?'

'Some big survey company?'

'Strike one. The Rand Corporation is what they used to call a think tank. They spend most of their time figuring out ways to fight World War III. Very nasty people when you get right down to it. Next we've got the Georgetown Institute for Strategic Studies. Ring any bells?'

'No.'

'Strike two. The Georgetown Institute is where old intelligence officers go when they retire. Kind of like an old boys' club for the CIA. Which brings us to Dr Chetwynd. You notice anything interesting in his bio?'

'He was an army doctor. I've heard about Walter Reed Hospital. That's where they send the president when he's sick, right?'

'Right. But what about Dugway, Utah?'

'I don't know. Except it sounds ugly.'

'Strike three and we're both out of the game if we've got any brains. Dugway proving ground is where they test chemical and biological warfare material. Poison gas and that kind of thing.'

'You really think all this has anything to do with Toby?' asked Devon.

'I don't really give a shit if it does or not. This whole thing is really beginning to stink, and I've got a feeling if we dick around with it much longer we're going to find ourselves in deep, deep trouble.'

'Great,' Devon said angrily. 'You don't think Toby isn't already in deep trouble?' She snorted. 'Pardon me, Mr Rubinek. I forgot, you don't give a shit. A little while ago all you cared about was the story, and now that's gotten a little too hot for you, so you forget about that too.' She shook her head sadly. 'You're really a chickenshit, aren't you, Mickey?' She stood up and stalked off, leaving him seated in front of the computer terminal.

She was right, of course. He *was* a chickenshit. It looked as if he had stumbled on a veritable black hole of child kidnappings, nationwide, and part of something that had been going on since the sixties, something big enough to involve the Rand Corporation, among others. It was right up there in Woodward and Bernstein territory, and he was willing to pass it up, kill it, just for the sake of his own skin.

He closed his eyes and tried not to think what he was thinking. All the people right back to his parents who had told him he'd never amount to a hill of beans, and now here he was, about to prove them right once again.

'Oh, shit,' he whispered. He stood quickly and followed Devon, regretting every step.

TWELVE

TRUE evil rarely gives itself away like the drooling, gore-drenched monsters in horror movies; instead it cloaks itself with all the trappings of normalcy, biding its time, overlooked until it's too late. The German army surgeon working on Adolf Hitler's leg in 1916 never gave the little man a second thought and Charlie Manson was nothing but a spare-change artist on Hollywood Boulevard before he began carving his way through Beverly Hills.

The nondescript brick building on the edge of the Georgetown University campus gave off no sense of evil, nor did the short, bald and slightly overweight man coming through the building's parking-lot entrance. The three-storey building was the home of the American Institute for Global Studies and the pudgy man was the institute's chairman, Dr William Andrew Gateskill.

Even though it was barely summer Washington was already a humid swamp and Gateskill sighed with relief as he stepped inside the air-conditioned building and let the door swish shut behind him. Instead of following the corridor from the side entrance to the building's main lobby he turned right, pushed through an unmarked swing door and paused in front of the narrow elevator door.

Placing his worn, bulging briefcase carefully down on the floor, he fumbled in the pocket of his rumpled tweed jacket until he found a ring of keys. Frowning, he riffled through them until he found the right one and inserted it into the lock beside the door. The door slid open. He pressed the lowest of the seven buttons on the panel, and the elevator began to drop.

The three visible storeys of the building really did contain the offices of the AIGS, and Gateskill was really the chairman,

67

but he had nothing to do with the day-to-day operations of the institute. At sixty-eight, William Gateskill had been an intelligence officer for more than half his life, the last twenty years spent as director of operations for the Inter-Agency Intelligence Administration, commonly referred to as IA-2.

Decades before it had become obvious to everyone in the American intelligence community that they were simply bringing in too much information to be properly processed and analysed. Major opportunities were missed simply because a vital element was overlooked and essential assessments of situations were skewed because information held by one agency had not been passed on to another. By the late sixties, with the computer revolution looming on the horizon, the major intelligence groups decided that there would have to be a central clearing house for information, a separate agency, loyal to no particular faction and with nothing to gain by favouring one group over another. IA-2 was born and Gateskill had been the unanimous choice for director.

Liked by few and loved by no one, he was respected by all as both a brilliant intelligence analyst and a man ruthlessly capable of swimming through the shark-infested waters of Washington's bureaucracies. Lyndon Johnson had referred to him as a 'heartless son-of-a-bitch with a lump of coal where his morals should be' and the CIA's William Casey had been the one to give him the nickname of the Georgetown Troll.

Five years previously, when the Phoenix Project became operational, IA-2 and Gateskill had automatically taken control of the plan's logistics, reporting directly to the president and a select group of cabinet members. Within a year, Gateskill was the de facto head of Phoenix with his own people in key security positions on the project, the most senior of these being a man named Gunnar Peltz.

The elevator door opened and Gateskill stepped out into a small reception area. He showed his pass to the uniformed duty officer, tapped out his ID code on the panel beside the main door into the command centre, then stepped into the large, brightly lit room. The door closed behind him and he stood for a moment, surveying the heart of his domain.

Unlike the dark, high-tech caverns depicted in science-fiction movies, the IA-2 command centre was as bland and antiseptic as a *Time* magazine subscription office. Banks of identical computer stations were arranged in aisles, each one manned by an operator wearing a headset, and the walls around the room were punctuated at regular intervals with numbered office doors. The room was flooded with light from recessed ceiling panels and the floor was covered with non-static, dark-blue industrial carpeting. A heavy stainless-steel door at the far end of the room opened onto a narrow corridor which in turn let to the super air-conditioned vaults for the high-speed Cray-2 computers and the chambers containing the massive Ampex log tape recorders, videotape recorders, data encrypters and photo-augmentation machinery.

Gateskill smiled briefly, nodding to himself with satisfaction. He moved slowly around the perimeter of the room, heading for his office. Everything seemed to be in order and order was why IA-2 had been created. Fibre-optic cables, dedicated to IA-2's exclusive use, led from the headquarters of seven major intelligence organisations directly to this room. Each day a hundred million shreds of information from human and electronic intelligence sources around the world funnelled into the fifty terminals and from there into the supercomputers next door. From that chaotic skein of myth, rumour and fact it was Gateskill's job to weave a tapestry of knowledge that went from the size of a Soviet satellite launch at Plesetsk to the thickness of barbed wire used by Israeli shepherds.

The AI-2 director's office was small by Washington standards, the walls white and bare, the floor covered in the same carpet as the command centre. The large, plain desk held only a computer terminal and a bank of telephones. Gateskill entered the office, leaving the door open, dropped his brief-case beside the desk and sank down into the high-backed office chair. He tapped a button on his telephone console and a few moments a later a tall, bony man in his forties appeared in the doorway.

'Morning, sir.'

'Morning, Brubaker.' Gateskill pointed to an armless chair on the other side of the desk. 'Sit.'

'Yes, sir.' Brubaker sat.

'Update me on Phoenix.'

Brubaker was prepared for this, having come to work before eight to get the latest information from the computers. 'So far everything appears to be on schedule. Peltz says there's some slight problem with the last consignment to Egypt Green, but nothing to worry about.'

'What kind of problem?' Gateskill asked.

'Girlfriend of one of the last ones we picked up. She's making a bit of a fuss.'

'Peltz is monitoring the situation?'

'Yes, sir.'

'Anything else?'

'Not much, Mr Gateskill. Detrick's on target as far as the shipments are concerned. One of the analysts there seems to think we're low on our estimates for domestic fatalities.'

'Nationwide or specific?'

'Specific,' Brubaker replied. 'New York.'

Gateskill turned slightly in his chair and keyed in a series of commands on his terminal. He stared at the screen thoughtfully.

'Seven per cent, most of it confined to the Bronx and Harlem.'

'The analyst at Detrick says it will be more like 12 per cent, still confined to the Bronx and Harlem but with a leakage into Manhattan. He says we forgot to work in the statistics for maintenance workers. According to him it skews all the information.'

'What's the numerical difference?'

'A little less than two hundred thousand.'

'Over how long?'

'Seven months.'

'Still acceptable.' Gateskill keyed out the terminal. 'Anything from Kulagrin?'

'Yes, sir. We had confirmation from him late last night. He says that Prussian Blue is up to its full complement.'

'Han?'

'Nothing yet, Mr Gateskill. China White is still 25 per cent away from optimum as far as we know. You predicted something like this yourself, if you'll recall.'

'I think the sons of bitches are stalling,' Gateskill said, anger is his voice. 'God damn it! I told the president they'd balk at the last minute.'

'It makes political sense, of course. They reap the benefits with none of the risk.'

Gateskill turned to his terminal again and keyed in a new set of instructions. The response was instantaneous.

'They get a 22 per cent overflow from Tibet and Afghanistan, 17 per cent through Shanghai and almost 40 per cent from Hong Kong. Hong Kong itself has a 72 per cent rate over less than a year. And that's without doing a damn thing.'

'Kulagrin picked up the same figures,' Brubaker commented. 'He thinks they're lying of course.'

'For once he's probably right,' Gateskill growled. He tapped his fingers on the surface of the desk, frowning at the computer terminal. Finally he nodded, coming to a decision. 'I'll want to talk to Kulagrin later on this afternoon.'

'On line or voice?' Brubaker asked.

'Voice. Maybe there's something we can do to light a fire under our little yellow friends.'

THIRTEEN

$\mathbf{A}$FTER leaving Toby, Peter Wolfe had followed orders, taking the green-lined corridor to the elevator and going down to green Level Three. Somehow he had been expecting echoing corridors and clanging cell doors, but stepping out of the elevator he was surprised to find himself in something that looked eerily like the lobby of a small hotel. The floor was carpeted in dark blue, the walls were a muted green and directly in front of him was a high, U-shaped counter, manned by three people in uniform, two of them women. The uniforms were simple, the women wearing dark-green military blazers over white blouses, the man in a dark-green officer's jacket with epaulettes and brass buttons. There were rank insignia on the cuffs of the jackets and the shoulder flashes were vertical lozenges in dark blue, filled with a gold capital P rising out of red and orange flames.

Wolfe stepped out of the elevator and approached the counter, trying to keep his expression neutral. The woman facing him behind the counter looked up and smiled. She was in her twenties, dark-haired and blue-eyed. The name badge over her right breast pocket said YARROW, D. She looked a lot friendlier than Berkowitz. There was a computer terminal built into the counter in front of her, and a complex-looking telephone panel by her right hand.

'Colonel Wolfe?' she asked brightly.

'Yes. I'd like to see someone in authority.'

'Of course,' answered Yarrow, D. 'Dr Hartshorn wondered if you could join him in the theatre.'

'Max Hartshorn?' asked Wolfe, surprised. 'NASA space medicine?'

'Yes, sir. I believe he worked for them at one time.' She

72

smiled again. 'Follow the corridor on your left and go to the end. The door will take you into the theatre.'

Wolfe nodded absently and turned away, following her directions. Madness compounded by lunacy. Max Hartshorn had been instrumental in developing the space-medicine programme for NASA as far back as the Mercury astronauts. What the hell was he doing here?

The corridor was narrow, metal walls enamelled off-white. There was a vague familiarity about his surroundings that didn't click until he had almost reached the oval bulkhead door. A ship. The place reminded him of the insides of an ocean liner.

Pulling open the bulkhead door he stepped into the fan-shaped, low-ceilinged theatre. In the half-light he could see a single figure seated in the front room, silhouetted against the broad, rectangular screen. Wolfe walked down the centre aisle to the front row, and as he approached the figure rose, one hand combing back a mane of snow-white hair. Max Hartshorn, looking as birdlike as ever, deep-set eyes like a hawk, with a hooked nose to match, and thin lips.

'Peter.'

'Dr Max.' Wolfe nodded formally. Hartshorn waved him to a seat and sat down himself. 'You mind telling me what the hell is going on, Dr Max?'

'In due time, Peter.' Hartshorn gave him a flickering smile. 'You are fit and well?'

'Presumably. That series of quarantine and sterilisation procedures I went through must have killed every bacterium I had.'

'I certainly hope so since that was the intent,' said Hartshorn in his heavily accented English. He told people he was Austrian but he had come to the State with Von Braun and the others, so he wasn't fooling anybody.

'You have been given quarters, yes?'

'No,' Peter said, shaking his head. 'I came directly here.'

'You have a private room on Level Nine. I will take you there when we have finished your briefing. Your room is close to mine.' The old man made a rasping, throat-clearing noise, then took a package of cigarettes out of his pocket. He offered one to Peter, who refused, then lit up, dragging deeply.

'I'm sure it's terrific, but Level Nine of what? Where the hell am I, Dr Max, and why was I brought here against my will?'

'Because you would not have come if we had simply asked. And because your presence here is necessary.'

'Necessary for what?'

'SAHARA.'

'The desert?'

'An acronym,' Hartshorn answered drily. 'It is something I have never become used to. Names for things which already have names.'

'What does it mean?'

'A number of things. A more important acronym is FORE-CAST. You know of it?'

'No,' Wolfe answered, irritation creeping into his voice.

'FORECAST is a computer program used by the JAD. My God! Another one. The Joint Analysis Directorate of the Pentagon.'

'War games.'

'Indeed.'

'So this FORECAST is a war game, and I'm playing?'

'Not exactly. FORECAST is much more than a war game. It had its origins with the National Security Agency, I believe. It is a monstrous database really, containable with only the most sophisticated supercomputers. Virtually every piece of data available to any official agency of the United States government is fed into the program and an analysis is made. Something of a Delphic oracle, you might say.'

'I don't see where all this is leading.'

'In due time, Peter; bear with me. As I was saying, the FORE-CAST program can effectively predict the future, at least in a limited way. It is very adept at broad situations.'

'Such as?'

'Nuclear war,' Hartshorn said blandly. 'Major conflict of any kind, actually. One of the FORECAST sub-programs, called the Strategic Conventional Intervention Model, SCIM for short, predicted the Falklands War, Afghanistan and Grenada. It also provided the strike scenario for the Libyan raid, among other things. For the last six years, however, FORECAST's main job has been to create and play out a variety of escalation ladders which might lead to nuclear war. Tiered escalation to nuclear war – TENWAR. There are twenty steps on the ladder. FORECAST predicts that once past the thirteenth step there is no way to stage down and that nuclear war is inevitable.

'Five months ago we reached stage ten and instituted

SAHARA. So far the FORECAST evaluation has been accurate. Last week we reached stage twelve, and according to the most recent evaluation we will reach thirteen within the next forty-eight hours.'

'You're saying that the whole world is about to go up in flames?' Peter said, unbelieving.

'Yes. FORECAST predicts a time scale of between seven to fourteen days from stage thirteen.'

'So what is this?' Peter asked, gesturing around the darkened theatre. 'Some kind of Noah's ark?'

'Very astute. Something quite close to that. You have heard of Mount Weather?'

'The special facility outside DC.' Peter frowned as he dug into his memory. 'Some kind of underground city for the bigwigs, isn't it?'

'Indeed.' Hartshorn nodded. 'Mount Weather was created in the late fifties, at the height of the Cold War. It has a capacity for 25,000 people and was intended to be a command and control centre for government in the event that Washington was no longer habitable. I and a number of my colleagues at NASA were asked to help design it. What we learned at Mount Weather led us to the establishment of SAHARA and eventually to the various compounds under its control.'

'Back to the desert,' said Peter.

'Safe habitat for repopulating America,' explained Hartshorn. 'A trifle melodramatic perhaps, but it does explain the process. There are four compounds: China White, Prussian Blue, Columbia Gold and this one, Egypt Green. The compounds are fully hardened, utterly secure and completely self-sustaining.'

'My God,' whispered Peter. 'How long has this madness being going on?'

'Since 1962. The Cuban Missile Crisis was the initial impetus.'

'But kidnapping children – ?'

'Saving them,' Hartshorn corrected. 'And the future of their country. This has a long historical precedent, Peter. In medieval times the women and children were taken within the castle keep during times of crisis, as they were protected behind the wooden palisades of your frontier forts during the Indian wars.'

'So you've been roaming around the country abducting kids at random and bringing them here?'

75

'It was hardly a random process,' Hartshorn said drily. 'The choice criteria for who would be brought to the compounds were laid down and in place before anything else.'

'Really?' answered Peter sceptically. 'And who played Solomon?'

'A computer,' Hartshorn answered blandly. 'Based on a long-range study developed by the Rand Corporation and our own group, the Phoenix Foundation.'

'Cute,' Peter said. 'Out of the ashes and all that.'

'The name was not my choice,' Hartshorn snapped. 'The study focused on a large number of American universities and identified the most intelligent students. The students were followed for a number of years and their offspring identified. It is those children who form the base community for the compounds.'

'How many?' Peter asked.

'Eight thousand, brought here over the last three months or so. There are roughly two thousand in each compound, slightly fewer boys than girls, all between the ages of twelve and sixteen.'

'Puberty.'

'Indeed,' said Hartshorn. 'Almost all are presently capable of reproduction.'

'*Lebensborn,*' Peter muttered, staring at the white-haired man. Hartshorn returned the look without blinking.

'I beg your pardon?'

'You know what I'm talking about, Dr Max. You were there at the time, remember? The *Lebensborn* camps. Baby factories with German and Austrian kids being impregnated by your classic Teutonic SS studs. Breeding brothels for the Führer and the Fatherland.'

'There is no basis for such a comparison,' Hartshorn said evenly. 'In the event of a global thermonuclear war approximately 165 million Americans will die immediately. Some 70 million will die within the first six months after the attack.'

'There will be some 40 million survivors after that, all suffering to a greater or lesser degree from radiation effects. Of their potential offspring, 15 million will spontaneously abort during the first three years after the war.

'The infant mortality rate will be close to that of the Dark Ages. Perhaps one in ten will survive. Within ten years the population of America will be reduced to 15 or 20 million, many of them sterile, the same number carrying mutated genes and the vast majority heading out of their childbearing years anyway. By the year 2000 America will have ceased to exist in any real way.'

'And your 8000 little geniuses are going to change that?'

'That is the hope. The compounds will be the wellsprings of an entirely new civilisation.'

'So fifty years from now they all come up into a nuclear wasteland, is that the idea? No agriculture, no culture, nothing. You're talking science fiction, Dr Max. A sick, Nazi science fiction.'

'Not at all,' Hartshorn said. 'The Department of Agriculture has maintained a seed-bank since the early seventies. There are two animal-embryo vaults now in existence and the Underground Vaults and Storage Corporation has been working since 1960. The entire Library of Congress is on microfiche. Every film ever made on videotape. And more.'

'You expect these kids just to sit still and take all of this?' Peter asked. 'You expect *me* to do nothing? Just accept it?'

'I don't see that you have much of an alternative, Peter.'

'Escape.'

'Egypt Green is a small, abandoned farming community twelve miles west of Hutchinson, Kansas,' said Hartshorn wearily. 'This complex is sealed 650 feet below it in a salt mine covering an area roughly one hundred miles by fifty. And even if you did manage to get out of the compound itself, what would you be escaping to? A holocaust which you would be helpless to prevent.'

'All right. So what do you need me for? I'm no genius. Where do I fit in and how come I'm one of the chosen few?'

'Initially you weren't. Siang Ping Lung was heading up our engineering department. I gather you knew him at one time. He spoke quite highly of you.'

'He was teaching at Western Tech up until a couple of years ago,' Peter said. 'He dropped out of sight.'

'Indeed,' said Hartshorn. 'We recruited him. Like you he was a specialist in the design and engineering of closed systems such as this one. Unfortunately he died of a cerebral haemorrhage ten days ago. We needed a replacement quickly. You were the next name on the list.'

'So you kidnapped me. For the greater good of the United States. Or your vision of it.'

'Not my vision, Peter. I am no more than a small part of this.'

'Just following orders, is that it?'

'A man doing his job. This project has been in operation for the better part of thirty years, and it has cost billions of dollars. Beyond that, it is perhaps the only humane outcome of a terrible scenario. Egypt Green is a small attempt to redress the horrors about to be visited on the world.'

'You can tell yourself that if you want, Dr Max.' Peter stood up, looking down at the old man. 'To me it's a bomb shelter, built by the same people responsible for the bomb. Humane, my ass. It's the same story all over again. Master race time. We blow the world to hell and gone, then crawl up out of the rubble neat and tidy, ready to start all over again. Except better this time. Wipe the slate clean and redo the experiment, and to hell with the three billion lab rats you lose in the process. Well, screw that.'

'You flew the Shuttle, Peter. You knew from the start that the Shuttle programme was essentially military, a weapons platform. You knew that, Peter, so you're just as much a part of what is going on as I or any of the others.'

'Why don't you show me my quarters?' said Peter coldly. Hartshorn nodded and stood up.

Peter followed him through one of the side exits to a small service elevator. There were fifteen buttons on the interior panel. The top three had letters instead of numbers, C-A, C-B, C-C, and could only be operated with a key. The bottom two were also key-operated and coded E and R. The middle buttons were numbered consecutively, one through ten. Hartshorn inserted a small magnetic-strip card into a slot in the panel and pressed 7. They began to descend slowly.

'The top three levels are command and control,' explained the old man as they moved downwards. 'E is engineering, R is the reactor level. The other ten serve a variety of purposes. The medical level is on Seven: hospital, laboratories, and accommodations for the medical, technical and science staff.'

'Where do you keep the kids?'

'So far they've been held in an assembly area. They'll be

moved into the main complex soon. Mostly Levels Three through Six.'

The elevator slid to a stop and the doors opened. They stepped out into another corridor and Hartshorn turned right. Once again Peter was struck by the similarities to a ship. Enamel-painted metal walls, bulkheads with oval hatchways every hundred feet or so and the low ceilings, lit with recessed fluorescent panels. After several turns they reached a dead end. Hartshorn led Peter to a door at the very end of the passage and opened it.

The room was small and narrow, eight or nine feet deep and about twelve feet long. There was a desk at either end with a wall-mounted lamp and two shelflike beds, one above the other, fitted into the long wall. The floor was covered in the same neutral carpet as the corridor, the walls were pale green and the ceiling was acoustic tile. Peter stepped past Hartshorn and looked around. There was a thick, plastic-wrapped parcel on the lower bunk.

'For the time being you'll have the room to yourself,' the old man said. 'But I can't promise privacy for long. Staff is being called in from all over now. You may have to share at some point.' He gestured toward the parcel on the bunk. 'You will find two changes of uniform in there as well as a shaving kit and a handbook on the organisation of the compound. The staff is grouped militarily and you have maintained your rank as colonel.'

'Who rates as the overall boss?' asked Peter.

'There are three. I am in charge of the scientific staff. Operations are headed by General Lucas Baird and the children are under the command of Brigadier George Armstrong Revik.'

'I've heard of Baird, he was on the Joint Chiefs, but who's Revik?'

'Brigadier Revik's last position was commandant of Fort MacLean Military Academy.'

'Peter had known a couple of Fort MacLean graduates at flying school. It was rated as one of the most highly disciplined military schools in the country and was euphemistically known by its alumni as Fort Fist. Hartshorn went to the door and then turned briefly.

'Someone will be by later to give you a general tour of the facility and to give you your documentation and an elevator key-card. Take today to familiarise yourself with the compound and report to me tomorrow as soon as you've finished breakfast.'

Hartshorn then left the room, pulling the door closed as he left. Peter slumped back against the bunk, staring at the door.

He tried to remember what he knew about Siang Ping Lung, the man he was replacing. Lung had been in his early forties, a hotshot theorist who was always coming up with bizarre megaprojects like tunnels linking New York and the European continent. Peter looked around the room. Utilitarian, sparse, military; not much different from a flight officers' quarters on an aircraft carrier. Nothing high-tech, nothing state of the art; hardly an environment for someone like Siang. Dr Max had said that the programme had been in place since the early sixties – almost thirty years. Would Siang have been content with a late-comers role? It didn't seem likely. Yet they had recruited him.

Peter stood up and began pacing off the narrow confines of the room. Four compounds, 8000 kids. Not much of a repopulation project, no matter how Hartshorn played with the numbers. A multi-billion dollar project with limited potential, recruiting people like Siang Ping Lung, but with enough clout to put together a massive onslaught of kid-snatching. He stopped in mid-pace and stared at the door, reaching out and touching it with the tips of his fingers. Solid, real.

He nodded to himself. Egypt Green was real all right, but Max Hartshorn was lying about its purpose. Something else was going on here, and standing in the empty room he smiled coldly. One way or another he was going to find out what that something was.

FOURTEEN

MICKEY Rubinek took a last drag from his cigarette, then flipped the glowing butt out into the Mustang's slipstream. Beside him, Devon Talbot swung her Sony Handycam in a long pan, taking in the lush greenery of the Monticello vineyards and the dusty hills beyond. It was early afternoon and the sun was almost directly overhead.

'You shouldn't do that,' Devon said, keeping her right eye to the viewfinder.

'Do what?' asked Mickey, pushing his sunglasses higher up onto his nose.

'Throw burning cigarettes out of a car window. You can start grass fires that way.' She checked the footage counter on the machine, then put it down on the seat. 'How much longer?'

They were just outside the town of Napa, less than ten miles from the Oakville sideroad that would take them up into the hills below Mount St John.

'Five, ten minutes,' said Mickey.

'I still think it's a waste of time,' Devon grumbled. 'Why would this Earthlab Resources place have any reason to kidnap people?'

'I don't have any idea,' said Mickey. 'Which is why we're going there for the royal tour.' He reached out and pulled a thick, spiral-bound notebook off the dash, then tossed it into Devon's lap. 'Make yourself useful and read me back what we got at the library this morning.'

'Earthlab Resources is an environmental, ecological and sociological consulting company,' Devon began. 'They were established in 1962, doing all sorts of surveys and things. In the seventies they got into a lot of environmental, ecology stuff, petroleum spills, land use, that kind of thing. They almost went bust in 1980 but they were bailed out by two high rollers from Texas, Robert Poundstone and Sam Hacker.'

She bowed over at Mickey as if expecting some comment. When none came, she continued. 'They made all their money in shopping malls. They had this idea of creating an enclosed environment for studying how different ecosystems work. They did a prototype in Florida called Earthlab 1 and made a killing out of the information they picked up about hydroponics. They set up another company to build that end of it, called Greenglass Industries. Five-pound tomatoes, hydroponic lettuce, that kind of thing. Then they decided to build Earthlab 2. According to the stuff I copied, E2, as they call it, is a full-scale project, rainforest, savanna, desert, marsh, even an ocean. They've got some deal worked out with the government and no one is quite sure exactly where the place is, except that it's somewhere in the Hawaiian islands. Eight hundred feet long, 420 feet wide, and completely sealed. They choose the people who'll be going inside – just like astronauts, except they're calling them econauts. Twenty scientists sealed up in this thing for two years.'

'What about Chetwynd?' Mickey asked.

'He's the project manager. Part of E2 is a monitoring station, computers, TV. Kind of like Mission Control.'

'Which means he's in Hawaii somewhere.'

'Right, but like I said before, I found an address for him here in the Napa Valley: 102 Dwyer Road, Napa Cellars, Oakville.'

'Presumably that's a hint,' Rubinek said, glancing over at her.

'If he is in Hawaii, then what's the harm in taking a look around his place?'

'It's illegal.'

'And you're Mr Law and Order,' answered Devon. 'Give me a break.'

Frowning, Mickey Rubinek increased his speed a little bit, hands gripping the wheel tightly. He wasn't at all sure he liked what the women's movement had done to the next generation, but more than that, the kid kept on pushing him into deeper and deeper water. He turned his head slightly, peering at her over the top of his sunglasses. The worst thing about it was that he was enjoying himself, even if he was scared shitless. Sighing, he turned his attention back to the road.

They found Earthlab easily enough and Mickey wheeled the Mustang into the large, shrub-camouflaged parking lot. The main building was a mirror-glass slab 200 feet long and five stories high, backed up to the foot of a low, tree-covered hill well off the main highway. A giant, gleaming ingot of silver dropped into the middle of nowhere. There was a wide set of concrete steps leading up to the front entrance and a small chrome plaque by the big double doors announcing that this was the home of Earthlab Resources.

The main lobby was cavernous, slate-floored and fitted out with enough potted *ficus benjamina*'s to start a rainforest. There was a small knot of university students huddled around an island of lounge chairs off to the left and a raised, circular reception desk in the centre of the lobby. The desk was manned by a woman wearing a high-tech headset and two green-uniformed security guards watching a bank of small television screens. To the right of the woman was a small pylon fitted with a security camera, a small red light below its lens flashing at precise one-second intervals.

Mickey and Devon crossed to the desk and Mickey gave the woman his name. She spoke briefly into her headset, nodded, then punched a keyboard hidden below the counter. There was a brief whirring sound and a few seconds later the woman handed them a pair of visitor's badges, plastic-laminated and including a small colour photograph taken by the camera beside her. It was an impressive display of very tight security.

'Please join the group over there,' the receptionist instructed, smiling pleasantly. 'Miss Teller, your guide, will join you in a moment. Welcome to Earthlab Resources and enjoy your tour. On leaving the facility please return your badges.'

'She sounds like one of those talking Coke machines,' Devon whispered as they crossed the lobby to the group of students.

'Just clip on the badge and shut up,' answered Mickey. 'They've got cameras everywhere, maybe they've got mikes too.'

The central security and communications command room for Earthlab Resources was located in a large, low-ceilinged chamber three floors below ground level. All communications within and without the Earthlab facility were monitored here, giant Ampex audio-video log recorders retaining everything for possible future use. A bank of IBM data encrypters filled one wall of the room, automatically coding every use of the nine big Cray-2 computers two floors above, as well as regularly running pilot checks through the entire system of several hundred terminals used within the building, sniffing out potential misuse. Every telephone line in the building funnelled though the command centre as did the intricate web of security devices. At any given time there were a minimum of twelve security officers manning the banked wall of video monitors and sometimes there were as many as twenty staff members on hand. Today they were running at minimum complement with one additional man, the tall, dark-haired man in the grey suit standing behind the officer in charge of the main floor monitors.

'Fifth floor wants a make on both of them,' said the grey-suited man, pointing at the lobby monitor showing Mickey and Devon. 'Roll back the entrance tape and get the licence number. It's a silver-blue '66 Mustang. Fax the photographs from their passes to Bluemount and get them to scan the composite files. They want it as fast as possible.'

'Yes, sir,' said the man at the monitors. He began playing the board in front of him like a pianist while the man in the grey suit watched. A few seconds later one of the preview monitors blanked, then cleared, showing the same photographs that had appeared in the passes given to Devon and Mickey. The pixels grew into digitised squares and then cleared, fed electronically to the waiting computer banks several thousand miles away. At the same time the tape-recording activities at the entrance to the facility rewound, then froze at the point where Mickey had driven into the lot. The licence number was clearly visible. Turning slightly in his chair, the man at the monitors fed the number into a flush-mounted terminal and waited.

'The car belongs to a Michael Rubinek. The address is a trailer park in Oakland. According to DMV he's listed as a journalist. They've got a dozen wants and warrants on him for parking. No criminal record but he's got an FBI tag on his file that goes back to the sixties.'

'How long to run it through NCIC?', Grey Suit asked, referring to the Federal Bureau's national crime-information computer.

'I'll have an answer before we get a response from Bluemount,' boasted the security technician. As it turned out he was wrong. The Bluemount information came in first. The refrigerated, ultra-quick supercomputers at the Bluemount facility had compared the digitised pictures with the images logged in their files and came up with a match for Devon Talbot almost instantly. There was no corresponding match for Mickey Rubinek. A few moments later the reply from the NCIC office in Washington appeared.

'The girl's name is Devon Talbot. She was logged in a peripheral file for the Mill Valley operation. The kid's a friend of the Hagen boy.'

'Shit,' said the man in the grey suit. 'What about Rubinek?'

'Not much, according to NCIC. Went to Berkeley, had a few questionable friends. The tag on his file is an out-of-date general surveillance.'

'Nothing since then?'

'Nope.'

'Get me a print-out of all of this,' ordered Grey Suit, staring at the screens. 'Send it up to the fifth.'

'Do we hold them after the tour?'

'No. Put a car on them when they leave and get me the number of our person in Oakland. Send it up with the print-out.'

'Will do.'

The man in the grey suit turned and left the darkened room. It was too close. A friend of the Hagen boy suddenly appears with someone who went to Berkeley during the test period. It couldn't be a coincidence, and that meant there was something wrong.

FIFTEEN

T HE move from the assembly area went without incident.
Under guard the children were led down a maze of sloping
corridors to their new accommodations. Compared to the
assembly area the new environment was luxurious; carpeted
corridors, several large dining halls, good-sized, if still spartan,
rooms and, according to the handbook each child was given,
a full spectrum of recreational facilities, including a swimming
pool.

The five 'house' designations were maintained. Kennedy,
Lincoln and Jefferson remained the houses for the older
children, while Owens and Bell were for the younger ones.
The three older groups, all boys, were installed on Level
Four, while Owens and Bell went to Level Five. So far
no one had seen any sign of girls, but Jason Sanchez said
he was sure they were around somewhere and the locked
bulkhead doors at both ends of their level indicated that
there was more to the facility than they were being allowed
to see.

Toby Hagen's group was kept together, sharing a large metal-
walled room roughly midway along the level. Within the first
few hours Corey Shire and Tony Deetz ran a quick scouting
mission and discovered that the level was approximately 400
feet long from bulkhead to bulkhead, and about 150 feet wide.
There were two long side corridors, connected by five shorter
ones at right angles. There was an area that looked like offices,
the dining hall, the pool and the gym, and six lift stations, all
key-operated.

There were seventy-five or eighty dormitory rooms, and if
they were the same size as the one Toby and the others occu-
pied, that meant there was housing on Level Four for about

375 kids. As far as Corey Shire and Deetz could tell they had free run of the level; on their scouting trip they had seen half a dozen uniformed adults, all wearing sidearms, but they had ignored the two boys completely.

'Pool or no pool, the place is still a fucking prison,' said Deetz, lounging on one of the lower bunks. The room was twelve feet long and eight deep, fitted with three pair of bunk beds, flush-mounted lockers, a shower and toilet cubicle, a tiny kitchenette with a hotplate and sink, a desk, a table and half a dozen folding chairs. The walls were pale blue, the floor was carpeted thinly in dark grey and the bedding was green. The overhead light was a recessed fluorescent. On the wall to the left of the door was an intercom.

'I still don't see why,' said Toby, seated at the table. He swept an open hand around the room. 'Us, this place.'

'*Lord of the Flies,*' Eric Lowery said quietly, leafing through the handbook, head propped against the wall of his bunk. He peered over the top of the book, owl eyes blinking behind his thick glasses.

'What's that supposed to mean?' asked Deetz. 'That was about kids cast up on a desert island.'

'Not just kids,' Eric explained, putting the handbook down and pulling himself upright. 'Private-school kids, in uniform. Survivors of a nuclear war.'

'I still don't get it,' Deetz said, shaking his head.

'I do,' Toby said coldly. 'He's saying this place is a big bomb shelter. We're survivors, right?' He turned to Eric.

'Something like that.'

'We haven't had a war,' Dick Dubrofsky argued, speaking from the bunk above Tony Deetz.

'Not yet' answered Eric. 'But maybe it's coming. Soon. And we were picked to survive.'

'Why us?' asked Toby.

'Brains, I think,' Eric mused. 'It's one of the first things I noticed. We've got all different shapes and sizes here, but no obvious dummies.'

'With the exception of the Dick. Sanchez, sitting across from Toby at the small table, laughed.

'Fuck off, Snatch,' Dubrofsky grunted pleasantly.

'He's right.' Deetz nodded. 'We're all pretty close to being top of the class one way or another. It's weird.'

'It makes sense,' Sanchez said. 'You're going to save people, you don't save the flakes.'

'A lot of trouble for a few hundred kids,' said Corey. 'A lot of money too.'

'Who says it's just us?' Toby remarked. 'Jason says he's sure there're girls around, and we know they've got a pretty good number of adults here.'

'And who says this is the only bomb shelter or whatever you want to call it?' Dubrofsky put in. 'What if they've got twenty or thirty places like this, spread out all over the country?'

'That brings up an interesting point,' said Eric. 'Just where in the country are we?'

'Some place hardened,' Corey said.

'Hardened?' Deetz echoed. Corey nodded.

'I did a paper on it for school once.' He swung his feet over the edge of the bunk. 'Hardened means being made strong enough to withstand a direct hit from a nuclear warhead. Most of the main missile bases are in the Midwest. The big nuclear-sub bases are in Virginia, Rhode Island and Washington State. None of them are really hardened. The only place I've ever heard about is the NORAD base inside Cheyenne Mountain, Colorado, and they're not even sure about that.'

'We're in Colorado?' said Deetz.

'We're somewhere that isn't targeted for a nuclear warhead.'

'Does it really matter?' asked Toby. He could see the hypothetical arguments going on for ever. 'The question is, what are we going to do about it.'

'Big X,' like I said before,' Deetz muttered.

'Oh God!' whispered Eric Lowery. 'Not this again.'

'What's Big X?' Toby asked.

'It's from *The Great Escape*,' Corey explained. 'Big X was the head of the escape committee.'

'Tunnels.' Eric sighed. 'Tom, Dick and Harry as I recall. Brother Deetz wants us to dig tunnels.'

'Back off, Zitface,' Deetz warned. 'All I mean is that we should be getting our act together. Figure out some way of getting out of here.'

The door slid back with a faint swishing sound and a short, broad-shouldered figure stepped into the room. He was fourteen or fifteen, his dark Irish good looks marred by a fist-sized burn scar on his right cheek. It was Jake Skelly, one of the boys Toby had seen on his first day.

He was greeted with a round of welcoming hellos, Toby noticed him passing a folded square of paper to Jason Sanchez. Snatch opened it, read it, then passed it across the table to Toby.

The intercoms are all bugged.
Watch what you say.

Toby nodded, then passed the note on as the small talk continued. Skelly disappeared into the toilet cubicle and came out a few seconds later with a wad of toilet paper. Approaching the intercom he slipped a tiny Swiss Army knife out of his pocket and unscrewed the blue plastic cover. Silently he pointed out a tiny pea-shaped microphone wired into the intercom circuit, then held up the wad of paper. Folding the paper carefully he stuffed it into the intercom box, then replaced the plastic cover.

'That should do it.'

'How did you know the intercoms were bugged in the first place?' Corey asked. Skelly shrugged.

'They'd be stupid not to have them bugged, so I checked.'

'How could they listen to all the rooms?' Sanchez asked.

'They couldn't,' Lowery said from his bunk. 'They probably have some kind of key monitor. The intercom picks up one of a whole bunch of key words and it automatically records what's going on in the room.'

Skelly looked around the room. 'You guys got anything going?'

'Like getting out of here?' asked Corey.

'Or at least finding out what the hell is going on.'

'Eric thinks we're in some kind of cosmic bomb shelter. A bunch of smart kids chosen to survive a nuclear war.'

'That's pretty close to what we've been thinking,' Skelly admitted. 'This place cost too much to be anything but government and we were all picked up within the last ninety days. That means they must think something is going to happen soon.'

'So what?' said Lowery, shaking his head. 'Why all the skulking around?'

'What's that supposed to mean?' asked Dubrofsky.

'It means, Dickhead, that he thinks we should join 'em rather than try to lick 'em,' said Tony Deetz. 'Right, Zitface?'

'Name-calling is the mark of an immature mind.'

'OK, Mr Lowery: *Pardonnez-moi.* But I am right, aren't I?'

'If our assumptions are correct we've been chosen by the government to survive some disastrous situation, and by all appearances we've been chosen for our intelligence. If that is the case, then what are we fighting? We've been honoured, given chance the rest of the world isn't going to get.'

'Including our families,' Corey put in darkly. 'We survive and they get incinerated. Have you thought about that?'

'Of course I've thought about it,' Lowery snapped. 'But there's nothing I can do about it, is there?'

'Jesus, you would have been great as a stand-in for Heinrich Himmler,' grunted Dubrofsky. 'I was only following orders, *mein Herr.*'

'He's right,' said Toby, speaking at last.

'What?' said Deetz, surprised.

'Not about that. About *Lord of the Flies.*'

'Grade 10 English.' Skelly shrugged. 'What about it?'

'Listen to us,' Toby said. 'Name-calling, arguing. Just like in the book. Give it a couple of weeks and we'll be running around with no clothes on, yelling, "Kill the Pig, spill her blood", and you'll have Eric's head on a stick because you don't like the things he's saying.'

'Make your point, Toby,' said Corey.

'The point is we're doing just what they want. The people running this place are relying on the fact that we can't get our own shit together. That's what all this crap with different-coloured uniforms and house names and all the rest of it is about. We can't come up with our own system of order, so we wind up following theirs.'

'The boy has a head on his shoulders.' Sanchez grinned. 'Go on. You've obviously got something cooking.'

'Not really,' Toby said slowly. 'Just some observations, some feelings. Like how lonely we are, how frightened. They're relying on that too. We're smart all right, too smart not to be shit-scared right now. I am anyway.'

'Don't worry,' muttered Dubrosky. 'You aren't the only one. It's just that none of us has got around to saying it.'

'Keep going,' Corey urged.

'OK. They think we're scared, they think we're disoriented, and they think we're going to adopt their version of order. That's a pretty standard *Psychology Today* kind of scenario. The question is, do we go along with that, like Eric says, or do we make like Rambo part thirty-five and maybe get our asses kicked?'

'Or worse,' Eric put in.

Toby nodded. 'Or worse.'

'Why don't we play it down the middle?' Corey suggested. 'Go along with them for now, but keep our eyes and ears open. Do a little snooping, a little scrounging, maybe look for some weak spots.'

'I'd go along with that,' Tony said. 'For now.'

'What about other people?' Jake asked. 'Russell Ching is going to want in. There're a few others.'

'Russell is it' Deetz stated. 'The more people, the more chance of getting caught. We're pretty sure the Lump is working for the bad guys, whoever they are. There could be others.'

'What about Mr Lowery over there?' suggested Dubrofsky.

'What's that supposed to mean?' asked Eric.

'Are you in, or are you out?'

'What you do is your business,' said the spectacled boy. 'Just don't get me involved, that's all I ask.'

'OK, how do we organise this?' Corey asked.

'Teams.' Deetz had obviously already been thinking about it. 'There's seven of us, Russell and Jake bunk together, so they're an obvious match. Me and Corey, Dick, Sanchez and Toby here. How's that?'

'Good enough.' Corey nodded. 'Snatch, Dick and Toby scrounge. Find whatever they can that might be useful. Russell is a computer freak. Maybe he and Jake can tap into whatever system they're using here. Tony and I will coordinate and see what we can find out about the place and how it runs. Agreed?'

'What about meeting?' asked Skelly. 'We can't use the rooms.'

'Tony and I will find somewhere safe,' Corey told him. 'We'll pass the word along.'

'OK.' Skelly nodded. 'Tony and I should get out of here. This is looking a bit conspiratorial already.'

91

Before Skelly and Deetz could move, the door swished open and they found themselves staring at the barrel-shaped figure of Ivan Lumby. His pudgy face was covered with a faintly glistening sheen of sweat and he was breathing hard. Toby watched the boy's small eyes flicker around the room, taking in the occupants.

'I'm supposed to tell everyone,' he said after a moment. 'All the senior kids have to go to the theatre on Level Three.'

'How do we get there, Lump, fly?' said Dubrofsky

'Go to the east end of this level,' Lump instructed. 'That's right as you go out the door here. The bulkhead is open and you'll find an escalator on the other side. When you get to the top, follow the signs to the theatre.'

Dubrofsky shifted his legs over the side of the bunk and dropped lightly to the floor. He stared sullenly at the short, fat boy in the doorway.

'What's it feel like to be a shit addict, Lump?' he asked. 'I mean, how far does your nose have to be shoved up their assholes to get a really good whiff?'

Lumby paled, his small mouth thinning even more. 'Why don't you leave alone?' he said. 'I'm just doing what they tell me. I'm just trying to keep out of trouble.'

'Watch you step Lump,' Dubrofsky warned. 'And keep your fucking little mouth shut, you got that?'

'Leave me alone,' the boy whispered. He took a last look around the room and then left, heading down the corridor.

'I think that was a mistake,' said Toby. 'Better to have him as a friend than an enemy. He could be dangerous.'

'The Lump? That greasy little tub of lard?' Dubrofsky laughed and slapped Toby on the back as they all filed out of the room, heading for the theatre. 'The only thing the Lump is dangerous to is himself.'

Toby paused and looked back over his shoulder, letting the others get ahead. Ivan Lumby was a hundred feet away, staring as a steady stream of kids moved around him, like a river splitting around a boulder. Even from that distance Toby could sense the fat boy's anger as the small, dark eyes bored into him, and in a terrible flash of insight he knew that he was seeing the eyes of a future rapist, sadist, or perhaps worse. Toby felt a chill go down his spine and he forced himself to look away.

Corey and the others were ahead, lost in the crowd that by

now had also swallowed Toby up. Faces, shoulders, voices, swarming around him. He bit his lip, trying to keep back the tears, thinking of Devon, wondering what she was doing, what she was thinking.

'God damn,' he whispered, and then he pushed ahead, trying to catch up with his new friends.

SIXTEEN

PETER Wolfe sat alone at a table in one corner of the staff
dining room on Level Six, leafing through the thick, blue-
covered binder given to him by the orientation officer the day
before. Like everything else he had seen of the Egypt Green
facility, the large room was plain and utilitarian. The most
colourful things in the room were the uniforms worn by the
half-dozen people seated at tables around him.

According to the information in the binder the civilian
personnel at Egypt Green were divided into seven categories.
All wore the same overall-style uniform, but each category had
its own colour. Green was security, yellow was science, blue
for communications, white for technical, grey for educational,
orange for life-support systems and brown for hydroponics.
Military personnel, like Peter, wore standard-issue US Army
summer fatigues, rank designated on the epaulettes.

The middle section of the binder contained a history of the
installation and a general description, including plans of each
level. Reading it, Peter was amazed by how logical and reasonable the whole proposition sounded.

In 1961 Ransom Air Force Base in central Kansas expanded,
swallowing the abandoned village of Egypt Green, a mining
town that never recovered from the Depression. This was
the height of the Cold War, and, on the basis of a MITRE
Corporation study on the possibility of developing secure
bases for Strategic Air Command personnel, a medium-sized
underground facility was constructed, incorporating several
Minuteman missile silos.

In 1963 Ransom AFB was deemed to be redundant, but
the Minuteman silos remained and the underground facility
expanded. In the event of a nuclear war the Egypt Green

facility would provide accommodation for SAC personnel and with the addition of secondary communications equipment it became a vital second line of defence. The project was so successful that three more installations were built, scattered around the continental United States.

By the late sixties, with the advent of more sophisticated missile and communications systems, Egypt Green and its sister facilities had themselves become redundant, but by that time so much money had been spent on developing them that they had taken on a bureaucratic life of their own, complete with offices in the Pentagon and a full-time comptrolling staff.

Facing redundancy, the United States Strategic Shelter Command, or USIK, went in search of a sponsoring agency that could protect its budget. USIK found what it was looking for within the Alternate National Military Command Center Program, the division of the Pentagon responsible for the Cheyenne Mountain complex housing NORAD headquarters, the National Military Command Center at Fort Richie, Maryland, and the Mount Weather underground complex in Virginia.

ANMC took an immediate interest in Egypt Green and the three other facilities because they offered relative security. Cheyenne Mountain, Fort Richie and even Mount Weather had long ago been targeted by the Soviets, but as far as any up-to-date intelligence could tell, the Russians had never heard of Egypt Green or the other facilities.

The Rand people and Hartshorn's NASA people had been running SAHARA for a number of years and the newly acquired ANMC facilities at Egypt Green and elsewhere were an obvious venue for their work. What had begun as a bomb shelter for a few dozen Strategic Air Command pilots and their crews had evolved into a huge, expensive, and entirely secret operational command within the United States military complex.

Philosophically the whole SAHARA plan was likened to the British mass evacuation of children during World War II and Peter could easily see how that idea could have taken root over a number of years. At first it had been nothing but a statistical study identifying the achievers within the United States university system. A little later someone with a more practical turn of mind rationalised that if you knew who the smart ones were you should make use of the information, or at the very least keep track of the group you had identified. From there it was a short step to the children of those people, and an even shorter step to establishing a plan to 'rescue' those children under the threat of nuclear obliteration. In its own convoluted way, SAHARA made sense.

It was also criminal, unconstitutional and utterly mad, Peter knew.

He flipped through the section containing the floor plans of the facility. The layout appeared to be vertically integrated, which made sense if the facility was built using an old mine. Levels One, Two and Three were much smaller, which meant they were probably built into the winch chambers of the mine's main haulage level. Somewhere on Level One there was almost certainly an elevator that used the mine's main vertical shaft to the surface. Levels Four through Ten probably used the various mine slopes and crosscuts, interspersed here and there with incline shafts leading down and which now contained elevators.

Peter couldn't help being impressed by the engineering of the place. It was an excellent way to utilise previously useless space, and the data collected from a closed environment like Egypt Green would be immensely helpful when it came to establishing some sort of lunar colony in the future.

Peter looked up as a figure sat down across from him at the table. A woman. Blonde shaggy hair, mid- to late thirties, pretty, with eyes like blue ice chips. The uniform was white with two gold bands around the stiff high collar, repeated on the cuffs and an ornate capital P on the shoulder flashes. White meant communications but he wasn't sure about the two gold bands or the P.

'The P is for Phoenix Project, the two gold bands give me the equivalent of a major's rank.' The woman smiled. Cheerful, but the ice-chip eyes were reading him like a computer print-out. Peter smiled back, keeping it carefully distant.

'Let me guess, you're the resident mind-reader.'

'Not quite. My name is Beth Scott. I'm head of the historical section. Dr Hartshorn asked if I'd show you around the place.'

'A historian, here?' asked Peter.

'Sure. Why so surprised?'

'Seems like a pretty esoteric job in a place like this.'

'Not really.' She shrugged. 'I keep track of all the historical material stored in the data banks and monitor all incoming communications, like your file for instance. Fighter pilot in Vietnam, astronaut, engineer, best-selling author . . .'

'Kidnap victim,' he added, a sour note in his voice.

'Why be difficult?' she answered smoothly, 'You were Navy Reserve. It would have been easy enough to change that to active status and order you here.'

'Why wasn't that done?'

'Security. This place was built on it, survives because of it. You weren't kidnapped, Colonel Wolfe, you vanished in a puff of smoke, literally. As far as the rest of the world is concerned, you're dead, and considering what else is going on upstairs I really don't think very many people give a shit.'

'Consider me appropriately put in my place,' Peter answered. 'Just what is going on "upstairs", or does Dr Max have that classified?'

'It's not classified. Later on I'll take you up to the communications centre and you can see for yourself.' She reached out and took one of Peter's cigarettes. 'Remember the arms deal we made with Burma? About six months ago?'

'Vaguely. They turned over a few buses in Rangoon to protest.'

'It was a little more complicated than that, but yes, that's the long and short of it.' She paused. 'Well, the Soviets got a little ticked and finally solidified their relations with Iran. They've just sent 40,000 troops in.'

'Shit.' Peter was no expert on the Middle East, but he knew that that was like throwing petrol on an open fire. 'Have we responded?'

'You bet. Pacific Fleet is moving into the Indian Ocean full strength and SAC has gone to DEFCON 4. Everything coming in from the Rand Strategy Assessment Center is looking sour.'

'Who are they?' asked Peter.

'RSAC is the Pentagon wargaming group.'

'The FORECAST program?'

'Yup. And everything they've run is pretty bad. They expect a Red D2 within a few days.'

'What's a Red D2?'

'Invasion of Europe. We go from the Pacific Fleet in the Indian Ocean to Rapid Deployment Forces dropping into

97

Egypt and Turkey. Soviets respond with a Red D2. From there it's all downhill. Conventional attack and response in the NATO countries and France. France asks for authority to use nuclear weapons, gets the authority, but the Soviets launch a pre-emptive first strike. We jump from there to a full nuclear response and that's the whole ball of wax.'

'The end of the world in a thirty-second description based on a bunch of guys in the Pentagon playing a sophisticated game of checkers. Christ on a crutch!'

'Dr Hartshorn said you wouldn't be an easy sell.'

'Is that what I am?' asked Peter. 'A sell? And you're the saleslady? I'm surprised you didn't show up in a slinky negligee with Chanel Number 5 in all the right places.'

'It's not my job to seduce you,' she said, blushing angrily. 'I just want you to understand. Dr Hartshorn said you were upset and confused. I wanted to change that.'

'Then start by telling me how you got involved in all of this.'

'It's pretty simple really. I wrote a PhD thesis called "The Future of History". It was a computer program actually, a database of historical events broken down into something like twenty-five different crucial components. Everything from the weather to the sexual mores of the specific period. I invented something called the Nishbik Theory.'

'Nishbik?'

'I know,' she giggled, obviously embarrassed. 'My thesis adviser at Princeton said it sounded like something you put on a bagel. It's actually NSHBK. It stands for nail, shoe, horse, battle, kingdom.'

'As in, "For want of a nail the shoe was lost, for want of a shoe the horse was lost", etcetera?'

'Right. I wound up calling the program OTLAS. The one-thing-leads-to-another syndrome. My adviser brought it to the attention of the people at the Phoenix Foundation and that eventually led here.'

'No moral qualms about what they've done?' Peter asked.

'At first, sure.' Beth nodded. 'But for me it was always a contingency plan. Something that might happen if worst came to worst. And now that it has, I feel pretty lucky to be one of the ones with a ticket on the ark.'

'Family, friends?' asked Peter.

'My parents are both dead and most of my friends are here.'

'Too bad the kids aren't that lucky.' Peter stood up. 'What about this tour you're supposed to take me on?'

'Brigadier Revik is giving his first briefing to the kids in a few minutes. I thought it might be interesting to start with that.'

'Lead the way.'

SEVENTEEN

'WELL, that was a complete waste of time,' Devon said as they left the Earthlab parking lot and headed back to the highway. 'Fish in tanks and tomatoes as big as volleyballs. Big deal.'

'Come on.' Mickey grinned. 'You have to admit it was educational.'

'Yeah, right.'

'Negative information can be useful.'

'It was negative all right,' Devon agreed. 'But I can't see it taking us any closer to Toby.'

'That place is five storeys high,' Mickey replied. 'And the whole greenhouse complex was at the back of the main level. They don't have that much security for a bunch of oversized tomatoes.'

'So?'

'So it means there's more going on there than meets the eye.'

'Like what?'

'I'm not sure. Did you notice the roof when we drove up?'

'Some antennae. So what?'

'Satellite dishes, microwave arrays, short wave, the works. Why do you need that much telecommunications stuff for a greenhouse? It doesn't make sense.'

'OK, what do we do now?'

'Take a run at Dr Chetwynd's place?'

'Now you're talking!' Devon grinned. 'Action at last!'

Mickey Rubinek sighed, shaking his head. 'You're going to be the death of me yet, kid.'

Dr Nelson Baines Chetwynd's house was a pseudo-Spanish monster that squatted just off the road almost completely

100

hidden by the remains of a fruit orchard which had been allowed to grow wild. The orchard, mostly peach and pear trees, continued up the hill behind the house, the gnarled trees unpruned, their long branches twisting together to form a briar-patch jungle.

'It looks like Dr C wasn't into horticulture,' Mickey commented as he turned into the lane leading to the house. Devon said nothing, her eye at the viewfinder of the Handycam, getting the scene down on tape.

Mickey pulled up in front of the main entrance and looked around. Shutters were up on all visible windows and the place had an abandoned air about it. He climbed out of the Mustang with Devon close behind and they approached the big front door, its surface sheathed in copper with a sunburst design done in hammered nailheads.

'Tacky,' murmured Devon. Mickey knocked on the door, then thumbed the ornate buzzer. No answer, and a damn good thing too since he didn't have the faintest idea what to say if there *was* someone home. They had called twice on the way down from the Earthlab complex without getting any answer, so he was reasonably sure the house was empty.

'How do we get in?' asked Devon. 'You going to use a 'loid?'

'A what?'

'A 'loid. You know, strip of plastic, credit card.'

'You been watching too much TV.' He laughed. 'That might have worked a long time ago, but locks are a little better than that now. Especially these,' he said, pointing at the door. 'Nice big deadbolt.'

'So what do we do?'

'Brute strength,' Mickey answered. 'Follow me.' He went back to the Mustang, popped the boot and took out the jack and the tyre iron. He also took out a pair of thick chamois mittens he normally used to wax the car, and handed them to Devon.

'What are these for?'

'Watch.' He went around the side of the house, skirting the garage until he came to a low stucco wall. He dumped the jack and tyre iron into the garden on the other side of the wall and boosted himself over. He helped Devon across, then they trotted across the brown, burnt surface of the lawn.

101

The back door to the house was plain wood with four panes of glass at eye level. Peering through the little windows Mickey could see that the door led into a narrow hallway with doors to the left and right. Left would be the garage, right would probably take them into the kitchen. He did a quick check, but he couldn't see any foil or alarm wires.

Over the past two decades he had come into contact with enough lowlifes of various sorts to get a boilerplate degree in everything from wiretapping to small-time arson, and he knew that most home alarm systems were wired into a control box within short reach of an entrance. There was none visible.

'Give me the mitts,' he instructed. Devon handed the chamois over and watched as Mickey put one of the mitts on the lifting tongue of the jack and the other over the baseplate. He turned the jack sideways, lining it up horizontally just below the level of the lock. It was a little wide so he inserted the tyre iron and cranked the tongue down until it fitted tightly into the doorframe. 'Hold this,' he said quietly, indicating the jack. Devon stepped forwards, holding the toothed main strut in place. Inserting the tyre iron again Mickey began to crank.

'What exactly is this supposed to accomplish?' Devon asked.

'People spend all sorts of dough putting in expensive dead-bolts, but they forget about the doorframes. Watch.' He kept on pumping the crank and Devon began to hear squeaking noises as the wooden frame was pulled apart, a fraction of an inch at a time. After less than a minute the frame had been pushed back enough to release the bolt and the door swung open.

They found themselves in a small mud-room. Rubinek opened the right-hand door and entered the kitchen. A quick check of the refrigerator and the shelves revealed no food, nothing in the freezer, not even any canned goods. No utensils or dishes either.

'Doesn't look good,' said Devon, swinging the camera briefly around the room. They continued on, checking out the main-floor living room, dining room and family room. Nothing except a few obvious places where pictures had been hung and dents in the thick, dark-green carpet to show where the furniture had been placed.

'The doctor is long gone,' Mickey said. He paused in the foyer and checked the wall phone. 'I take that back.' He frowned. 'Still a dial tone.' They went up the carpeted stairs to the second floor. Three bedrooms, a big bathroom complete with a Jacuzzi tub, and a large den that looked out over the back yard.

In one corner of the den there was a stack of boxed photocopy paper and a mark on the carpet where the machine had been. Screwed to the wall to the right of the window was a large bulletin board. Apart from that the room was empty.

'I'm going to call a friend of mine at the telephone company, see if I can find anything out,' Mickey said.

'I'll be right down,' Devon said, staring at the bulletin board. Mickey shrugged and turned away. Devon put the Handycam down on the pile of boxes and approached the bulletin board, biting her lip thoughtfully. The board looked almost new, with virtually no wear at all, but something had hung there because she could see the holes left by quite a few drawing pins or thumbtacks, forming a strangely familiar pattern on the fibre.

There was a chalk tray with a few felt markers at the base of the board. She picked up one of the markers and highlighted the pinholes. She stood back from the board, picked up the Handycam and shot the outlined pattern for a long moment, just in case it turned out to be important. She stopped tape and shook her head, knowing that the meaning of the pattern was lying just on the fringes of memory.

Downstairs she found Mickey hanging up the wall telephone.

'Anything?' she asked. Mickey consulted his notebook.

'Long-distance calls all made over the last two weeks. Four to the Earthlab office in Honolulu, Hawaii, two to a residential address in Hawaii, five to Washington DC. That number belongs to something called the New World Health Foundation. He also spent some time with his computer linked to the Center for Disease Control database in Atlanta and another one in Washington, something called INFOCGIAR, whatever the hell that means. The last call was collect from a number in San Francisco. My friend at the phone company says it was the number for the San Francisco office of something called Phoenix Holdings Ltd.'

'Was?' asked Devon.

'It's shut down. Out of service. The interesting thing is that the call was placed almost exactly twenty-four hours after your

103

boyfriend was snatched.' Mickey tucked the notebook into the back pocket of his jeans. 'It's too much of a coincidence.'

'Now what?'

'Go back to my place. I want to make a few calls. Then we bring in the cops.'

Mickey and Devon left the house the way they had come, removing the jack and climbing back over the low garden wall. As far as Mickey could tell no one had seem them enter or exit. They spent the next hour and a half making their way south, Devon listening to the radio and brooding while Mickey drove, trying to ignore the synthetic rock and roll being hurled at him from KFRC.

They hit Sonoma Boulevard at rush hour and crawled onto the Carquinez Bridge. Mickey paid the toll, then reached out and hit the black plastic buttons on the radio. The dial slipped along to KCBS 740, the all-news station, as they funnelled across the bridge to Richmond and El Cerrito.

'Turning again to our top story this hour . . . an interesting and sinister twist to the recent kidnapping of Mill Valley high-school student Toby Hagen. The young man's girlfriend, Devon Talbot, also a student at Mount Tamalpais High School, has disappeared. At this point foul play has not been established but Mill Valley and San Francisco police are not ruling out the possibility. Local tabloid journalist Michael Rubinek is wanted by police for questioning in connection with the case . . .'

'Holy shit.' Devon stared wide-eyed at the radio. Mickey could feel sweat breaking out on his forehead and it was all he could do to keep the Mustang moving across the bridge.

'This is crazy,' he said, his voice catching.

'I don't understand,' said Devon, 'I never mentioned you to anybody, I swear. How did they know?'

'It doesn't matter. They know now and they think I've fucking well kidnapped you, which means they think I probably kidnapped your friend as well. Shit!'

'Pull off,' said Devon, trying to keep her voice even.

'Screw that,' Mickey shot back. 'I'm going to the cops, now!'

'Pull off the goddamn road!' Mickey glanced quickly across at her. She glared back at him, her face suddenly that of a much older woman. 'Pull off the fucking highway, Mickey, or we're both dead.'

The next exit was the Pinole Valley Road, heading east

toward Martinez and Concord across Sobrante Ridge. A mile off the interstate Mickey pulled the Mustang onto the shoulder and parked.

'Talk,' he said.

'I didn't tell anyone anything. You have to believe that.'

'OK, for now I believe it. Go on.'

'If I didn't tell anyone, then how did they know?'

'Tell me,' Mickey said drily.

'Say the kidnappers were setting up Toby for quite a while before they took him. They'd have seen me with him, right?'

'More.'

'The kidnappers know me, and the only way they could know who you were is if they saw us together. That means they must have seen us today at the Earthlab place.'

'You forgot one thing. You found me by getting your friends at the Mill Valley cop shop to run down my licence number. Maybe your old man called from wherever he is and found out you weren't staying with your aunt. He calls the cops, they remember you asking about the car and suddenly I'm a fugitive.'

'No,' Devon said firmly. 'Daddy wouldn't call. Not this early on a shoot. Someone tipped the police. It has to be the Earthlab people, or Phoenix, or whatever they call themselves.'

'OK, what if you're right? Now what?'

'Kidnapping is a capital crime, isn't it? Like murder or armed robbery?'

'No shit.'

'They think you snatched Toby and now me. I don't think they'll be too friendly if they catch you.'

'So?'

'So, we have to get rid of the car and split up. Meet later.'

'Why not just split up, period?' said Mickey. 'You go home to your aunt and I'll call the cops and tell them it's all a big mistake. If you turn up safe and sound they won't have anything to charge me with.'

'I don't think it's the cops we have to worry about,' Devon murmured darkly. 'If this Phoenix bunch have the power to kidnap that many kids and get away with it, they sure as hell can make us disappear. What if they're waiting for me to show up at my aunt's, for instance? I wind up getting raped and mutilated or something and they put what's left of me

105

into some ditch. Who do you think they're going to blame, Mr Rubinek, sir?'

'Maybe you're just being paranoid.' Mickey did not really believe it even as the words came out of his mouth.

'Jesus, what does it take to convince you?' Devon wailed, shaking her head.

'OK. Say you're right. How do we get ourselves out of this mess?'

'Vanish. Drop me off somewhere where I can catch a bus. I go east, maybe Reno. You dump the car, sell it if you can, then get to Reno yourself. We meet at some prearranged spot and then catch a plane.'

'And just where do we go?' said Mickey.

'Take your choice. Chetwynd was calling Washington and Hawaii. One or the other. We can choose later.' She sat back in her seat, staring at Mickey in the gathering gloom.

He tapped his fingers on the steering wheel, looking out through the windshield. The whole thing was blowing up in his face and common sense told him that the smart thing to do was turn himself into the cops, and the sooner the better. On the other hand there were all those missing kids. If his instincts were right there were a hell of a lot more than just the ones he had been able to uncover, and that meant that Devon was right: these people had power.

'What will you do for money?' he asked.

'I've got my dad's credit cards but they might he tracing them. They won't be able to trace the cash cards, though. I've got one for Citibank and a BankAmerica one as well. Dad told me I could get five hundred a day from each one if I had an emergency. I think this qualifies. What about you?'

'I've got maybe a hundred in cash on me. More in the bank in San Leandro.'

'They'll be watching for you more than me.' Devon dug into the inside pocket of her jean jacket and pulled out a battered wallet. She pulled out the BankAmerica instant cash card and handed it to him. 'The ID code is my dad's birthdate, two-six-five-four-five. May 26, 1945, okay?'

'May 26, '45,' Mickey repeated.

'Reno,' Devon said briskly. 'I've been there twice, I think, a long time ago. How well do you know it?'

'Not very.'

'Then let's make it the bus station, wherever that is, OK?'
'I guess.'

Still not sure he was making the right choice, Mickey put the Mustang in drive and headed east. Forty minutes later he deposited Devon at the bus terminal, then followed the signs to the Bay Area Rapid Transit station. He left the Mustang on a side street, walked back to the station and bought a ticket on the next train to Oakland.

EIGHTEEN

V LADIMIR Ivanovich Kulagrin drove the antiquated
Mercedes northwards on the Leningradski Prospekt,
squinting in the fading evening light and staying in the outside lane in an attempt to avoid the steady traffic heading for
Dynamo Stadium.

As director general of the Moscow University Biological
Institute, he could easily have had a better car, but the
Mercedes had been with him for almost thirty years and was
the closest thing to family he still had, even if the parts for it
took up almost a third of his salary every month.

Manoeuvring through the darting traffic on the wide
thoroughfare he occasionally reached over and touched the
document case on the seat beside him. The risk of their joint
venture was enormous, but if the information in the document
case was ever made public it would almost certainly mean a
catastrophe capable of destroying the Soviet Union.

Half a mile beyond the stadium he turned left at the lights
and drove hesitantly into the huge parking lot between the
two slab-sided buildings marking Aeroflot City. One of the
buildings was the Aeroflot Hotel, used by transit passengers
on their way to and from Sheremetievo Airport, while the
other housed the Civil Aviation Authority. Between them was
the concourse where passengers were ferried to the airport by
bus or helicopter, depending on their station in life.

Kulagrin wasn't flying anywhere, however. He parked the
Mercedes and locked it, keeping the document case firmly
under his arm. He stood beside the car and within less than
a minute a large black Zil limousine pulled up beside him. He
climbed into the rear of the unmarked but obviously official
vehicle and sat back against the comfortable seat.

The uniformed driver, a corporal in the GRU – Soviet military intelligence – eased the car out of the parking lot and followed a service road that led onto the old Khodinsky Field, Moscow's first airport, now home to the Soviet Space Authority, the Moscow Aeronautics Institute and the Aquarium, notorious headquarters of the GRU.

The trip to the GRU compound took less than five minutes. Entering by the rear gate the driver took Kulagrin directly to the tall, glass-enclosed building which gave the headquarters its name, depositing him at the main entrance. Getting through the complex set of security checks took the scientist longer than the ride from Aeroflot City, but he finally reached his destination and was ushered into the top-floor office of General Arkady Zotov, chief of the GRU.

The slim, immaculately uniformed intelligence chief was in direct contrast to the bearlike, gravel-voiced Kulagrin, but the two men had been close friends since their earliest school days and greeted each other warmly. After the inevitable glass of ice-cold vodka from Zotov's personal refrigerator, the two men got down to business.

'You really think we are to trust the Americans' information?' Zotov asked, leaning back in his chair, feet up on his immense oaken desk.

'Yes.' Kulagrin nodded. 'They have as much to lose as we do.'

'It has been more than forty years since we were allies,' Zotov replied, shaking his head. 'I'm not sure I feel comfortable with the relationship.'

'I am afraid we have little choice in the matter, Arkady,' Kulagrin answered. 'We have gone too far to back out now.'

'Why not?' Zotov offered. 'By all appearances that is what our friend Comrade Han is doing.'

'The esteemed Chinaman in question is of little importance,' Kulagrin said, pouring another glass of vodka from the tray on the table, and helping himself to the silver case of cigarettes beside it. He lit one of the Russian-made Marlboros and dragged in a lungful of smoke. 'Han has lost control of the situation.'

'The Americans think the problem can be resolved,' Zotov said quietly. 'What is your opinion?'

'Their plan is a sound one.' Kulagrin put down his glass and unzipped the document case. He took out a sheaf of papers and slid them across the Zotov. The GRU head ignored them for the moment. 'It is a matter of increasing the number of potential vector sites,' Kulagrin continued. 'They will provide the . . . material . . . if we will put it in place.'

'Where?' Zotov asked.

'North Korea, Hong Kong, Vietnam, Kampuchea, Afghanistan and along the northern border. According to the Americans we can triple the number of potential targets.'

'What about the effect on our own people?' Zotov asked. It was the key question, of course, but Kulagrin answered without hesitation.

'Marginal,' he replied. 'The northern border is only lightly populated on our side, and what population there is in the area is military; they can be protected.'

'You know the men in the Kremlin better than I,' Zotov mused. 'What of their reaction?'

'We are all bound by the Leukertal Accord of 1968,' Kulagrin responded. 'All of us. The accord remains in place.'

'And if things go wrong?' Zotov asked. 'People change their allegiance quickly when faced with failure.' He smiled bleakly and Kulagrin knew his old friend was thinking about the horrors they were about to unleash on an unsuspecting world. The big man shrugged his shoulders and reached for the vodka again.

'Wrong is a subjective word,' Kulagrin said. 'We are all going to burn in hell for what we are about to do. All we can do is burn a little longer, my friend.'

'All right.' Zotov nodded. 'We will join the Americans this one last time.' In a single sentence he had given the death sentence to almost a hundred million people.

'And may God have mercy on our souls,' Kulagrin whispered. Zotov laughed.

'It is one of the benefits of a Marxist-Leninist state, old friend – we don't have to worry about the wrath of God, and we have no souls for him to offer his mercy.'

'Perhaps,' Kulagrin said quietly. 'Or perhaps it is only that we lost them long ago, you and I.'

NINETEEN

T OBY Hagen and his roommates sat together in a group as far back from the stage as they could get. The seats fanning out below them were slowly filling with kids, dressed like them in the coloured jump suits designating the four houses. For the moment the stage was empty except for a polished wood podium, a large, rectangular rear-projection screen looming behind it.

'Reminds me of a high-school assembly,' whispered Dick Dubrofsky seated on Toby's left.

'I think that's the general idea,' Sanchez said from the row behind them. 'Except in school I had this incredible girl named Shannon O'Leary who sat beside me on one side and another one named Bev something or other on the other side. It used to drive me crazy. I'd sit there sniffing Chanel on the left and Obsession on the right. I'd come out of those assemblies bent over at the waist.'

'You're disgusting, Sanchez,' Eric said from the shadows behind Toby.

'A man ruled entirely by his glands,' Dubrofsky snorted.

Below them the auditorium was almost full and the house lights were dimming. Then a single spot on the stage began to brighten, bathing the podium in a halolike glow. The four entrance doors to the theatre closed and a few seconds later a figure appeared on the stage. The man was short and pot-bellied, dressed in an ordinary business suit. He was almost totally bald except for a curly fringe of hair around his ears and he wore thick, heavy-framed glasses balanced precariously on a large Roman nose. The man crossed to the podium, adjusted the microphone slightly and leaned forwards, pudgy hands gripping the edges of the stand.

111

'Good afternoon. My name is Lucas Baird and I am the operations chief of the Egypt Green facility. I am sure you have a number of questions and concerns, all of which will be addressed over the next few days. Many of you are confused and perhaps frightened by what has happened to you. This is understandable, but let me make it clear that you are not alone.

'Egypt Green and its sister facilities were designed as a solution of last resort in the event of a potential nuclear holocaust. All of us, including I might add, the president of the United States himself, hoped and prayed that what we refer to as the SAHARA contingency would never be necessary. Sadly, those hopes and prayers have not been answered.

'Some of you may be aware of Strategic Air Command's alert system, but for those of you who are not, let me explain. SAC has a four-stage alert which goes from DEFCON-4, defence condition four, to DEFCON-1, their highest main alert. This facility is in contact with SAC headquarters in Omaha, Nebraska, and as of twenty minutes ago we were at DEFCON-2, which is only one step removed from a war status. In addition to the SAC alert there is also a long-range computer program called FORECAST used by the Pentagon, which has its own alert codes, going from Trigger through Cocked Pistol, Hammerstrike and Headshot. According to the FORECAST program we are now at Cocked Pistol.

'In practical terms this translates as a near-war situation. For the last six months we have been following a number of indicators which pointed to an escalation of world tension that would be impossible to back down from. In the last twenty-four hours that escalation has become critical. It seems certain that the Soviet Union is about to invade Iraq in depth. If that happens the United States and NATO will have no choice but to retaliate. From that point the FORECAST program gives us less than twenty hours. It would appear that the Soviet Union would respond by using their variant A plan which calls for nuclear war in Europe. We in turn will respond with a full-scale strike on the Soviet homeland. Our best-guess estimate for the first nuclear exchange is thirteen hours from now, with full-scale global involvement coming some time between the fourteenth and fifteenth hour.

'I realise that all of this must be quite bewildering, especially with regard to your own position here. At this point all I can tell you is that the Egypt Green facility is totally safe from the effects of any nuclear exchange, and that it has been designed to ensure the survival of its occupants for as long as five years. The facility is located more than 600 feet below ground in central Kansas and is powered by a pair of small nuclear reactors of the same type used in our nuclear submarines. Two full levels of the facility have been given over to aquaculture and hydroponics for both food and oxygen production. We have just about everything you'll need for the duration, however long that may be.

'That's about all I have to say for now, except that for anyone interested in what's going on in the outside world, we have a newswire screen being set up in the recreation centre on Level Five. Oh, and one more thing. If any of you are having trouble sleeping, or just want someone to talk to, we have a staff of counsellors. Use your intercom and make an appointment or go to the administration desk on your level. Now then, do we have any questions?'

'Everybody keep your mouth shut.' The harsh whisper came from the darkness behind Toby. It was Corey Shire's voice. 'We keep a low profile.'

There was a scattering of questions from the theatre, most of them having to do with contacting parents or leaving the facility. Baird deflected them all, telling the kids to go to the administration desk, or to see one of the counsellors. Finally someone asked the obvious question.

'What about girls?' The voice was anonymous, coming from roughly the centre of the theatre.

'I've been waiting for that,' Baird said. 'For the time being the girls' section is being kept segregated from the boys'. And in case anyone is wondering, there are about 25 per cent more girls at the facility than boys.' He looked around the hall and then lifted one hand. 'Anyway, enough questions for now. At this point I'd like to turn the proceedings over to the man who will be in charge of the four houses making up our "school" here, a man, by the way, who has a great deal of experience in this field, Brigadier George Armstrong Revik.'

Baird stood away from the podium and looked to the right. He began to applaud lightly as a uniformed man came striding out onto the stage. Automatically the kids in the theatre picked up the applause as Revik approached the podium. He was tall, at least six four, broad-shouldered and beefy under the dark-green uniform jacket. The right breast was slathered with medals and ribbons and he carried a thick binder under one arm. His hair was a salty-and-pepper brush cut.

'This one's bad news,' Sanchez whispered. 'Check out the hair.'

The applause died abruptly as Revik took over the podium, turning his head slightly and nodding Baird off the stage. Revik grasped the front edge of the speaking platform lightly. He stared out into the audience, then flipped open the binder in front of him.

'I'll keep it short. A few of you already know me, but most of you don't. For you new boys, let's get a few things straight,' he said. The voice was firm and strong with a faint trace of a Southern accent. 'I'm the boss, and I've chosen who'll lead each house. Each housemaster automatically has the rank of captain.' Revik glanced down at the binder. 'From what I can see here there are roughly thirty rooms in each house with four or five men apiece. I've divided each house into three squads of ten rooms, A Squad, B Squad, C Squad. Each squad in each house will have a squad leader who will report in turn to the appropriate housemaster captain. Squadleaders automatically have the rank of lieutenant prefect. Each room can elect a leader who will be given the rank of corporal. Lists of housemasters and squadleaders will be posted at the administration desks on each level later today. By tomorrow I want all of the rooms to have chosen leaders and their names given to the administration officer on each level.' Revik paused and looked out into the theatre.

'Over the next four or five days we'll be doing a number of tests on all of you to see just where you're best suited to fit in around here. We'll also be running system checks on the facility itself. Use this time as an orientation period. Get to know your way around, ask questions if you want to. When the testing is over I want you all to know this place backwards and forwards.' He paused and closed the binder, slipping it under his arm again.

'My office is on this level, just to the right of the administration desk. I'll see the housemasters there at 1800 hours tomorrow, immediately following the evening meal.' Revik stepped back from the podium, turned sharply on his heel and walked off the stage. The house lights began to go up and Toby blinked.

'Your basic fascist,' Dubrofsky said, standing up and stretching.

'He's dangerous,' Toby remarked thoughtfully.

'What's with all this military crap?' asked Sanchez, stepping in beside Toby as they headed up the aisle to the exit.

'He's smart,' said Toby. 'Rank hath its privileges and all that. He makes the room leaders responsible to the squad leaders, the squad leaders to the housemasters. You can bet he's got some pleasure-pain deal in the works too.'

When they reached the door leading out of the theatre an elbow thumped painfully into Toby's side as an adult figure stumbled into him. He felt a brief pulling sensation and then something was pressed into his hand. He turned, surprised, and for a split second he thought he spotted Peter Wolfe, now dressed in a uniform with a woman beside him. Then they were gone. It felt like a folded piece of paper in his hand but he didn't dare look at it surrounded by so many people. If it had been Wolfe he had done his best to hand over the note without being seen.

Toby, the Dick, Corey and the others followed the crowd to the escalators and went down to Level Seven. They reached their room and filed in, each boy heading for his own bunk. It was obvious than none of them felt like talking. Toby crossed to the toilet cubicle, closed the door and latched it. He sat down and only then did he open his clenched fist. The note was from Wolfe, scrawled hastily on the back of what appeared to be a diagram of Level Seven.

> *TOBY*
> *Remember what Dorothy said to her dog?*
> *Meet me at 0200*
> *change room at the pool.*
> *Don't tell your friends.*
> *Wolfe*

For a moment Toby wondered if the man had gone right out of his mind. Who the hell was Dorothy and why would he know

115

what she had said to her dog? Then it dawned on him and he remembered something Baird had said before introducing Revik. He had described the Egypt Green facility as being located in central Kansas.

'Well, Toto, I don't think we're in Kansas any more,' he whispered to himself. But if they weren't in Kansas, why would Baird lie about it, and why would it make any difference anyway?

He took a deep breath and let it out slowly. The only way he was going to find out was by meeting Wolfe at the pool and to do that he'd have to sneak out past Corey and the others. He closed his eyes and leaned back against the cool enamelled wall of the cubicle. Christ! What he'd give to be back with Devon right now, bitching and complaining about how boring it was to be a teenager in Mill Valley. Thinking about Devon he felt a tightening in his groin and swore out loud. He had to be the biggest bastard in the world to be thinking about sex with someone who was about to be incinerated. And he had to be an idiot to even consider meeting Wolfe.

He wadded up the note into a tight little ball and tipped it into the bowl of the toilet. Standing, he turned and flushed, then unlocked the cubicle and went out to join his friends.

TWENTY

B ETH Scott and Peter Wolfe came out of the administration
office on Level Seven and watched the last of the kids leave
the theatre.

'So there goes the future of America,' Peter commented. He
paused, clipping his plastic-coated security pass to his collar.
The young woman gave him an angry look as she put on her
own pass.

'Are you always this much of a cynic?' she asked. Peter
shrugged.

'Only when I've been buried alive by my own government,'
he answered. They were alone in the broad foyer in front of
the theatre entrance and Peter wondered what the Hagen boy's
reaction would be to the note he had managed to pass. He
had spotted Toby before the lights went down and midway
through Revik's speech he excused himself to go to the big
public washroom just outside the theatre entrance. Slipping
him the note had been risky, but necessary. If he was going
to make his plan work he'd need an ally and the boy was the
only one he could trust.

'Being buried alive is better than being up there,' said the
historian, poking a thumb towards the ceiling.

'That's a matter of opinion,' Peter argued. 'I still like the idea
of free will.' He did his best to smile. There was no sense in
making an enemy unnecessarily and he was pretty sure she'd
be reporting back to Hartshorn. It was time to backtrack a little.
'Look, you've had a lot more time to absorb this whole thing,
I'm still winging it. Why don't we call a truce and you can take
me on this tour you've been promising?'

'All right, truce,' she agreed. 'You've seen Levels Four, Five,
Six and Seven so we'll go down from here.' She looked up,

117

checking the large digital clock on the opposite wall. It was now 1540 hours – twenty minutes to four. 'Dr Hartshorn said he'd meet us down on Level Fourteen at 1830. Fourteen is the reactor level and that's where you'll be working.'

'I'm a mechanical engineer, not a nuclear one,' Peter pointed out. 'I don't know diddley about reactors.'

'Fourteen is the big expansion level too,' she explained. 'The long-range prediction is that Egypt Green and the other facilities like it will be in use longer than it's necessary for us to remain here. The computer is calling for a resident population of about 15,000 within twenty years.' She put her key-card into the slot by the elevator doors and waited.

Peter frowned, doing some fast calculations in his head. There were about 350 senior boys in the facility and another 200 juniors. If there was an equivalent number of girls, as Baird suggested, that meant a total population of a little more than 1200. Even if Hartshorn had some bizarre *Lebensborn* plot to keep the girls pregnant all the time for the next decade, that would only give a population of 6000, not to mention the fact that the place would be swimming in babies and toddlers. Somehow that didn't seem likely. Another anomaly.

The elevator doors slid open and they stepped inside. Using her key-card again, Beth punched the Level Eight button and they descended. Level Eight contained the junior school, complete with its own dining, recreation and sleeping facilities for boys between the ages of five and seven. They were dressed in dark-blue overalls and the staff were all women.

'Have they been told?' Peter asked as they returned to the elevator from the brief tour. Beth shook her head. 'No. About half of them are staff members' children, so they see their parents all the time. The rest have been told that their parents had to go on a business trip or to visit someone. There's also a staff of three child psychologists here. According to them most separation trauma is over within a few weeks, and given a little more time the kids will block off most memories. At that age they're pretty adaptable.'

Like the other levels reserved for adult staff, Level Nine ran continuously from end to end without a dividing bulkhead. About half the area was made up of suites for married staff and a number of smaller rooms for single men and women. There were two lounges, a small gym and a good-sized pool as well as a video theatre, complete with a bar. The other half of the level was given over to a well-equipped but not particularly high-tech hospital including several operating suites and two twenty-bed wards. There seemed to be no private rooms and, even stranger, Peter saw nothing in the way of a maternity area – no nursery, no incubators, no delivery rooms. Where were all these babies going to be born? He decided to say nothing.

Except for the aquaculture area, most of Level Ten seemed to hold various science labs, none of which apparently were on the tour.

The aquaculture section took up almost half the level, and stepping through the bulkhead doors Peter immediately felt a wave of warm, humid air. The tanks, each one at least fifteen feet across, were arranged in long rows with a criss-cross grid of catwalks above them. Each tank had its own computer terminal which was linked to a central workstation in a small, cluttered office at the far end of the chamber.

'I'll introduce you to Mike Whitefather, our resident fish freak,' Beth said as she led Peter along the catwalks to the office. Below them he could see thousands of fish in each of the tanks, so densely packed that he was sure they'd be starved for air and food.

The office was really no more than a floor and four glass walls suspended between two of the tanks at the far end of the level. A tall, desperately thin man was seated at a battered desk, feet up, reading a large volume. There was a computer on a stand beside the desk and the floor was stacked high with more books and reams of computer paper. As they stepped in, the man lowered the book, and Peter saw a face that could have come right off the buffalo nickel. Big nose, high cheekbones and jet-black hair streaked with white, tied back in a long pigtail. The only thing missing was a feather.

'Mike, this is Peter Wolfe, our new engineering man.' Peter extended a hand but the Indian just stared at it.

'Know anything about fish, man?' Whitefather asked.

Peter grinned, surprised at the man's nasal New York twang. 'They eat worms,' he answered.

'Right.' Whitefather nodded, 'I see where you're head is at.' Whitefather picked a bag of Red Man chewing tobacco off the desk and poked a wad into his cheek. Peter couldn't

119

help smiling at his choice of brands. 'Something funny?' asked Whitefather.

'No.'

'Know anything about aquaculture? Tilapia, buffalofish?'

'Not a thing.'

'How about Venturi drains?'

'Venturis I know about.'

'Maybe we can do business together. I'm looking to build some small algae ponds in between the big ones. Fertilise them with piss and keep them going with all the sediments we get pumped up from the hydroponics people downstairs.'

'Piss?' Peter asked, eyes widening.

Whitefather nodded. 'Sure. Male human urine. Nothing like it for growing up a crop of *Scenedesmus* scum. Eats ammonia and makes oxygen. You smell any piss out there?'

'Not a whiff,' said Peter, grinning.

'What'd I tell you, man? Nothing like *Scenedesmus*, unless maybe it's a batch of *Golenkenia*. Very far-out stuff, *Golenkenia*. Not your average pond algae, that's for damn sure.'

'I thought you could show Peter around,' Beth said. 'Aquaculture's not really my field.'

'True.' Whitefather nodded. He unhooked his legs from the desk and stood up, towering at least four or five inches over Peter.

Beth dropped into a metal folding chair. 'I'll wait for you here.'

Standing outside the office Whitefather pointed out the organisation of the section.

'Exactly one hundred tanks, five rows of twenty, each tank with 1400 gallons of water. Right now I've been getting about 250, 300 pounds per tank per crop, but I could probably double that by screwing around with the ammonia concentrations in the water.'

'What kind of fish are they?' asked Peter as they headed out along the catwalks.

'Blue tilapia mostly. Some perch, trout, like that.' He gestured towards a twisting nest of pipes and valves below them. 'That's the central recirculation system. Designed it myself, but it's too complicated so I spend half my time on maintenance. Think you could do it better?'

'Maybe.' Peter shrugged. 'I'd have to have a closer look.'

'You're new here, right?' Whitefather's voice had dropped to something just above a whisper.

'That's right.'

'They been scooping people like I here?'

'Scooping?'

'Kidnapping, man.'

'That's how I got here.'

'Shit,' Whitefather said, frowning. 'I don't get upstairs much, you know, don't hear everything that's going down. I heard that, though, but I didn't really think it was true.'

'How long have you been here?' asked Peter.

'Almost two years.'

'Are you serious?'

'Sure, man. Two years, just about done my time.'

'You make it sound like a jail sentence.'

'Kind of like that,' Whitefather answered, smiling for the first time. 'They needed someone who knew about aquaculture, ads in all the right places, you know. I went for the interview and they hired me, Said I'd have to be in isolation for two years.'

'They?'

'Earthlab. A closed-circuit demonstration project. Some long-range thing to do with the space programme. Anyway, that's what they said.' He paused, looking at Peter thoughtfully. 'Then about three, maybe four months ago all these military types started showing up and now I hear that this place is really some kind of big bomb shelter and they've been scooping kids, just like I've been stocking these tanks. I don't go for that kind of shit, man.'

'You want out?'

'Maybe. I want to find out what's going on, I know that much. I'm hearing rumours that they're about to press the big button. What about that?'

'That's what they say.'

'You believe it?'

'I'm not sure.'

'What about little old Beth?' Whitefather asked, looking over Peter's shoulder towards the office. 'I've met her a couple of times before. Once with Baird and then again with the German, Hartshorn. She seems pretty straight'.

'A true believer, I'm afraid. She's taken the whole thing, hook, line and sinker.'

'Hey, man, no fish jokes,' Whitefather said, grinning. 'Look. We shouldn't talk too long or she'll get suspicious, but if you get anything going or you need something, you let me know, OK? I know this place pretty well, especially the lower levels.'

'I'll remember that, Mike.'

Peter went through the rest of the tour on automatic, nodding when he was supposed to and asking the right number of appropriate questions. Level Eleven was hydroponics, a neatly ordered jungle of every edible plant known to man, all growing in nutrient solutions, monitored by computer and harvested on an automated conveyor belt. Twelve and Thirteen were both engineering levels, crammed with refrigeration and heating equipment, generators and ducts. Finally they reached Fourteen, the reactor level.

Beth took him quickly through the control room and then out into the reactor chamber, a sprawling, high-ceilinged room about the size of a small-town hockey arena. The reactor itself looked like a three-storey-high windowless office building. Above it was a complex web of catwalks and rails for aerial cranes. Except for a dull, throbbing hum the room was silent.

'Not the most impressive sight in the world, is it?' said a voice from behind them. It was Dr Max. He was wearing a white lab coat and carrying a clipboard.

'I thought you said there were two reactors,' Peter commented.

'There are. The other one at the far end of the level, separated by several dozen yards of reinforced concrete and lead shielding. Only one reactor is used at a time. The second is kept for emergencies and maintenance checks.' Hartshorn smiled. 'Beth has taken you everywhere?'

'I saved the best for last,' the young woman replied, smiling back.

'It's interesting,' said Peter, nodding towards the reactor.

'But not very exciting?' said Hartshorn, still smiling. He let out a short, barking laugh. 'Beth and I are having a little joke. For all its power there is nothing in the world so boring as a nuclear reactor.' He took Peter by the elbow. 'Come, let me show you where you will be working.'

They crossed the chamber to an oval bulkhead door fitted with a locking wheel. Beth turned the wheel and Peter heard a faint hissing sound as the pressure equalised. Stepping over the sill Peter found himself in a tubular passage, and from the exposed cables strung from the curving roof he assumed they were headed into some kind of construction area. The passage went on for three or four hundred feet, then curved downwards abruptly. A few moments later they reached another airlock door and once again Beth spun the locking wheel. She pulled the door open and beckoned to Peter.

'Close your eyes and then step through' she instructed. 'It's more exciting if you get the impact all at once.'

Peter did as he was told and stepped through the opening. He heard Hartshorn and Beth follow.

'Now,' said Hartshorn. 'Open your eyes.'

Peter did as he was told.

It was, without any doubt at all, the most extraordinary thing he had ever seen. So extraordinary that he closed his eyes and opened them again, not quite sure if he should believe what he was seeing.

'Jesus Christ!' he whispered.

He was standing on a metal platform suspended three or four hundred feet in the air. Below him a curving web of girders and metal plates seemed to stretch out infinitely. There wasn't much to scale things by, but he knew that the chamber he was looking down into had to be a mile long and at least as wide.

Above him the girders arced like the ribs of some unbelievably gigantic beast forming a magnificent dome at least two hundred feet above his head. The roof-girders were strung with thousands of lights and in the distance Peter could see the winking, white-hot flames from scores of welding torches as dozens of work crews laboured to put down the floor of the cavern. More crews were building jutting tiers and platforms, some already enclosed, creating a metal landscape of cliffs, slopes and plateaus.

'My God,' said Peter, suddenly realising what he was seeing. 'It's O'Neill's Island One.' O'Neill was Gerard O'Neill, the Princeton physicist and the man at the heart of the NASA space-colony effort.

'Not Island One,' Hartshorn corrected, coming to stand beside Peter at the edge of the platform. 'What you saw today with Beth was always seen as a temporary measure. Camping out, if you will. 'He raised his arm and swept it over the vista before them. '*This* is the real Egypt Green.'

123

TWENTY-ONE

THE man in the grey suit was alone in the command centre. He watched the various screens in front of him, his fingers on an outsized keyboard, a hands-free telephone headset over his ears.

'This is Peltz,' he said quietly, speaking into the microphone that curved in front of his mouth. 'What have you got for me?'

'The trailer was a mess,' came the slightly tinny reply. 'I'd say he was some kind of half-assed private investigator or a journalist. Both maybe.'

'Any connection to the girl?' Peltz asked.

'There was a clip file on Hagen.'

'Nothing else?'

'We found the car. Parked outside the bus terminal in Concord.'

'Shit,' said Peltz.

'Right,' said the voice in his ears. 'We figure they got spooked by the story we fed to the media.'

'Where did they go?'

'We're working on it. Except for some local runs the only thing that fits is an express to Reno.'

'We have anyone there?'

'Sure.'

'Get on it. I'll be in touch.'

'Right.' There was a click and the line went dead. Peltz tapped a sequence on the keyboard. The response was almost instantaneous.

'Transportation.'

'Peltz. I'm booked on the Falcon in an hour. Tell McCann I want the flight plan changed. Oakland to Reno with about a two-hour layover and then on to Bluemount. ETA for

124

Bluemount will be around 9.30 a.m. Eastern Standard Time. And wind up the Hughes, I'll be at the pad in ten minutes.'

'Done,' answered the voice. Peltz keyed out the line and took off the headset. He stared at the screens for a moment. Things were getting critical and what he didn't need now was a couple of outsiders screwing it all up. He glanced at the digital clock clicking off the seconds on one of the screens. In seven minutes he'd be on board the helicopter heading for Oakland Airport. If things went according to plan all the loose ends would be cleared up within the next few hours. He stood up and left the command centre.

Mickey Rubinek, exhausted, sat slumped in a chair, blindly watching the cable news network while he listened to Devon showering. In front of him on the coffee table lay the littered remains of Chinese take-out while beside him on the floor were a half dozen pieces of brand-new luggage. He lit a cigarette and inhaled blearily. A week ago he had been leading a reasonably normal life and now he was a fugitive from justice, lying low in the White Rose Motel in Reno with a smartass fourteen-year-old as his companion in crime.

But you had to give the kid credit. He was already bone-tired when he hooked up with her at the bus terminal downtown, but she had been full of piss and vinegar. Within an hour she had organised a car rental, bought clothes and toilet articles, and kitted them out with luggage. She even ordered the food after they had booked into the motel.

Which was all very nice, but it was getting out of control. Whether she liked it or not, it was time to bail out. If she wanted to play games with the bad guys that was fine, but he was heading for the hills. Canada maybe; they had their fair share of sleazeball tabloids he could work for.

She came out of the bathroom wearing the robe she had bought and towelling her hair dry. Yawning, she dropped down onto one of the twin beds and stared at him.

'You look like shit,' she said, grinning. 'Have a shower, it'll get the blood flowing through your veins.'

'Out of my wrists it'll come more likely,' he muttered, momentarily slipping back into a Yiddish phrasing he had all but forgotten.

'What's your problem?' she asked, dropping the towel onto

the bed beside her. In the robe, with the wet hair, she looked about ten years old. 'We pulled it off, we got away.'

'Right. Across a state line too,' he answered gloomily. 'I've got breaking and entering, kidnapping, illegal use of credit cards, and to top it all off I've got the Mann Act, taking a juvie across a border. That means we could have local cops, state and FBI on us, not to mention Chetwynd's people. You think they're going to give up now?'

'How will they find us?'

'Don't be stupid, kid.' he sighed. 'They've got pictures of both of us. They've got my car in Concord. I paid cash for my flight and used a phoney name, but if they work at it they'll pin it down. I figure maybe twelve hours before they're banging on the door.'

'So?' Devon shrugged. 'We leave in the morning, bright and early. You've got those numbers Chetwynd was calling. We go to Hawaii or DC, one or the other.'

'Not a chance,' Mickey said, shaking his head.

'What's that supposed to mean?' Devon asked, startled.

'It means I'm going to take a shower, and then I'm going to sleep. When I wake up I'm out of here, all on my own. You can do whatever you like, but I'm bugging out.'

'You can't!'

'Watch me.'

'I've got those tapes.'

'So I add illegal wiretapping to the list. Whoopee shit, kid.' He stood up and began unbuttoning his shirt.

'What about Toby?' she asked.

'He's shit out of luck, sweetheart. I think maybe he always was. I don't know what Chetwynd, Earthlab or these Phoenix people are up to, but I do know they're heavy hitters and I don't want anything more to do with the whole damn thing.'

'You're a bastard,' Devon whispered, staring up at Mickey coldly.

He shrugged. 'Hey, I'm sorry you feel that way, but if that's what it takes to survive, then I'm a bastard and proud of it.' He turned away, stripping off his shirt, and headed down the short passage to the bathroom.

Ten minutes later, feeling clean if not particularly refreshed, he came back into the bedroom, two towels covering him modestly. He had expected the lights to be off and Devon to be curled up in one of the beds, but the lights and the TV were still on and Devon had vanished. He panicked for a moment, then saw that she had left all the new clothes behind, and her purse was on the bedside table. Wherever she had gone, she was coming back. Using the privacy he slipped into a fresh pair of jockeys, killed the TV and the lights and climbed under the covers of the bed closest to the big picture window. He allowed himself half a minute to wonder where the kid had gone, then let go of it all. Before the other half of the minute had passed, he was asleep.

As the unmarked, French-built Dussault Falcon business jet went into its approach for Reno-Stead Airport, Gunnar Peltz, in the luxuriously appointed passenger salon, was going over his briefing notes for the Bluemount meeting later that day. He glanced at the heavy Rolex on his wrist and frowned. Two thirty. The Falcon was one of the fastest aircraft of its kind, capable of speeds of over 450 knots, but unless things went very smoothly in Reno they were going to be late. Almost on cue the radio phone on the bulkhead wall buzzed softly.
    'Peltz.'
    'Reno.'
    'Go ahead.'
    'How far away are you?'
    'Five minutes, maybe ten.'
    'Good.'
    'You found them?'
    'Yes. Place called the White Rose Motel on Oddie Boulevard just north of I-80. You coming into Stead or Reno International?'
    'Stead.'
    'Perfect. Less than five miles away.'
    'You sure it's them?' asked Peltz.
    'Positive. And they're both in the room.'
    'How can you tell?'
    'Aimed an OTIS at the window. Came up with two hot spots. It's them or a couple of hibachis full of charcoal.' OTIS, Peltz knew, stood for observer thermal imaging system, a high-powered heat-sensitive night sight.
    'You have some way to take them?'
    'Pick the lock, toss in a can of BN nerve gas and wait five

127

minutes. One whiff and they'll be down for ten to twelve hours. Good enough?'

Peltz thought for a moment. 'Do they have a car?'

'Rental Chev, parked outside the room.'

'Make sure it's taken care of. I want this to be very clean.'

'No problem. We can have them there in forty-five minutes.'

'Fine. Do it.' Peltz hung up the phone and sat back as the jet nosed down to the airport. He smiled. Maybe he'd be on time for the meeting after all.

TWENTY-TWO

TOBY Hagen lay on his bunk in the darkness, listening to the sleep sounds of his roommates. With a little imagination he could transport himself out of the cell-like room and pretend that he was at camp again. Instead of a cubicle deep underground, the darkness hid the faded cedar planks of his hut, and beyond the door was the thin screen of trees that stood between the camp buildings and Lake Torrance.

But it didn't work for long. The cubicle smelled of old metal and instead of a soft breeze making ghostly sounds outside the door there was only the faint click-whirr of the ventilation system. Camp became prison in a single heartbeat.

The confusion and fear he had felt were fading, though, replaced by something else, an adult anger that made him want to scream out his defiance. He had listened to Baird and then to Revik, his jaw setting and his heart turning to stone. The uniforms and ranks and soft talk pretending that this was some kind of private school were as childish as his own fantasies about Egypt Green being his old summer camp. It was neither camp nor school – it was a tomb, and they were the walking dead.

If what Baird had said was really about to happen then it meant the end of the world. Baird made it sound as if they were going to be heirs to some kind of paradise, but all Toby could envision was an underground existence, like the grunting horrors in H. G. Wells's *Time Machine*. He shook his head against the pillow, gritting his teeth. Screw that. He'd take earthly hell over Baird's subterranean paradise any day of the week.

He sat up quietly and swung his legs over the side of the bunk, hooking his toes into the lower rungs of the built-in ladder. He eased himself off the bunk and swung down to the floor, pausing for a moment, listening. Nothing; they were all asleep.

He reached the door and opened it, peering down the long, narrow corridor. According to the manual, this was a sleep period, hence the dim red light. The manual had also mentioned that during sleep periods any unauthorised movement outside assigned quarters was a serious offence. In other words, there was a curfew.

During their first reconnaissance of the level neither Deetz nor Corey had noticed anything in the way of high-tech surveillance. There were no obvious cameras anyway. Not that it meant anything; there could be motion detectors, infra-red, anything, and he'd never know until it was too late.

He took a deep breath, stepped into the corridor and eased the door shut behind him. He waited a full minute, every sense on full alert, waiting for an alarm to go off or a swarm of Revik's goons to appear. Still nothing except the machine-breathing of the vent system. He could feel his armpits getting damp and a trickle of sweat slid down along his cheek even though the air was cool. He had a flashing memory of his first swimming lesson and the terror he had felt letting go of the edge of the pool. It was the same now. With one hand on the doorhandle he could slip back into the room and safety; released, he was swimming on his own and vulnerable.

He headed down the corridor, walking quickly, his bladder suddenly burning like a hot coal below his stomach, his mouth parched. He pushed it all into the back of his mind, concentrating on what was ahead. He was scared shitless, but that was just fine, because, by God, he was actually doing something for the first time since he was snatched. He grinned, feeling his lips pull back over his teeth. A little bit of free will went a long way.

Out of the corner of his eye he kept a count of the room numbers. His own room was N-47, the N supposedly meaning north. The other main corridor on the other side of the level was S and the cross corridors connecting them were all E and W. The swimming pool was located at the far west end of the level between the two long corridors and was accessible from either side and also from the last of the cast-west linking corridors.

He kept moving, pausing at every linking corridor and peeking around the corner. From the looks of it, Revik didn't post any kind of guard. At N-6 he reached the last link corridor and turned down it. There were no doors at all on his left –

that was the swimming pool, and the doors on the right weren't spaced equally and had long numbers and no letters. Probably service areas of one kind or another.

Two-thirds of the way along the linking corridor he spotted a door on his left and tried the handle. It went down with a click and the door swung open. The room beyond was completely dark and Toby felt the slightly burning tang of chlorine in his nostrils. He stepped into the room, shutting the door behind him, and reached out with one hand, palm flat, running it down the invisible wall on his left. He found a light switch and flicked it. There was a crackling sound and a few seconds later a bank of fluorescents in the ceiling popped into life.

Toby blinked, momentarily blinded. He was on some kind of observation deck. There were a dozen or so theatre-style seats and a huge picture window looking out into the pool. To one side there was a doorway while on the other there was a table set out with coffee-making paraphernalia.

He walked to the window and looked out at the pool. It wasn't quite olympic-size, but it had a two-tier diving platform and the sign on the wall said the deep end was fourteen feet six inches. Everything was done in tile, the floor in a deep green, the walls and slightly arched ceiling in white. The pool itself was a regulation blue, the water utterly smooth, like a huge rectangular turquoise set in a Navajo brooch, gleaming in the faint ghost light from the observation area. There was no sign of Wolfe, even though the big clock on the wall at the shallow end showed it to be exactly 0200. Two o'clock in the morning, at least in this world.

He frowned. Enough of that. There was no other world, no Devon, no mother or father, no US Cavalry coming to the rescue. He snorted; the US Cavalry had been the ones who nabbed him in the first place, so any rescue was going to have to come from the Indians. And since that wasn't going to happen either, he was on his own.

He froze. A sound echoed somewhere close by. A door? He lunged for the light switch, plunging the room into darkness again. He dropped to the floor and crawled back to the big window. Lifting himself onto his elbows he looked out. A puddle of light swinging back and forth giving little glimpses of the diving board, the silent, empty pool. A guard, it had to be.

The light swung around and Toby dropped to the floor as

131

the beam crossed the window. He could hear footsteps on the tile around the pool edge. Closer. He swallowed hard. Two options: freeze where he was or try and get to the door and the corridor outside. He could visualise the long corridor leading back to N-47. It had taken him almost ten minutes to get here and it would take that long to get back. He'd be a sitting duck.

'Shit,' he whispered. Flat on his belly he crawled across to the rows of seats and squeezed down between them. If the guard came into the room and turned on the light it would be all over, but he might go unnoticed if the man only used his flashlight. The footsteps grew louder and Toby's heart lurched as he heard the handle on the pool-side door rattle. A pause, another rattle and then the footsteps again, receding this time. Toby let out his breath in a long gasp. He waited for a long minute, then stood slowly, levering himself up on the seats, remaining in a crouch.

'He's still there, don't move!' the harsh whisper came from only a few feet away in the darkness.

'Corey?'

'Shut up!'

Toby dropped as the flashlight beam swung into the room again, much closer this time, the light almost crossing his face. The guard must have doubled back. The light moved back and forth again, then vanished. Toby closed his eyes, counting out the silence. At two hundred, nerves screaming silently, he heard the footsteps receding for good. He waited another minute, then spoke.

'Corey?'

'Who the hell else would it be? I'm right behind you.'

'You followed me.'

'Of course I followed you, asshole. You get up at two o'clock in the morning and go for a walk, my curiosity gets aroused. What the hell are you doing?'

'At the assembly, Wolfe, the man I came in with, passed me a note. He asked me to meet him here and not tell anyone else.'

'Why?'

'I'm not sure. All the note said was to remember what Dorothy said to her dog.'

'Dorothy as in *The Wizard of Oz*?'

'I guess.' Toby groaned, the pins and needles in his arms

132

and legs beginning to hurt. 'You think maybe I could get up now?'

'I suppose so. I think the guard's gone.'

Toby sat up and dropped into one of the seats. He began massaging his knees. There was a brush of movement and then Corey slid into the seat beside him.

'What the hell did he mean?' he asked. Toby shrugged.

'Well, Toto, I don't think we're in Kansas any more,' he quoted. 'You figure it out.'

The overhead lights in the room blossomed again and Toby almost cried out. Both he and Corey whirled around in their seats. Standing just inside the corridor entrance was Peter Wolfe in full uniform, a long black halogen flashlight in his hand.

'It means exactly what it says,' said the astronaut.

'Jesus!' said Corey, 'I almost wet myself.'

'Who's he?' Wolfe asked, gesturing towards Corey with the flashlight.

'A friend,' Toby answered defensively.

'I told you to come alone.'

'I followed him,' Corey explained. 'He didn't know anything about it.' He looked at the flashlight. 'Was that you out by the pool?'

'Yes. Toby wasn't in the change room so I went looking for him. I saw the light here and then it went out, but the pool door was locked.

'We thought you were a guard,' said Toby.

'I might have been,' said Wolfe. 'In which case you two would be getting grilled by Brigadier Revik right now. Try and be a little more careful next time, OK?'

'If there is a next time,' Corey said. 'I'm not sure I was cut out for a life of action and adventure.' He gave Wolfe a long cold look. 'Not that you have any say in what we do or don't do. So far you haven't given me any reason why I should trust you either.'

'Don't be a smartass,' Wolfe answered wearily. 'I'm not in the mood, frankly. And I'll be in just as much trouble as you if I get caught off my level at this time of night. If we want to get out of here we're going to have to trust each other.'

'Just exactly where do you think "here" is?' asked Toby.

'Baird said Egypt Green was built in a salt mine in Kansas. Your note says no.'

'I don't know where we are, but it sure as hell isn't Kansas,' the ex-astronaut told him.

'You sound pretty sure of yourself,' Corey said.

'I am. I don't know if Toby mentioned it, but when we were brought here they kept us in some sort of quarantine for a while. I recognised some of the components in the place as being NASA. When I got here I was introduced to an old colleague of mine, Dr Max Hartshorn; he used to be a big wheel in the space-medicine programme.'

'Great,' Corey smirked. 'We're on the moon.'

'Just listen,' Wolfe said. 'For a while I swallowed the whole line about this being some kind of massive bomb-shelter programme, a civil-defence thing spun off the NASA space-station plans. They've even got a giant extension to this place under construction off the lower levels.'

'So?' said Corey.

'So it's bullshit,' Wolfe stated. 'A whole lot of things didn't add up, and then I discovered the cruncher. According to Max, I was brought here to replace their top engineer. I know the man, and this place could never have been designed by him — too utilitarian, too basic, and way too old. From the looks of it this installation has been in place for quite a while.'

'OK.' Corey shrugged. 'So he lied. What does that prove?'

'Nothing. But it got me thinking. I was trying to date the original construction, so I managed to steal a screwdriver during the tour they gave me. I went back to my cell or whatever you want to call it, and I unscrewed the ventilator in the ceiling. You can usually figure out how old a building is by the engineering components and I wanted to have a look.'

'What did you find?' Toby asked.

'Sheet-metal vent housings, steel beams, heavy-duty wiring. Most of it looked fifteen, maybe twenty years old.'

'What does that have to do with Kansas?' asked Corey.

'By itself, nothing,' Wolfe said. 'But some of the beams still had their shipping chalk.'

'What's that?' asked Toby.

'Big shipments of steel always have the mill name, the date and the shipper's name chalked onto them before they go out. That way shipments don't get confused. It's especially important when the steel is for a complicated installation like this.'

'Get to the point,' said Corey.

'The point is, the chalk wasn't in English. The alphabet was Cyrillic.'

'Russian?' said Toby, his eyes widening.

'Russian.' Wolfe nodded. 'The steel came from shipyard number 199. That's Komsomolsk at the mouth of the Amur River in Siberia. They specialise in building the big Soviet submarines; the same kind of steel you need in a pressurised underground installation like this. According to the chalk I saw, that particular shipment went out on 23 September 1977 on a ship from Nikolayevsk called the *Mitsenek*. So how does a shipload of Russian steel get used in what's supposed to be a disused Strategic Air Command facility a thousand feet under the wheatfields of Kansas?'

'This is crazy,' said Toby. 'It doesn't make any sense at all.'

'It does to someone, and that's what we have to find out,' Wolfe said. 'I think all of it – the bomb shelter, Kansas, even the big bang we're supposedly counting down to – is all a cover for something else.'

'This chalk,' Corey put in, 'did it have any kind of destination marking? Anything to tell you where it was being delivered?'

'Yes,' said Wolfe. 'Not that I can figure it out. The destination was one word: OKEAH.'

'Which means?' asked Corey.

'Ocean.'

TWENTY-THREE

ICKEY Rubinek woke up with a stunning headache and a taste in his mouth that defied description. His body felt as though it was made of rubber and he didn't seem able to open his eyes. The only thing close in his experience was how he had felt coming out from under the gas when they wrenched out his wisdom teeth, but this was much worse. He was sure that if he moved he'd shatter into a thousand pieces and there wouldn't be the slightest chance of putting him back together again.

He phased in and out a few times over the next hour or so, and finally he regained full consciousness and risked cranking open one eye. It didn't look promising. Directly overhead he could see bare concrete and a triple tube of fluorescents behind wired glass. He closed the eye, groaned, and then opened both at once, swallowing the nausea and waiting until things came into focus.

It was a jail cell, that was clear enough. An eight-by-eight cube in cinderblock and concrete. The bed was a metal shelf built into the left wall, there was a toilet and sink at the back and a windowless green metal door in front. No pillow and the mattress was a one-inch-thick slab of foam rubber covered in green ticking to match the door.

'Goddamn,' he groaned, swinging his legs onto the floor. The headache was receding, stabbing into his brain now and again as it retreated. Standing, he wobbled to the sink and splashed water on his face, then rinsed out his mouth. He urinated, weaving in front of the bowl with his eyes half closed, then sat down again. He was wearing the same clothes he had had on in the motel and from the feel of it, he had been wearing them for at least a couple of days. He had a fleeting image of Devon, then groaned again. Jesus! What had happened?

136

He had been snatched, of course. Probably Devon as well. They were statistics, just like the others. Except now there was no half-assed quasi-journalist sniffing along the trail with his teenaged Tonto for sidekick. The adventure had become reality, just as he had been afraid it would all along. Play with fire and you were going to get burned eventually.

They had been slick, that was for sure, because he only had the haziest memory of being taken. Sleeping lightly in the motel he had been aware of a bright light, a stunning concussion, and then nothing except the vague feeling that he was flying. The whole thing probably hadn't taken more than a few minutes. Half a dozen guys in suits, quick flash of fed ID to the motel manager, and then the assault. He and Devon come out in body bags and get loaded into a van, the manager gets a number to call to report the damages and then it's over. Two fugitives bite the dust in a Reno motel. It sure wasn't going to get a big play on the wire services.

So now there were only two questions: where was he and what was going to happen next? The second question was the easiest to answer. Mickey Rubinek and Devon Talbot were going to be snuffed – loose ends to be tied up permanently.

He glanced around the barren cell. No graffiti on the walls, no signs of wear. The stockade in some little-used military facility? He stood up and shuffled to the door, putting his ear to the hairline crack between the door and the wall. Nothing, silent as a . . .

'Tomb,' he said aloud, his voice croaking. He went back to the sink and took another mouthful of water. Whatever they had drugged him with had been powerful. He sat down again, thinking about Devon and Toby and the rest of it. The kidnappings, Earthlab, the motel snatch, this place. It was all slick and professional and with the exception of himself and Devon, it had all gone off without a hitch.

Big money and big government had come together to hatch this project back in the sixties, and it had grown like crabgrass, spreading out from the original study, gaining power ad maintaining near-perfect security. At first it was all about establishing some sort of brains trust, identifying who the smart up-and-comers were. Then it got more complicated. Whom did the 'brains' marry, where did they live? And now the grand finale: snatching their kids. Dozens, scores, maybe hundreds of the smartest children in the United States. A high-tech Pied Piper leading the children of Hamelin into the subterranean depths of some mountain.

Was that it? Earthlab sets up a completely sealed environment, an ark, in an utterly secret location. In it, under it, or around it is a storehouse of snatched kids, put on ice. For what?

The door to the cell opened suddenly, banging back into the wall. Mickey's head jerked around and he saw a figure standing under a bright light in the corridor outside. The man was tall, well dressed and had a bland, reasonably attractive face. Somewhere between thirty-five and forty-five. Beside him was a younger man in military uniform without any insignia. The man in the suit stepped into the cell, leaving the door open. The uniform stayed out in the corridor.

'Mr Rubinek?'

'Yes.'

'My name is Peltz. Come with me.' He stepped aside and gestured towards the door. Mickey stood up and did as he was told. Peltz had bland enough features but there was something dead and cold in his eyes. Peltz was one of those people who followed orders – any orders – without compunction.

The uniform took the lead, Peltz and Mickey behind. Mickey could detect the faint sour smell of raw stone through the concrete and without any real proof he knew he was underground. He counted ten cells on each side as they went down the corridor, then passed through a mesh gate. Two left turns, a ramp leading up, another gate, another short corridor and the uniform came to a stop in front of an office door. The uniform opened the door and stepped aside. Peltz ushered Mickey inside and closed the door after himself.

The office was bare. A desk, three filing cabinets, a chair for the desk and two metal chairs for visitors. There was a computer terminal and a telephone on the desktop and nothing on the walls except a big square ventilator grille behind the desk. As in his cell, the walls were cinderblock. The floor was linoleum.

'Nice place you've got here.'

'Shut up and sit down,' sat Peltz, going behind the desk. Once again Mickey did as he was told. Peltz keyed in the computer terminal and sat staring at the screen for a moment.

Then he turned to Mickey. 'You're in a great deal of trouble, Mr Rubinek.'

'Tell me about it.' He shrugged. There was no reason to be polite. Peltz, if that really was his name, wasn't about to do him any favours.

'Do you know how long we've had you here?' Peltz asked.

Mickey shrugged again. 'I shaved before going to bed in that motel in Reno. I've got two, maybe three days' stubble.'

'Three days.' Peltz nodded. 'We've interrogated both you and your young friend several times since you arrived.'

'Scopolamine. Drugs.'

'Yes.'

'Find out anything interesting?'

'Other than the fact that you're a very bitter and frightened man, no. You've really been inept, Mr Rubinek.'

'Then why am I here?'

'Because I wanted you here.' Peltz leaned back in his chair. 'Think of me as someone who removes flies from ointment.'

'What about Devon? Are you and your friends afraid of a kid?'

'Somewhat more than we are frightened of you, Mr Rubinek. The child has a better intuitive grasp of what's going on, we discovered that much.'

'You're snatching kids and hiding them away in some kind of Noah's ark,' Mickey said. 'Presumably because you think the shit is about to hit the fan. My guess is someone up there is about to press the button.' Mickey took a deep breath and let it out slowly. The headache was coming back. Peltz laughed, but there wasn't any humour in the sound.

'Very good, Mr Rubinek, a little bit of last-minute bravado.' The man shook his head wearily. 'All for nothing.'

'Why don't you get to the point?' Mickey said. 'You said you interrogated me and you didn't find out anything. You tell me that Devon and I are flies in the ointment. Fine, so let us go or blow out the candle. If you're about to kill us, why don't you give me a cigarette as my last request?'

'A psychiatrist could make his life work out of you, Mr Rubinek.' Peltz smiled. He opened a desk drawer and took out a package of Winstons and a book of matches. He tossed them to Mickey. 'I want the matches back.'

'Sure.' He lit up and slid the matches onto the desk.

139

'Do you know where you are?' asked Peltz.

'A government reservation of some kind. It feels like its underground.'

'Quite right. Have you ever heard of a place called Mount Weather?'

'Big government bomb shelter outside Washington. Way out of date. The Russians have got about fifty SSBs locked onto it. It's supposed to be super-secret but every once in a while somebody rams a plane into the mountain and it hits the newspapers. Some kid back in the sixties did some drawings of it from outside and there was a big stink.'

'You have excellent recall,' said Peltz.

'Stock in trade,' Mickey answered. He took a deep drag on the cigarette and tried to keep calm. Mount Weather was supposed to be about forty-five miles from DC – West Virginia?

'We could keep you and your friend here indefinitely,' Peltz said. 'Why do you assume that we intend to have you killed?'

'Because it's expedient. And any group that can kidnap dozens of kids won't hesitate to kill if that's what's necessary.'

'It astounds me, all of this paranoia,' Peltz remarked. 'Why is it so fashionable for the public to believe the worst of its government and its leaders? These children haven't been kidnapped, Mr Rubinek, they've been saved. What we're doing is no different from Winston Churchill ordering the children of London to be evacuated into the countryside. These children represent the future of the United States, perhaps even the world.'

'So the means justify the end?' asked Mickey. 'You and your pals get to pick who'll survive while the rest of us have our eyeballs liquefied in some nuclear firestorm? Horse puckies, Mr Peltz. This whole thing is a crock, an obscene crock of shit.'

'You're entitled to your opinion, Mr Rubinek, but that aside, I can assure you that we have no intention of killing either yourself or Miss Talbot. At the moment we are in a critical situation that may lead to nuclear war. If we manage to weather the crisis the children will be returned to their parents and you will be released. For the present, you and Miss Talbot will be taken to another facility in Maryland.' Peltz picked up the telephone on his desk and hit three buttons. He listened for a moment, then hung up. 'Miss Talbot

140

is waiting on the next level,' he said. 'The guard outside will escort you.'

Mickey stood up and leaned over the desk. He had nothing to lose and the only risk was that Peltz would put a bullet in his head now rather than later.

'You're a little bureaucratic shit, Peltz. And if you believe all of what you just told me, then you're an even bigger idiot than I am for ever getting involved in all of this.' The man behind the desk stared up at Mickey blandly and smiled. Mickey turned away, went to the door and opened it.

'Goodbye, Mr Rubinek.' Mickey went out into the corridor and fell in behind the uniformed guard, hands jammed into the pockets of his jeans, fingers curled around the book of matches he had palmed when he leaned over the desk.

TWENTY-FOUR

HANDCUFFED to a metal eyebolt and with an armed guard beside him, Mickey went on a golf-cart tour of the tunnels of the Mount Weather 'special facility' as they worked their way up to the surface. Despite his bravado and palming the matchbook, Mickey was paralysed with fear. For years he had been writing stories about the most absurd events and conspiracies, but nothing he had ever concocted was a match for this.

He felt as though he was on the detailed set of a science-fiction film, complete with uniformed bad guys and underground bunkers, but he knew that it was all horribly, monstrously real. There really *was* a Mount Weather, there really *was* a big front company called Earthlab that was kidnapping children, and he and Devon really *were* going to be taken out into some anonymous backwoods and shot. And unlike what happens in a movie, no Rambo-style gladiator was going to come to their rescue.

Mickey let his head fall back against the seat rest, his eyes on the bright pans of light hanging down from the rough stone ceiling. The whole place had a rancid basement smell and the fat little tyres on the golf cart hummed busily as they beetled along. He sat up, blinking, trying to throw off the dumb, frozen fear enshrouding him. These bastards were leading him off to his own execution and he was just sitting there, letting them do it, not even *thinking* about a way out.

He cursed silently. That was the biggest crime in his books – not thinking. He might not be Sylvester Stallone, but he had a brain, and if ever there was a time to put it to work, it was now.

With the handcuffs on he was helpless. The guard driving the cart had a holstered automatic pistol on his web belt and the one beside him had both a pistol on his belt and some kind of small machine gun held loosely in his lap. Mickey tried to relax, breathing slowly, biding his time. The chances were good that Peltz wouldn't foul his own best by having them blown away too close to the Mount Weather installation. He swallowed, working his tongue around in his mouth, trying to get some saliva into his parched throat. Think, turkey! How will they do it? The cart turned a corner and the incline started to get steeper; they were getting closer to the surface now and there was other cart and pedestrian traffic in the corridor.

Peltz was a professional, so he had probably done his home-work; that meant they had a dossier on him and some kind of quickie psychological profile too. What would it say? Failed journalist, mediocre writer, unsuccessful with women . . . coward? Whatever the details were, Peltz wouldn't be expecting any trouble.

Well, screw that. *Something* had made him take those matches, and it wasn't the off chance of getting a final cigar-ette from his firing squad. Peltz expected cowardice, so he'd get the opposite, or at least a reasonable facsimile.

The corridor levelled off and the golf cart was slowing down. A hundred feet ahead Mickey could see the corridor widening into a big rectangular compound half filled with military jeeps and a few automobiles, blazingly lit by banks of overhead sodium lights. Hell's garage in a sick, jaundiced colour. At the far end of the parking area there was a guard post and a floor-to-ceiling chain-link gate. The way out.

The driver turned the cart into the garage and pulled to a stop in front of a windowed guard station with a metal door to one side. He stepped out of the cart, went to the window and handed a clipboard through a slot in the glass to the uniformed attendant inside. Turning, he hooked a thumb over his shoulder and the guard beside Mickey prodded him out of the cart. There was a push-button console to the right of the entrance and no knob. The door was controlled from within.

It was opened, and the guard poked Mickey through. Mickey found himself in a small, windowless antechamber with another door fitted into the rear wall. The guard undid his handcuffs and vanished back into the parking garage, leaving Mickey alone. Not for long. A few seconds later the inner door swished opened and another guard appeared, a two-foot billy club dangling from his right hand.

'In here.'

The next room looked like an infirmary, complete with examining table, cabinets marked with large red crosses and a pair of oxygen tanks. Using the tip of the truncheon the guard prodded Mickey towards yet another door, also fitted with a push-button lock. The guard opened the door and pushed Mickey through, closing it behind him.

'Mickey!' It was Devon, looking like hell in wrinkled clothes, with lank hair and a tear-streaked, grimy face. She jumped forwards, wrapping her arms around him, pressing her cheek against his chest. Embarrassed, he let her hug him for a moment, surprised at how pleasant it felt, then untangled himself, silently furious at the flush he could feel rising on his cheeks.

'You OK?' he asked, stepping back.

'I guess. I think they drugged me or something. I feel like I could drink a gallon of water. Do you know what they're going to do with us? The guy who was asking me all these questions said we were being taken to some kind of quarantine . . .'

'They're going to kill us,' Mickey said, cutting into her enthusiastic babbling. This was not time for subtlety.

'What?'

'Kill. As in murder, assassinate, tie up the loose ends. To use an old cliché, we know too much, kid.'

'But – '

'Shut up,' he said coldly. There were no visible cameras, but there was a good chance the room was bugged. He looked around slowly. An office, probably for a duty nurse or doctor. There was a computer terminal, a bookcase full of medical books and computer-program manuals and a steel cabinet. Mickey put a finger to his lips, pointed around the room, then used his hand to do a duck-quacking imitation. Devon frowned, her brow wrinkling, and then she got it and nodded. She began talking again, keeping up a continuous stream about what she remembered of her capture while Mickey went around the room. The cabinet was locked, there was nothing useful on the shelves and the computer terminal had a security bar over the keyboard.

While Devon kept on talking he tried the desk drawers.

The right-hand file drawer was locked but the narrow front drawer and two on the other pedestal were open. Rubber bands, Federal Emergency Measures Agency stationery, a can of screen cleaner for the computer and some tissues, half a dozen pencils with FEMA imprinted on them, paperclips, an open package of Beemans. He picked up the pack of gum, slid out two sticks and handed one to Devon. She took it without breaking the flow of her monologue and put it into the pocket of her jeans.

Mickey stopped dead and stared down at the open centre drawer of the desk. The screen cleaner. James Bond in what? *The Man with the Golden Gun*? *Diamonds Are Forever*? There was a snake in the bathroom and Bond had fried it with a match held to a can of hairspray. An aerosol flamethrower. Mickey dug out the four-inch-high cylinder of screen cleaner and squinted at the list of substances. Iso-propyl alcohol was at the head of the list. He took the matches out of his pocket and turned, showing both matches and can to Devon. She nodded, still talking, and took the can from Mickey's outstretched hand. She stowed it under the belt of her jeans and Mickey put the matches into his shirt pocket.

When the door opened two minutes later Devon was still talking and she kept it up all the way to the parking garage and into the dark-green unmarked car waiting for them. Mickey slid in beside her and she finally shut up. The only other person in the car was the driver, separated from them by a metal grille. Sitting forwards Mickey could see that the car was equipped with a cellular phone and a riot gun in a clamp holder. There were no door-lock releases or window cranks in the passenger compartment.

The car moved forwards carefully along a relatively narrow tunnel that did a long S-curve before it reached the massive front doors. They must have tripped some kind of sensor because the doors began to roll back into the rock walls on either side, revealing a steadily broadening band of natural light.

They drove through the opening into a large fenced compound. Beyond the chain link and barbed wire Mickey could see forest everywhere.

'What are they here for?' asked Devon, pointing to the left. Mickey turned and spotted a convoy of half a dozen

145

cube vans, all with large cartoon polar bears on the side and the name MR FREEZE Ltd in icicle-dripped letters. Over the cabs each lorry was equipped with a large refrigerating unit.

'Beats me,' said Mickey. 'Maybe they eat a lot of ice cream in there.'

'Weird,' Devon muttered, looking back over her shoulder as they passed.

The car stopped at the outer barrier gate. The driver rolled down his window, showed his ID to the armed guard and then put the car in gear again as the gate began to open. As they drove through Mickey made a coughing sound and bent over, slipping the matches out of his pocket and into his hand. He sat again, sliding the matchbook under his thigh.

They moved upslope, doing a steady fifteen miles an hour, turning past a number of barrack-style buildings nestled in the trees. Reaching a narrow plateau they turned left, then right, weaving between more buildings. The sky was clear and from the position of the sun it looked as though it was early in the afternoon. Here and there Mickey could see uniformed figures walking between the buildings and he spotted one group at a picnic table under a stand of trees. Lunchtime. Between twelve and one then.

Beyond the buildings the roadway was shaded by large pines on either side. They were moving downslope now, the road twisting around large rock outcroppings every hundred yards or so. Eventually they reached another gate and guard house. Beyond it Mickey could see a paved road and a cluster of signs. 'Appalachian Trail', 'Clarke County Route 605', 'Frogtown 3 miles', 'Morgan Mills 5 miles'.

The gate opened and they turned left. Frogtown or Morgan Mills. Neither one sounded like a whole lot of fun to Mickey. If Peltz was telling the truth and they really were being taken to some kind of quarantine area, the driver would head for a main road. If not they'd turn onto some byway where the dirty deed could be done in privacy.

The driver followed 605 for less than five minutes, driving under thirty and giving Mickey and Devon a fine view of the broad, thickly treed hollow far below. It was beautiful, but Mickey couldn't help wondering how many bodies were buried in that rich, dark earth.

A sign on the right announced that they had arrived in Toy Hill, a hamlet of half a dozen run-down houses using the crossroads of 605 and 604 as an excuse for existence. The driver swung the car to the right. According to the sign, Virginia State Highway 7 was fifteen miles away. Mickey swallowed his chewed-out stick of Beemans, his muscles tensing, the matchbook feeling as though it had spontaneously exploded under his leg. This was it; somewhere along this stretch of road the driver was going to pull off and blow their brains out. He nudged Devon.

'Huh?'

'Pretty country,' he said inanely, watching the reflection of the driver's eyes in the mirror. The flicker seemed to come at about seven- or eight-second intervals. Not much but it would have to do. 'I wonder where we're going?'

'I hope it's better than the last place,' Devon answered. She slipped the can out of her belt and switched it from her left to her right hand, keeping her palm over it on the seat.

Mickey looked left and right. They had turned off the slope, following a narrow valley with a creek that meandered alongside the road. Turning slightly he checked the road behind. No second car riding shotgun. They'd reach the halfway point between the crossroads and the main highway within five minutes and there was no way of knowing when the driver would find his spot. He couldn't wait, it had to be soon. Keeping his eyes on the mirror Mickey pulled the book of matches out from under his leg, Devon appeared to be looking out of the window, but then he saw that she was watching him out of the corner of her eye.

'*Now!*' he screamed. He struck a match, turning it back on the rest, so it became a torch. He lifted the flaming book quickly, holding it up to the grill, and Devon brought up the screen cleaner, her finger down hard on the button. A two-foot-long tongue of flame whooshed out of the can, turning the back of the driver's head into a fireball. The man bellowed in pain but Devon kept her finger on the button as he swung around, raising his arm to ward off the flame. Mickey saw the inevitable approaching and dragged Devon down onto the floor as the car swerved off the road to the right, running up the slope and sideswiping a tree. The engine coughed, then died.

147

Suddenly it was silent except for the sound of the engine ticking as it cooled, and the air was full of the reek of burned hair.

Mickey dragged himself back into his seat, now tilted at a thirty-degree angle. The man's hair had stopped burning and he was slumped against the door, a thick stream of blood running down his roasted cheek.

'You OK?' Mickey asked Devon.

'Fine', she groaned, jammed between the seat and the door. 'What about our friend up there?'

'Out cold, bleeding, flame-broiled, but still breathing . . . I think. Now let's get out of here.'

'How? You can only open the doors from the outside.'

'Move out of the way,' said Mickey. Holding on to the grille with one hand and gripping the back of the seat with the other, he smashed down with both feet on the window glass, praying it wasn't bulletproof. It wasn't. The window burst outwards with a satisfying crunch. There was a two-foot gap between the window and the ground, just enough to squeeze through.

Devon manoeuvred herself through the opening. Mickey followed, feet first, ducking his head to one side to avoid a razor-edged shard. Finally, wonderfully, he was standing in the open, filling his lungs with fresh, cedar-scented air.

'Amazing,' he said, and laughed.

'What is?'

'We're out. We made it.'

'Not if we don't get out of here fast,' said Devon, looking around. There was nothing to be seen but trees, the steep hills and the blue sky. 'We're no more than ten miles from the place. If our driver there doesn't report in they're going to come looking for him.'

'You're right.' Mickey went back to the car and pulled open the driver's door. Their victim slithered out onto the ground in a heap. Most of his hair had burned off, leaving raw, blistered scalp, and his cheek was the same. There was a bump high on his temple and a lot of blood was coming from a long shallow cut on his forehead.

'What do we do with him?' Devon asked.

'We'll put him down there when we're done,' Mickey said, pointing to a culvert that went under the road. 'Search him, see what you can come up with. I'm going to get the car going if I can.'

Mickey managed to rock the car onto four wheels and backed it carefully down the slope to the shoulder. Except for the nostril-twitching smell of burnt hair and a four-foot crease on the right side, the vehicle seemed fine.

'Anything?' asked Mickey, joining Devon beside the still unconscious man.

'Wallet, credit cards, hundred and sixty in cash, a pair of handcuffs and this.' She reached under the man's jacket and pulled out a dull-metal automatic pistol. 'It says Desert Eagle on the side, and Israel Military Industries.' She handed it to Mickey, who put in in his jacket.

'Cuff his hands behind his back,' Mickey instructed. 'Take his wallet too.' Devon rolled the man over and snapped on the handcuffs, and together she and Mickey carried him over to the ditch and down to the culvert. They pushed him into the corrugated steel tube, head first and face up.

'Now what?' asked Devon.

'We run like hell.'

TWENTY-FIVE

THEY drove as far as Leesburg, West Virginia, and parked behind Courthouse Square. They risked five minutes to clean themselves up in the public washrooms at the visitors' information centre, then joined a group of tourists returning to an English doubledecker sightseeing bus on its leisurely way back to DC. According to the courthouse clock it was 2.00 p.m.

'This is insane,' Mickey muttered. 'They'll find the car and figure it out.' Whatever courage he had managed to summon up back at Mount Weather had vanished. The escape had been a wildly lucky break and nothing more than a brief stay of execution. As far as he was concerned, the next step involved the first available means of transportation to the Canadian border.

'They won't figure it out,' Devon said. 'Who's going to look for us on a doubledecker bus that says "Oxford Circus" on the front?'

'Who was he?' asked Mickey, changing the subject.

'His name was George Carlaw. According to his driver's licence he was born 18 November 1955. Six-two, brown eyes.'

'Anything else?'

'Social Security card, Red Cross card that says he's AB negative, and an ID card with a picture that says he works for Southern Air Transport Corporation, 2210 E Street, Washington.'

'Oh, shit.'

'What?'

'Southern Air Transport is a CIA-owned company. Jesus! It looks like everyone in the world is involved in this thing.'

'Well, he's also got cash and a whole folder full of credit cards. At least we're not going to starve.'

'Wonderful,' Mickey said. 'We can have the condemned's last meal at the Palm before a flock of spooks put matches under our toenails and pull out our teeth with pliers.'

'You were pretty hot back there in the mountain,' said Devon quietly. 'Lose your nerve or something?'

'I never had it in the first place,' he answered. 'I didn't have any choice.'

'You still don't. This thing isn't over yet.'

'It is for me,' Mickey told her. 'We get to Washington and I'm hopping on the first bus to Canada. Mrs Rubinek's boy is going on a vacation. A long one.'

'I thought we had this conversation back in Reno.'

'We're having it again. Nothing's changed.'

'Suit yourself.' Devon shrugged and turned in her seat, looking out across the rolling countryside. She stayed like that all the way into Washington.

At three thirty the bus disgorged its chattering load on Constitution Avenue, directly in front of the White House. There were half a dozen other buses waiting to take their charges back to their hotels, and within fifteen minutes Mickey Rubinek and Devon Talbot were alone on the pavement, staring at the large white mansion a thousand feet away behind the high, wrought-iron fence.

'We need fresh clothes and a place to really clean up, and we need a telephone. Do you know Washington at all?' Devon asked.

'I've been here once or twice, a long time ago.'

'So where do we go?'

'There's a Howard Johnson's across the street from the Watergate,' said Mickey. 'It's close, and the Watergate has a whole shopping mall.'

'Let's go,' said Devon.

Gunnar Peltz stood on the shoulder, arms folded, watching as the ambulance crew pulled Carlaw out of the culvert. To his right, up the slope, he could see the fresh white scar on the tree trunk where the car had hit it. The road itself was swarming with people and vehicles. Give it another half-hour and the press would show up. The whole thing was turning into a circus.

He swore softly. He hated inter-agency projects and this one was by far the most complex he had ever orchestrated. The fact that Carlaw had been done over by Rubinek and the child was incredible and he knew he was going to have a hard time explaining it to his superiors. Just then Renquist, one of his own crew, came down the gravel shoulder, walkie-talkie in hand.

'What kind of condition is he in?' asked Peltz.

'Concussion, scalp wound. Nothing serious except for the burns. It looks as though someone took a blowtorch to him. They're going to take him to the base hospital at Detrick.'

'No,' Peltz said, coming to a decision. 'Kill him.'

'Pardon?'

'Get all these idiots out of here, now, and then kill him. I want him dead and in that culvert, understand?'

Renquist stared at Peltz, wondering if he had suddenly lost his mind. On the other hand, Peltz insane simply meant it was wise to expedite his wishes even faster than usual.

'Yes, sir.'

'Good. What about the car?'

'They found it in Leesburg, on a street behind Courthouse Square. I checked. There were all sorts of tour buses coming in and out, two Trailways buses, and then there's the car-rental agencies. Assuming they're using Carlaw's ID and credit cards, they shouldn't be hard to trace.'

'They won't have rented a car. They'll head for DC. If I know Rubinek he'll rabbit the first chance he gets, either New York or across the border into Canada. Cover it all and put out an advisory. The car will have his prints on it. Is Carlaw's gun missing?'

'Yes.'

'Even better. Make it an armed and dangerous. He's already wanted in California, he's done a Mann Act with the Talbot kid, and now we can add Carlaw's death as well. Blow the son of a bitch away on sight and if the kid happens to get it, that's just too bad. Oh, and while you're at it, get me Peter Tananga on the horn.' Peltz checked his watch; it was already four o'clock. If Rubinek was dumb enough he'd opt for one night in a hotel before he made his move; there was still time to wrap it all up before the operation got under way.

'So, what do you think?' Mickey asked, coming out of the bathroom in their room at the Howard Johnson's. Both of them had used Carlaw's American Express card with gay abandon in the Watergate complex across the street.

'My God, I don't believe it,' said Devon, putting a hand to her cheek in mock surprise. Mickey was a changed man in a houndstooth linen suit, clean-shaven, groomed and stylish.

'You're no slouch yourself kid.' Mickey smiled. Devon had opted for the Ralph Lauren look from head to toe. 'I hate to say it, but we could make a really good father-and-daughter act.'

'Good,' Devon said, grinning, because that's sort of how I booked us.'

'Booked us where?' Mickey asked, the smile vanishing.

'Honolulu International. The flight leaves at nine tonight and gets into Hawaii ten o'clock their time.'

Mickey slumped down onto one of the twin beds. 'Don't you think they'll be checking any reservations made with Carlaw's credit card?'

'They'll be looking for reservations made by Carlaw in his name,' Devon explained. 'I made the reservations under the name Lucas.'

'As in George, I suppose?'

'That's what gave me the idea. I always call him Uncle George at the studio. I told the reservations lady that you, that is, Mr Lucas, were a friend of my mother's, Mrs Birmingham, but that I call you my uncle, and that my father, Mr Carlaw, was paying for your ticket as well as mine because you were being helpful sending me out to my mother who lives in Hawaii, and that my name is Birmingham, because my parents divorced and when she remarried she kept her maiden name, Birmingham, and I stuck with that even though my stepfather's name is Sloane.'

'She believed you?' said Mickey, staring.

'Sure.' Devon nodded. 'I know kids at school who have weirder pedigrees than that. If Peltz or whatever his name is checks reservations there won't be any Carlaw, just a Birmingham, Miss Julia, and a Lucas, Mr Bob.'

'Bob?' he said weakly.

'It was about as far from Mickey Rubinek as I could get.'

'I don't want to go to Hawaii,' said Mickey. 'I told you that.'

'You know as well as I do that they'll be watching for us to try and leave the country. Any border we cross is going to be a rope around our necks. Hawaii is still in the United States. No passports, no ID, nothing. It's five thirty now, that gives us an hour before we catch the shuttle to the airport. There's one of those cash machines over at the Watergate and he's got Amex, Visa, Mastercard and Citibank. That's two thousand in cash we can pull out before we get on the bus.'

'They'll trace the transaction,' Mickey argued.

'Not in an hour,' Devon said, shaking her head. 'And when they do, all they'll get is a cash machine at the Watergate. By then we'll be long gone.'

'When did you figure all this out?'

'On the bus,' Devon answered blithely. 'It's the only thing that makes sense. We have to find out the key to this or eventually Peltz and his gang are going to find us, and the next time they won't make any mistakes.'

'Let's say you're right. I presume you chose Hawaii because of the Earthlab connection, right?'

'Earthlab 2 is in Hawaii, and Chetwynd made a lot of long-distance calls to the Earthlab office in Honolulu. If I had a whole bunch of kidnapped people to deal with, Hawaii wouldn't be a bad place to stash them. Nice and isolated.'

'OK, so we waltz into Honolulu, drop in on the Earthlab offices before we hit the beach, and demand they spring your friend Toby and all the others – is that the game plan?'

'Why do you keep on making fun of me?' Devon asked. 'Just because you're an adult you think nothing I have to say is valid.'

'That's got nothing to do with it, believe me,' Mickey answered. 'But you have to admit that this whole thing is insane. You've got a clapped-out reporter like me and a teen-ager like you trying to figure this thing out all by ourselves. It's suicide.'

'I don't know about that.' She shrugged. 'We've been doing all right so far. That trick with the spray can was pretty good.'

'Yeah, it was, wasn't it?' Mickey grinned. It suddenly occurred to him that Devon was right. They were doing fine so far, and even if there wasn't a chance in hell of bringing it off, at least he was doing something that had some meaning beyond making enough money to keep up the payments on his trailer. He laughed, thinking about his cruddy little home by the airport.

'What's so funny?' Devon asked.

'Nothing, really. I'm just thinking about all the bridges I've burned behind me lately.'

'Does that mean you're coming to Hawaii?'

'Yeah, I guess that's what it means.'

At first it all appeared to be going smoothly and on schedule. They packed their old clothes in a pair of new overnight bags, left the hotel without bothering to check out, and used Carlaw's credit cards to draw the maximum for each card. They boarded the bus for the airport and were on their way out of Washington at exactly six thirty.

As they crossed the Beltway and headed north on the Baltimore Washington Parkway, Mickey noticed that Devon seemed worried. He let it ride for a while but the mood wasn't passing and she kept on moving anxiously in her seat.

'If you had to go to the bathroom you should have done it at the Hilton, we had time,' he whispered, leaning over in his seat.

'There's nothing wrong with my bladder,' she hissed back.

'Then what's bugging you?' Mickey asked.

'Four rows back on the right, the aisle seat, but don't look.'

'What's going on?'

'A man.'

'This bus is full of men. Women too, and three or four kids.'

'He was at the hotel,' she answered harshly.

Mickey felt a large, cold, phantom hand squeezing his heart.

'Are you sure?'

'He's black, he's wearing a dark-blue suit and dark glasses. He's built like a football player.'

'I left Carlaw's gun in the wastebasket at the hotel.'

'I know. I took it out. It's in my bag.'

'Are you nuts! What about the metal detectors at the airport?'

'See, there you go again, underestimating. I was going to ditch it before we got on the plane.'

'OK, so we've got a gun. What do you want to bet he's got a bigger one? Not to mention the fact that he probably knows how to use it.'

'So go back there and turn yourself in,' she said sourly.

Mickey stared blankly out the window, trying to think it through. Finally he turned to Devon.

'Maybe we could lose him, split up or something.'

'How? We have to pick up our tickets at the American Air-lines counter. As soon as we do that he's going to know what flight we're on. All he has to do is wait at the departure gate and arrest us.'

'He could have arrested us back at the HoJo, or before we got on the bus. Either he's just tailing us, trying to figure out where we're going, or he's got instructions to kill us. I think he wants to kill us.'

'Then we'll have to kill him first,' Devon said calmly.

Forty-five minutes after leaving the Capitol Hilton the shuttle bus arrived in front of the monumental, red-pillared airport, taking the upper ramp to the departures level. With only one small bag each Mickey and Devon managed to squeeze quickly out of the throng of people around the baggage compartment of the shuttle and enter the terminal through the central entrance. Devon spotted the American Airlines ticket counter at the far end of the slightly curving concourse and grabbed Mickey by the sleeve of his jacket, pulling him in the opposite direction.

The airport, recently expanded and renovated, serviced more than a hundred major destinations with forty departure gates and five projecting departure piers. At this time of night most of the international flights were loading and the depar-ture level was a sea of people, baggage and flight attend-ants. A quick glance at one of the suspended TV monitors showing departure and arrival times told Mickey there were more than a dozen flights scheduled to leave within the next hour and almost twice that many arriving at the lower-level gates.

'Down,' said Devon, pointing towards an escalator. 'Find a newsstand.'

'This isn't going to work.'

'It has to,' Devon answered firmly. They stepped onto the escalator, wedging in between two large women dragging lug-gage carts piled high with souvenirs from Walt Disney World.

The arrivals level was even more crowded than the depar-ture concourse, especially around the main doors leading to the access road and the parking lots.

'There,' Devon said, pointing. 'A newsstand. Hang around and keep his attention focused on you.'

Mickey did his part, twirling the paperback racks, reading titles, wondering if he could pull off the next part of the plan without passing out. An airport had hundreds of security people, some in uniform, some in plain clothes and all of them armed. Their tail was leaning against a pillar twenty feet away, leafing through a copy of *Time*.

'OK.' Mickey felt a touch on his arm and jerked around. It was Devon. 'I've got all of it. You ready?' She had a shopping bag in one hand and the overnight bag in the other.

'Oh, sure. I'm either going to puke or lose control of my sphincters. Both of them.'

'That's disgusting. Which way is the ladies' room?'

'Down there,' Mickey said, pointing with his chin.

'Wait outside for me,' she said, taking his elbow and moving off. 'When you see me come out, start walking. Do something to make sure he has his eyes on you, not me.'

'Like what?'

'Anything. Bend down to tie your shoe, drop your bag. Stop and turn in his direction, anything. I'm going to need about thirty seconds and then I'll catch up with you.'

'OK.'

The ladies' room was located in an alcove a hundred feet along the concourse from the newsstand. Fibreglass seats were lined up on either side of the alcove and Mickey found an empty one where he could see the doorway into the restroom. He lit a cigarette and leaned back, letting his head rest against the cool marble of the wall, his eyes closed to slits. The football player continued flipping through the magazine, but Mickey could see his head come up every few seconds, checking the door to the ladies' room and then Mickey.

He wasn't sure if it was imagination but he was almost positive he could see a bulge under the right shoulder of the man's neatly tailored suit. He kept watching through his eyelashes and spotted the flash of a gold watch bracelet on the right wrist. Gun and watch on the right would mean he was left-handed. Something to remember.

Devon poked her head out of the washroom doorway and Mickey was instantly on his feet. He kept his eyes on Football Player and veered left, taking the man away from the alcove, keeping himself between the doorway and the tail. He let his overnight bag slip out of his hand, praying that the gun wouldn't

157

go off accidentally, watching as the black man's eyes flickered downwards.

Mickey bent down, fumbled for a few seconds, then stood up, making sure he jostled the shoulder of a man going in the opposite direction. He apologised and continued walking, hoping he had given Devon enough time. A few seconds later he heard running footsteps and then Devon's arm poked under his.

He turned towards her as he walked forwards. She was wearing a kiddie version of a pilot's cap, there was a pair of plastic wings on the breast pocket of her blouse and she was carrying a clipboard.

'You're kidding,' he whispered. 'They bought that?'

'Absolutely. I think it was the clipboard. What about our friend?'

'He just gave you a weird look.'

'Fine, maybe we'll get him worried. You ready for stage two?'

'Do I have a choice?'

'OK. Let's find an arrival.'

The arrival turned out to be at a TWA gate and from the looks of it the flight was the last of several that day bringing in a load for the United States Association of Service Clubs. Shriners, Lions, KCs and Kinsmen. Gate 31 was an undulating, cheering, hooting maelstrom of hats – everything from beanies and fezes to straw boaters and bowlers.

'This is it,' Devon said. 'Go right for the middle and then split. I'll go left, you go right.'

They pushed into the packed crowd, Mickey managing to unzip the overnight bag and pull out the butt of the automatic pistol as he veered away from Devon. Repeating a mumbled series of 'Excuse me' and 'Pardon', Mickey cut to the edge of the crowd, then squeezed along the observation window for fifty feet before heading back into the swarming mass of mildly inebriated humanity. He stepped on a dozen feet and jostled twice that many elbows on his way, but no one seemed to notice.

The football player was caught in the middle of the herd, looking left and right for his quarry. Mickey worked his way behind the man, took a deep breath and hauled the pistol out of the bag, poking the barrel into the base of the man's spine. The football player froze.

'Good man,' said Mickey, trying to keep his voice from breaking into a soprano croak. 'You just stay like that. What you're feeling is the working end of your friend Carlaw's forty-five.' Christ! He sounded like something out of *Dirty Harry*.

'Who's Carlaw?' the black man said. The voice was deep and smooth, like the bass pipe of a church organ.

'A colleague of yours.'

'Don't know him.' The man was calm and relaxed. Mickey felt sweat beginning to trickle down into his eyes.

'Don't worry about it. Just do as you're told.'

'You haven't given me any orders,' the man said easily.

Mickey remembered the bulge in the man's jacket. 'Put your left hand in your pants pocket.'

'What?'

'Just do it!' Mickey snarled. He could feel his hands going clammy, slicking the pistol grip. That was all he needed, drop the gun just as you're trying to make this halfback son of a bitch do what you want.

'Now what?' asked the black man, putting his left hand in his pocket.

'Go right,' said Devon, coming up beside the man, hooking her arm around his elbow. Mickey set his jaw and shook his head; the kid had more guts than he did, that was for sure. 'Come on, mister, just smile and move it or my friend might accidentally blow out your spine.'

They moved slowly out of the crowd, Mickey making sure that the gun barrel was firmly against the man's back at all times. They went downstream with the current, sidestepping gladhanders and hat-wavers, eventually beating their way back to the newsstand and then the washroom alcove. Devon's taped, felt-marker sign on the plain back of a giant postcard was clear and very much to the point:

BROKEN WASTE PIPE
NO ENTRY!
TOILETS OUT OF ORDER

'This should be educational,' said the black man evenly. 'I haven't been into a girls' washroom since high school.'

The man's casual attitude was getting on Mickey's nerves, as though the gun in his back was a slight inconvenience that could be dealt with any time he chose. And that sounded too close to the truth.

'What's your name?' Devon asked when they were inside.

'Smith,' the black man answered, smiling. 'John Smith.'

'Imaginative.' Mickey backed away from the man, but kept the gun pointed at his back.

'Turn around,' Devon answered. The man did so. This close Mickey could see that Smith had poor skin, small cratered scars from a childhood bout with chickenpox or acne. The eyes were dark brown and intelligent.

'You were following us,' Devon said.

'Yes.'

'Why?'

'I was told to.'

'By who?'

'Whom,' Smith corrected gently. 'I have no idea. He knew the right words, that's all.'

'We're wasting time,' Mickey interrupted, his voice nervous. 'Let's get this thing done.'

'OK. Watch him.' Devon went to the last stall, came out with her overnight bag and the shopping bag she had had at the newsstand. She pulled out a plastic package containing a folded Mylar 'Dragon' kite and a Baltimore souvenir pocket knife. She opened the bag, took out the kite and sliced through the cord with the knife. 'Nylon fishing line. That should hold him.' She smiled at Smith. 'Strip.'

'Pardon me?'

'Take off all your clothes, but first put your gun on the floor.'

'With your right hand,' said Mickey, watching him carefully. The black man sighed and eased the right side of his jacket aside, revealing a holstered .38 police special. Using thumb and forefinger only he plucked the gun out of the dark leather holster and bent down slowly, keeping his eyes on Mickey. He put the weapon on the floor and gently pushed it in Devon's direction.

'While you're down there, undo your shoes and take them off,' she ordered. Smith began working on the laces.

'They want you dead, they'll have you dead, Miss Talbot, it's just a matter of time. You too, Rubinek. Swim with sharks, you get eaten.'

'Just take the clothes off,' said Mickey. Much longer and

he was going to blow some kind of mental gasket. He bit his lip, gripping the pistol, wishing all of it would just . . . stop, at least for a little while. Still crouching, Smith shrugged his broad shoulders and went back to his shoelaces.

The move came with appalling swiftness, taking Devon and Mickey completely by surprise. Smith's empty left hand swept up to his ankle and suddenly he was holding a Detonics .44 derringer. Uncoiling like a giant snake, the black man reared up, his left leg lashing out in a snap kick aimed at Mickey's gun hand.

Devon screamed and did the only thing she could. She flung the overnight bag towards the two men. The bag came between Mickey and Smith's steel-capped toe, deflecting his aim. Mickey, horrified, jerked backwards and slipped on the smooth terrazzo floor as Smith fired both barrels of the gun with a sound like a backfire in an echo chamber.

The massive recoil threw Smith's arm up as Mickey hit the floor, his elbow smacking hard and his trigger finger jerking spasmodically. Carlaw's automatic went off and with Mickey's finger momentarily paralysed by the crack to his funny bone, it continued to go off in a series of cannonshot explosions, emptying all eight soft-nosed bullets into a various parts of Smith's body.

The multiple impacts threw Smith off his feet and out of his unlaced shoes, sending him reeling back to fall in front of a toilet stall. He had taken three shots in the upper right shoulder, almost severing the arm and spraying blood all over the room. The other shots had hit his face, neck, chest and groin.

Shaking, Mickey stood up, wincing with pain and holding his elbow. He stared at the corpse of the man he had just inadvertently killed and felt the sour, hot stink of vomit burning at the back of his nose.

'Oh, jeez,' he whispered, blinking. 'Oh, jeez.' White-faced, Devon staggered to her feet and made her way to Mickey.

'Are you OK?'

'My elbow,' he mumbled, unable to tear his eyes away from what was left of John Smith.

'Check the door,' she said, gripping his uninjured arm. 'See if anyone heard the shots.'

'What?' Mickey's ears were still buzzing and some distant part of his brain knew that he wasn't far from fainting.

'The door, goddamn it!' said Devon. 'Check the door!'

He nodded, then turned, still holding his elbow. Dazed, he opened the door an inch and looked out. The arrivals concourse was still a milling crowd of noisy people.

'I don't think anyone heard,' he said. He looked down at the body again, trying not to believe that less than a minute ago he had killed someone.

'Shouldn't we . . . do something?' he asked.

'With the body?' Devon said. Mickey nodded and she shook her head. 'No time and no point. We've got to go.'

'Where?'

'Hawaii, remember?' she said gently. She picked up her overnight bag and took him by the arm, leading him out.

'What about the door?' he asked. 'What if someone comes in even with the sign?'

'I've got it covered,' she said, taking a small tube of Krazy-Glue out of her jacket pocket.

'You think of everything, don't you, kid?'

She stared at the sealed entrance to the makeshift mortuary they had just created.

'No, not everything,' she said quietly. 'I didn't think anyone was going to die. I didn't think about that.'

TWENTY-SIX

TOBY Hagen and Jason Sanchez moved forwards awkwardly in the narrow confines of the ventilator duct, the makeshift knee and elbow pads shredded after only twenty minutes in 'the Hole'. The Hole was their name for the Egypt Green vent system and the pads were made with rubber bands and stolen napkins from the dining hall.

Toby and Corey Shire had met with Peter Wolfe only once since their first rendezvous at the pool, but they already had what Toby considered to be a fairly reasonable plan.

Based on the assumption that Hartshorn and the rest were lying about the purpose of the Egypt Green installation, escape seemed like the logical course of action, and to escape required some fundamental organisation, equipment and information.

With Revik in command their days had been tightly regimented along distinctly military lines. Wake-up at 0600, inspection by a uniformed pair of goons at 0630 and a hup-one-two to the dining hall at 0700. Assembly in the theatre at 0730 followed by three hours of high-school-level classes starting at 0800, an hour's free time until lunch, then another two hours of classes, an hour of physical education, an hour in the pool and an hour of drill.

By then it was time for dinner with only two hours before lights out. After that Revik's goons were on patrol in the corridors and it was worth your life to be caught outside. Revik knew this job: keep your charges busy and physically exhausted to make sure they don't have time to think. But he hadn't counted on the combined brainpower in N-47 or the complicity of Peter Wolfe.

During a second meeting between the former astronaut and Corey Shire, Wolfe brought them a hand-drawn schematic of

163

the installation based on the official plans he had been shown by Beth. He told them to keep the plans to themselves and agreed that the fewer people who knew about their efforts the better. Besides the occupants of N-47, Jake Skelly and Russell Ching were the only ones who knew what was going on.

The fact that Eric Lowery categorically refused to become involved in their efforts was worrisome, but there wasn't much to do about it except keep a close watch on him. They also arranged a system of passing notes to Wolfe during the assembly period, and he in turn tried to get them what they needed.

Using the vent system had been Toby's idea and so far he and Snatch Sanchez had been the only ones to check it out. The grilles in the individual rooms were too small to move through, but Toby had assumed, accurately as it turned out, that the small opening close to the ceiling would have to lead to larger ducts, probably running across the ceilings or behind the walls.

It turned out to be the walls, specifically the back wall of the shower enclosure. It took Corey Shire and the Dick the better part of an entire night carefully to cut through the heavy fibreglass, using a hacksaw blade passed to them by Wolfe at the morning assembly. When the two-foot-square trap was replaced and the edges filled with soap, the cuts were almost invisible.

The area behind the wall was a maze of pipes, electrical lines and ventilating ductwork. Using the hacksaw again they cut through a bend in the largest section of duct, discovering that it was easily large enough to crawl through. The interior of the duct was spiked and clawed with jagged-edge interior joints, making the knee and elbow pads a neccessity; a bad cut needing medical attention, or even superficial scratches visible during their swimming sessions at the pool, could ruin everything.

The night following the opening of the duct, Toby and Snatch, the two smallest of the group, entered the ventilation system on a reconnaissance expedition. From lights out to midnight they snaked through the walls and ceilings of their own level, pausing at the larger grilles to orient themselves, Toby noting down each twist and turn on a scrap of paper. The next night they went even farther afield, bracing feet and elbows to crab their way both up and down the levels.

For their third expedition Toby decided that it was time to do something practical, so he suggested to the others that he and Sanchez should try to go as high as they could in the system. If Wolfe was right and they were in some sort of converted mine, the ventilators would have to exit on the surface, or at least lead to some major service level close to the top. If they could reach that point they might be able to find a way out of Egypt Green.

'You have any idea where we are?' asked Snatch, his voice ringing hollowly in the narrow duct. Sanchez was ten feet behind Toby, working his way along by touch. Both boys were crawling in absolute darkness, broken only when they were within a few yards of a central grille.

'We've done three up-walks, so this is Level Four. From what I can tell we're somewhere in the middle of the level at ceiling height.'

'How long?'

'Hour and a half so far, about,' Toby answered.

'Another hour and we start back. We've got to have a margin.'

'Right.' Two and a half hours was the agreed maximum from the room, based on the assumption that on the way back they'd be tired and it would take longer, perhaps three to four hours. On the other hand, they would be caught anyway if there was a surprise bed check. It hadn't happened so far, but there was always a first time, Toby tried not to think about it; bad enough to feel like a rat in a maze without worrying about the rat-catchers waiting for you when you got back home.

Home. A joke and a fast-fading memory. More and more now he was beginning to think of the dormitory room as a permanent residence and Egypt Green as the real world. It didn't even matter if Wolfe was right and there was no imminent war about to explode outside. War or not, they were prisoners, and unless they found a way out, they were going to be prisoners for a long time to come.

'Shit!'

'What?' asked Toby, pausing.

'Nicked myself on a weld. These mitts are useless.'

'Bad?'

'No.'

'Let's keep going then.' Toby began to move forwards, suddenly aware of the air in front of him in motion.

165

'You really think we're going to get out of here?' asked Snatch after a few minutes.

'Yes,' Toby said, not sure if he meant it. 'I think Colonel Wolfe is right. We're not hand-picked survivors from a war. We're something else.'

'Like what?'

'I don't know. And I don't want to wait around to find out. That's why we have to escape.'

'And if we do? What then?'

'I don't know,' said Toby, irritation rising in his voice. 'I'm going to leave that to Wolfe.'

'You trust him?'

'I don't have any choice. Now let's shut up and keep moving, OK?'

The farther they went, the stronger the breeze. That usually meant a main grille, and sometimes an intersection of major ducts, but there was no sign of any light ahead. A few minutes later Toby's napkin-shrouded hands bumped into a right angle in the duct. The breeze was coming from directly in front of his face.

'Hold on,' he whispered. He leaned his shoulder against the side of the duct and took the padding off his left hand to feel around.

'What is it?' Snatch hissed.

'Grille, and an upturn.'

'How come no light? There's always been a light when there's a vent.'

'First time for everything.'

'What do we do?' Sanchez asked.

'Check it out.' Toby took the padding off his right hand and felt around the perimeter of the grille. As in the other ones they had found, the steel mesh was welded to a framework of angle iron that fitted into the ducts without screws, held in place by friction alone.

Grunting, Toby rolled over on his side and opened the hand-made pouch on his belt. He took out one of the knives they had stolen from the dining hall. With a file Wolfe had passed to them the day before. The handle of the knife had been honed down at one end in the rough shape and thickness of a screw-driver, and the blade had been worked to a needle-sharp spike. Toby poked the screwdriver end under the fitted angle iron and

166

levered it up on two sides, giving himself enough space to give his fingers purchase.

He put the knife back into his bag and began jiggling the grille frame until it was loosened on all four sides. Twisting and pushing simultaneously he jerked the frame out entirely, hanging on, fingers straining. Working blindly he tilted the frame with his arms outstretched, then brought it carefully in through the opening, gently putting it down against the far wall of duct.

'Anything?' Snatch asked anxiously.

'No. Pitch dark. Lot of air movement.' Toby edged forwards until he was right beside the opening. He poked his head through and reached out with one arm, waving it invisibly in front of his chest. With his head through the hole he could definitely hear the distant sound of an electric motor. 'Jesus!' he whispered, pulling himself back into the duct.

'What?' Snatch said startled.

'It's an elevator shaft,' Toby answered, realising that he had been hanging out over a yawning hole in space. He swallowed, his mouth suddenly parchment dry. Another foot or two and he would have taken a dive.

'What do we do?'

'Shut up for a second, I'm thinking.' Toby stared out into the darkness of the shaft, trying to remember what he knew about elevators. It wasn't a whole hell of a lot. He knew there were two parts to the shaft, and two sets of rails, one for the elevator itself and the other one for the counterweight. The counterweight was supposed to be as heavy as a fully loaded car, and when you got onto the car it went down or up depending on the position of the counterweight in relation to the car. The brakes were electrical and if something went wrong there was a safety cable and big clamps that snapped around the car rail to keep it from dropping all the way to the bottom.

'Service ladder,' he said to himself.

'What?' asked Snatch, who had moved up close behind him.

'They usually have a service ladder, steel rungs set into the wall.'

'So?'

'So, follow the shaft to the top and see what's there.'

167

'You're nuts. What if an elevator comes while you're on the ladder?'

'I think the ladders are set in behind the rails; there should be enough room.'

'You think, but you don't know, and you can't see a thing.'

'Wait.'

'What now?'

'It's coming up.'

The motor sound Toby had heard before began to deepen and even in the darkness he was aware of something moving directly in front of him a few feet away. The safety cable? Shit, what he wouldn't have given for a book of matches! Chancing decapitation he poked his head out again and looked down. Far below he thought he could see a spot of light. The longer he looked the brighter it got. Some kind of safety lamp on the roof of the elevator? He kept watching and the light continued to enlarge. From above he could hear a steady rumbling noise as the counterweight dropped along its guide rails. Everything seemed to be moving slowly and he wondered if this might not be a freight elevator.

Finally the elevator rose to within twenty feet of them, the small maintenance light on the top of the cab throwing a weak glow around the shaft. For a few seconds Toby could make out details of the rails, the I-beams making up the shaft, and less than a yard to his left on the nearside wall he could see the metal U-bolts of the service ladder. Then the elevator groaned by and everything was dark again. Toby sat back against the duct, thinking hard, heart thudding with excitement.

'OK, so it's an elevator,' said Snatch. 'Why so interested?'

'Because it's still going up,' Toby said quietly. 'It's gone way higher than four levels.'

'So?'

'It was a lot bigger than the elevator cars they use for people. It's a freight elevator.'

'What are you getting at?'

'If it goes higher than the top level on Wolfe's plans, maybe it goes all the way to the top.'

'A way out?'

'Maybe. There's only one way to find out.'

'You're kidding.'

'No.' Toby, prayed that his resolve was firmer than his voice.

'I'll go up the ladder as far as I can and take a look. The ladder is recessed between the rails, so even if the elevator comes back down again I won't be caught.'

'What about getting down again?'

'I can handle it.' If there was one thing that really scared him it was heights, but now wasn't the time to mention it.

'You're nuts, but I guess I'll hang around and see how it comes out.'

'An hour, no more,' Toby warned. 'If I'm not here by then, get back to the others.'

'I don't have a clock in my head like you,' Sanchez complained. 'How am I supposed to know when an hour is up?'

'Count to thirty-six hundred,' Toby laughed. 'Slowly.' He eased his head and shoulders out through the hole. 'Hang on to my ankles,' he instructed Sanchez. Easing farther out he twisted, reaching for the ladder with his left hand. He caught a rung and hung on, wrapping his fingers tightly around the slick, oily metal. Taking a deep breath he pushed himself out beyond the point of no return, balancing his hips on the edge of the grille. He dug his toes in and pushed again, tipping out and corkscrewing his body, right hand groping for the iron rung. For a split second he thought he had missed his mark and his stomach churned, a scream rising in his throat. Then he had it and he let his legs swing across the wall of the shaft until his toes found a hold on a lower rung.

'Tobe? You OK?' Sanchez's voice seemed small and distant, echoing in the shaft. For the first time Toby was thankful there was no light. If he had been able to see down the shaft he never would have attempted this.

'Yes,' he answered, biting off the word, pressing himself against the metal rungs like a leech. 'I'm OK. Start counting.'

'You too,' Snatch suggested. Count the rungs so you'll know when you're back opposite the vent.'

Beth Scott and Peter Wolfe rode the central core elevator down to Level Ten. For several days Wolfe had been using any excuse to spend time with the historian, at first telling himself that he was trying to pump her for information. Now he wasn't so sure; something else was creeping in – affection, lust, a frustrating desire to convert her to his way of thinking about what was going on at Egypt Green, or perhaps all three. This evening,

169

however, it was Beth who had called on him. According to her, Mike Whitefather had asked her to bring Wolfe down to the aquaculture level after the dinner hour. The historian was concerned because Whitefather had been very insistent that no one else come along.

'Any idea why he's being so secretive?' Beth asked as the elevator doors opened on the Level Ten main corridor.

'Does he think we've been having secret meetings?' Wolfe asked, grinning, but half serious at the same time. He still found himself wondering if she wasn't some kind of spy for Hartshorn.

'No, not at all,' she answered, flushing slightly. 'I just thought you might have an opinion.'

'Maybe he's had some fish escape and he wants Revik to arrange for a search party,' said Wolfe.

'With such a big chip on your shoulder I wonder why Dr Hartshorn wanted you here so badly,' she remarked as they made their way to the bulkhead at the far end of the passageway. 'All you do is make jokes and smart cracks.'

'That's how I always act when I'm kidnapped against my will, buried alive and given a job with no apparent function. I've been here more than a week and I haven't been given any kind of assignment.'

'Maybe that's got something to do with your attitude,' said Beth, cracking open the bulkhead. 'You haven't exhibited what I'd call an overwhelming spirit of cooperation.'

'You've been reading my psych profile,' exclaimed Wolfe in mock dismay. He followed her through the open bulkhead and into the aquaculture section. As before, he was instantly aware of the humidity and smelled the faint odour of wet earth.

They made their way over the catwalks above the breeding tanks, eventually reaching Whitefather's greenhouselike office. The thin, serious-faced man was waiting for them, an LA Dodgers cap tipped back on his head. He was at the computer when they entered and he turned to greet them.

'Why don't we go out and check on the fish?' he said. From the look on his face it was more than a suggestion.

He led them out over the catwalks to an eight-by-eight metal-grille platform roughly in the centre of the gymnasium-sized facility. Even through the maze of overhanging pipes and drooping tentacles of plastic tubing they had a clear view in all directions. The only eavesdroppers were the massed tanks of fish ten feet below them.

'You know what UNMAP is?' he asked Beth.

'It's a United Nations project, isn't it? Uh . . . United Nations Medical Assistance Programme. It's one of the joint operations run by the World Health Organisation.'

Whitefather nodded and pointed towards the ceiling, twenty feet over their heads. 'That's what I was doing upstairs in the library this afternoon. Checking on them. Found out all sorts of things.'

'Like what?' Wolfe asked.

'Like for instance they have free medical clinics set up in all the Third World countries. The Russians and the Chinese and the French and the Germans and who-all try to compete with each other. Like, hey, the Russkies put three clinics into Guatemala and the US puts six into Honduras, like that. The whole thing is financed privately, and UNMAP, through the World Health Organisation, gives them administrative help.'

'So?'

'They've got 630 clinics in all,' Whitefather continued. 'From the Philippines to Botswana. Every poor, overpopulated, underfed and unhappy place in the world.'

'I don't see where this is leading,' Beth said.

'You know what carbol fuchsin is?' asked Whitefather.

'No.'

'It's a stain,' Whitefather explained. 'It's used in lab tests. I was down on Level Fourteen today, getting some nitrates from supply, and I spot them loading these crates onto skips. A whole lot of them. The crates all had UNMAP stencilled on the sides. The guys loading were army types, uniforms and stone-faced. First thing I thought was . . . what are they doing with Rangers lifting and hauling?'

'They were Rangers?' Wolfe asked, surprised.

'That's what they looked like. Hard, you know?'

'Yeah, I know,' said Wolfe. 'Go on.'

'OK, so I figure these guys do not want me here, so I'd better keep low. But I was curious, so when I noticed one of the crates open I took a look inside.'

'And?' Beth prodded.

'I found these. Maybe two hundred in each crate.' He pulled a small package out from the chest pocket of his coveralls. It

171

was dark-green plastic, and the size of a packet of cigarettes. He popped the small box open with his thumbnail and showed it to them. Two small vials and a rubber-bulbed pipette.

'What the hell is it?' Wolfe frowned.

'A test kit,' Whitefather told him, putting the box back in his pocket. 'Carbol fuchsin.'

'You said it was a stain,' Beth reminded him. 'For . . .'

'You use it for staining bacteria on a slide. One bacteria in particular. *Pasteurella pestis.*'

'Jesus Christ!' the astronaut breathed.

'What's *Pasteurella pestis*?' Beth asked.

'Plague,' Whitefather said. 'Bubonic and pneumonic, take your pick.'

'I don't understand,' Beth said, confused. 'Why would we have these test kits here?'

Whitefather laughed. 'You think that's weird? Try this. I'm playing the invisible man, looking for a way out of there, and I hear them talking, but it's not English. These guys I thought were Rangers were speaking *Russian.*'

By Toby's count he had climbed 162 rungs when the elevator descended again. Pressing himself against the ladder he closed his eyes and waited. It went past without incident and he began to climb again. At rung 308, his knees and arms beginning to weaken, he heard the car returning. He estimated that he had already been in the shaft for almost forty minutes and there was no way of knowing how far he still had to climb.

Moving cautiously he turned himself around on the ladder, elbows hooked around the rung above his head. Taking a deep breath he risked a glimpse down and saw the dim light far below. He waited, following the growing circle of light, and when the car had come almost level with his position he simply unhooked his arms and stepped off onto the roof of the elevator. It was as simple as that. He turned, crouching, careful not to make any noise, and began counting rungs again as they appeared in the faint puddle of light from the maintenance lamp. Being off by two or three wouldn't matter, and riding the car down to the vent would save an awful lot of time.

The elevator was slow, but it was a lot faster than going up the ladder. Within less than two minutes the rung count was up to 575 and the elevator was slowing down. As the car continued upward Toby was suddenly aware of a strange but familiar smell that was cutting through the thick odours of ozone and grease. It took him a few seconds, but then he had it. Salt. Like a sea breeze. Risking a quick look upwards he saw a dim wash of light. Natural light.

The elevator kept on rising slowly and now Toby could see a web of heavy I-beams forty or fifty feet above his head. And above that, seemingly illuminated from the side, he could see smooth concrete and rough, dark stone. The top of the shaft? Sure, and the light was coming through the slats of a vent. He had done it, he had reached the surface!

At rung 659 the elevator stopped with a brief shudder. With the rungs about twenty inches apart that meant he had risen close to 1400 feet. Blinking up at the faint bars of light that scored the beams above him, he came to a quick decision. Below his feet he heard the elevator doors rumble open and then the faint sound of voices. Reaching up he grabbed the nearest beam and boosted himself off the roof of the elevator.

Crouched spiderlike among the beams at the top of the shaft, Toby waited, and within two or three minutes he heard the elevator doors close. The cab began to descend, leaving him staring down a steadily deepening chasm, the growing well beneath him marked by the shrinking dot of light from the rooftop lamp. He closed his eyes for a second, praying that the elevator hadn't made its last trip for the day, stranding him, and then he stood up, balancing himself on the main beam.

He worked his way slowly towards the vent, a six-foot square on the far wall of the shaft housing. There was no doubt about it now: the light was natural, and so was the salt-tang breeze that touched his face. Where the hell *was* he?

After what seemed like an eternity on the beam, he reached the wall and moved one hand up to the vent. The slats were angled downwards and there was nothing at all to see, but he pressed his nose against one of the openings and breathed in great lungfuls of the clean, fresh air. Voices again, this time clear, no more than a yard away. Silence, the unmistakable click of a lighter and then more talk.

'*Eeleh tow yest?*'

What the hell kind of language was that?

'*Oshem.*'

Emphatic. A number maybe?

'*Chi Rossinskye son to?*'

Rossinskye had to mean Russian. What about the Russians? Jesus!

'*Oneh yush scoinchiwie.*'

Followed by a long bitter laugh. The -ski ending on Rossinskye might be Polish. Questions, answers, numbers and Russians, spoken in Polish with a sea breeze behind it.

Definitely not Kansas.

TWENTY-SEVEN

GUNNAR Peltz paced back and forth in front of the picture window and glanced out at the scattered lights and curtained windows of the Watergate on the other side of the street. Behind him, four of his men were methodically tearing the room apart. A Landmaster briefcase encrypter was connected to the room phone and Peltz wore a hands-free headset as he paced. It was almost five o'clock in the morning and his temper was becoming shorter with each passing minute.

'When did you last talk to Tananga?' he asked, speaking into the headset microphone.

'He called from the Capitol Hilton. He said he had them in sight buying tickets on the airport shuttle.' The reply came from their mobile unit at Baltimore International.

'When?'

'Six fifteen. The shuttle was leaving at six thirty and he was going to tail them.'

'When was his next check call?'

'Eight.'

'Nothing?'

'No, sir. He did say that the six fifteen shuttle was for flights leaving between eight and nine.'

'You get a list of those flights?'

'Yes, sir.' He read them off.

'Hang on.' Peltz pushed the microphone away from his mouth and turned to the men working the room. 'Anything?' One of the men came out of the bathroom, silently holding up a crumpled Waldenbooks bag and a strip of cash-register tape. Peltz motioned the man over and examined the two-inch strip of paper: date, time, travel section, $13.95 and an ISBN number: 013–384529–X. He pulled the microphone to his mouth again.

175

'Still there?'

'Yes, sir.'

'Keep this line secure. Get me the duty desk at OCR.' There was a pause, a double click as the line was shifted and then a new voice on the line.

'Office of Central Reference. Please state your code.'

'Watchdog,' Peltz said.

'Thank you, Watchdog. What can we do for you?'

'ISBN 013 dash 384529 dash X as in X-ray.'

'Just a moment.' The answer came back almost instantly. 'On your request, that number refers to *Insight Guides Hawaii*, APA Productions listed as publisher, Prentice Hall as distributor.'

'Thank you, OCA.'

'You're welcome, Watchdog.' The line clicked off and the Baltimore mobile came back on.

'It's the Continental flight to Hawaii,' Peltz said. 'What time does it arrive?'

'Five twenty-five a.m., that's our time. Just after midnight in Honolulu. Right about now, actually.'

'Who's closest in Honolulu?'

'Kaiser.'

'Get him there, fast. And for Christ's sake find out what happened to Tananga.'

'Yes, sir.'

Peltz pulled the headset off and tossed it onto the bedside table. He frowned, staring out the window. They were amateurs, playing without rules, and the whole operation was coming apart. Hawaii might have been a random guess, or just the first available plane, but he doubted it.

'Goddamn!' he said angrily. He turned and snapped his fingers loudly. The men in the room stopped what they were doing and looked at their superior, waiting. 'One of you get on the horn,' Peltz ordered. 'Tell McFee I want the Falcon gassed up and ready to go inside thirty minutes. Flight plan is DC to Oakland, Oakland to Oahu.' He turned back to the window. They were getting too close and they had to be stopped. Now.

Continental flight 482 hit the reef runway at Honolulu International Airport four minutes early, the light impact of the 747's tyres bouncing Mickey Rubinek out of a light sleep while beside him Devon Talbot yawned and pushed back the blanket covering her shoulders.

'It's raining,' he said, surprised. 'I didn't think it rained in Hawaii.'

'Of course it rains in Hawaii,' Devon said, sitting up.

The jumbo jet slowed and then U-turned, finding its taxiway to the main terminal. With only carry-on luggage to deal with, Mickey and Devon made it through the arrivals area quickly, even managing to avoid the Hawaiian Tourist Board hula girls with their flower leis.

'Where exactly are we going?' he asked as they got into a cab.

'The Waikikian,' Devon told him.

'Why there?' Mickey asked.

'The guide book said it was moderately expensive and low rise. And on the map it looks as though it's right downtown. It also said they have terrific eggs benedict, which I happen to like.'

Mickey shrugged; there were worse ways of picking a hotel than by its menu.

Even in the nighttime darkness it was obvious that they were travelling through a heavily industrial area: warehouses, wrecking yards, used-car lots and ranks of oil tanks. In the distance, the crescent moon of lights marking the hotels along Waikiki were like beacons gleaming in the steady rain.

A few minutes later they were at the hotel where Mickey registered them as Mr John Tananga and his daughter Helen.

'Why Tananga?' asked Mickey, groaning as he kicked off his shoes. Devon had whispered the name to him as they crossed the lobby to the reservations desk of the old-fashioned hotel. Now she reached into her bag and tossed a worn lizard-skin wallet across to him.

'You took it off the guy in Baltimore?'

'I thought it might come in handy.'

'Not if we want to rent a car.' Mickey warned, holding up Tananga's Maryland driver's licence. 'I'm not going into the local Hertz office in blackface.'

'His birth certificate doesn't list his colour. We can take it in to the licence bureau tomorrow, tell them you lost yours and they'll issue you a temporary.'

'Are you sure you're only sixteen?' asked Mickey, shaking his head.

177

'Seventeen in two months,' she answered, pulling off her sneakers.

'OK, seventeen in two months. What do you propose we do, now that we're in Hawaii? God help me.' The whole thing was mad; less than twenty-four hours before they had been locked inside a mountain in Virginia.

'Sleep first,' suggested Devon matter-of-factly. 'Then check out the Earthlab office.'

'We didn't give Peltz the slip, you know,' Mickey said. 'He'll track us down eventually.'

'I know. We'll just have to keep a step or two ahead of him until we find Toby.' She fluffed up the pillows at the head of her bed and leaned back against them, arms limp at her side. Mickey sat up and lit a cigarette, watching her for a moment.

'He must be some kid,' he said finally.

'Huh?'

'Toby. You know, the guy we've been running around trying to find.'

'What about him?'

'You said he was a friend.'

'That's right.'

'I think he's more than that.'

'Why don't you turn out the lights?' Devon muttered turning her head on the pillow so he wouldn't see the tears forming in her eyes. 'I'm pretty tired, Mickey.'

'Sure,' he said softly. 'Me too.'

TWENTY-EIGHT

P ETER Wolfe, summoned that morning at the assembly by a
hastily passed note, arrived at the storeroom meeting place
on Level Seven and found Toby, Corey Shire and Tony Deetz
waiting. There was still an hour to lights out but the boys were
obviously nervous. As soon as Wolfe entered the closetlike
room Deetz jammed a folding chair under the inside knob.

'Who goes first?' the ex-astronaut asked. 'You called the
meeting, but I've got news of my own.'

Toby, seated on a trolley used to move cleaning supplies
around, reached into the pocket of his uniform coveralls and
took out an irregularly shaped piece of dark stone.

'You said you trained as a geologist,' Toby began. 'Any idea
what this is?'

Wolfe took the fist-sized rock and examined it under the dim
light of the single overhead fluorescent. The stone was light,
aerated with hundreds of tiny holes with small, pale intrusions
of some other material.

'Pumice,' said Wolfe, perplexed. 'Pumice with coral intrusions. This is some kind of home-grown concrete. Where in
hell did you get it?'

'At the top of a freight-elevator shaft,' Toby told him. He
gave Wolfe a quick rundown on his escapade of the night
before.

'You think they were speaking Polish?' Wolfe asked, when
Toby finished his story.

'Some kind of middle European language.'

'And you smelled salt air?'

'That's right.'

Wolfe tossed the lump of stone from hand to hand, nodding
to himself. 'It's beginning to fit,' he said finally.

179

'What is?' Corey asked.

'There's a man named Whitefather,' Wolfe explained. 'An old hippie type. He runs the aquaculture section on Level Ten. He said he was getting supplies on one of the lower levels and he heard several people speaking what he thought was Russian.'

'Are you saying this is some kind of Soviet operation?' Deetz asked.

Wolfe shook his head. 'No. I worked with Max Hartshorn, and Revik probably checks for commies under his bunk every night before he goes to sleep.' Wolfe looked at the piece of stone in his hand again, turning it over and examining it.

'So?' Corey prodded. 'What do you think *is* going on?'

'Whitefather stole a lab-test kit,' Wolfe said. 'The Russians or whoever they are were loading them onto an elevator, probably the same one you rode up to the surface. According to Whitefather the kits are used to test for plague.'

'As in bubonic?' Toby asked.

'Bubonic and pneumonic. Whitefather says the pneumonic is the worst. He also said the crates the Russians were loading were all marked UNMAP; that's the United Nations Medical Aid Programme.'

'Are we some kind of test group they're keeping in isolation?' Deetz asked.

'I don't think so,' Wolfe answered. 'The crates were going out, not in. Whitefather says he heard Russian, Toby here says he heard Polish. There's also the question of the markings I saw on that girder. The best I can come up with is that it's some kind of joint Soviet–American operation involving biological weapons. Your chunk of rock here fits too and so does the sea breeze you smelled.'

'How?' Toby wanted to know.

'It's volcanic and old. The coral is much younger geologically. You don't get much coral in the Atlantic so it has to be the Pacific. That means some place like Midway, Guam or American Samoa. I'd bet on Midway, simply because it's been in American hands for a long time and it's close to Hawaii – easy to supply.'

'OK, so what do we do about this?' Toby asked. 'Obviously we're part of what's going on, people to use either as guinea pigs or as survivors.'

'We have to get out of here,' Wolfe answered. 'A few of us, anyway.'

'What good is that?' Deetz asked. 'If you're right we're on a goddamn desert island somewhere.'

'If it's Midway there's an airbase,' Wolfe told him. 'And in case you hadn't noticed, I'm wearing a colonel's uniform. If we can bluff our way onto some kind of transport, I can fly us out.'

'With a flock of F-16s on our tail, probably,' Corey snorted. 'It's hopeless.'

'Well, I don't know about you guys, but I'm willing to take the chance,' Toby said. 'We can whine as much as we like, but it's the only way out of here.'

'I still don't see how we can manage it.' Deetz sighed. 'You and Snatch are small enough to go through the vents, but we're too big, and the colonel here would be impossible. Not to mention the fact that one person jumping onto the roof as the elevator goes by is risky enough; half a dozen is something else again.'

'He's right,' said Corey. 'How do we even get onto the elevator, let alone escape after that?'

'It's a problem,' Wolfe admitted. He checked his watch. It was almost curfew time. 'It's late, we should be getting out of here. Let me talk to Whitefather, maybe he can think of something.' He looked around at the three boys. 'In the meantime I want you to choose which of you are going to come along. I don't think we can risk more than four.'

Toby thought hard. The events of the preceding evening had been terrifying, and he knew that if he balked now, whatever courage he possessed would desert him. He had never thought of himself as being particularly brave, but he instinctively knew that if he stayed in Egypt Green much longer he'd turn into a lump, content to go along with the flow, giving in to an existence over which he had no control. Wolfe might have all sorts of high-minded thoughts about blowing the whistle on Dr Hartshorn and his buddies, but all *he* wanted to do was get the hell out. Before it was too late.

'When do we go?' he asked.

'If Whitefather can figure out a way to get us on the elevator I'll pass you a note at assembly. Be ready to go some time in the next two or three days.'

181

Mickey Rubinek awoke, amazed at how clearheaded he was. He turned and looked at Devon, asleep a few feet away. No matter what Devon thought, Mickey knew in his heart of hearts that they weren't going to get out of this thing alive. The chances were good that Toby Hagen had already bought the farm and Peltz wasn't going to let them get away with Tananga's killing.

He felt strangely calm about it all and wondered if there might be some hormone squirted into your body when you were in imminent danger of death. Something to make you accept it as front-and-centre reality. Or maybe the last few days had changed him. He smiled at the thought. A week ago he had been Mickey Rubinek, ace putz, sneaking through life like a thief in the night, and then he had stepped into another world full of people like Peltz, Tananga and the phantom Dr Chetwynd.

And Devon over there, too smart for her age, with a face that looked sixteen only when she was sleeping. Playing Tonto to his Lone Ranger. He laughed, then reached for his cigarettes on the bedside table. If anything, it was the other way around.

'What's so funny?' Devon asked sleepily.

'Private joke, kemosabe,' he grinned. 'Old Mick here has just been indulging in some hotel-room metaphysics, that's all.'

Devon eyed him thoughtfully from the other bed. 'Sometimes you're very weird.'

'I can accept that,' he said, nodding philosophically. 'The clan Rubinek has always been known for its weirdness.'

'How come you're in such a good mood?' Devon asked. 'It's out of character.' Yawning, she threw back the bedspread and swung her legs out onto the floor.

'Late-night flights and island air,' he shot back. 'Heavy doses of reality.'

'I have to pee.' Devon disappeared into the bathroom.

Running his tongue across his teeth Mickey promised himself a toothbrush at the earliest opportunity, and then, with cigarette in hand, he began poring over the Honolulu telephone directory.

'Who are you calling?' Devon asked when she emerged.

'No one. I was just looking up the number and the address for Earthlab.'

'Find it?'

'It's on Ahui Street, wherever that is.'

'We can ask at the front desk,' Devon said. '*After* the eggs benedict,' she added firmly. 'I'm starved.'

Devon ordered from room service and, while Mickey was savouring a perfectly brewed cup of Kona coffee, she had an idea.

'Norman Opana,' she said, beaming.

'Who?' asked Mickey.

'The cab driver we had last night. His name was Norman Opana. Instead of going through a whole lot of crap getting a licence and renting a car, why don't we just rent him?'

'Because he was on the night shift and he's probably sleeping.'

'I'm going to try anyway.' She got up from the small table and went to the phone. Mickey shook his head wearily and ignored her.

Devon was back at the table a few minutes later.

'Well?' Mickey asked. 'Was he asleep?'

'No,' she said, triumph in her voice. 'He was not sleeping, and for a hundred bucks he'll be glad to take us anywhere we want to go for the entire day, and in his own car.'

'He's crazy,' Mickey scoffed.

'No, he's saving up to get his pilot's licence. His brother-in-law owns an air charter service.'

'Oh.'

'He'll be down in the lobby in fifteen minutes, so finish your coffee.'

In true aloha tradition, the thin, dark-haired young man was dressed in a blindingly colourful, flowered shirt, white duck pants and emerald-green flip-flops. He greeted Devon with a smile and Mickey with a nod, then took them out to his car, an enormous 1959 Cadillac hardtop Coupe de Ville, jet black, rocket-finned and chromed at every opportunity.

'Well,' said Mickey, staring at the gigantic piece of nostalgia. 'This is nice and inconspicuous.'

'Eight point two litres,' Opana said proudly, slipping the shift into drive. 'Biggest production engine ever made. When Dad retired he let each of the kids choose a car, and I took this one.'

'What kind of business was he in?' asked Devon.

'He had a funeral home. That's how my brother-in-law got

183

into the charter business.' He eased the car around the hotel drive, heading for Ala Moana Boulevard.

'Makes sense,' said Mickey. 'Funerals to aeroplanes.'

'Not so crazy,' Opana said. 'None of us wanted the hearses, so Rick took them and started up a courier service in town. Small parcels mostly. He wound up spending half his time going to and from the airport, so he made a lot of connections. The business took off, and he diversified, started buying planes. Kahala Air Transport.' He looked in the rearview mirror. 'Which way you people want to go?'

'123 Ahui Street,' Mickey told him. 'Place called Earthlab Resources.'

'Never heard of it,' said Opana. 'What do you want to go there for? Except for John Domini's Restaurant there's nothing but a bunch of government offices and warehouses, right down to Point Panic. I can take you places a lot nicer.'

'Maybe later. Right now we've got some business to attend to,' Devon explained.

'Suit yourself.' Opana shrugged.

'I need to get a camera,' Devon said. 'Do you know somewhere?'

'There's a photography store in the Ala Moana Center,' Opana told her. 'It's right up the street.'

Opana steered the big car across the bridge over the Ali Wai Canal, then turned into the parking lot of the sprawling shopping mall. Opana and Devon left Mickey in the car, contentedly watching the bikini-clad ladies strolling through the park on the far side of the boulevard. The weather was travel-poster perfect, little shreds of pure white cloud against a crisp blue sky, mimicking the brushstroke foam on the rolling surf curling into the beach at the edge of the park.

Mickey breathed deeply, taking in sweet lungfuls of the tangy salt air, enjoying the simple moment until he found himself thinking about how long it would last. During the flight from Baltimore he had told himself that he was doing the prudent thing by getting as far away as he could from a clear and present danger, but even the bright Honolulu sunshine wasn't enough to blind him to the truth. It was the old cliché come true – you can run but you can't hide.

He sighed and lit a cigarette. Staking out Earthlab was probably tempting fate yet again, but by the same token, it might bring things to a quicker end, one way or another, and any conclusion would suit him better than the constant, nagging threat of Peltz and his pack of bloodhounds on their trail.

Devon and Opana came out twenty minutes later. Devon had picked up a pocket 35-mm camera and half a dozen rolls of film.

Opana wheeled out of the parking lot, following Ala Moana to Fisherman's Wharf and the Kewalo yacht basin, then he turned off onto Ahui. Except for the big restaurant on a rocky point overlooking the yacht basin, Opana was right; Ahui Street was nothing but warehouses and efficient-looking government buildings.

Unlike their operation in California, Earthlab's Honolulu office was a nondescript blockhouse structure three storeys high and windowless on the street side. There was a large fibreglass-roofed carport on one side big enough for half a dozen vehicles, and a grey metal door. The only thing at all interesting about the place was the cluster of antennae on the roof, and three black mesh satellite dishes. There was no identification on the building other than the numbers, painted in red on the front door.

'Don't get too close,' Devon warned. Shrugging, Opana pulled to a stop on the far side of the street fifty feet beyond the building. In front of them was Point Panic and a small waterfront park.

'You do business, you drive up to the front door and you knock,' said Opana, switching off the engine. 'You're acting like this is some kind of stake-out.'

'It is,' Mickey said.

'You want to explain?' Opana asked. 'I booked on to tour you people around, not play James Bond.'

There was a long pause. Devon looked at Mickey, but he just shrugged. It was her show. 'Which do you want, a lie you'd believe or the truth, which you wouldn't?'

'The real goods,' said Opana, turning in his seat to face her.

Devon took a deep breath and launched into the story, from Toby's disappearance to the death of Tananga in the Baltimore airport ladies' room. It took ten minutes and the Hawaiian's expression never changed. When Devon finished he just nodded.

'Fascinating,' he said after a few seconds. 'You obviously just escaped from the nut house, but it's a good story.' He shook his head. 'Maybe later on you'll show me where you keep the miniature submarine that turns into a car.' He turned on the ignition and fired up the engine. 'I'm going to take you back to the hotel, and you can keep your hundred bucks.'

'I don't have time for this shit,' Mickey said. He dug into the pocket of his jacket and pulled out Tananga's wallet, flipping it open to the dead man's CIA identification card, complete with blue, red and orange seal, photo and an office address at 2430 E Street in Washington DC. 'Satisfied?' he asked. 'The son of a bitch tried to kill us. I killed him first, accidentally. Believe what you want, but everything Devon just told you is the truth. Earthlab is a front for a group who've been monitoring a whole generation of America's brightest people, and now for some reason they're kidnapping those people's children. Hundreds of them, maybe thousands.'

'Well, they're not in there,' said Opana, hooking a thumb over his shoulder.

'No, but a man named Chetwynd is,' Devon said. 'He was one of the people who started this whole thing. If we trail him he might lead us to Toby and the others.'

'Which brings up a logistical problem,' Mickey said. 'How do we find out if he *is* in there?'

'Shouldn't be too hard,' said Opana, looking over his shoulder at the building. 'Hang on.' He climbed out of the car and walked across the street. Devon and Mickey squirmed around to watch him through the rear window.

The Hawaiian walked in under the carport as though he belonged there, checking the parked vehicles. Devon's heart was thumping painfully against her chest and her mouth had gone dry. 'Do you think he believes us?' she asked Mickey, keeping her eyes on Opana as he opened the driver's side door of one of the cars.

'He'd have to be out of his mind,' Mickey answered. Opana moved on to the next car, a Toyota Land Cruiser. 'But yeah, I think he believes us, or at least he believes that *we* believe, which is good enough for me.' Opana suddenly appeared, strolling calmly out from the shadows of the carport. He crossed the street again and got in behind the wheel.

'Well?' asked Devon.

'*A'ole hou*,' said Opana. 'No sweat. It's the Land Cruiser.'

'I'm impressed,' said Mickey.

'Don't be.' Opana laughed. 'I was trying for registrations, but then I saw this retaining wall and signs. Each space is reserved. The Toyota is parked in a spot that says "Reserved for Dr Chetwynd."'

'OK, now what?' asked Mickey.

'We wait,' Devon said.

'What if he's in there all day?'

'Relax, man,' instructed Opana. 'I'll teach you some Don Ho songs to pass the time.'

Midway through the second song a muscular, grey-haired man with a full beard appeared in the Earthlab Center and walked over to the Land Cruiser. Like Opana, he was dressed in a garish, short-sleeved shirt and a pair of baggy shorts. He was carrying two large aluminium cases of the kind used by photographers as well as an attaché case. Using a key he opened up the back of the Land Cruiser, dumped the luggage and then got into the driver's seat. Opana gave him a fifty-yard lead, then followed.

Devon sat forward, hands on the dashboard, eyes glued to the Toyota's taillights. Her first look at Chetwynd had been disappointing. No sinister dark glasses, no bodyguards or bulging shoulder holster under the flower-print shirt. Just a faintly academic-looking man with grey hair driving a slightly battered dark-green Land Cruiser. She loaded her camera and took a few shots through the windshield, but her heart wasn't in it. She felt a wave of depression sweep over her and she gritted her teeth angrily as her eyes began to water.

At first the whole thing had been like one of Uncle George's movies: an honourable quest for a friend in distress. But all that was fading now, and had been ever since the sordid horror of Tananga's death. She had been thinking a lot about that, realising that she could have been killed or, worse, been responsible for Mickey's death. Now she had managed to rope Norman Opana into her little fantasy adventure, putting him in danger as well.

'This is crazy,' she muttered hopelessly, sitting back with her arms folded across her chest. 'This is going to get us all killed.'

'What's the matter, kiddo, having second thoughts?' asked Mickey, who had been watching her. 'Me too.'

'And?'

'We're doing the right thing,' he said quietly. He reached up and gave the back of her neck a gentle squeeze, surprised at how nice it felt; it had been a long time since he had been affectionate towards someone without lust being his prime consideration.

'I hope so,' she answered.

Eerily, the Land Cruiser retraced the exact route they had taken from the Waikikian, and for a moment Mickey thought that was where Chetwynd was heading. At the last minute, after crossing the Ala Wai Canal, he turned right onto Harbor Lane.

'He got a boat, this man?' asked Opana, keeping two or three cars between him and Chetwynd. A forest of masts and rigging marked the yacht club on their right.

'I don't know,' Devon said. Chetwynd seemed to be heading for the end of the private lagoon owned by the Hilton. Opana slowed, then pulled the Caddy off onto a triangular patch of unused ground.

'Why are we stopping?' asked Devon

'Because I know where he's going,' Opana said. 'And we don't want to run up his tailpipes and let him know we're here.' He pointed towards a parking lot. 'It's the Duke Kahanamoku Heliport,' he said. 'Two or three shuttle companies work out of there.'

'How do we find out where he's going from here?' Devon asked.

'He has to file a flight plan. All I need are his registration numbers.'

A few minutes later a small, bubble-nosed helicopter appeared over the line of palms that screened the heliport. Devon leaned out of the window and took three fast shots as the helicopter went overhead, calling out the numbers painted on the underside of its passenger compartment.

'N8485E. The name on the side says Tradewinds.'

'It's an old Bell Ranger,' said Opana. 'He's not going off island in that.' He got out of the car and went to a public telephone at the side of the road. Three minutes later he returned, climbed in behind the wheel and launched the Caddy in a dust-belching turn that took them back onto Harbor Lane.

'We've got him cold,' Opana said happily. 'I called my brother and asked him to check on the chopper. He didn't have to. According to him Chetwynd is on a scheduled jump to the strip at Ford Island. It's perfect.'

'What's so good about it?' Mickey asked.

'Ford Island is a navy airfield, but they've turned over most of it to commercial operations. It's the old auxiliary for Hickam. Anyway, that's where my brother has his charter company. He said he'd have one of the guys check on the Tradewinds chopper and see where our man goes.'

Ten minutes later they were at the ferry terminal for Ford Island. Opana drove onto one of the broad-beamed barges that cruised back and forth across the half-mile channel. They passed the bright-white floating mausoleum that marked the USS *Arizona*, already swarming with camera-clicking tourists, and continued on to the Ford Island dock. Opana wheeled the car off the barge with a thump as they dropped from the ramp, then drove down a broad, tree-lined dirt road to a clump of weatherbeaten hangars and low wooden offices. He stopped in front of a freshly whitewashed building with a windsock on the flat roof and a sign over the front door: Kahala Air Transport.

They were barely out of the car before an enormous Hawaiian appeared in the doorway, dressed in a pink, green and purple shirt and white shorts stained with grease. The man was at least six foot four, with a massive bald head that appeared to sit directly on shoulders broad enough to be used as bridge pylons.

'Hey, bruddah, what's all this cloak-and-dagger bullshit?' the big man asked, coming down the short flight of wooden steps. The whole stoop shuddered when he moved. Mickey tried to imagine the man flying a light plane, but couldn't raise a reasonable image in his mind.

'My brother-in-law, Tommy Akano,' said Opana. 'These are my friends Mickey and Devon.'

'Aloha.' Akano stuck out a giant hand. Mickey was surprised at how gentle the grip was. Akano turned back to his brother-in-law, frowning. 'So what gives, Norm? Why the interest in Earthlab all of a sudden?' Akana turned back to Mickey and Devon. 'You don't look much like journalists.'

'How did you know about Earthlab?' asked Mickey, his interest quickening. Akano turned on his heel and pointed with a meaty index finger. In the distance a blue-and-gold business jet was hurtling down the single runway. Within a hundred feet of the harbour it suddenly vaulted into the air, fanjets screaming, and began to climb away, heading out to sea.

'That's one of their jets,' Akano explained, squinting as the aircraft dwindled in the distance. 'BAe 800. They've got a Falcon, too, comes in here once in a while. When they first announced the Earthlab project a couple of years back we had newspaper people all over us, trying to figure out where the place was. None of them ever found out.'

'You know where it is?' asked Mickey.

Akano shook his head. 'No way.' His smile looked like a knife cut in a cantaloupe. 'Not to say that I don't have some ideas. They just never asked the right questions.'

'What's the range of the BAe 800?' Mickey asked. Akano laughed, then punched Mickey lightly on the arm.

'This is one smart *haole* you got here,' he said, grinning at his brother-in-law. 'That jet could take you maybe 2500 miles at full load.'

'What is there within that range?' Mickey asked, continuing to play Akano's game. 'With an airport that has a field long enough to land her on?'

'She got thrust-reversers,' said Akano. 'First thing I noticed about her. She's rated for just over 2400 feet, but the reversers could cut that down a little. That means she could hit just about every airport in the islands.'

'You ever check the flight plans?' Opana asked.

'Sure. I'm as curious as the next person. Always the same. She logs in for Princeville on K'Auai, but that's a lot of bullshit because the runway's too short.'

'So she overflies Princeville,' Mickey said. 'What is there after that?'

'Nothing,' Akano said. 'Except Midway and the old coast-guard strip on Kure Atoll. If she was flying into Midway she'd have to transmit an approach sign because it's a restricted air-space. And I've never heard of anyone spotting her squawk-ident on radar.'

'You're saying it's Kure?' Opana prodded.

'I'm not saying it's anything, bruddah.' Akano warned. 'That plane comes in and out of here with some pretty strange people on board, a lot of them in uniform. I mind my own business.' He gave his brother-in-law a dark look. 'Maybe you should mind yours too, Norman Opana. *Ho'omana haole hiki au m'aka'u loa,* if you catch my drift.'

'*Da kine kaiko'eke.* I hear you. Thanks for the information.'

'No problem, just remember what I said.' Akano went back into his office. Mickey, Devon and Opana got into the car.

'What did he say?' asked Devon.

'Roughly translated it means, "Remember, white people can be dangerous". Don't worry about him, though, Tommy's a pussycat.'

'Do you know anything about this Kure Atoll place?' asked Mickey.

'It's the oldest and farthest out of the Hawaiian chain,' Opana answered. 'I'm not sure, but I think a long time ago it used to be called Ocean Island.'

TWENTY-NINE

SIR James Stephenson leaned on his cane in the faint pre-dawn light and watched as the first of the Vulcans slipped batlike into the sky, its massive, dead-black delta wings briefly blotting out the few remaining stars. As the huge bomber climbed away to the south the old man shivered and used a gloved hand to draw the lapels of his overcoat close around his throat. The crumbling, deserted buildings around him dated back to World War II when Lavesham had been an American 8th Air Force base. Until now he had never been to this particular airfield, but he had seen others like it during his own service.

He shook his head, feeling the cold in his bones and the ache in his knees. So long ago, he thought. At twenty-five he had completed his degree in economics at Oxford, trained as a pilot and brought down two Heinkels over the Channel. He smoked a pipe and was positive that there was little in the world he didn't already know.

How wrong he had been! His service in the war had been no more than a semicolon in his life, an exciting interlude. And neither it nor the years that followed had prepared him for this night. For more than twenty years, all that time since Leukertal he had treated Phoenix as no more than a series of hypotheses. To him it had always been a game, a fanciful extrapolation of figures and facts, projections and potentials.

He had played with the numbers, responded to them with scenarios to counteract them, and passed the results on to his colleagues in France and the United States. Dussault had played the game and so had Chetwynd, each with his own territory, watching with satisfaction as their predictions came to pass, but always sure there would be some other way out

192

of the steadily expanding quagmire into which the world was sinking.

There was no other way, he knew that now. The computer program he had created almost single-handedly some ten years before proved that beyond any question. Ironically, it was that same computer program which had earned him his knighthood. Sir James Stephenson, Knight Commander of the British Empire. Sir James Stephenson, sole creator of LUXOR, the twentieth-century incantation that had opened Pandora's box. With it, the scientists involved in Phoenix could predict death rates and resulting economic problem sites with pinpoint accuracy.

Originally Stephenson had seen the program as a way of exorcising his guilt. With it, thousands of lives, perhaps millions would be saved from needless tragedy. In the end, though, he had seen it for what it really was – a tool to create what Dussault had once referred to as a 'phantom war' with no allies and no enemies.

A second Vulcan roared into the sky and then a third. In all there would be ten bombers on this first flight, carrying their cargo to its remote destination in the Pacific. After that it would simply be a matter of time and not even a thousand installations like Egypt Green and their own Cobalt Blue would make a difference.

The Four Horsemen of the Apocalypse had been unleashed on an unsuspecting world and the responsibility for their savage harvest rested squarely on his shoulders. Chetwynd, Dussault and the others had described the problem and explained the solution, but he had been the one to make the implementation of that solution possible. As the fourth Vulcan took off from the deserted airfield in central Sussex, the old man turned away, limping towards the shell of a concrete building that had once housed the Lavesham control tower.

Making his way with difficulty he clambered through the rubble, finally reaching the ancient, rusted staircase bolted to the rotted concrete wall. He paused there, catching his breath, staring into the darker puddles of shadow in the gloom, trying not to remember all the voices from his past, all the faces, all the talk of honour and bravery under fire.

Gathering himself together he began to climb the stairs, stopping as each of the Vulcans thundered into the air, then banked

193

away. He reached the top of the tower building just as the last of the black-painted bombers lifted off from the cracked and windblown runway. He stepped out onto the observation deck and took a deep breath, his eyes fixed on the lightening line of the eastern horizon. Dawn was coming up, but the morning sun would find nothing changed here. The fuel lorries and generators would be gone, the flight crews vanished like their aircraft.

Stephenson hooked his cane over the creaking guardrail and slipped off his thin doeskin gloves. He reached into the pocket of his topcoat, drew out his old gunmetal case and lit a cigarette, coughing at the first inhalation. He stood silently, bare hands on the cold railing, waiting for the sun fully to appear; he'd give himself that much at least.

His wife had died years ago, his only child was killed in Margaret Thatcher's useless weekend war in the Falklands, his past was nothing more than a fading album of obscure memories. His future? A footnote in the history books if any were written. Sir James Stephenson, signatory of the Leukertal Accord, designer of the LUXOR program. Mass murderer. He felt a tear stinging his eye and gritted his teeth. Perhaps it was better that Michael had died on that wretched archipelago; at least he wouldn't have to bear the shame of his father's outrage.

The old man finished his cigarette, dropping the short end onto the floor of the observation platform and grinding it out with his heel. He reached into the other pocket of his topcoat and drew out the .38 calibre Webley and Scott automatic pistol he had carried since the war. A methodical man, Stephenson had done some research and knew that placing the barrel under the chin or in the mouth was not necessarily fatal. Instead he placed the end just below his left eye, pressing slightly to ensure that the muzzle was within the orbit. Tears spilling freely now he watched as the sun rose over the trees at the far end of the runway, the sky turning from deep cobalt to a softer blue.

'Forgive me,' he whispered softly, knowing that there could be no forgiveness for a man guilty of murdering half his world. He squeezed the trigger and died, blood and brain matter fountaining into the clear morning air.

THIRTY

DEVON, Mickey and Norman Opana sat at the rear of the upper deck on the SeaFlite hydrofoil and watched the Honolulu skyline recede in the sunshine. The double-decker passenger ferry travelled at a sizzling fifty miles per hour in good weather, making the ninety-five-mile trip from Honolulu to Kauai in just under two hours.

'So who exactly is this Willy Chang person we're going to see?' asked Devon.

'Like I told you,' Opana said, 'he's what they call a "sportsman's guide". Flies a floatplane out of Port Allen, takes fishermen out, scuba parties to the out islands, that kind of thing. I went to school with him.'

'I don't get it,' Mickey said. 'How come you think he'll fly us to this Kure Atoll and your brother-in-law wouldn't?'

'Willy's a bit off the wall,' Opana explained. 'He swears his great-grandfather was the first *pake* crime lord in Hawaii, "Brilliant" Chang. He was supposed to have had a whole string of opium dens and brothels. Willy likes to think of himself as being the same kind of guy.'

'He's a crook?' Devon asked, frowning.

'Some people might call him that.' Opana grinned. 'He, uh, has connections with the seedier side of Hawaii.'

'Dope?' Mickey asked shrewdly.

'I'm not saying.' Opana shrugged. 'Let's just say he knows his way around, and when I called him he agreed to get you to Kure.'

The hydrofoil reached Nawilliwilli Bay at 2.45 in the afternoon, cutting its engines and dropping down onto its hull. They coasted in to the small ferry terminal at the end of the breakwater and disembarked with the hundred other passengers who had

195

travelled with them from Honolulu. Norman Opana shooed away the rickshaw drivers and cabbies crowding around the terminal and they walked the half-mile to the incongruous pair of slab-sided eleven-storey hotel blocks sitting stolidly at the end of the manmade rectangular bay. To the left Mickey and Devon could see a cruise ship docked at an old sugar terminal, and far in the distance, nestled under a low mountain, they could make out the low-rise cluster of buildings marking Lihu'e proper.

Reaching the hotel Norman rented a car and followed the signs down the main drag of the little town until they reached the intersection of Highway 50 and the Kukui Grove shopping centre. Norman pulled into the diminutive plaza and returned a few minutes later with a bag of groceries and two six-packs of bottled Budweiser as a present for Willy Chang. He pulled the car back onto the street, then turned left onto the main highway, heading for the pass through the low, greenery-shrouded *pali* of the coastal range.

Half an hour later, the windows rolled down to fill the car with the deep, rich scent of the surrounding trees, they hit the coast again at Port Allen and the town of Hanapepe, a tiny, slightly down-at-heel town straddling a narrow river that wound its way back into the hills behind. With the sea on their left they crossed the river and continued along the coast highway for another few miles to Waimea, a smaller town than Hanapepe, but a lot more prosperous by the looks of the modern housing. A mile beyond the village, almost midway to Kekaha, the next hamlet on the coast, Opana turned off onto a narrow dirt road that ran through a thick stand of trees down to the sea.

The road ended abruptly in front of a small, sun-bleached cottage on a low bluff above the beach. To one side was a large engine of some kind up on blocks, while on the other side an ancient chicken coop was bleeding an incomprehensible ooze of aircraft and truck parts from every window and door. A brutalised Dodge truck in a camouflage design of primer and rust squatted beside the chicken house and the ground directly in front of the cottage was permanently stained with engine oil. A windsock fluttered idly from the peak of the roof.

Opana turned off the engine and they all got out of the car. While Norman carried the beer and groceries to the cottage, Mickey and Devon walked to the bluff. It was less than fifteen feet high, with wooden steps leading down to a stone and packed-earth jetty stretching a hundred yards or more out into the crystal green water. At the end of the jetty was a large, rectangular floating dock topped with a little shack of some kind. Beside the shack was a petrol pump that looked as though it belonged to another age.

'Rustic,' Mickey commented, raising a sceptical eyebrow.

'It's pretty,' Devon said defensively, watching the light surf roll in, sliding along the wall of the jetty to curl up over the dark sand beach. The tide was out and the air was full of the sweet-rot perfume of wrack and trapped pools of marine life. She turned slightly to her right, shading her eyes with one hand, squinting at the northern horizon. There was nothing to see except a fine, pale haze in the distance, but from the map she had pored over in the guide book she knew that Kure Atoll was out there, eight or nine hundred miles away, a speck of coral and age-old lava hiding a secret she had travelled halfway around the world to unravel.

She shivered, even though the air was warm. It wasn't fear, loneliness, or even being homesick; it was the emptiness of it all. In her mind's eye she saw herself, no more than a speck, standing on the bluff, on a tiny island in a huge ocean, and no one in the world she loved or really trusted had the slightest idea where she was. It was as though her mother, father and every friend she had ever had were gone, vanished into thin air, except that was wrong, because she was the one who had vanished, and the only thing worse was the fact that it was even more terrible for Toby. If he was still alive. She squashed *that* thought like a bug, and shivered again.

'Cold?' Mickey asked.

'A little,' she lied. 'Let's go back to the cottage.'

They walked back to the little house and went up the creaking wooden steps to the open porch. There was an old-fashioned swing and a bench, the paint long worn off and a big green Castrol Oil thermometer nailed up beside the screen door. Both sides of the porch were in deep shade created by the jungle of poinciana and lavender queen-flower blossoms. Chang had strengthened the cavelike effect by placing huge cut-down oil drums here and there, filled with green spreading ferns. The obvious interest in plants seemed at odds with what they had heard about the man.

The interior of the cottage was equally contradictory. Stepping through the doorway Devon and Mickey found themselves in the perfect recreation of a Japanese tatami room, complete with grass mats, low benches and sliding paper screens. There was a modern kitchen to the left, fitted out with everything from a microwave to a garbage compactor, and to the right of the main room was a simple sleeping cell. The only decorations in the house were carefully placed terracotta vases of various cut flowers.

'I thought you said he was Chinese,' said Mickey to Opana as he stepped into the kitchen. 'All of this looks Japanese to me.'

Opana put the last of the beer into the fridge and stood up. 'It is,' he agreed. 'He's a Nipponophile.'

'He seems to have the money to do it right,' Mickey commented, looking around the kitchen. 'Not that you'd know from the outside.'

'Willy's always been one to hide his light under a bushel,' said Opana, finishing off a beer. 'He says it gives him an edge, and he's probably right.' Opana frowned, cocking his head slightly. 'Speak of the devil.'

Mickey listened and thought he could hear the faint sound of an aeroplane engine.

They went outside and walked down to the bluff. They could all hear the engine sounds now, but neither Mickey nor Devon could find the aircraft in the sky. The insect buzz was rapidly turning into a full-throated roar, but the source of the noise was still invisible.

'Where the hell is he?' said Mickey, feeling a little foolish as he peered up into the sky.

'There,' said Opana, pointing. 'Off to the left, coming parallel to the beach.'

'What in the name of God is that?' Mickey asked. The body of the aircraft was shaped like a streamlined pelican, heavy towards the nose. The wings seemed to be impossibly high on the fuselage and the engines appeared to be mounted backwards.

As the aircraft angled towards the jetty and its floating dock, Mickey could see that it was painted a pale whiteish-blue on the belly and the underside of the wings, the colour deepening as it climbed the fuselage until it was a rich ultramarine, swirled with lighter blue patches and strips of white.

'That,' said Opana, 'is Willy's pride and joy.'

'It looks like a duck having a spaz attack.' Devon giggled.

'It's a Piaggio 136,' Opana explained. 'They called it a Royal Gull in the US, but that particular one is Greek. Olympic Airways bought it, then sold it to Aristotle Onassis. One of his people bellied into a hardstrip landing without putting down the auxiliary wheels and it was written off. Willy was doing some stunt flying for a movie in Europe and bought it from the insurance company for peanuts. It took two years and every dime he had to put it back into shape.'

'What's with the colour scheme?' Mickey asked. As he spoke, the Piaggio touched down with a minimal splash, cutting through the light sea like a hatchet blade. Mickey didn't know much about flying, but he was pretty sure he had just witnessed a perfect landing.

'Willy calls it coast-guard blue,' said Opana, watching as the aircraft turned towards the jetty, the twin pusher-mounted engines thundering loudly. 'From above the colour looks exactly like the ocean and from below it looks exactly like the sky. Almost invisible. It took him about a month to get the fading just right.' He waved a hand. 'Come on, let's go down to the dock and help him tie up.'

They reached the end of the jetty and stepped out onto the floating dock just as the high-winged aircraft puttered up, engines dying in a final fading rattle, the triple-bladed propellers whining to an abrupt stop. A hatch opened in the rear of the fuselage a few seconds later and a hand appeared, then tossed a rope to Mickey. He looped it around a cleat on the dock and the hand vanished. A second hatch opened, this one forward, and a second line appeared. Opana cleated this one down, leaving the Piaggio safely moored. Finally the cockpit hatch was thrown back and Willy Chang came into view. Following him like a pungent, invisible fog was the sweet, strong odour of freshly cured marijuana.

Chang stepped down onto the dock, smiling at Norman Opana. The pilot was of medium height, athletically built and wearing a dark-blue jogging suit and sneakers. His hair was jet black and very long, pulled back off his forehead by a broad white headband marked with red Japanese characters, his eyes invisible behind a very expensive-looking pair of Ray-Bans. He looked like a cross between an American Indian actor on a coffee break and a kamikaze pilot.

'Hey,' said Chang, giving Opana a backslapping hug. 'Been

too long, Norman Opana, your brain is going to rot from all the big-city fumes.'

'Don't talk to me about fumes, man!' Opana laughed.

Chang looked over at Devon and Mickey. 'These your friends?' he asked.

'Pretty girl with the blonde hair is Devon Talbot. The curly-haired one with no tan is Mickey Rubinek. *Haole malahini,* but good people.'

'I hear you're into some heavy shit,' Chang said.

'Heavier by the minute,' Mickey answered.

'OK.' Chang nodded. 'Let's go up to the house and I'll make us some tea. Then we can talk about it.'

They sat cross-legged around the low table in the central room as Mickey and Devon told their story for the second time that day. The sun was sinking, its light filtering through the foliage outside and into the room, turning it into a green-gold island of tranquillity. To speak softly seemed natural, and Devon felt herself relaxing for the first time in days.

When they finished their story, Chang got up and padded across the room to one of the sliding screens. Pushing it back he revealed a deep cupboard fitted with narrow map drawers. He returned to the table with a set of charts and spread them out on the dark, laquered surface. The top one appeared to be a general map of the entire Hawaiian chain.

'It all fits.' Chang nodded, looking down at the map. 'If it wasn't for all the weird shit I've seen going down recently I would have said you were crazy . . . but it all fits.'

'What do you mean?' Norman asked.

'I've got a little place not many people know about,' Chang said. 'Out here on Pearl and Hermes Atoll. That's about eighty-five, ninety miles from Midway, say 160 miles from Kure . . . here.' He pointed out each island on the chart. In comparison to the bigger islands like Kauai and O'ahu, Pearl and Hermes was a flyspeck and Kure was almost invisible.

'Not even the helicopter tours get out as far as Pearl and Hermes,' Chang continued. 'It's more than 800 miles from here and it's got maybe seventy or eighty acres above the water. Guano and coral and not much else. I can spend a week out there and not see a single soul. At most you might see the contrails from a few jets on manoeuvres out of Midway, but that's about it.

'For the last three, maybe four months I've been seeing all sorts of action. Choppers on low-level recon, big SeaKings in navy camo but no markings, and something I swear was a Soviet Hind, one of the five-bladed jobs they used in Afghanistan. I've also seen a Brit Vulcan and a couple of Harrier jump jets, right in there with the F-16s out of Midway, and to top it all off, last week I spotted a Hercules. Now what the hell is a Herky-Jerk doing a thousand miles away from its base at Hickam? The only thing I could think of was some kind of war-game thing, but I've never heard of PacCom manoeuvres where they invited the Soviets. The other problem is that the type of aircraft I've seen need carrier support. The Vulcan might have the range if it was taking off from somewhere in India, but the Harriers and the Hinds have to be coming off carriers, so that means we've got something like the *Ark Royal* and the *Kiev* sitting out there somewhere out of sight.'

'The *Enterprise* hasn't been in Pearl for a while either,' Opana put in. 'Maybe you can add her to the list.'

'Maybe you should throw in a couple of nuclear submarines,' Mickey said with a snort. 'It sounds insane.'

'So does your little tale.' Chang shrugged. 'I'm just telling you what I've been seeing, I'm not saying I understand what it means.'

'I don't understand what any of this has to do with Kure Atoll, or Toby, or the rest of it,' Devon said.

'I'm pretty sure that your Earthlab closed environment is on Kure,' Chang offered. 'That fits too. Up until a couple of years ago there was a twenty-man coast-guard unit on Kure to operate the Loran satellite navigation system. Then all of a sudden the coast-guard unit pulls out and the whole thing is automated. The new air charts show Kure as being a restricted flying space to 40,000 feet, and if you get within fifty miles, Midway comes on the radio advising you that you're travelling in a military zone and if you go any farther they'll blow you out of the air. They mean it, too.'

'So how are you going to get us there?' Devon asked. 'You make it sound impossible.'

'I'm not sure I am going to get you there,' Chang said blandly. 'Not until I know what you're going to do when you arrive. Running up the beach with guns blazing isn't going to do anyone any good, that's for sure, so if you're planning to play Rambo, count me out.'

'We need evidence,' Mickey said slowly. 'Hard evidence we can give to newspapers. We need to find something to make people believe what we say is true.'

'What will that accomplish?' Chang asked. 'You've got a story about a bunch of kidnapped kids, and I've got a story about all sorts of strange military activity going on in the same area. It sounds nuts, but the worst thing that could happen is that we find out we're right. I've seen military hardware from the Soviet Union, the United States and the United Kingdom. If they *do* have some secret operation going on, and it *is* tied in with this Earthlab place, then we might as well slit our throats now and save them the trouble.'

'You had this all figured out before I called you,' Norman said. 'That's why you were so quick to agree on taking us to Kure.'

The pilot shrugged. 'I was halfway there,' he agreed. 'Your two *haole* friends have just filled in a few blanks.'

'So we're damned if we do and damned if we don't. Is that what you're saying?' asked Mickey.

'Something like that,' Chang answered. 'I've got the Kauai County cops on my ass everywhere on the island, and since all the out islands are part of the city and county of Honolulu, I've got HPD watching me too, not to mention the coast guard, customs and a freak named Dillaway who works for the Drug Enforcement Agency. I've been playing peek-a-boo with all of them for years now, so it's only a matter of time before they catch me.'

'What are you saying?' asked Devon.

'I'm saying that if I don't take a fall pretty soon they'll set me up for one anyway. It's inevitable. So I figure we can do this Kure thing, take some great pictures, and if we don't get shot in the process, maybe I'll be able to turn myself into some kind of local hero, get out from under.'

'Bull.' Norman laughed. 'You just want to go up against the feds and win, that's all.'

'Not all,' Chang answered with a quiet smile. 'Just some.'

'So when do we go?' Mickey asked nervously.

'Tonight,' Chang told him. 'No time like the present.'

202

THIRTY-ONE

'I'T'S tonight,' Toby said dropping into a chair, his hair still wet from his afternoon swimming period. 'Colonel Wolfe passed me the note this morning. I've already told Tony and he'll pass the word to Jake Skelly and Russell Ching.'

'Are they still pissed about not going?' Corey asked from the other side of the table. The Dick, Snatch Sanchez and Eric Lowery were still in class and the two boys were alone in the room.

'I don't know.' Toby frowned. 'We chose by lots. They lost. The colonel said four people, so that's it.' The seven boys involved had written their names on slips of paper and four had been drawn. Skelly, Ching and Dick Dubrofsky wouldn't be making the escape attempt.

'It's too bad about the Dick,' Corey said.

'He seems pretty cool about it.' Toby shrugged. 'If we make it out of here we've got a chance of blowing the whistle on this thing and getting everybody out. If we try and take out too many now we could screw up the whole thing.'

'We're putting a lot of faith in this guy Wolfe,' Corey remarked. The expression on the teenager's face was clear: Wolfe was Toby's man.

'I trust him,' Toby defended. 'As much as I trust anyone in this place. We came in together, after all.'

'He could have been a plant,' Corey suggested evenly.

'What's so special about me that I'd be chosen to have someone planted?'

'I don't know,' Corey answered wearily. 'I guess I'm getting paranoid. I still don't understand any of this shit about plague and Russians and all.'

'We don't have time to think about that now. Our first priority is getting out of here.'

'Alive. Which is something we won't be if Revik and his rat pack find out.'

'Has the Lump been snooping around?' Toby asked.

'No more than usual. He tried to sit down at the same table with me at lunch today. Offered me his fucking sponge cake. Jesus!'

'What about Eric?'

'What about him?' Corey shrugged. 'He knows we've been going through the vent system, I mean, shit, he lives in the same room with us. I just think he doesn't want to get involved in anything. Hear no evil, see no evil.'

'Do you think he knows we're planning something?'

'I'd know if I was in his place,' said Corey. 'Every time we have a meeting it's either when he's not in the room, or we go somewhere else. He's not an idiot.'

'That's the trouble with this place,' Toby said. 'Everyone's too smart, and Revik knows it. I can't help thinking he's going to be waiting for us at the top of that elevator shaft tonight.'

'Him and a dozen Russians?' Corey snorted. 'Now there's nightmare for you.'

'Wolfe's note said we're supposed to meet at the storeroom exactly an hour before curfew. I guess this Whitefather guy has something figured out.'

'I hope so,' Corey said quietly. 'Because if he doesn't, we're dead.'

The Level Six lounge was quiet except for the hum of the ventilator fans and there were only a few people in the large, softly lit room, watching taped movies, reading or writing in the small cubicles lined up against the far wall.

Beth Scott and Peter Wolfe sat across from each other in an isolated corner of the lounge, a low perspex coffee table between them. According to Beth she had been in the library for most of the day, seeing what she could discover about Whitefather's incredible discovery.

'I've got top clearance here,' she said, keeping her voice low. 'And all I could get was the basic orientation stuff for new people. Damn it, I wrote most of it!'

'What about UNMAP?' Wolfe asked.

'The same. Not much more than the kind of entry you'd find in an encyclopedia. All very positive, helping out our Third World neighbours, that kind of thing.'

'So what do you think?' asked Wolfe. She was clearly confused by the situation and just as obviously upset. Still, she was one of Hartshorn's early converts and it would take a lot to make her abandon Egypt Green.

'I don't know what to think,' she answered after a long pause. 'Mike Whitefather has been here for two years, longer than just about anyone. Maybe he's got cabin fever or something, just wants out.'

'So he comes up with a story about Russians and bubonic plague? If Hartshorn and his FORECAST program are right then the whole world is going to be turned into an overcooked marshmallow within the next few days. Cabin fever or not, do you think Mike is suicidal?'

'No,' Beth admitted, her expression anguished. 'No, he's always been pretty down-to-earth.'

'So Hartshorn is lying,' said Wolfe. 'They all are. This place has got nothing to do with surviving a nuclear war.'

'I did notice one thing while I was going through the computer files in the library.' Beth paused, frowning down at the clear-topped table in front of them. When she looked up again Peter Wolfe could see the fear in her eyes.

'What was it?' he prompted gently.

'Do you know how the library here works?'

'Vaguely. Everything is on computer, all the terminals linked with a mainframe that has everything stored.'

'There's also a whole lot of interconnected datalinks. Networks access to existing databases.'

'What are you getting at?'

'I was trying to find out if Mike Whitefather's information was accurate,' she explained. 'So I asked the computer to check around and see what it had on file about bubonic plague. I got a lot of general stuff, but I wanted more detailed information so I went deeper. The computer eventually connected me to a Dbase called BIOTOX. I tried to get into it but I guess my security clearance wasn't high enough because all I could get was a general log of the contents and any updates. The two main programmers were listed as Dr Lionel Chetwynd and Dr Max Hartshorn.

205

'Max I know; who's Chetwynd?'

'I'm not sure,' said Beth. 'He was part of the selection committee when I was hired on. I think he's some kind of statistician involved in medicine.'

'OK, forget him. What about the contents?'

'It was a list of diseases and countries. I wrote them down.' She took a small slip of paper from her coveralls and gave it to Wolfe.

Lassa fever A .... Central and
   West Africa
Ebola A .... Sudan/Zaïre
Marburg virus B .... South Africa
Argentine haemorrhagic fever .... Argentina,
   Bolivia, Chile, Columbia
Congo-Crimean haemorrhagic fever .... Pakistan/
   Central Asia/Iran
Chikungunya ['breakbone fever'] .... India,
   Thailand, Bolivia, Trinidad
Rift Valley fever A/B .... Central Africa/Ethiopia
Sindbis A .... Central Africa
West Nile encephalitis B .... Africa/Middle East/
   tropical Asia

'I thought it was strange,' Beth said, watching as Wolfe went over the list again. 'All the diseases listed seem to relate to Third World countries. Then I thought about what Mike Whitefather said – all the boxes being marked United Nations Medical Aid Programme. UNMAP only operates in countries like that.'

'Mother of God!' whispered Wolfe, staring at the list, the pieces of the puzzle suddenly falling horribly into place. 'They're going to use the health clinics!'

'I don't understand.'

'Look at the list. Every Third World country or area you could think of, every military hot spot for both East and West, and I'll bet you anything that each of those countries has an UNMAP clinic. Jesus! Of course the Russians are involved. Maybe even the Chinese!'

'What are you talking about?' Beth asked.

'All these diseases . . . the As and Bs are probably DNA-altered variants. They're going to use the UNMAP clinics to start epidemics and create plague reservoirs.' Wolfe balled his hand into a fist, crumpling the list.

Beth Scott's hand went to her throat.

'Oh God!' she whispered. 'It would work too,' she said softly. 'And it would take a long time for people to suspect.'

'The big problem for Hartshorn and the others involved would be leaks,' Wolfe said, spinning it out in his mind. 'Immigrants, people visiting relatives. There'd almost certainly be epidemics in the West too. Not as bad perhaps, but pretty catastrophic. Even a 10 per cent mortality rate would mean 30 or 40 million dead in the United States. You'd have anarchy.'

'For a while,' said Beth. 'But then you'd have places like Egypt Green to put everything back in order.'

'It's diabolical,' Wolfe whispered. He looked at Beth. She was staring blindly into space, jaw tight, shaking her head slowly from side to side as her expression hardened.

'I want to go with you,' she said coldly. 'I want to see these bastards crucified.'

Mickey Rubinek stared down into the darkness, trying to spot some sign of land in the endless ocean a hundred feet below the cockpit of the seaplane. They had been in the air four and a half hours, most of it at wavetop level. He tried to sleep in the cramped passenger compartment with Opana and Devon but the noise and vibration made it impossible. At least sitting up front he could see where they were going and Chang seemed to enjoy the company.

'How much longer?' Mickey asked.

'Ten, maybe fifteen minutes.'

'You haven't said what happens when we get to Pearl and Hermes.'

'We go for a boat ride. Make your vacation complete.'

They flew on, Chang paying close attention to the compass. After five minutes he began delicately to push the yoke forwards, dropping the nose of the aircraft and sending them into an almost imperceptible approach.

'I can see more breakers now,' Mickey said, looking down. 'No land yet, though.'

'You won't see much land even in broad daylight,' Chang told him, gripping the mated pair of throttles and drawing them back slightly. 'The atoll is about fifteen miles long but the total land area is something like sixty-five acres. Most of it is shoals, underwater. There're two islands that stand about ten, twelve feet above sea level. Southeast Island is the one we're headed for.'

'What's on it?'

'Coral and birdshit.' Chang cut back the throttles and the engine sound deepened. To Mickey it looked as though he could reach out and touch the frothing water.

'Twenty feet,' Chang said. He reached up and threw a toggle switch on the overhead console. 'Time to turn on the lights.' As he spoke, the big halogen Sungun mounted on the underside of the nose flared on, sending out a blinding cone of light. 'Instant glide path,' he said. Dead ahead Mickey could now see a huge area of broken water and dark, irregular lines of coral reef. Chang throttled back even more, bringing up the nose at the same time, and they dropped another five feet, almost sitting on top of the roiling water.

'Jesus!' whispered Mickey, goggle-eyed. 'You're not landing here?'

'Watch me,' said Chang, keeping his eyes forward and one hand on the throttle. Without warning the breaking water vanished, replaced by a sheet of calm the size of a football field. In a perfect series of fluid movements Chang tucked the throttles fully back, killing the engines, lifted the nose again and hit the flaps. The sound of the engines died, replaced by a razor hiss as the keel of the aircraft touched the water.

As the hull began to settle Chang lowered the flaps even more and both side windows were covered by arcing sheets of spray. Directly ahead now, illuminated by the Sungun, Mickey could see the starkly outlined shape of a tiny island, slightly higher at the left end than the right. From where he sat it didn't appear to be more than a few hundred feet long.

'This is it?' Mickey gaped.

'This is it.' The aircraft had slowed to a walking pace now, the barely revolving props giving them headway. Hearing a yawning groan, Mickey turned in his seat. Devon was stooped in the narrow doorway leading back to the passenger section.

'Where are we?' she asked, yawning again.

'Nowhere,' Mickey said. 'Right in the middle of nowhere.'

Devon and Mickey stood on the coral-sand beach watching

as Norman Opana and Willy Chang finished mooring the amphibian, tying her off to a pair of rings set into large concrete blocks on the shore. Without the glare of the halogen light, the island was nothing but a low hump of shadow, outlined by a phosphorescent line of water where the sea broke gently on the beach.

'What's that stink?' asked Mickey as Opana and Chang approached. 'It smells like someone dropped a couple of million gallons of cleaning fluid.'

'Like I said before –' Chang grinned in the darkness – 'birdshit. Natural ecologists, the gooney birds never crap in the water.'

'I'm freezing,' Devon said, arms wrapped around herself. Tropical island or not there was a chill breeze blowing in off the water. Mickey could feel it too.

'Follow me,' Chang said. He began heading up the beach to the high end of the island and the others fell in behind him. After 200 yards or so Mickey could see a small hill rising in front of them. Approaching it he frowned. It seemed a little too perfectly curved to be true. The hill ran almost down to the beach and then stopped abruptly, as though someone had neatly chopped off the seaward end of it.

'What's that?' he asked, pointing.

'That's the Bat Cave,' Chang told him. 'Come on.'

He led them to the beach side of the hill and rounding the corner Mickey saw that it wasn't a hill at all, but a perfectly shaped cave opening leading back towards the middle of the island. Even in the darkness Mickey could tell that there was something artificial about it; the curve was almost mathematically perfect and the walls of the cave seemed too smooth. Reaching out, he let his hand play over the surface. It was fabric of some kind. Pushing with his hand he could feel something firm and regularly shaped behind the cloth.

'This place is a phoney,' he said.

'Burlap and chicken wire mostly,' Chang agreed. 'It's braced with the support struts from an old navy Quonset hut I found on a trip to Molokai once. The top is covered with a nice layer of birdshit the gooneys add to all the time. Looks perfect from the air.' Mickey heard Chang grunting with effort and then there was a muted thump. Suddenly the stars outside the mouth of the cave were blotted out.

'What the hell was that?' Mickey asked, startled.

'Blackout canvas.' Chang's voice came out of the pitch darkness. Mickey heard movement and then a stuttering roar as some kind of small engine started up. There was a clicking sound and the cave was filled with light. Mickey stared. The cave was actually a roofed-over dock with a wooden walkway around three sides and a slipway in the middle. To the left a large canvas drop cloth covered the mouth of the bunker, dropping down into the water. Floating in the slip was one of the blackest, meanest-looking boats Mickey had ever seen.

'Holy . . .' whispered Devon, standing beside him. She turned to Chang. 'What is that?' she asked.

'It's a PT boat,' Mickey said, before Chang had time to answer. 'Right out of a World War II movie.' The boat, eighty feet long and twenty-four feet wide, filled up almost the whole slip. The brutal, spade-shaped bow stood high in the water, the small, tank-style cabin squatting broodingly amidships.

'Right in one.' Chang grinned. 'My sweetie-pie. Made by the Elco Division of the Electric Boat Company in 1942, sold to the Malaysian navy as US Navy surplus in 1947, bought by me from an unnamed source three years ago.'

'What a brute,' said Opana. 'You never told me you had a monster like this.' The taxi-driver ran an appreciative hand along the hull. 'It feels like it's made of plywood,' he said surprised.

'It is. No radar profile at all. She could do better than forty knots when she was new but by the time I got her the engines were shot to hell. I took them out and replaced them. Now she'll do almost sixty knots standing on her head. With the cannons, torp tubes and depth charges gone, she's about a ton lighter than when she was configured. She's a hot, sweet ship.'

'What do you call her?' asked Opana.

'*Willy's Girl*, what else?'

Dr Lionel Chetwynd sat in the dimly lit master control room of Earthlab 2 and watched the screens broadcasting from eleven different locations in the complex. Three other monitors, dark for the moment, were also capable of receiving any signal he punched in from the Egypt Green complex several hundred feet below. To his left, banked against one long wall of master control, was the security console, equipped with half a dozen radar scopes, IR monitors and comlinks, and manned by three Earthlab employees in standard dark-blue uniforms, wearing sidearms.

Chetwynd leaned forwards, tapped a button and watched as the monitor directly in front of him switched to the view from the main rotating camera on top of the complex. It showed nothing except for stars and the occasional glimpse of sea, but he enjoyed the view even at night; it reminded him of the splendid isolation of this place and the secret power of its anonymity.

He dropped back in his chair and pulled a battered old pipe from the pocket of his corduroy jacket. Strictly speaking smoking wasn't allowed in master control, but since he was the one who had made the rule, he could just as easily unmake it and tonight was a time for celebration, however slight.

Twenty-nine years ago he had brought his first inklings of the problem to the attention of the president's science adviser. For the first few years no one really believed in what he was doing, but then the evidence began to mount, and so did interest in Phoenix and the concept of SAPCON, selected artifical population control.

Even though the evidence was clear, few people wanted to think about it, so Chetwynd and his slowly expanding group of colleagues were quietly funded through the Phoenix Foundation and treated as 'Contingency Plan Development', an obscure and overlooked division of the Federal Emergency Measures Agency. At first Chetwynd had been annoyed at being swept under the bureaucratic carpet, but as time went on he began to see, and relish, the anonymity of their position.

No one bothered them, they were allowed to grow and expand virtually without checks from outside, and they were safely hidden from both Senate and Congressional investigation by the non-governmental status of the Phoenix Foundation. Over the years Chetwynd discovered that, contrary to established protocol, one did not have to exercise power to keep it, one only had to continue accumulating it as discreetly as possible. Chetwynd was very discreet, and you could accumulate one hell of a lot of power in thirty years.

The key to it all, of course, was believing in what you were doing, and Chetwynd's faith had never faltered. In the late fifties, almost as a hobby, he had begun taking statistics from a variety of agencies and correlating them. Even though computer technology was in its infancy then, he had enough data to reach several startling conclusions about the world around him.

The first was the easiest and most obvious. Unless population was severely controlled in India, Africa, Asia and Central and South America, there would soon be more of them than there were of us. He wasn't the only one working in the field and the whole idea of the population explosion became a briefly held political issue during the late 1960s. Then it was forgotten, put on the back burner as old news, and supposedly negated in some magical way by the Western world's lowered population growth rate.

Food was the second problem Chetwynd had identified all those years ago, even though it wasn't as obvious in the beginning, and eventually led to subtler but equally catastrophic situations. At first the Western world, long since primed as a consumer society, saw the increasing population of the world in strict business terms: more people meant more consumers, and more Third World people meant cheaper labour to produce goods.

What the West hadn't counted on was that the cost of producing enough food for everyone made the price of that food prohibitively high for the Third World countries who were supposed to be busily manufacturing cheap goods. If you can't eat, you can't labour, so the United States and a number of other Western countries began lending the Third World immense amounts of money to keep the cheap labour working. The whole structure was completely artificial and was bound to collapse eventually.

Underlying that particular problem was a steady and dangerous use of chemical agents to increase food production. Pesticides and steroids became more and more apparent within the food chain, irrevocably altering the very soil in which the food was produced. Equally problematical was the fact that the feed given to the animals slaughtered for the West's protein was more expensive than the protein produced.

It was a merry-go-round Chetwynd had seen from the beginning. Any solution to the problem of population and famine was merely an avoidance of the only real solution, and one that was as old as mankind itself.

Death, and the meeting in Switzerland where it had all begun.

In ancient and medieval times, and even into the present, massing of population in a given area always led to disease, which then led to a regulation of the population back to manageable levels. Any biologist or botanist or epidemiologist could quote you the statistics, but somehow twentieth century man refused to listen. Antibiotics and modern medical practice had destroyed dozens of those death-dealing countermeasures, which merely added to the problem.

Perfectly good diseases like plague and yellow fever had virtually been eradicated, and others like smallpox, poliomyelitis and anthrax had been defeated altogether. Even rabies and distemper had been dealt with, leading to a potentially terrifying increase in the dog and cat populations of the world, which, as a sidelight, ate better than most people in Africa or Latin America.

To Chetwynd it was the height of insanity. Those diseases had been the world's population thermostats; with the thermostats removed the furnace was running wild. Until now.

He leaned forwards again, pipe clamped between his teeth, and tapped out a series of commands on the keyboard. The modified large-screen terminal immediately began to pour information onto its amber screen. Chetwynd keyed the scroll command and watched as the list of UNMAP clinics rolled by. Three hundred and seventy-one clinics in seventy-six countries, each one dispensing medical aid to tens of thousands of potential vectors, each one capable of infecting a geometrically increasing number of new carriers.

Within weeks the plague reservoirs of medieval times would be firmly re-established. The new diseases, created at Fort Detrick in the United States, Porton Down in England, Compound 19 at the Sverdlovsk Institute of Microbiology and Virology in the USSR, and a dozen other places around the world, would soon be doing their work.

It wouldn't happen overnight, of course, and there would be sacrifices. In the West they were assuming a potential infection rate of 20 to 25 per cent with a projected total mortality count of 100 to 150 million over the next seven to ten years, most of it in Europe. In the Soviet Union and China, with stricter movement control, the relative death toll would be somewhat less, probably on the order of 35 to 40 million in the USSR and 150 to 200 million in China, most of those from areas close to plague sinks like Tibet, Afghanistan, Pakistan and Bangladesh.

The long time period involved and the resulting societal problems were the reasons for Egypt Green and its sister compounds, as well as comparable installations built in Europe, China and the USSR. Disease tended to be completely democratic in its course, so protecting a high-level cross-section of each signatory nation's gene pool was imperative, if for no other reason than to salve the guilt feelings of the powers involved.

Chetwynd frowned at the thought. The whole SAHARA Earthlab project had cost more than all the biological agents to be used and in the end would accomplish virtually nothing, yet every signatory nation to the account had insisted on construction of the facilities before the real SAPCON operation began.

At meeting after meeting, at home and abroad, he had tried to make them see the urgency of initiating the actual toxification programme as soon as possible, but no one listened. He might be the creator of a plan that would almost certainly provide a better world for future generations, but he was also a pariah among his peers – the man who had forced them to open Pandora's box and look inside. Lately he had even found himself wondering if Peltz or one of his thugs had orders to bring about his expedient demise as soon as the project was well and truly launched.

One way or the other, news of SAPCON would leak out eventually and it might be better for all concerned if there was no spokesman like himself, willing to tell the story straight and without equivocation. He was useful now, but he might later be perceived as an embarrassment. He smiled grimly; he had covered that base long ago. If Peltz or anyone else saw fit to remove him, he had enough documentation safely hidden away to implicate entire nations as well as literally hundreds of highly placed people.

He brushed the thought away; this was no time for paranoia. He turned in his chair and signalled to one of the duty officers at the security board. 'Give me general status, please.'

The senior officer punched keys on the console in front of him and a large plasma screen on the end wall of the darkened room lit up. Kure Atoll stood in the centre of the screen, marked by a glowing green square. At the edge of the board Midway blinked on and off as a red dot. 'Russians?'

'*Kiev's* on station,' the senior officer said. He touched a key and a small red dot pulsed a scale sixty miles to the north of Kure. The aircraft carrier was still at anchor. Chetwynd shook his head. The Russians should have finished up two days ago and they were still only loaded to 65 per cent.

'French?'

'*Suffren's* on station,' the officer said, referring to the French missile cruiser. 'We've got two Mirage coming in about an hour from now. They're almost done. The *Amatsukaze* radioed in earlier. She'll be on station by dawn.' Trust the Japanese to be punctual.

'If we can get the Russians out of here we'll be on schedule,' Chetwynd said. No ship involved was more than six days from a home port; from then it would take another four days to distribute the material.

Chetwynd suddenly found himself wondering if those in the vast complex beneath the Earthlab installation would ever thank him for giving them the future.

THIRTY-TWO

D R William Gateskill sat alone at the conference table in the Crisis Room hidden below the east wing of the White House and found himself wondering why the world's most important meetings always seemed to be held below ground.

The long, low-ceilinged room had changed very little since its first use during the Cuban Missile Crisis. It was still panelled in wood, still lit by hidden fluorescent tubes in the acoustic tile ceiling, and still smelled vaguely of disinfectant. The only changes were at the head of the room; instead of a thick roll of pull-down maps and a blackboard, the end wall was now filled by a liquid-crystal screen that could give the people in the room access to anything from the war-room status maps at NORAD beneath Cheyenne Mountain to ABC *Wide World of Sports*. At the moment it was blank.

A few moments later the president appeared and took his place at the opposite end of the table. He nodded wordlessly to Gateskill and the IA–2 director began his last-minute briefing.

'Good morning, Mr President.'

'Good morning, Dr Gateskill. I understand we have reached the last stage of this affair?'

'Yes, sir.' Gateskill nodded, and launched into his prepared briefing.' At this moment the various inventories of biotoxins are being distributed from our Kure Atoll base. Over the next fourteen days they will be delivered to the more than three hundred United Nations Medical Aid Programme clinics throughout the world, providing us with our primary vector. Secondary vectors are the responsibility of the individual countries concerned. In our case that means Mexico City, Rio and Bogota. Special teams from Fort Detrick are presently in place within these cities.'

216

'How soon before we begin to see the first results?' the president asked.

'For our on-site teams the results will be visible within the first twenty-one days. Publicly we estimate about three times that.'

'And here?' the president asked.

'Ninety days,' Gateskill responded crisply. 'Primarily in New York City, Los Angeles and San Francisco. Mostly through immigration and tourists returning home. We can also expect a vector through Chicago, Montreal, Toronto, Vancouver, Boston and Miami.'

'What about precautionary measures? I believe you mentioned some sort of inoculation programme at our last meeting.'

'Yes, sir,' Gateskill said. 'We initiated the programme almost two years ago, in fact. Our people leaked several stories about an upsurge in new strains of polio and the Surgeon General made a number of announcements. The idea was to get people to bring their children in for polio and diptheria boosters. It worked quite well. The boosters were augmented according to location. Miami was given a plague vaccine additive, New York plague and hepatitis B, LA and San Francisco were boosted with the vaccines we have for the various Asian biotoxins. We ran the effects through the LUXOR program and it showed a 61 per cent gain rate. That's a lot of lives saved, Mr President.'

'Not Sir James Stephenson's,' the president commented, staring down at the red-covered report on the table in front of him. Gateskill cleared his throat and continued.

'No, sir. Sir James's death came as a shock to us all.' He paused briefly and went on. 'At any rate, the Phoenix Project is now operationally underway, and my main purpose in coming here today was to reiterate my earlier suggestion that no mention should be made of our own government's involvement or the involvement of any of the Leukertal Accord signatory nations. Security at this stage is vital.'

Gateskill stood, picking up a small black device that looked like the remote-control unit for a television set. He pointed it at the large screen behind him and pressed a button. The screen lit up, depicting a huge outline map of the United States. Scores of red lights were blinking on it like small glowing wounds. The IA-2 director turned back to the president.

'Twenty-five years ago the world's leading scientists, econo-

217

mists and military strategists devised the Leukertal Accord, much of it based on work previously done by Dr Nelson Baines Chetwynd. At that time, the accord was treated as a contingency plan, with the hope that it would never have to be used. Unfortunately, time has proven that the Leukertal Accord and the Phoenix plan were the only viable alternatives to an inevitable global thermonuclear war between the superpowers.' Gateskill turned to the map and made a sweeping gesture with his arm.

'What you see here is a diagram of the fatalities resulting from Phoenix. Slightly less than seven million dead over a three-year period with a resultant drop in the loaded population rate of almost 20 per cent over the next two decades. With the exception of some minor long-term medical effects from the biotoxins and the possibility of a mutated virus or two, *no* effect on the gross national product, *no* loss of industrial capability and virtually no damage to property except for that caused by civil disobedience.'

Gateskill pointed the clicker again. The outline map remained the same, but now it was almost entirely red with only a few open spaces scattered along the central spine of the Rockies.

'On the other hand we have *this*,' the intelligence man offered. The third-day scenario for global thermonuclear war. To hell with the nightmares cobbled up by the Freeze people – this is the reality: 95 per cent kill rate, 97 per cent loss of GNP, 94 per cent loss of industrial capacity over fifty years. Hopeless. Suicide.' He tossed the remote-control unit down on the table.

'That was our choice, Mr President,' he said coldly. 'And it doesn't take a Solomon to see why we went with Phoenix. With the Egypt Green facility keeping our best minds safe and protecting the germ tissue necessary for repopulating our country with virtual genetic purity, we stand a chance of being in a better fiscal position within five years from now than in the boom years of the fifties. We'll have stable markets, cleaner air and a lot fewer mouths to feed. Mouths we never *intended* to feed. We've got a second chance here. We have to put aside whatever moral qualms we might have and think about *that* future.'

'Seven million dead?' the President murmured, staring at the scarlet-stained map on the wall.

218

'That's right, Mr President,' Gateskill said firmly. 'Seven million over three years or 230 million in seventy-two hours. A world cleansed or a world destroyed.'

'You make it seem so simple, Dr Gateskill,' the president remarked. 'Yet both worlds are hypothetical. Neither one exists.'

'Not yet,' Gateskill agreed. 'But we all know that one or the other of them will eventually. The difference here is that Phoenix gives us choice and a chance to recover.'

'The lesser of two evils?'

'Yes, sir.' Gateskill nodded. 'All I need is your approval to set the final implementation in motion.'

The president of the United States was silent for a long moment, his eyes never leaving the map glowing on the far wall. Finally, sadly, he nodded.

'All night, Dr Gateskill,' he said wearily. 'You have your approval.'

THIRTY-THREE

ERIC Lowery looked up from his book and watched as Corey Shire and Toby Hagen zipped on fresh coveralls and prepared to leave the Level Seven room. Tony Deetz and Sanchez had already started out for the storeroom rendevous, while Dick Dubrofsky, Jake Skelly and Russell Ching were watching the side corridors for the Lump or anyone else who might cause last-minute problems.

'Going somewhere?' Lowery asked. 'It's pretty close to curfew.'

'Relax, Eric,' Corey said. 'We know how to tell time.'

'So you'll be back before then?' the boy insisted.

'Of course.' There was a tone in Lowery's voice Corey didn't like – a smirking sound.

'Dubrofsky and Sanchez, they'll be back on time as well?' Lowery prodded.

'Probably. I'm not sure what they're doing.'

'Bull,' Lowery said coldly. He dropped the book onto the floor and swung his legs off the bunk, pulling himself into a sitting position. 'They won't be coming back and neither will you.'

'What makes you say that?' Toby asked, his heart pounding.

'Because I can read both of you like a book,' answered the thin, bespectacled teenager. 'You've been up to something for a long time, and this is the big moment. You've been walking around on tiptoe all afternoon and neither one of you ate anything at dinner tonight. Nerves.'

'You think you're pretty perceptive, I guess,' Corey said. He sat down at the small table in the middle of the room and stared at Lowery. He was everyone's idea of the bookish nerd, right down to the glasses, the zits and the clothes that never seemed to fit properly. The kind of kid who grew up to be a cost accountant or a civil servant.

'I think I don't get enough credit for being just as smart as the rest of you,' said Lowery, brittle anger in his voice. 'You've got your own little club and people like me are always excluded. It was the same at home. It was always the same.'

'You're full of shit, Lowery,' Corey said. He leaned across the table, staring at the boy crouched on the bunk. 'You could have been part of all this, but you always kept on the outside, you never wanted to get involved. People like you? Who are they, Eric? Are they the people who hang around on the edge of things, waiting for something to go wrong so they can say "I told you so"? Is that who you mean? The people who won't take risks?'

'You're going to try and get out, aren't you? That's right, isn't it?'

'Why do you want to know?' Corey asked angrily. 'So you can tell the Lump, or squeal to Revik?'

'No,' Lowery said flatly. 'I want to come with you.'

'What?'

'I want to come with you. And if you don't let me I *will* tell Revik. I'll stop you.'

'Shit,' said Toby, slumping onto his bunk. He looked at Corey.

'Now what do we do?'

'Tie him up and gag him?'

'Don't try it,' Lowery said, 'I'll kick and scream and have everybody on the corridor in here.'

'It's dangerous,' Toby said quietly. 'I'm pretty scared myself, Eric. Maybe you want to think again. The plan we have may not work and the way out of here could kill us. And even if it doesn't there's a good chance we're going to get caught.'

'I don't care.'

'I thought you liked it here,' Corey said.

'I hate every minute of it. I hate not knowing what's going on, I hate Revik, I hate all of it. I want to go home.'

'I know how that feels,' said Toby, his voice softening. He looked at Corey and the other boy shrugged.

'I guess we don't have much choice. Either we take him or he squeals.'

'I don't think he'd do that,' Toby said, looking at Lowery

221

thoughtfully. 'I think he wants to get out of here just as badly as we do.'

'What about Dick and the others?' asked Corey. 'It's not fair if we take Lowery and leave them behind.'

'It's too late,' answered Toby. 'We have to choose. Now.'

'All right.' Corey looked at Lowery, his eyes hard. 'You screw up or get hurt or get scared and we leave you, got that?'

'Yes.'

'Then let's go,' Corey said.

Mike Whitefather's plan was simple and straightforward. Once or twice a month he would bring all his computer files up to the documentation centre on Level Four and return with one or two dollies loaded down with blank spools. He always used one of the core elevators, travelling directly from the Level Ten aquaculture facility to Level Four, returning the way he had come. Occasionally he'd stop at the lounge on Level Six, but normally he went straight back down to Level Ten.

This time, instead of going up to Four, he would get off the elevator on Level Seven and head for the storeroom rendez-vous, dragging two of the computer dollies behind him. The dollies were made of brushed steel, four feet long and three feet high, each one with two removable shelves for the big computer tapes, and locking doors. Each dolly could be used separately, but they were also fitted with ball-socket hitches so that several could be joined together. Wolfe and Beth Scott would meet him at the storeroom, and after dumping the com-puter tapes and removing the shelves, the four boys would cram themselves into the dollies, two in each one. Then Wolfe, Beth Whitefather would haul the containers back to the core elevator and ride down to Level Ten. It seemed foolproof.

'We've got a problem,' Wolfe said, helping Whitefather pull the heavy carts through the doorway and into the storeroom. The former astronaut checked up and down the corridor. It was empty. Dubrofsky, Ching and Jake Skelly were in position to warn them if anyone got too close, but they could only stay until a few minutes before curfew. They had less than ten minutes now.

'What problem?' Whitefather asked as Wolfe closed the store-room door.

'Him,' Wolfe said, nodding towards Eric Lowery. 'A last-minute addition.

'Shit,' said Whitefather. 'I set this up for four, you know that.'

'There was no time to warn you,' Corey said. 'I'm sorry.'

'Screw sorry,' sighed the fish-breeder. 'We got room for four, not five. That's all there is to it. Somebody's going to have to stay behind.'

There was a long silence and then Toby spoke up, trying to ignore the terrible ache in his chest as he did so.

'I'll stay.'

'No,' said Wolfe, staring angrily at Lowery. 'We'll all go.'

'How?' Whitefather asked.

'Let me handle that,' Wolfe said. 'Now let's get these carts unloaded.'

It took only a few minutes to dump the tapes and remove the shelves. When they were done Beth and Wolfe helped Deetz and Corey into one dolly, Jason Sanchez and Lowery into the other.

'What about him?' Whitefather asked, looking at Toby.

'This is the story,' said Wolfe. 'The hitch broke on the dolly while you were upstairs and Beth got you one of the kids to help bring them down to Level Ten. Anyone stops us, let me do the talking.' He crouched down and spoke to the four boys who had been squeezed into the storage carts. 'Anyone sneezes, anyone makes any sound at all and we're dead meat, understand?' The boys nodded as best they could. 'Good,' said Wolfe. 'Play possum for the next fifteen minutes and we should be OK.' He eased the doors shut on the first cart and then the second. 'Toby, you push the first cart on ahead. The Chief and I will be right behind you. Anyone comes along, you just play dumb, OK?'

'OK.'

'Good.' Wolfe cracked the storage-room door and checked the corridor. Satisfied, he opened the door wide and waved Beth, Toby and Whitefather out of the room. Wolfe closed the door and fell in step with Beth, one hand on the handle of the computer dolly.

They moved through the maze of corridors as quickly as they could, Wolfe's eyes occasionally sneaking a look at the digital clocks mounted at every main intersection. As they reached the bank of core elevators it was four minutes to curfew. Wolfe took the elevator key-card from the pocket of his uniform shirt, but before he could stroke it through the slot the elevator door opened and Ivan Lumby stepped into the corridor. The squat, pumpkin-faced boy stared at Toby Hagen, his surprise quickly changing to suspicion.

'Hi, Lump.' It was the best Toby could do. The elevator doors began to slide closed and Toby quickly rolled his cart forwards jamming it into the opening. The doors slid back automatically. Lumby glanced up at the clock suspended from the ceiling and then down at Toby again.

'Three minutes to curfew, Hagen, how come you're out of your room?'

'He's here on my authority,' Beth said quickly, stepping forwards and looming over the boy

'He shouldn't be out after curfew,' the Lump insisted. 'It's against the rules. I'm supposed to report things like this.'

'Come on, kid, ease up,' Whitefather put in. 'The hitch broke on one of the carts so I needed someone to help me take this stuff down to Level Ten.

'Why doesn't *he* help you?' Lumby asked, nodding towards Wolfe.

'Because he's a fucking colonel, kid, that's why. Colonels don't push computer dollies around the complex.'

'I'll have to report him being out after curfew,' the fat boy said primly.

'It's not curfew yet,' Toby said smoothly. 'I've still got time to get back to my quarters. Then maybe you can help Mr Whitefather, how's that?'

Lumby eyed the heavy-looking cart jammed in the elevator doorway. 'I have to do my rounds,' he said finally. 'Check all the corridors on this level.' The fat boy's eyes slitted thoughtfully and he looked at Beth. 'I guess it's OK, as long as you're taking the responsibility.'

'Don't worry,' she answered calmly. 'If you have any problems I'll speak to Brigadier Revik personally.'

Lumby nodded, obviously still suspicious, and stepped aside. Toby and Beth wheeled the first dolly into the elevator, followed by Wolfe and Whitefather with the second. The doors slid shut and Toby let out a whooping breath. Wolfe ran his card through the key slot and pressed the Level Ten button. There was a deep whining sound and the elevator began to drop.

'I thought I was going to faint,' Beth said, leaning against the side wall of the elevator and closing her eyes.

'Close,' Wolfe admitted.

'It's not over,' Toby said, frowning. 'The Lump may be a fat little toad, but he's not stupid. It might take him a while, but he'll report the fact that I was out this close to curfew. He'll cover his ass.'

'OK, so we speed things up.' Wolfe turned to Whitefather. 'What about the freight elevator?'

'There's a hatch in the roof,' the Indian said. 'The only trouble is there's no panel on the inside, just a key slot. It's a robot. They've probably got the panel topside. A couple of guys get sent down, load up, then key the slot. Guys up top bring the elevator to the surface.'

'So how do we do it?' Wolfe asked.

'Only way is to get up through the hatch and wait until someone brings the elevator up.'

'Let's hope it's not too long,' Wolfe commented.

They reached the bottom and the doors slid open, revealing a broad, empty corridor. Curfew had gone into effect and the lights had been dimmed. They quickly pushed the carts to the far end of the level, finally reaching the warehouse area and the freight elevator. It too was empty. They wheeled the dollies behind a pile of crates and helped the four boys out of their cramped hiding place.

'I must have been having hallucinations,' Corey said, uncoiling himself from the dolly with Deetz. 'I could have sworn I heard the Lump.'

'You did,' Toby said, then looked over his friend's shoulder. Eric Lowery was standing apart from the others, ignored. Toby turned his attention back to Corey. 'He was going on his snoop rounds.'

'Was he suspicious?'

'Yes.'

'Shit,' Corey muttered. He stared at Lowery. 'If the Lump reports us, remember that it was your fault.'

'Leave him alone,' said Toby. 'He's just as scared as the rest of us.' He turned, Wolfe's hand suddenly on his shoulder.

'I want you to describe exactly what it was like at the top of the shaft,' the astronaut ordered. 'Quickly.'

'A blockhouse above ground level,' Toby answered, trying to remember as much as he could. 'Sort of a cage of steel beams and a platform to hold all the elevator equipment, winches and pulleys and a big set of wheels. There's a steel-pipe ladder fitted into the wall on the left, set in between the elevator guide rails. The air vent to outside is about six or seven feet above the end of the ladder.'

'Can you get to it from the steel cage or whatever it is?'

'I think so.'

'How close does the elevator come to the top?' asked Whitefather.

'Very close. Three feet maybe. All you have to do is grab one of the beams and pull yourself up onto the platform.'

'What about the vent? How is it fitted into the wall of the blockhouse?'

'I can't really remember,' Toby answered. 'Nothing special, really. Screws?'

'Any sign of an alarm system?' Wolfe asked.

'Not that I could see.'

'OK,' Wolfe said. He turned to the others. 'Anyone here got any problems with heights? When that elevator goes back down it's going to look like a pretty deep hole.' Wolfe turned to Whitefather. 'What about tools to get the vent off?'

Whitefather reached into the front pocket of his bib overalls and brought out a shiny-looking cold chisel and a small rubber mallet.

'This should do it.'

'What about the doors, you sure they'll open?'

'I jammed a little piece of plastic pipe between them at floor level,' the Indian explained. 'They look closed but you can pry them open, even if the cage isn't there.'

'Good enough,' Wolfe said. 'OK, we make for the elevator, go up through the hatch and wait. Anyone with second thoughts, say so now.'

Nobody moved.

'Do you really have the slightest idea where we're going?' Devon asked, raising her voice slightly over the steady drone of the engines. She was standing beside Chang at the helm of the former torpedo boat. There was a small companionway door just to her left, leading down to the galley and crew quarters. Opana was asleep in one of the bunks and Mickey was making coffee in the galley. There was almost no wind and the black sea was calm. *Willy's Girl* was cutting through the water at a steady forty-five knots with barely a roll or tremor.

'Sure I do.' The long-haired Hawaiian nodded. 'You don't need radar or Loran to know where you are.'

'How close can we get without being spotted?' Mickey asked.

'The boat passage is to the south, too close to the old coast-guard station. The best thing to do is drop you off in the *Zodiac* a bit to the west. There's an opening in the coral, but it's too shallow to take *Willy's Girl* through. If a storm comes up, we'll have even better cover.'

'Presumably by *Zodiac*, you mean that rubber raft tied down at the back?' said Mickey, trying to forget the comment about the storm.

'Not back, stern, and yes, that is the *Zodiac*.' Chang sighed. 'You two and Norman can take your pictures and then scuttle off, this time using the boat passage. Tides will take me around to you. Just remember, the longer you stay, the more dangerous it gets. For all I know they'll have guards posted every ten feet.'

'What about weapons?' Mickey asked.

'Forget it.' Chang shook his head firmly. 'I've got some on board, but they're more trouble than they're worth. Get caught sneaking up on a guard with an M-1 in your hands and he's likely to blow you away.'

'What if we can see some way of getting to Toby?' asked Devon. 'I mean, if there's a chance we can rescue him?'

'Nice thought, kid.' Chang laughed. 'But not likely. The best thing is to get in and get out with your pictures. With what I've seen in the last few weeks I doubt that a division of Green Berets could get your friend out.'

'If that's true, how are we going to get in at all?' Mickey asked.

'Because, my man,' Chang said, grinning, 'sometimes a mouse can slip into a hole that a big old bear can't.'

Gunnar Peltz entered master control and sat down at the console beside Chetwynd. Peltz had checked on the doctor's where-abouts before coming to master control and the duty officer had told him that Chetwynd had been there for hours, staring at the various monitors and occasionally calling up informa-tion on the big plasma screen. Peltz had already been warned that Chetwynd's behaviour was becoming steadily more erratic.

That was half the reason for Peltz's presence at the Earthlab complex. Although the doctor was supposedly his boss, the security director knew where the real power was, and it didn't lie with Lionel Chetwynd. He also knew that if the doctor's behaviour got out of hand he had carte blanche to do as he wished. Chetwynd's usefulness to the project, it appeared, was rapidly drawing to a close.

'Anything to report?' the doctor asked, not aknowledging Peltz's presence with so much as a look.

'They're en route, just as I predicted. When we found out they'd broken into the Napa house we realised they'd eventually track you to Honolulu.'

'You failed to stop them at the airport in Baltimore.'

'It wasn't our show. I had no control over that. The point is that now we've got them coming to us. They won't be a problem any more.'

'What method of transportation are they using to reach Kure?' asked Chetwynd. 'And who is supplying it to them?'

'They fell in with a man named Norman Opana, a Honolulu taxi driver. He in turn put them together with someone named Willy Chang, a small-time hood based on K'auai. He supposedly operates a charter seaplane operation for tourists and drivers, but he has a fat jacket with the FBI and HPD. They both think he's got a go-fast boat hidden somewhere in the out islands that he uses to pick up dope dropped from freighters. Presumably he'll be using that to get here – the seaplane would be too obvious.'

'This young girl and her friend appear to be quite resourceful,' Chetwynd remarked. 'You're sure you can handle this invasion from the sea?'

'I can have an F-16 bounced from Midway at the first sign of a radar squawk. It would be here in less than two minutes.'

'No.' Chetwynd looked at Peltz for the first time. 'Let them land if that's their intention. When they do, bring them to me.'

'Why? They're a nuisance. Why take any more chances?'

'Because I say so, Mr Peltz.'

'Whatever you say, doctor.' Peltz stood up and walked out of the room, trying to control his anger. He allowed himself a single, brief smile. He'd do as the good doctor ordered, but it would be the last time.

THIRTY-FOUR

T HINGS began to go wrong almost from the moment the five teenagers and three adults pulled themselves up through the elevator hatch and onto the roof of the cage. With the hatch back in place the only illumination came from the small maintenance light and even Toby felt a claustrophobic tightening sensation in his chest. The air was thick with the odour of grease and hot oil, and in the dim light the rough concrete walls around them seemed to be pressing in closer and closer. The snaking safety and high-tension cables trailed upwards into the darkness and to the left Toby could make out the bare metal rungs of the ladder as they climbed up the wall of the gloomy shaft.

'Everyone find a spot and stick to it,' Wolfe instructed, his whispering voice echoing faintly in the chimneylike enclosure. 'Keep away from the side walls and the cables.'

'I don't think I can handle this.' Deetz was crouching a few inches away from Toby. The boy's voice was cracking and Toby could almost feel the fear rolling off him.

'Just relax,' Toby said quietly. 'There's nothing to it. When we reach the top you just step off. Once we start moving it'll be over in five minutes. We'll be out, free.'

'You don't understand. It's not just heights, it's little places. Closets, locked rooms, anything. It makes me crazy.'

'You have to hang on,' said Toby. He reached out and gripped the other boy's shoulder. 'It's too late to back out now.'

As he spoke there was a grinding sound and then a thump as the doors on the cage opened automatically and closed again. The grinding was replaced by a rising whine from far above and the cables attached to the centre of the cage began to twitch and swing. The cage began to ascend, speeding up as the whining motor sound increased. Toby kept a firm grip on Deetz, listening

229

as the boy began to moan softly.

'Shut him up,' Whitefather whispered.

'He'll be OK,' Toby answered, staring upward into the darkness. He remembered how it had felt when he was on the upper platform and the cage had started down again. It had been like tightrope walking over a bottomless pit. The platform had seemed small enough when he was alone – what would it be like with eight of them on it?

'Oh, jeez!' Deetz moaned. 'I think I'm going to be sick.'

'No you're not.' Toby pushed his fingers as hard as he could into the other boy's arm. 'You're going to be fine.'

The elevator was moving at maximum speed now, the walls on every side a blur in the weak light of the lamp. Then the motor whine began to fall and the cage slowed. Toby let out a long, ragged breath and squeezed Deetz's arm.

'See, almost there,' he whispered.

'Right, sure. A few more minutes,' Deetz managed.

'As soon as the cage stops we move,' Wolfe hissed. 'Go fast, but keep it quiet. Whitefather first, then Corey, Jason, Beth, Lowery, Toby and Tony. I'll go last and help Tony up, OK?'

'I'll stay on the cage,' Toby said quickly. 'You help Tony from the platform, you're stronger.' Toby was pretty sure that he was the only thing standing between Deetz and blind panic. The cage slowed even more; they were almost at the top.

'All right,' Wolfe agreed. 'You OK?' he asked, turning to Beth.

Her face was streaked with grease and dirt but she managed a weak smile. 'Fine. Not the kind of thing graduate school prepares you for, though.'

'Sorry you came along?'

'A few things left unresolved,' she answered. She leaned over and gave him a fast, hard kiss on the mouth. 'If we're lucky maybe we'll get to them later.'

The elevator was slowing rapidly, the web of girders and the mesh-steel platform less than twenty feet above them. Wolfe stood up cautiously, motioning the others to do the same. He tensed, craning his neck and waited. A few seconds later there was a jerking thump and the elevator stopped.

'Now!' Wolfe whispered harshly.

They went up in the order he had given them, Toby standing beside Deetz, hand still on the teenager's arm, watching as the others hoisted themselves off the roof of the cage and up into the girders. Finally it was their turn and Toby guided Deetz to the centre of the cage.

'Just reach your arms up,' Toby whispered. 'Colonel Wolfe will grab your arms and I'll boost you up.'

'OK.' Deetz sounded right on the edge, his voice like taut wire.

'Keep looking up,' Toby ordered. 'And hold on tight.'

Wolfe was on the lowest girder, straddling it, Eric Lowery at his side, waiting for room to move higher. Wolfe reached down, arms outstretched.

'I'll grab your arms,' he said quietly. 'Just keep looking at me.'

Toby edged Deetz closer to the centre and the boy numbly moved his arms upwards.

'Lift up your foot,' Toby said. He bent down, cupping his hands into a stirrup, guided Deetz's foot into the pocket and looked up, waiting until he was sure that Wolfe had a firm grip.

'OK, I've got you,' the older man said calmly.

The movement came almost without warning. As Toby pushed upwards, feeling the weight coming off his hands, the elevator started up loudly and a split second later the cage began to drop. Before he could react the girders were ten feet out of Toby's reach. Tony Deetz's legs dangled over him, the boy's terrified scream ringing in his ears.

Toby acted instinctively, lunging to the left and clawing for the ladder fixed between the elevator rails. He looped one elbow over a rung and felt the roof of the cage slide out from under his feet. The elevator raced downwards and within seconds Toby found himself looking straight down into the shaft.

Swallowing the bile in his throat he forced his eyes upwards, fumbling for a foothold. On the girders, thirty feet above, Wolfe was trying to keep his grip on Deetz. The boy was hysterical, his screams echoing in the dark confines of the shaft. The only light now came from the air vent and as he began clawing his way up the ladder Toby saw the dim shape of another figure drop down beside Wolfe on the lowest girder. Another arm reached down, trying to haul Deetz upwards, but the boy had gone out of control, desperately trying to outwit gravity, thrusting his legs upward in a vain attempt to reach the girders.

231

Toby went up the rungs as fast as he could, trying to reach Deetz, but it was too late. He saw his friend reach out to the person beside Wolfe, gripping an ankle. Toby saw the foot slip on the girder and then they both fell, cartwheeling out into the shaft before they plummeted, shrieking, down into the abyss. In the instant before they vanished Toby caught a glimpse of the second figure, clutching Deetz in a final embrace. Eric Lowery.

'Oh God!' he whispered.

'Come on, Toby!' It was Wolfe, any attempts at keeping things quiet abandoned. Toby took a last look down into the shaft but there was nothing to be seen and no sound to be heard. He looked up again and began to climb, his mind numbed by the horror of what he had just witnessed. As he found the last rung of the ladder and reached out to take Wolfe's outstretched hand, the first alarm siren began to wail.

Kure Atoll is located at the intersection of 178 degrees 20 minutes west longitude and 28 degrees 25 minutes north latitude and is closer to Vladivostok than it is to Los Angeles. The atoll is composed of four small islands and a ring of submerged coral. The largest land mass is Green Island, totalling 237.4 acres, rising twenty feet above sea level and spread out in a leaf shape one and six-tenth miles long by half a mile wide.

The atoll was discovered in 1823 by a Russian sea captain named Kure who ran into it with his cargo ship, which promptly sank. Except for a succession of guano miners, feather hunters, mother-of-pearl divers and turtle rustlers, Kure was forgotten until the battle of Midway when half a dozen torpedoed Japanese sailors starved to death there.

Because it is part of the Hawaiian Islands National Wildlife Refuge, official permits are required to land on Kure and with the exception of a small coast-guard station there to service the Loran C navigation equipment, the atoll has never been permanently inhabited. The Loran station was automated in 1985 and within two weeks of its closure the single runway airstrip on Kure was officially closed even to emergency traffic and the airspace above the atoll was designated 'restricted'.

With the exception of a small group of Pentagon and Defense Intelligence Agency officials, few people knew that Kure had been used as a forward missile-tracking station for several decades before the closure with the coast-guard operation as a front. A geological team investigating the atoll in the mid-fifties, looking for appropriate nuclear test sites, had discovered that the sub-surface of Green Island was riddled with ancient lava tubes that went down more than a thousand feet into the submerged caldera of the prehistoric volcano. The geologists' reports were immediately classified and an underground listening post was created.

The listening post on Kure coincided with the introduction of Polaris missile technology in the United States and it quickly became obvious that a secret missile base within 2500 miles of both the Soviet and Chinese coastlines might prove useful. Even larger areas beneath Kure were excavated and by 1961 three dozen Polaris III launch tubes and their missiles were in place.

That much activity didn't go unnoticed by the Russian navy's large fleet of 'fishing' trawlers and during the Cuban Missile Crisis of October 1962 the not so secret base on Kure became a phantom bargaining chip. In the end the Russians pulled their SS-4s out of Mariel and the United States shut down their bases in Turkey and on Kure.

The abandoned subterranean base, empty since the sixties, was brought back to life by Lionel Chetwynd and his organisation in the mid-1980s, its cover story now the Earthlab installation. Even before Chetwynd's group began enlarging the immense volcanic cavern beneath Kure, the installation was already gigantic, with almost forty miles of corridor on a dozen levels, the entire project created with hardly anyone knowing of its existence.

'See anything?' Devon asked. She lay beside Mickey in the small rubber raft while Opana rowed them steadily towards the shore. Dawn was beginning to break, a hard silver light throwing the tiny island into silhouette. Behind them, banks of low-lying storm clouds were building in ragged ranks just as Willy Chang had predicted. Rubinek was scanning the beachline with a pair of high-powered binoculars from the PT boat.

'Looks quiet,' said Mickey, panning the glasses along the beachline. 'Some seals swimming around close to shore and a lot of birds. Seagulls, I guess.' He paused and adjusted the focus. 'To the left, some buildings. Looks like a small aircraft hangar or something.'

'How much farther to shore?' asked Opana, digging in with the oars.

'Two hundred yards,' Mickey said. 'And keep bearing to the left.'

Five minutes later they felt the crunch of coral under the thin floor of the boat and Opana gratefully put down his oars. They clambered out of the boat, Devon carrying the camera she had bought in Honolulu as well as a Nikon with a telephoto-zoom lent her by Willy Chang. He had given her four rolls of film for the Nikon and she had three cartridges for the Instamatic tucked in the breast pockets of her jean jacket; more than enough film as long as they found something to shoot.

She helped the two men drag the *Zodiac* up onto the beach, then followed them in a crouch to the crest of the low, sawgrass-covered rise that marked the upper tideline. They peeked over the rise and Devon drew in her breath.

'Unreal,' she whispered.

They had made landfall within a hundred yards of the airstrip and on its far side they could see a huge, one-storey structure at least 500 feet long, flat-roofed and windowless, its entire surface covered with a massive camouflage net that draped down to the ground in an irregular, undulating line. From the air it would be completely invisible.

'Is that the Earthlab place you were talking about?' asked Opana. 'It looks more like Hitler's bunker.'

'It sure as hell doesn't look like the model we saw,' Rubinek said. 'In fact it doesn't look like anything I've ever seen at all.' He swallowed hard.

'There's some kind of opening way off to the left,' Devon said. She had the Nikon up and was peering through the viewfinder as she snapped off three or four exposures.

'Got it,' Rubinek said, checking with the binoculars. 'A loading dock and the entrance to a big freight elevator, maybe.'

Devon panned the length of the massive concrete structure, taking several more shots, then twisted the zoom to focus on the buildings at the far end of the runway. There was a cluster of four buildings around a low control tower, all of them whitewashed with shutters over the windows. There were three vehicles in front of the tower, painted in pale camouflage like the net over the bunker and without any numbers or symbols she could see.

Standing beside them, like huge gunmetal insects, were a pair
of Huey Supercobra helicopter gunships. She took shots of
the buildings and the vehicles, then pushed the zoom further,
pointing the camera at the end of the runway.

There were four aircraft: the business jet they had seen taking
Chetwynd out of Honolulu; another, smaller business jet; and
two giant transports, one in US coast-guard colours, the other
as black as Willy Chang's boat.

'What are those?' she asked, putting down the camera.

'The big planes?' Mickey asked, peering through the binoculars. He shrugged. 'Beats me. One of them is coast guard, I
think.' He handed the glasses to Opana while Devon took more
pictures. 'You know planes, what are they?'

'C-130s. Hercules,' said the taxi driver, looking through the
binoculars. 'The white one is a coast guard air-sea rescue and
the other one looks like a Dragonship.'

'What the hell is that?' Mickey asked.

'During the Vietnam war we called them Spookies. The Viet
Cong called them Dragonships. They were equipped with about
ten different cannons that could shoot something like 6000
rounds a second. Noisy.'

'What are they doing here?'

'Beats me.'

'It doesn't matter,' Devon said. 'Except for that big concrete
thing we could be anywhere. We've got to get closer.'

'To what?' Opana asked.

'That freight elevator. It's got to go somewhere. This just isn't
good enough.'

'You're crazy,' Opana said. 'They've probably got all sorts
of alarm systems around the runway. Maybe mines, for all we
know.'

'I don't care,' Mickey said calmly, not believing himself as he
spoke. 'Devon's right. We didn't come 10,000 miles for some
snapshots of a fucking airstrip.'

'Maybe I should stick around and guard the boat,' Opana said
weakly.

'Suit yourself.' Mickey shrugged. He tapped Devon on the
shoulder and smiled, throwing her a quick salute. 'Come on,
kiddo, it's your play.' Without waiting for her response he came
up out of his crouch and sprinted for the broad, pale line of
the airstrip, arms pumping and head low. A split second later

Devon came up beside him, camera banging against her chest, then pulled ahead, aiming for the drainage ditch on the far side of the runway.

They were halfway across the concrete strip when Mickey heard the thunder. The low rumbling became a stupendous roar and he looked around frantically, trying to locate its source. It was an aeroplane, a Hercules like the black one, coming in off the sea at less than fifty feet, the unwieldy bomb-bay undercarriage dropping down as the monster gunship howled along the glidepath.

'Oh, shit!' Mickey wailed, his cry lost in the booming roar of the aircraft's four spinning props. He caught up with Devon and turned his head just in time to see the blunt black spike of the aircraft's nose race towards them, seemingly only yards away. For a terrible instant he was sure they'd be impaled on the radar antenna and then they were rolling into the shallow ditch on the far side of the runway. Mickey winced, eardrums battered by the hurricane of sound, and then his eyes were filled with dust and grit as the backwash of the passing Dragon pushed them towards the bottom of the ditch.

'Did they see us?' Devon asked, yelling over the bruising noise of the passing aircraft.

Coughing the dust out of his throat, eyes watering, Mickey lifted himself out of the ditch and looked down the runway. A brace of black parachutes had blossomed from the afterdeck of the Hercules, slowing it down as it rolled ponderously towards the tower and the other planes. Suddenly, faint but definitely audible over the fading engine sounds, came the rise and fall of a siren.

'They heard us.'

'What now?' Devon asked.

'They'll be here in a couple of minutes, no more. We go back to the boat and we'll be sitting ducks. Head for the loading dock over there and . . .'

'The loading dock,' Devon said.

Mickey nodded, then gripped her shoulders and grinned insanely. 'You're going to be the death of me, kiddo, but I've never felt this good in my entire life!'

'You're crazy.'

'You're right!' Together they raced across the packed earth. Mickey felt a deep, stabbing pain in his chest and for a moment he thought he had been shot by some hidden sniper, but the pain grew into strength as his body tapped some hidden source of adrenalin. He pulled up short, breath ragged, squinting in the light, not believing what he saw.

Beside the heavy elevator doors at the rear of the loading dock a ventilator grille had suddenly popped outwards and people were crawling out. Lots of people, Mickey stared. An American Indian with a pigtail wearing a rumpled lab coat, a woman in a grease-smeared jump suit, three kids in coveralls and a big guy with a patch over his eye wearing an absolutely filthy US Air Force uniform.

Mickey stood there, stunned. He had come within an inch of knowing the meaning of life and death, he had gone through hell and back, he had committed every crime in the book including homicide and now he had lost it. He really *was* crazy. Devon left his side and ran ahead.

'*Toby!*'

THIRTY-FIVE

T OBY, numb, exhausted and disoriented by his sudden rebirth onto the surface, stared open-mouthed as the familiar figure raced towards him, and then Devon was in his arms, her face buried in his neck, her arms tightly wrapped around him. The sudden preliminary squall engulfing the island with sheets of blinding rain drenched them both in seconds, but neither noticed. In the distance, swallowed up by the rain, the Hercules had vanished but the sound of her engines was still audible, and so was the alarm siren.

'Uh, I don't mean to be wet blanket,' said Wolfe, tapping Toby on the shoulder. 'But maybe you should introduce the young lady and tell me what the hell is going on. Fast.'

Toby stepped back, wet hair plastered down, his eyes wet with more than rain, and grinning from ear to ear. 'Colonel Wolfe, this is Devon Talbot, she's . . . Oh, shit, sir, she's . . .'

'Your basic knight in shining armour,' Mickey Rubinek offered, climbing up the ramp to the loading platform. 'The fair damsel come to rescue the lad in distress, you might say.'

'And just who are you?' Wolfe asked, blinking the rain out of his eyes, trying make sense out of what was going on.

'The fifth estate. My name is Rubinek,' Mickey answered. 'And I recognise you, colonel, which brings up a lot more questions than it answers, not that we have time for that now.'

Another, shriller siren had joined the first, underlining Rubinek's assessment of the situation. Wolfe thought he could also hear the sound of a half-track, its mufflers popping and growling.

'What are we looking at, Mr Rubinek, and where exactly are we?'

'Kure Atoll, colonel,' Mickey told him. 'We've got a high-speed boat about a thousand yards from here. They've got three tracked vehicles, some of those Blue Thunder helicopters and three big transports I believe you call Spookies, one of which just landed. There're also a couple of business jets. We're running out of time, colonel. Our friend waiting in the boat says they can call up fighters from Midway and have them here in two minutes if necessary. We've already lost one.'

'They won't be able to use the fighters, not in this weather. Nor the helicopters for that matter,' the colonel said, squinting up into the rain. 'Is this just a little blow or what?'

'Willy says it's a full-fledged storm. I saw lots of clouds in the west just before we got here.'

'Who's Willy?'

'A Chinese-Hawaiian dope smuggler and philosopher. And he won't wait out there for ever.' Mickey nodded towards the far end of the island, a quarter of a mile away. He could feel some satisfaction in bringing Devon and her boyfriend back together, but Wolfe taking command so easily was a different matter.

'He won't have to wait,' Wolfe said after a moment, staring in the opposite direction, towards the hardstand end of the runway, invisible in the driving rain and gusting wind. 'We're flying out.'

'What?'

'This is a local storm,' Wolfe explained tautly. 'We get caught out in some dope freak's speedboat and the fighters from Midway will blow us out of the water as soon as the weather clears. How far are we from some kind of civilisation?'

'About 800 miles.'

'Even at fifty knots that leaves us out in the open sea for sixteen hours. You really think the storm will last that long, or they won't be able to call up any other kind of air support?'

'So what are you going to do?' asked Mickey, even though he knew the astronaut was right. 'Steal one of those planes?'

'That's exactly what I'm going to do, Mr Rubinek. 'You can go back to your friend on the boat or come with us, but make up your mind fast.'

He turned away from Mickey and began guiding his charges across the loading platform to the lorry parked near the elevator doors. Abandoned, Mickey stood in the downpour, the cold rain chilling him. He hadn't come 10,000 miles to take snapshots; he had come all this way to be treated like a piece of shit.

239

On the other hand, Wolfe, Toby and the others were far better evidence than any number of photographs.

Willy Chang might think he was capable of outrunning a Sidewinder missile, but Mickey wasn't much for long shots. Not that Wolfe's plan was a shoo-in by any means.

'Screw it,' he muttered, making his choice. 'Hang on!' he called out, starting across the loading platform. 'I'm coming with you.'

Ivan Lumby's report to Brigadier Revik and Dr Max Hartshorn was delivered within minutes of the *Zodiac*'s breaching of the Kure perimeter radar defence. Peltz, with orders from Chetwynd to let Rubinek and Devon land on the island, merely monitored their movements after their arrival, losing them briefly during the communications flutter of the Hercules landing and then watching them vanish into the screening downpour.

Deep below the bunkerlike upper structure of the Egypt Green complex, it took Revik and his security people another three minutes to check Toby Hagen's dormitory room and an additional two minutes for the correlation of the report from the crew using the freight elevator.

By the time the two bodies were discovered, pulped on the roof of the elevator, and the alarm sounded, the squall preceding Willy Chang's storm had already hit the atoll, effectively negating most of the security systems. The strategically placed video cameras and ground-vibration sensors were drowned and blinded in a drumming roar of rain, and both infra-red and side-scanning intrusion radar systems showed nothing but a whirling pattern of electronic snow.

Beyond that the flight officer in the small control tower at the end of the island's airfield announced that his latest meteorological update on the WeatherFax showed a storm system sixty miles across and ninety deep that would take at least an hour and a half to pass. The edge of the storm had already reached Midway, sixty miles away, shutting down the field on Sand Island.

Chetwynd, sleeping in his surface quarters when the alarm sounded, stormed into master control and found Gunnar Peltz already there, dressed in a full flying suit, complete with sidearm. Peltz was standing behind his two monitoring officers, trying to decipher the garbled signals pouring into the complex.

'What the hell is going on, Peltz? Why is the general alarm siren sounding?' he demanded.

Peltz barely looked at his superior. 'Because we have a GA situation, doctor.'

'I told you to bring them to me when and if they arrived,' Chetwynd shouted. 'You've disobeyed a direct order!'

'I'm not talking about Rubinek and the girl, doctor. According to your Brigadier Revik, we have a security breach and possible exit from the lower levels.'

'That's impossible!' Chetwynd said, but he sank into the chair in front of the central computer terminal, his face suddenly ashen.

'It's not impossible,' Peltz snapped, 'It's happened. Two of the children are dead. Apparently they fell down the main shaft of the freight elevator.'

'Was there anyone else?'

'They can't find Wolfe, the new engineer you wanted brought in, and another adult. We don't know yet if there are any other children missing.'

'They can't get away,' said Chetwynd.

'You'd better hope not, doctor.' Peltz frowned, pressing the earpiece of the headset with one hand. 'Shit!' he grated. He tore the headset off and spoke to the senior officer at the security console. 'Get one of those Apaches fired up and get me a gunner. Tell the tower I'm on my way over there. If he gives you any crap about the weather, tell him I want full clearance in four minutes or I'll blow his fucking brains out.' Jaw set and eyes flashing, Peltz pushed past Chetwynd and headed for the door. The doctor's voice stopped him momentarily.

'Peltz! Stay where you are!'

'What would you like . . . sir?' said Peltz, half turning, one hand on the holstered sidearm at his waist.

'I demand to know where you are going. What's this about a helicopter?'

'Somebody's just fired up the engines on one of the C-130s out there, Dr Chetwynd, and it's not one of our people.'

'That's preposterous!' Chetwynd stormed, clambering to his feet. 'This Rubinek isn't a flyer.'

'I don't think it's Rubinek, doctor, I think it's Wolfe. And

241

I think your whole operation here is going to be down the shithole unless I stop him.'

'I insist that you remain here,' Chetwynd demanded. 'If you leave you will be deserting your post.'

The tall, cold-eyed man in the flight suit calmly drew the heavy automatic pistol out of its holster, stepped forwards and placed the end of the barrel against the exact centre of Chetwynd's forehead.

'One more word and I turn your head into porridge,' Peltz threatened quietly. 'I don't work for you any more, Dr Chetwynd; in fact, I never did. A good part of my job has been to make sure that you don't do anything stupid. You might say that the people I work for have never quite trusted your stability, and I've got absolute authority to deal with you as I see fit.'

'This is monstrous!'

'No,' said Peltz. 'It's expedient. So you just sit there and listen to the radio calls, and do exactly what my men here tell you to do. And pray, Dr Chetwynd. Pray that I get whoever's in that Hercules before they get us.' Peltz eased back the hammer of the pistol and slid it carefully into its holster. He gave the seated man a long, piercing look, then turned on his heel and left master control.

'Sit,' Wolfe commanded, pointing to the co-pilot's seat in the cockpit of the Hercules. 'I'm going to need your help.'

'Are you nuts?' Mickey cried. 'I don't know anything about flying!'

'You don't have to, just sit down, for Christ's is sake!' Wolfe turned to Beth, who was standing behind them. 'The kids all strapped down?' She nodded. 'Yes, but that back door thing is still open. I – '

'Don't worry,' Wolfe said. 'I'll deal with it. Just get back there and stay with them. You see anyone close to the ramp in the next thirty seconds, give a yell.' The astronaut eased himself around the throttle console and dropped into the left pilot's chair. He reached down beneath the seat and pulled out a holstered .45 calibre automatic pistol. 'Standard Operating Procedure' he grunted, pleased with himself. 'All I need now is a good cigar.' He began flicking switches, muttering a check-out list under his breath. Beside him, Mickey stared at the scores of dials, lights and switch panels, and then out through the eight-paned cockpit windows. The rain was coming down in full force, a grey shroud of water so dense that he could see nothing of the runway.

Their getaway had been remarkably simple; with the rain to cover their movements they had skirted the far side of the bunker in the lorry, following the wall until they reached the edge of the runway. Driving blind, two wheels on the runway and the other two in the ditch, Wolfe had followed the concrete strip until the huge, two-storey-high aircraft appeared in front of them.

Both the black-fuselaged Spookies were deadhauled on the hardpan, wheels chocked and without power, but the Hercules painted in coast-guard colours had been prepared for takeoff just before the rain began. A generator lorry was connected to her by a snaking cable that ran up into her belly and the rear loading ramp was down, lights in the cargo bay shining brightly.

There didn't seem to be anyone around so Wolfe simply drove the lorry up the ramp and into the cavernous cargo area. Once inside he had given Beth and Toby a quick course on how to loop the big wire cables around the axles of the truck and clip them to the tie-downs, then he and Mickey had headed to the cockpit.

'How many men does it take to fly this thing?' Mickey asked, watching as the lights and dials in front of him came to life.

'Four. Pilot, co-pilot, engineer and radio operator.' Wolfe turned to Mickey and grinned. 'Under the circumstances I think we'll try to get the bird off with just you and me, OK?' He reached out and flipped the engine-start buttons one after the other.

Mickey closed his eyes and kept on telling himself that Wolfe had once piloted the Space Shuttle. It didn't do any good. The Space Shuttle was not a transport plane full of kids about to take off in the middle of what seeme

'What if we run out of runway?' he asked.

'No problem,' said Wolfe, watching the dials as the engines spooled up to an earsplitting wail. 'Almost ready. Another minute. You see a button over on your side that says RATO?'

'Raytow?'

'R.A.T.O,' Wolfe said, spelling it out.

'Yeah, I've got it.' The button was large and bright red.

'Why?'

'Push it when I give you the word.'

'I don't – ' Mickey was interrupted by a harsh typewriter clatter. It sounded as if someone was pitching stones at the aeroplane.

'*DOWN!*' Wolfe roared. He reached out and grabbed Mickey's arm, pulling him to the floor. The clatter turned into a rhythmic series of splintering explosions as a stuttering burst of machine-gun fire ripped through the starboard windshield of the cockpit. Wolfe didn't hesitate. 'Hit the button!' he yelled.

'What?'

'*Hit the goddamn button!*'

Mickey did as he was told, slamming his palm on the button, keeping his head below the level of the demolished windscreen. He was completely unprepared for what followed. There was a blast-furnace roar from somewhere at the rear of the Hercules and Mickey was instantly thrown back against the lower edge of the seat, smashing his forehead hard. The transport lunged forwards like a runaway train and Wolfe hauled back on the yoke an instant later, his feet braced hard against the metal strut beneath the wheel.

Bellowing madly, engines at full power, the Hercules vaulted into the air, rolling through less than a thousand feet of runway before she was airborne. By the time Mickey had pulled himself back up into his seat, rain was sheeting into the cockpit on his right and Kure Atoll had vanished.

With his left hand Wolfe eased slightly forward on the yoke, bringing the nose down, using his right hand to depress the throttles. The roar of the engines evened out and he slumped back in his seat, letting out a long, snorting sigh of relief.

'Son of a bitch,' he whispered. 'For a minute there I didn't think we'd make it.' They were flying at less than 3000 feet and the sky ahead was a thick, roiled mass of low-lying storm cloud, solid, with no sign of the ocean below. Beside him, Rubinek was dabbing at a thin stream of blood oozing down from his scalp, wincing slightly as his fingers prodded the growing lump on his forehead.

'Tell me,' Mickey asked, keeping his voice as mild and unconcerned as someone making small talk at a cocktail party. 'Just what does R.A.T.O. stand for?'

'Rocket-assisted takeoff,' said Wolfe.

'Ah,' said Mickey, nodding. 'I thought it might be something like that.'

'The standard C-130 Hercules is capable of taking off with a roll of less than 2000 feet at full power, but RATO packs can cut that length almost in half,' Wolfe explained.

The eight canisters of solid fuel strapped to the rear of the main landing gear had each developed a thousand pounds of forward thrust within an instant of Mickey pressing the cockpit control button. This accomplished two things: it got them off the ground and into the air within twenty seconds, and it also incinerated the two-men security team which had been firing at them.

'How fast can this thing go?' Mickey asked.

'About 300 miles an hour,' Wolfe told him. 'But we won't get anything like that much speed in this kind of soup.' He looked back over his shoulder. 'Get me those charts, will you?' he asked.

Wobbling slightly, Mickey stood up in a crouch and retrieved the plastic-coated chart pack from the little table behind his seat. He handed it to Wolfe and sat down again. The storm turbulence was enough to rock the plane nastily every few seconds and Mickey swallowed hard, trying to keep down the ultimate embarrassment.

With his feet on the strut and keeping the yoke steady with his knees, Wolfe examined the maps, checking headings against the compass in front of him. 'The closest non-military field is Port Allen on Kauai.' He peered at the fuel gauges and nodded to himself. 'Full tanks; we can push her hard, say four hours, maybe less if this weather fades.'

'Then what?'

'I'm not sure. Ask me in four hours.'

Gunnar Peltz stood on the hardstand, examining the cindered stain on the concrete that marked Peter Wolfe's abrupt takeoff point. The security chief shook his head and turned away, pulling the green-visored helmet onto his head against the pummelling rain. The visibility was still less than fifty yards, but at least the wind was dropping; it was safe enough to fly.

He reached the sinister-looking helicopter, crouched like some evil dragonfly in the lee of the control tower. The gunner he had asked for was already in the lower section of the two-step cockpit and the rotors were spinning on idle.

The two Apache gunships, fully armed, had been used as escorts for the various aircraft that shuttled back and forth between their waiting motherships ranged along the International Date Line, less than a hundred miles away, but this morning one of them at least would demonstrate its true effectiveness. Peltz had flown Hueys and HH-3s into Laos for Air America back in the sixties, and he had kept up his rating over the years. Now it seemed that he'd have one last crack at combat flying.

He hoisted himself into the upper cockpit, settling down on the narrow seat. A foot below him he could see the back of the gunner's seat. He tapped the man on the shoulder, then reached up and pulled the canopy down. The gunner had already done the pre-flight, so there was nothing left to do but plug in and take off.

Peltz waggled the stick between his legs, getting the feel of it, then dropped the visor on his helmet. He plugged himself in to the pilot's helmet heads-up display console and instantly the inner surface of the visor became a grid of lines and arcane symbols. He moved his head from side to side, feeling the vibration under his feet as the Hughes chain gun in the chin of the helicopter moved.

The weapons system for the Apache was a 'look-see'; when his eyes followed a target, the gun would track. The same applied to the four Sidewinder missiles and nineteen folding-fin aerial rockets bolted to the helicopter's outriggers. The chain gun alone, powered by an electric motor, could deliver 650 rounds a minute, enough to vapourise a ten-ton lorry before the 1200-round magazine was emptied.

The Apache was also equipped with extra fuel tanks and one of the most sophisticated computer tracking systems in the world. The tanks would give her enough range to reach Kauai, Wolfe's most likely destination, and with a top speed of almost 200 knots Peltz wouldn't be more than a few minutes behind the lumbering transport. He smiled thinly behind the visor. It wasn't going to be a fair fight at all.

246

THIRTY-SIX

THE Hercules flew out of the storm pocket slightly more than an hour later, bursting out into brilliant sunshine. Peter Wolfe dropped the big transport down to a thousand feet, keeping well under both civil and military radar. Assuming that the people on Kure wouldn't simply let them fly away unhindered, he activated the entire avionics board on the aircraft, including the dual high-frequency radio, very high frequency and ultra-high frequency systems, the VHF navigation system, the DME, the radio direction finder, Tacan, and the ground-proximity warning system.

The only thing he left off was the autopilot, preferring to keep control himself since they were flying into a field with no beacons of any kind. If he gained another thousand feet the Hercules would light up radar scopes like a Christmas tree for a thousand miles in every direction, but Wolfe knew that it was more important to monitor any enemy radio traffic; there were only so many places he could be going and the people on Kure would almost certainly have them covered.

Mickey returned to the cockpit after a quick check on their passengers. The blood had dried on his forehead, and except for feeling hungry he was in reasonably good shape. He had used the tiny galley behind the cockpit to make himself and Wolfe coffee; unfortunately the built-in refrigerator had been empty except for a jar of non-dairy creamer.

'How are they?' Wolfe asked as Mickey slid back into the co-pilot's seat. Rubinek handed his companion a steaming mug and settled into his chair, looking out over the glistening ocean unreeling below them.

'Most of them are asleep,' Mickey answered, sipping his coffee and trying to ignore the draft from the windscreen

247

behind him. They had plugged the hole with a clipboard and a plastic tray from the galley, strapping the patch together with one of the tie-down wires from the hold. Even so, there were leaks and the wind whistled through with a thin, irritating shriek. 'The Indian guy, Whitefather? He's keeping a lookout in back and your lady friend is in the cargo bay with the kids. Very romantic; they let Devon and Toby have the crew bunk right behind us. The two of them are twisted together like a pretzel. Platonic as hell, mind you.'

'Toby's a good kid,' said Wolfe. 'They brought us in at the same time. Never lost his cool through the whole thing. At that age I would have been completely out of it.'

'Same with Devon,' Mickey told him. 'Kid's got no nerves at all. Made me feel like an idiot sometimes.'

There was a long silence as the two men stared out through the windscreen, trying to deal with the events of the past days.

'I had a little talk with Whitefather,' said Mickey after a while. 'He filled me in a little on the whole epidemic thing. Very scary stuff, Colonel Wolfe.'

'I'm still not sure I believe it.'

'I do,' said Mickey. 'In fact, I find it really easy to believe under the circumstances.'

'It couldn't have been done on the up and up,' Wolfe said. 'It has to be some kind of fringe group in the Pentagon or something.'

Mickey laughed bitterly. 'Bullshit, colonel. It could *only* have been done on the up and up.' He shook his head. Wolfe might have orbited the earth a few times but he was remarkably naive politically.

'Since when has it been American military or government policy to kill its own people?' Wolfe asked. 'Dr Max and his cronies down there were lunatics.'

'I think they call it acceptable losses,' Mickey said. 'You have to admit it all makes a lot of sense if you look at things in the long term. No more Third World debts, no more Middle Eastern hot spots. And the whole thing was getting as bad for the Soviets as it was for us.'

'You're talking about genocide,' Wolfe said angrily. He gestured out through the windscreen. 'This isn't Hitler's Germany, Rubinek – there's no Auschwitz in Honolulu.'

'If I remember correctly there was a Japanese internment

camp on Sand Island just outside Pearl Harbor,' the journalist answered quietly. 'And the way Whitefather described that Egypt Green place, it comes pretty close.'

'A final solution,' Wolfe muttered.

'Something like that,' Mickey nodded. 'You've got to remember who these people are, colonel. They're professional paranoids. They spend their lives in missile silos, tapping phones, or digging themselves into places like Mount Weather or Cheyenne Mountain. It drives them crazy, and it leads to things like Egypt Green.'

'OK,' Wolfe said. 'You seem to have all the answers. What do we do once we get on the ground? This man Peltz you mentioned, what about him? Not to mention blowing away a fed in the Baltimore airport. How do we play it?'

'I'm not sure,' Mickey admitted, sighing wearily.

The reappearance of Wolfe, Toby and the other children might make a little ripple, but the people behind Egypt Green had connections and assets far beyond anything he or Wolfe could muster.

Mickey frowned, staring at the distant cloudbank. Somehow he had to find some leverage, a hook big enough to stop the whole evil project dead in its tracks. He sighed again. Mickey Rubinek takes on the entire military and governmental might of the United States, Soviet Union and Europe. Jesus! Whom was he trying to kid? They were doomed, and their little joyride in the hijacked Hercules was just delaying the inevitable. Unless . . . He took another sip of the coffee, now cold, a little drifting mote of a thought floating into his memory. It was something Chang had said, back there in the night on *Willy's Girl*. Something about a mouse being able to go where a big old bear couldn't.

'We've got problems – and dead ahead and something coming up behind,' Wolfe said suddenly.

Mickey squinted out through the forward windscreen. The bank of clouds had resolved itself into a large, low-lying island, green at the base, with a whipped-cream topping of clouds. It had to be Kauai. He heard sounds of movement behind him and turned. Mike Whitefather was standing in the cockpit doorway, big hands braced on the green metal bulkhead.

'I don't mean to make a joke,' he said, his face deadly serious. 'But we've got an Apache on our ass.'

'You're sure?' Wolfe turned in his seat.

'I've been watching out for the last two hours, waiting for something like this. He came out of nowhere and now he's sitting about half a mile back, maybe two, three hundred feet under our tail.'

'What's he doing?' Wolfe asked. Behind him at the navigator's position the horn continued its plaintive bleating: the radar announcing the helicopter's presence.

'Nothing,' Whitefather said apprehensively. 'He came up like a bat out of hell and now he's just sitting there. I don't get it.'

'I think I do.' Wolfe took the headset down from the overhead hook and pulled it over his ears. Fiddling with the dials on the radio console, he listened intently, then nodded to himself.

'What is it?' asked Mickey. He didn't know much about helicopters, but the ones he had seen through the binoculars on Kure had death written all over them.

'It's a Wardair jumbo out of Vancouver,' said Wolfe. 'He was getting ready for his approach into Honolulu when we popped up on his radar. I don't think he's picking up the Apache, but he's calling Dillingham air force base asking why we're flying out of the corridor. He's pretty pissed off; says we're a navigation hazard.' The astronaut smiled grimly. 'Whoever's flying that Apache won't make any moves until we're off the Canadian's scope.'

'It's Peltz,' Mickey grated. 'I can feel the bastard.'

'How long do we have?' Whitefather asked.

'Ten minutes, maybe less. The jumbo's flying a lot faster and higher than we are,' Wolfe told him.

'What do we do?'

'Die,' Mickey muttered.

Wolfe ignored the comment. 'Go back and wake everyone up,' he ordered Whitefather. 'Get them all into the back, but clear of the freight truck. I saw a pile of tarpaulins and shipping blankets back there. Get them wrapped up as close as you can to the tail bulkhead. I may have to do some fancy flying.'

Whitefather disappeared into the rear and Mickey started to get out of his seat.

'Where are you going?' Wolfe asked.

'You said you wanted everyone in the back.'

'Strap in,' said Wolfe. 'I may need you.'

'But – '

250

'Just do it.'

'Now what?' Mickey asked when he was strapped in again.

'We're about twenty miles off the coast,' Wolfe told him. 'If we can stay in that jumbo's radar shadow for another five minutes we might have a chance.'

'You've got a plan?' Mickey asked hopefully.

'Not even a glimmer.'

K'auai is the oldest of the main Hawaiian islands, built on the foundation of a volcanic eruption which began ten million years ago 15,000 feet below the surface of the Pacific Ocean. The island, covering an area of roughly 700 square miles, is circular, made up of a single-shield volcano, Mount Waialeale, or Rippling Waters. The crater, long since dormant, is now filled by the Alakai Swamp, a treacherous sinkhole of bogs and primordial ooze almost constantly shrouded in fog and pelted by rain. The summit of the volcano is 5243 feet above sea level and is commonly referred to as the wettest place on earth with an annual rainfall of 500 inches.

The swamp below the summit, dreary though it may be, is the source of K'auai's beauty. Acting as a cistern, the Alakai feeds seven main rivers and an uncounted number of streams which race between the scores of ridges which fan out from the ancient crater, gouging out spectacular canyons and sharpening the thousands of knife-edge cliffs which make up the almost inaccessible Na Pali coast in the northwestern section of the island.

The Na Pali coast has resisted two hundred years of man's attempts to civilise it, and even now, much of the eighty-mile strip of land is impossible to get to except by boat or helicopter. Apart from a few bands of nomadic and very hardy back-to-the land types, it is also uninhabited, and for good reason.

The coast is made up of scores of razorback ridges, some as high as 3000 feet, which drop straight into the ocean, leaving only narrow lines of beach and unclimbable cliffs. Even if the cliffs could be scaled they lead to narrow, vegetation-choked valleys unmarked by any kind of trail. Ridge overlaps ridge, valley overlaps valley, and all of it leads back to the jungle depths of the Alakai.

The vegetation is so thick and transportation so difficult that the Na Pali has been ignored even by the local marijuana

251

farmers. The Hercules, piloted by Colonel Peter Wolfe and co-piloted by Mickey Rubinek, was on a compass bearing that neatly bisected the Na Pali at Honapu, the Valley of the Lost Tribe, the narrowest, nastiest, most isolated valley on the island.

Gunnar Peltz kept the Apache straight and level, the bright-white pip of the Hercules dead centre in the firing grid of his helmet. His gunnery officer in the forward seat had logged all the projected ranges and target data into the fire-control computer but there was nothing they could do until the stupid airline pilot took his lumbering 747 out of radar range.

Peltz cursed loudly, letting his hands off the control stick for a moment and flexing his fingers. The flight through the storm had been difficult, burning more fuel and taking more time than he had expected. So far he had kept radio silence, but he would have given his right arm to know how much fuel the Hercules had on board.

The Apache was already running on reserve now, so unless he took out Wolfe and the Hercules within the next few minutes he was going to have to break for Dillingham to refuel – and that might cause some problems. Peltz had no offical designation except for his standing clearance code from the Joint Chiefs. That would take a good hour to check if he was forced to detour into Dillingham and that in turn would give Wolfe enough time to get the Hercules down somewhere.

'Guns!' he barked.

'Sir?'

'How deep into the scope?'

'On the edge, sir. Two minutes maximum.'

'Good. What's the range?'

'Four miles now, sir. I can bring us in closer if you want.'

'Not yet. We turn on the power to those missiles and the jammer goes on automatically. The Hercules has DFE so he's going to know we're getting ready to fire. I don't want him doing anything hinky at the last second. Hang back.'

'Yes, sir.'

'I want Sidewinders out first, all four. Then we close and go with the rockets and the chain gun.'

'I doubt there'll be anything to shoot at by then, sir,' the gunnery officer answered blandly. 'She's a pretty big target.'

'Just don't screw up,' Peltz instructed. 'The man flying her isn't an idiot.'

'No, sir.'

Peltz glanced down at the helmeted head of the man in front of him. He didn't even know his name. Too bad, because he'd have to go when this was over.

'Give me a count on the scope when it's down to a mile. I'll monitor the radio.'

'Yes, sir.'

Peltz leaned forwards, twisting the dial on the radio slightly. The Canadian pilot was till talking to Dillingham, asking to be patched through to the coast-guard base at Pearl. He wanted to lodge a formal complaint unless the Hercules was on an actual rescue mission. Peltz made a small sound in the back of his throat. There'd be no rescues today.

'Uh, don't you think we should be turning or something?' Mickey asked, staring out at the hunched, bony spines of rock surging up out of the green glass ocean a mile or so in front of them.

'Not yet,' Wolfe said, hands gripping the yoke tightly. 'According to the charts, Port Allen is about fifty miles south of here, so all we have to do is follow the coast until we reach it . . . and I don't want that bastard behind us to know what we're doing until the last minute.'

'Can we outrun him?' asked Mickey.

'No way.'

'So what do we do?'

'Outthink him.' The cockpit suddenly filled with a shrill buzzing sound. 'Shit! He's making his move.' The buzzer came from the navigator's position and indicated that their radar was now being jammed. Wolfe knew that meant the Apache had gone into target-aquisition mode. His headset was already on and he lunged forwards, switching over to the DFE channel, waiting for the 'ping' announcing missile lock.

'There should be a box clipped onto the right-hand side of your seat,' Wolfe said quickly. 'It should have a flare gun inside. Get it out and load it, and tear that shit out of the broken window.'

Mickey didn't hesitate. He felt for the box, found it and opened it. He pulled out the fat-barrelled flare gun, snapped it open and inserted one of the shotgun-shell cartridges. There were six more in the box. He tore away the makeshift window patch, turning his head away as the cockpit suddenly filled with shrieking cold air.

'Now what?' he yelled, raising his voice over the howl.

'Fire when I tell you to!' Wolfe shouted back. 'And keep on firing. Aim the gun straight up if you can.'

'Right!'

Wolfe eased back on the throttles slightly and increased flaps, bringing the nose up a fraction as he touched the yoke lightly. He hoped the pilot of the Apache would read that as a preparation for climbing over the cliffs, now less than a thousand yards away. An instant later he caught the faint telltale sound in his headphones and the roller-coaster ride began.

'Fire!' he bellowed to Rubinek. At the cracking explosion of the flare gun Wolfe backed the throttles off by half, reversed the flaps and pushed the yoke as far forwards as he could. Starved for fuel, the engines almost failed, then caught as the nose-down attitude threw the Hercules into a heart-stopping dive and peeling turn, increasing their speed.

Ignoring the repeated explosions of the flare gun, Wolfe held the yoke down for as long as he dared, watching as the jagged cliffs twisted in front of his eyes, the windscreen filling with a gyrating image of bare rock, jungle and then ocean once again. At the last possible moment he kicked the rudder hard and slapped the throttles back to full power, straining, feet braced as he brought the yoke into his tensed stomach.

The massive aircraft stood on one immense wing, its belly almost kissing the stone of the cliff, then straightened again, less than two hundred feet above the narrow strip of beach. From far overhead Wolfe and Mickey both heard a series of crackling explosions followed by a downblast of air that almost put them onto the beach. Wolfe grunted, still fighting with the yoke, and then they were flying relatively level again, the powerful screaming of the engines deafening in the cockpit.

'Sweet Jesus!' Mickey whispered, eyes bulging. 'What in God's name was that?'

'They were heat seekers. We dropped out of his pattern so fast they went after the flares.'

'Where'd you learn how to do that?'

'I saw it in a movie once. I didn't really think it would work.'

'Great!' Mickey moaned.

'Son of a bitch!' Wolfe grated. The ping was back, a lot louder this time. 'He's got another lock!'

The astronaut knew he had almost no time to make a decision. Out of the corner of his eye he spotted a thin black slash in the rock cliff on their left, no more than a quarter of a mile away. He reacted instantly, praying that the slash was shadow and not some anomaly in the geology. Slamming the rudder heavily he dropped the nose frantically and jerked the yoke over. Once again the Hercules swept into a wing-up turn, this time to the left, sliding between the towering stone portals of the Honapu and into the dark, narrow valley beyond.

The Hercules wingspan was 132 feet, leaving barely a hundred feet on either side as they tore along the valley's jungle floor. For a moment Mickey was sure they were going to drift into the solid stone parapet at the end of their turn, but Wolfe regained control, straightening them out in a yawning slide that left them less than fifty feet above the tangled vegetation below.

'I think we did it!' Wolfe howled triumphantly. 'I think we –'

He never finished the sentence. From behind them Peltz stroked the Apache's collector smoothly, whipping the buglike machine into direct line with the tail of the Hercules, a stark white target against the blurring background of the valley floor. The duck dive and the flares had been a neat trick, and so was the pop turn into the valley, but neither would save the people in the aircraft as it clicked into the grid field on his visor. Moving the collector fractionally, he edged the image closer to the centre, and then he saw the lock-light flare. In the end, as he had known from the start, it hadn't been a fair fight at all.

'Bye-bye,' he said quietly, and then the brace of rockets fired, streaking from the weapons pods, vapour trails marking the line to the point-blank target. An instant later the rockets reached the broad tail section of the Hercules and suddenly Peltz's field of vision erupted in a solid wall of flame. He pulled the Apache up quickly to avoid any debris and at the same instant he heard the buzzing of the fuel-warning alarm in his ear.

Pushing the Apache up over the ridge he craned his neck, hoping for a last look at his quarry. He almost felt sorry for Wolfe. Another minute or so and he might have made it. But Peltz was a realist, and he knew full well that few stories in this world have happy endings.

255

THIRTY-SEVEN

A FRACTION of a second after the brace of missiles impacted, every alarm in the Hercules cockpit began to sound, horns and sirens mixing with the thunderous explosion from the rear of the aircraft. Mickey had no time to react as the yoke was jerked out of Wolfe's hands and the huge plane rolled right in a nauseating, uncontrolled turn. For an instant the windscreen filled with the mottled floor of the jungle no more than 200 feet below them and then it slid away, replaced by a solid square of bright blue sky. He could hear screams from the rear of the plane, and over everything there was the crackling roar of rising fire.

'Oh, Jesus!' he moaned, feeling his stomach.

'Shut up!' Wolfe reached with one hand to grab the yoke, using the other to slam the throttles forwards. 'Grab the wheel! Hold it steady!'

Mickey did as he was told, while Wolfe struggled with the throttles. The missiles from Peltz's Apache had taken out almost the entire tail section of the aircraft, destroying the control surfaces and incinerating Whitefather and Snatch Sanchez in the process. With the hydraulics gone, Wolfe was vainly trying to steer the crippled bird by manipulating the throttles, but it was a losing battle. The nearest airport was well out of reach and their chances of even getting above the canyon wall were almost nonexistent.

'I'm going to ditch!' yelled Wolfe, bellowing over the aircraft's raging death rattle. 'When I give you the word, pull the yoke back as hard as you can!'

Mickey nodded, eyes glued to the blurring horror of the jungle canyon floor as it rose up to meet them. He didn't have the faintest idea what Wolfe was going to do, but he knew that

256

whatever it was, it wouldn't work. The Mickey Rubinek good-luck account had long since been overdrawn.

A final horn added its screech to the avalanche of discordant sound filling the cockpit. They were at sixty feet and the 'no gear' alarm was sounding. There was no more than twenty feet of clearance on either side and directly below them was the canyon, a death trap of jutting rocks and dense, obstructing undergrowth.

'*NOW!*' Wolfe roared. Mickey jerked the yoke back into his stomach, letting out a woofing breath and squeezing his eyes tightly shut.

Then everything faded, as though a switch had been turned. The siren sounds and the raging noises of the fire seemed to recede, as though someone had stuffed cotton in his ears. Opening his eyes he watched lazily as Wolfe heaved back on the yoke, then turned his attention forwards, gazing at the thick green hell rushing up to meet them. For a brief, aching instant Mickey Rubinek realised just how perfect life could be, how much he had left undone and unresolved. Then they hit and the lights went out.

He came to ten minutes later and found himself stumbling through a swamp supported by Peter Wolfe and Corey Shire. Blinking the caked and drying blood out of his eyes he was vaguely aware of Toby Hagen and Devon squatting on a rocky outcrop a hundred feet away, fitting a makeshift splint onto Beth Scott's arm.

They reached the rock platform. He dropped down onto the ground, listening to the hammer rhythm of his heart begin to slow.

Wolfe groaned as he lowered himself gingerly. His face was spattered with a mixture of soot, swamp mud and blood, half his shirt had been torn away and one leg of his trousers was torn up beyond the knee Devon and the others were no better off and Mickey suspected that he probably looked just as bad.

He rolled over, spitting out the remains of a splintered tooth and a mouthful of dirt. A hundred yards away, back along the valley, the remains of the Hercules fumed and hissed in the light rain that had begun to fall. Staring, Mickey realised how lucky they were to be alive. The wreckage was only barely recognisable as an aircraft, pieces of twisted metal scattered like huge, scorched modern sculptures up and down the floor of the high-walled, jungle-choked canyon.

'Holy shit,' he whispered, awestruck and astounded that he had survived the crash.

'Exactly,' Wolfe agreed, pulling himself into a sitting position. 'By rights we should all be dead, not just Whitefather and Sanchez.'

'Dead?' Mickey repeated blearily, gently prodding at his forehead, trying to establish the extent of his wounds.

'They were in the tail when the missiles hit,' Corey explained. 'They didn't have a chance.'

The six survivors stared silently at the steaming, littered wreckage, watching as the metal cooled in the misty rain, each of them aware that their lives had been saved by something close to a miracle. Had they stayed in the air any longer, the flames that had engulfed the tail section would have reached the almost empty wing tanks and the vapours trapped in the massive reservoirs would have detonated with the explosive power of a bomb. As it was, Wolfe, with Mickey's help, had pulled the nose up just in time.

With the nose up, the remaining root of the tail struck the ground first, tearing the fuselage in half and taking the fire with it. The forward section and the cockpit, suddenly freed from the rest of the plane, had shot forwards and then bounded up, finally coming to rest on the soft and slightly more forgiving surface of the swamp's perimeter.

'We can't stay here much longer,' Wolfe said at last. 'We'll have to get going.'

'Get going where?' Beth said from behind them, her face still grey from the shock of her broken arm.

'I don't know.' Wolfe shrugged, turning. 'Away from here, that's all I know.'

'Why?' Corey asked.

'Peltz. The bastard in the helicopter,' Mickey grunted, standing up, using the remains of his shirtsleeve to dab the muck away from his face. 'Colonel Wolfe is right. The son of a bitch will be back. You can bet on it.'

'He was probably low on fuel, that's why he didn't follow us in to make sure of the kill,' the astronaut explained. 'The rain might slow him down a bit, but this wreckage will stand out like a homing beacon.'

'And it's not like the US Cavalry is about to come to the rescue either,' Devon put in, her arm around Toby's shoulder. She nodded towards the smoking entrails of the Hercules. 'We just trashed a few million bucks' worth of federal government aeroplane, not to mention what we did back on that island.'

'Which way do we go?' Corey asked.

'How long were we in the air from the time I turned the Herc into the valley?' Wolfe asked. 'One, two minutes?'

'More,' Mickey said. 'Closer to five.'

'Call it three,' Wolfe said. He frowned, trying to put the figures together in his head. 'We were going close to 200 miles an hour when the missiles hit. Four minutes at a steadily decreasing rate from 200. We're maybe seven or eight miles up the valley from the coast. If we head inland we're bound to hit a road eventually. The coast looked pretty barren.'

'Which island is this?' Devon asked.

'K'auai,' Wolfe answered.

'That's what I figured,' she said. 'Which means that heading for the coast is the *only* way to go.'

'Why?' Mickey asked.

'I remember from the guidebook I read on the flight. This is the place that Puff the Magic Dragon in the song came from.'

'I don't get it.' Mickey frowned.

'You know,' She grinned. 'Da-da-da, 'frolicked in the autumn mists in a land called Hanalei.'

'What are you getting at?' Wolfe asked.

'Hanalei is right in the middle of the island,' Devon explained. 'It's supposed to be the wettest place in the world or something. The point is that there's this place called the Alakai Swamp which is just about impossible to get across.' She made a sweeping gesture with her hand. 'I think the Alakai Swamp is where you crashed the plane. We're right on the edge of it.'

'OK,' Wolfe said. 'So much for the geography lesson. We'll rest here for a little while, then head west, towards the coast.'

Hours later, with the sky beginning to darken, Wolfe estimated they had made less than half the distance towards the coast and they were exhausted. The valley, never more than five or six hundred yards across, was a rotting, frustrating gauntlet of vines, muck and dense foliage so thick and tangled that it often took them an hour to travel a few hundred feet. Above them the sky was a blanket of dull grey lead, the mist and

259

rain coming so low that they were never able to see the clifftops on either side and their only guide was an intermittently visible stream that snaked along their path.

As night began to fall Wolfe knew they were in serious trouble. All of them were exhausted, plagued by a mind-boggling selection of sucking, biting and stinging insects, and starving. Worse, Beth's arm was beginning to swell alarmingly and she was developing a fever, her faltering pace slowing them even more. They were going to have to rest for the night, but he knew that the longer she went without medical attention, the worse the arm was going to become.

A few minutes later it seemed as though the undergrowth was beginning to thin out, and then, abruptly, they found themselves moving through a sea of high, spindly foliage almost as dense as the jungle they had just come through.

'What the hell is this?' he asked, turning to Mickey.

Mickey stripped some leaves off the nearest plant and rolled them between his fingers. He cupped his hands and lifted them to his face, breathing in deeply through his nose. 'Here,' he said, smiling broadly in the failing light. 'Take a whiff.'

The astronaut sniffed the handful of crushed leaves. 'Dope?'

Rubinek nodded. 'Cannabis sativa. A whole plantation of it.'

'That means there should be people around.'

'Probably,' Mickey agreed. 'The only problem is they may not be too pleased to see us coming out of their patch like this. From what I hear, your average mainstream grower is pretty antisocial.'

'We don't have any choice. Beth is sick, we have to get her help, fast.'

They continued on, Wolfe leading, pushing open a path for the others through the forest of ten- and twelve-feet-high marijuana plants, the rain and mist covering the long, deeply serrated leaves and turning them a rich, deep green.

After ten minutes of relatively easy movement they reached the end of the 'patch' and Wolfe stopped cold, the straggling group behind him finally catching up.

'Very weird,' Devon commented, looking out into the clearing in front of them.

In the last light, the half-acre clearing under the looming shadow of the canyon wall seemed like a ghostly vision from some prehistoric past. In the clearing's centre a fire smouldered, a thin line of smoke drifting up to the overhanging rock a hundred feet above. Ranged around it were half a dozen low, hutlike structures, thatch-roofed and open-sided. At the far end of the clearing, protected by the canyon wall, stood a tall, log-walled structure at least forty feet across, apparently built right into the face of the cliff. In front of the building dozens of tightly wrapped bales were piled up, neatly covered by clear plastic dropsheet.

Squinting in the dusk light, blinking the rain out of his eyes, Devon could see that there were people in the open-walled huts. Women, bare-breasted and deeply tanned, wearing roughly made short skirts; children, completely naked; and a few grown men wearing knotted loincloths. All of them had long hair, the women's done in pigtails or left straight and free, the men's hair most often tied back in ponytails or circled with headbands.

'Nineteen sixty six' Mickey whispered, turning to Wolfe. 'It's like something out of a *Life* magazine pictorial.'

'Hippies,' said Devon. 'This is some kind of commune.'

'No one move, please,' said a strange voice.

Wolfe's head snapped around and he found himself staring at a tall, perfectly muscled man with flowing grey-blonde hair that fell well past his shoulders. He was wearing a narrow cloth band that cupped his genitals and a broad leather belt fitted with a long-bladed hunting knife. He was also holding a five-and-a-half-foot compound bow, complete with wheels and pulleys, a full-length, tungsten-bladed hunting arrow nocked on its string, pulled back so far the pale feathers on the fletching were brushing against the man's right ear. From such a short range Wolfe knew the arrow would barely slow down as it sliced through him.

'Greetings,' the man with the bow said, smiling down the length of the shaft. 'Welcome to the Valley of the Lost Tribe.'

It didn't take the grey-haired bowman long to convince himself that Peter Wolfe and his bedraggled band of wanderers weren't really narcotics agents, especially since the bowman, who introduced himself as Simon, had been inspecting the marijuana patch when the Hercules crashed.

Wolfe gave the aging hippie a severely edited version of their story and Simon responded by telling them something about

261

the valley. According to him he had been a graduate student in anthropology at the University of Hawaii when he received his draft notice and, rather than go to Vietnam or exile himself to Canada, he decided, along with a group of his close friends, to establish a commune deep in the interior of K'auai. Bringing a minimum of twentieth-century goods they made their way to Kalalau Beach and headed inland.

Over the years some of the commune members had returned to straight society while others had joined the group, but Simon had remained as leader. They had their own migratory patterns, moving from the beach area to long-established camps higher up the valley, but the compound hidden under the giant, protective shelf of the overhanging cliff was their only real home.

Simon had heard of other groups like his, hiding hermitlike along the twisting valleys and trails of the Na Pali, but had never run into them. According to him, the only contact they ever had with the outside world was with the dealers who came to buy their harvest two or three times a year. Listening to his story, Mickey Rubinek was reasonably sure that Willy Chang was one of those dealers, but he kept his mouth shut. Simon seemed likable enough but ten acres of high-grade dope was serious business and knowing too much could be dangerous, especially since Simon kept his nasty-looking bow within arm's reach at all times.

Simon showed the group around the compound while two of the commune members helped Beth to a bed in the rear of the high-roofed log building. Simon told them that the main building was used by everyone as a meeting place and communal dining hall, then took them into the winding network of tunnels and caves behind it. Some of the caves were used for storing goods brought in by the dealers they traded with, while others were private sleeping accommodation for those who needed it. During the tour Mickey noticed that several offshoot tunnels had been fitted with heavy wooden doors, complete with iron hinges and modern padlocks, but once again he said nothing.

Eventually, after a tasty meal, Wolfe's group wandered off to various beds in the log house and the cave network, leaving Wolfe and Simon alone, seated on a long bench just outside the doorway of the main building. The sky had cleared, and beyond the overhanging canopy of stone they could see a narrow band

262

of stars. The two men sat silently for a long time, then Simon spoke.

'You didn't tell me everything, did you?'

'No more than you,' Wolfe answered. 'You have people to protect and so do I.'

'I can dig that,' Simon said. 'The only difference is, I can smell trouble, man, and you're it.'

'So why did you let us stay?'

'You needed a place.' The hippie shrugged. 'Your lady needed rest.'

'She needs a doctor.'

'So we get you out. We'll rig up a stretcher tomorrow and take her down to the beach. Three, maybe four hours. Easy going if you know how.'

'That doesn't get her a doctor.'

'Jungle telegraph.' Simon grinned. 'Don't worry, pilot man, we'll have her back to civilisation before tomorrow night, take my word for it.'

'I guess I'll have to.' Wolfe shrugged.

'That's right, man.' Simon stared at Wolfe, his eyes dark and cold. 'You have to trust me and I have to trust you.'

'What's that supposed to mean?'

'It means what I said before, man. You're trouble, and I don't need it. I'm not turning you away, but I'd like to know what kind of shit I'm getting into.'

'Like what?'

'Like should I be expecting heat? You told me you had a fire on that Herky Jerk you bounced. Screw that, man, you got taken with incoming, maybe some kind of air-to-air, like a Sidewinder. Somebody did you, man, I want to know who.'

'Pretty knowledgeable for a draft-dodger anthropologist,' Wolfe commented drily. The language was a dead giveaway. Somewhere along the line, Simon had been in combat, probably as a grunt in Vietnam. A deserter? Or someone who just couldn't hack it back in the world?

'Some people you tell things they want to hear,' the grey-haired man answered. 'Others you tell the truth.'

'And you want the truth from me?'

'If it concerns my people, yes.'

There was a long pause. Wolfe sighed wearily. 'His name is Peltz,' he answered finally, the words coming slowly. 'He's just

the tip of the iceberg, but he's the one you have to worry about'
'He'll be looking for us, probably not tonight, but he'll come,
and not alone.'

'What kind of firepower?'

'You name it, he can get it.'

'Shit,' said Simon.

'That's one word you could use,' Wolfe agreed.

'I can't sleep,' Devon whispered, staring up at the flickering,
candle-lit shadows on the ceiling of the tiny cave. She twisted
nervously on the thick, moss-filled burlap sack that served as a
mattress.

'Me neither,' Toby answered from his own bed a few feet
away. The cave was little more than a closet-sized alcove in
the main passage leading back into the cliff, the low, arched
doorway covered with a thin, ragged beach towel, the hard
stone floor softened by a small woven mat.

'We could all have been killed,' Devon said, her voice
starting to break. 'When the plane went down and there was
all that screaming and flames I thought we were going to die
and I thought . . .'

'Shhh,' soothed Toby. He rolled off his mattress and crossed
the floor of the cave. He crouched down beside her, one hand
gently brushing the mud-matted, shaggy bangs away from her
forehead. 'It's OK,' he whispered. 'We didn't die, we're safe.'

'Bullshit,' she sniffed, using the back of her hand to wipe
away the tears and streaking dirt from one side of her face to
the other. 'We're not safe and you know it. Your friend Wolfe
knows it, too. That bastard Peltz is going to come back looking
for us and I'm going to die in the middle of some stupid dope
farm . . . for nothing!'

'I don't know about that,' Toby answered, his hand rubbing
the soft hollow between her throat and shoulder. 'You came a
long, long way to find me, Dev; that's not nothing.'

'That feels nice,' she murmured, lifting a hand to cover
his.

'I know.' He grinned. 'It feels nice to me too.'

'What were we talking about?'

'How you came looking for me, and how that wasn't nothing.'

'No, I guess it wasn't.' She let her eyes close, soaking in the
hot, sweet ripples of sensation rising from somewhere deep in

her belly. They stayed that way for a long time and then she spoke again. 'Tobe?'

'Umm?' he answered, still stroking.

'Would it bother you if I told you I loved you? Not just best friends and I don't mean all syrupy or anything, but, oh, shit, you know.'

'Sure, I know.' He smiled. 'I love you too, kiddo.'

'Tobe?'

'What?'

'Last summer. That time we went to Cascade Park?'

'What about it?'

'We went in swimming and then we lay on the rocks to dry off, remember?'

'That was the day I found that lighter and gave it to you.'

'That's it.'

'And?'

'When we were lying there did you . . .' She let it hang.

'Absolutely.' He smiled.

'So why didn't you?'

'Chicken.'

'What about now?'

'Not chicken any more.'

'Me neither.'

He leaned down and kissed her, tasting blood and sour earth and sweat and then the cool sweet wetness of her tongue. Mouths together they pushed and tugged and slid the ragged remains of their clothes off until they lay together on their sides, arms and legs entwined, still tasting each other, making small sounds as they explored each other slowly.

'Much bigger than the last time I felt it,' she said softly, laughing lightly.

'So are these,' he answered, letting the palm of one hand brush across her breasts. She drew in a breath, astonished that his touch could feel so different from her own, and in a single motion they moved together, she falling back, he moving forwards, hips breaking the curving wave of her thighs, touching the hidden hearts, the soft pads of her fingers playing on the smooth skin of his back, then gripping hard as he pushed, filling her for ever.

Not for nothing, she thought as he began to move, not for nothing, and then she didn't think at all.

The bloated, evil-looking machine thundered ponderously up the valley in the first light of dawn, eighty-foot rotors chewing at the air as it swung its bulbous nose back and forth in steady rhythmic movements. Gunnar Peltz sat crouched in the open doorway of the Hind-24 attack helicopter borrowed from the Russian aircraft carrier *Kiev*, still waiting on station off Kure Atoll.

Using a Soviet aircraft and crew galled him deeply, but it was the only way to scout for the crash site and still maintain operational security. He shrugged off the feeling, eyes glued to the heavy, high-powered, infra-red binoculars. The interpreter back at Kure had assured him that the pilot and crew were the best, all of them veterans of Afghanistan, bloodied in dozens of firefights over terrain that made the Na Pali and Kalalau Valley look like a walk in the park. The helicopter itself was a monster and although not as manoeuvrable or as fast as the Apache, it was much more heavily weaponed. Four pods on the stub wings just behind the doors held a total of one hundred and forty-eight 57-mm rockets and four Swatter anti-tank missiles; there were four side-mounted 50-mm cannons, and the swivel nose mount carried a twin-barrelled chain gun. If that wasn't enough, in the cavernous belly of the beast, eight silent and blank-faced Spetsnaz commandos sat woodenly, waiting to clean up anything the gunners left standing.

Peltz glanced at his watch and tried to ignore the sour ulcer-taste building in his guts. Five thirty in the morning and he was playing bloodhound on a Russian assault helicopter. He grimaced, then lifted the binoculars again, scanning the shadowed floor of the canyon. Between Chetwynd and Wolfe's grandstand escape in the Hercules he was just about ready for a nervous breakdown. The call from Gateskill in Washington hadn't helped either. The IA-2 director hadn't left anything to his imagination. Check out the Hercules, kill anything that moved and report back immediately. Blow it, let Wolfe or any of his people get back to civilisation, and his head was on the block.

'*Lyeyah!*' he yelled, spotting a movement below, trying to remember the command words the interpreter had taught him. What the hell was the word for slow? Then he had it. '*Myedlyenah! Myedlyenah!*' The engine noise deepened

266

as the pilot slowed, easing slightly to the left as Peltz had directed.

If they had been flying any higher than a hundred feet he would have missed it, and even with the electronically enhanced vision of the infra-red binoculars the cluster of huts under the overhanging canopy of the cliff had almost escaped him. He squinted, panning left and right. At first he thought the settlement was abandoned, but then he saw movement. A human figure showing up like a bright red mannikin in the eyepiece, was walking slowly forwards, out from beneath the protective shelf of rock.

'Neeskayah!' he demanded, and on command the pilot began to bring the heavy vehicle down, searching for a landing spot. Peltz kept his eyes to the lens and then looked up. He was close enough not to need the binoculars any more. 'I'll be a son of a bitch,' he whispered. It was Wolfe, filthy clothes torn, waving a white flag. 'He wants to give himself up.' He turned briefly, craning his neck to look up into the pilot's cabin. Making a flat hand gesture for the pilot to land, he turned again and crooked a finger at the closest Spetsnaz.

'Dietee menyah,' he ordered.

'Shtoh?' the man queried, frowning.

'The gun, idiot, the gun!' Peltz snapped, pointing at the man's Tokarev sniper's rifle. Fuming, he reached out, grabbed the weapon from the startled commando and braced himself in the doorway of the helicopter. Before it had fully landed, he shot the bolt of the rifle home, cocked it, and dropped down onto the ground, ducking under the dropping blades of the main rotor, then striding towards Wolfe's motionless figure.

'Colonel Wolfe, I presume?' Peltz asked, grinning as he approached the waiting man.

'Mr Peltz.' Wolfe nodded.

'I'm impressed.' Peltz smiled. 'You know my name.'

'Mickey and Devon told me all about you.'

'They made it, too?' Peltz raised his eyebrows. 'Now I'm really impressed, colonel. You must be one hell of a flier.'

'Good enough.'

'Where are they?'

'In there.' Wolfe pointed his stick-and-rag truce flag in the direction of the log building.

'I'm surprised you gave up so easily,' said Peltz, gesturing at the flag with the barrel of the Tokarev. 'I thought you were going to give me some sport.'

'I'm not giving up,' Wolfe murmured quietly, allowing himself a a brief, tight-lipped smile. 'You are.'

'Did I miss something?' Peltz laughed. 'I've got a Russian chopper armed with enough ordnance to start a small war and eight very uptight Afghanistan vets who want to get this over with so they can go home for a nice bowl of borscht and a shot of vodka.'

'You missed quite a bit, as a matter of fact,' Wolfe said easily. 'There's a slightly whacked-out drug and arms smuggler named Willy Chang we whistled up on the big short-wave they've got here. He's hiding in the second hut from the left with another guy named Opana. They've got one of those fire-and-forget one-man rocket launchers armed with a HEAT round. That's for the chopper and your hungry vets. Your old friend Mickey is standing in the shadows there by the door of the log building and he's got an RPG anti-tank gun they spent an hour showing him how to use. That's for you, or maybe the chopper if his aim is off.' The astronaut turned, pointing over his shoulder towards the densely planted patch of marijuana. 'And just for the hell of it we've got Simon the long-haired hippie freak and a few of his friends over there in the tall grass. He tells me they're all pretty good shots with the bows they use.'

'Nice.' Peltz nodded. 'Silly, but nice.' He shook his head. 'And how do we get these mythical merry men of yours to come out and play?'

'Either you surrender to me here and now and send your Russians back where they came from, or I drop the flag. The flag drops and so do you.'

'Bullshit,' Peltz snorted. 'This is a bluff, colonel.'

'Then call it.' Wolfe shrugged. 'But don't say I didn't warn you.'

Peltz lifted the Tokarev, resting the butt on his hip, the barrel pointing up towards Wolfe's chest.

'Locked and loaded, colonel, drop the flag or I'll blow your fucking lungs out through your spine.'

'Suit yourself, Mr Peltz.' And he dropped the flag.

Two hours earlier Mickey Rubinek had been dragged out of the first decent sleep he had had in days to find himself staring into the grinning face of Norman Opana. Five minutes later, the Hawaiian had shoved the five-foot tube of an RPG into his arms and launched into a lecture on how to use it. While Opana droned on about muzzle velocities, Mickey had been vaguely aware that the members of the commune were quietly packing up a few belongings and slipping away into the darkness.

The flurry of activity had all been leading up to the moment. Peter Wolfe dropped the flag in the middle of the clearing, but the only thing Mickey remembered with any clarity was Willy Chang, pure white scarf around his head as he moved people into position, armed like some oriental Rambo, faint starlight glinting on the crossed bandoliers of machine-gun ammunition looped over his bare chest, twin short swords in his belt and the rocket launcher in its canvas sling on his back. He was probably stoned, undoubtedly crazy, and Mickey couldn't think of anyone else he'd rather have on his side as dawn began to break.

From his vantage point in the shadowed doorway the events following the flag's fluttering descent seemed like some terrible parody of the Fourth of July. Even before the scrap of cloth touched the ground, Simon and the other communards let fly. They had all clearly been aiming at the same target as five yard-long arrows sprouted dead centre in Peltz's chest. Magically, the man seemed unharmed, and Mickey knew instantly that he was wearing some kind of protective body armour beneath his camouflage fatigues.

There was a snapping sound as Peltz fired the Tokarev from the hip, but Wolfe had already dropped to the ground, rolling left out of the line of fire. Mickey didn't hesitate. Pulling the RPG higher on his shoulder and squinting through the slotted sight, he squeezed the trigger of the device, screaming as the round ignited, almost rupturing his eardrums. The anti-tank round shot across the open space, flight line marked by a sheeting trail of flame, and then it struck, tearing out most of Peltz's left side and flinging him back a dozen feet before the high explosive charge erupted in a tight white ball of fire. A split second later the HEAT round from Willy Chang's rocket launcher took out the waiting Hind, the thunderous explosion lifting the sixty-ton machine a dozen feet into the air before it blew apart, flinging shrapnel in all directions like a thousand madly spinning Catherine wheels and Roman candles.

Mickey yelled again and dropped the RPG as something

soft and hot from the helicopter slapped against his cheek and then he ducked out of the way as more bits and pieces began to fall, hot coals of fused metal, flesh and plastic hissing on the wet ground of the clearing. After a few seconds the deadly rain stopped falling and Mickey stood again. There were fires everywhere and the lightening air was filled with the foul stench of hot metal, burning plastic and aviation fuel, but Mickey ignored it all and ran out into the clearing, skirting small tongues of smouldering wreckage as he headed for Wolfe. Willy Chang beat him to it, eyes glittering wildly in the light from the crackling flames.

'You OK?' the Chinese man asked, helping Wolfe up. The astronaut nodded, wincing as he got to his feet. There was a dark stain on his right shoulder.

'I guess I didn't hit the deck fast enough.' Wolfe grimaced. 'I think he nicked me.'

Chang leaned forwards, fingers delicately pulling open the gaping shirt. 'Just a flesh wound,' he said. 'Make a nice scar.'

'I guess we did it,' Wolfe mused, looking around at the carnage surrounding them. The wounded man smiled, extending his good hand to Mickey. 'Deadeye Dick.'

As the others slowly came forwards into the clearing, Willy Chang frowned, the rage in his eyes shifting as he surveyed the battleground.

'Sometimes you have to make a stand,' he said philosophically. 'I guess this was it.'

'I'm not so sure of that,' Mickey said tightly. 'This was just a skirmish. The final battle is still to come.'

THIRTY-EIGHT

'THIS is amazing!' Devon said peering through the view-finder of the Minicam from the eleventh-floor suite in the Hotel Washington. 'If it wasn't for those hedges you could see right into the White House sunroom.'

'Blame that on Nancy Reagan,' Mickey said, seated at the table in the middle of the room with Wolfe and Toby. 'The hotel was offering weekend "view" packages. You'd get a room that lined up with the White House like this one and you could spend the whole day spying on Ron and the family. She found out and had all the greenery planted.'

Wolfe laughed. Mickey watched as Toby got up from the table and joined Devon by the window. He put his arm around her and she leaned right into him, her own arm snaking possessively around his waist.

Mickey grinned, pleased with himself. They had been in Washington for three days now, getting things ready, and Devon had been sharing the other bedroom with Toby. It was fun watching the two of them together, and playing Cupid was a whole new role for him. Wolfe had agreed right from the beginning: both the teenagers had been through too much not to be called adults now. They'd be back home soon enough anyway, so why shouldn't they have some fun before the parental boom was lowered and they went back to being high-school kids?

Mickey glanced down at the table and the open suitcase he had carried away from the wreckage of the Hercules. On the other hand, if they didn't work fast, Devon and Toby might never have the chance to be high-school kids again.

'You really think this is going to work?' Wolfe asked, following the journalist's glance. The open suitcase was fitted with a foam pad with holes cut out for sixteen plastic and glass

271

containers the size of a small Thermos bottle. Eight of the holes were empty.

'Yeah' Mickey nodded, sighing. 'I think so.'

He gingerly removed one of the canisters and rested it on the table. Then he gently closed the suitcase and put it on the floor. 'According to the reading I did yesterday at the Library of Congress, there's probably enough bubonic-plague virus in this canister to wipe out all of Washington DC overnight. Beth and Corey Shire have the other canisters in New York, and even we don't know where they are. If we're not here to take their call and give them the right response, they release their eight bottles from one end of US to the other.'

'You're threatening the entire government,' said Wolfe.

'Right. We can't do this half-assed. Either they release every kid in Egypt Green or we let the bugs go. That's a whole hell of a lot worse than going to the *New York Times*.'

'The story will get out eventually,' Wolfe said. 'They must know that, plague or no plague.'

'Sure' Mickey nodded. 'But at least we'll leave them some kind of control. And it gives them time too. They can pull back all their germs from the UNMAP clinics. And you can bet your ass everyone else will pull out as soon as the US does; none of the other countries wants to be left holding the bag.'

'I guess you're right,' Wolfe said wearily. 'We don't have much choice, really. I can't see any other way out of this.' He glanced at his watch. 'It's two thirty. When do we go?'

'Now'. Mickey stood up and eased the plastic bottle into the pocket of his jacket. It barely made a bulge. 'The tickets I picked up are for the three o'clock tour and there's usually a bit of a lineup.' He turned to Devon and Toby. 'We'll call you in an hour, one way or the other. If you don't hear from us by then, take the suitcase and get out of Washington as fast as you can. Beth will call at the number I gave you.'

'No sweat,' Toby assured him. 'We'll be fine.'

A few minutes later Wolfe and Mickey got into a cab.

'Where to?' asked the driver.

'1600 Pennsylvania Avenue,' Wolfe said.

The driver gave a long-suffering sigh. 'You mean the White House, right?'

'Right,' Mickey said. 'The place where the president of the United States lives. He's expecting us.'

272

Author's Note

THERE are probably a number of you who, after reading *Egypt Green*, are sceptical about the possibility of such a scenario actually happening. If that is the case then be sceptical at your own risk. There really was a study made of the brightest university students in America during the 1960s and the study has been updated, using government resources, right until the present. The Mount Weather installation described in the book exists in exactly the geographic spot in which I have placed it. Kure Atoll also exists in the location named in the book and cannot be visited without prior permission.

Although the government of the United States was signatory to the Geneva Accord banning the use and production of chemical and biological warfare agents, a stockpile of such agents existing at the time amounted to approximately 30,000 tons. Because of the way in which the protocol is worded, the agents could not be stockpiled within the continental United States. Instead, following the letter, if not the spirit, of the protocol, the agents were removed and are now stored on a remote Pacific atoll, Johnston Island. The toxic death rate for the stockpile can be computed at 30,000 multiplied by 3 billion, or roughly 90 trillion units.

The United States is certainly not the only country stockpiling such weapons. France, Germany, Canada, Italy and the Soviet Union continue to create and store the agents for possible use. Both the United States and the Soviet Union have distinct military units for the use of chemical and biological warfare material, and both countries have covertly tested their vectoring systems on their own populations at one time or another. Various Western and Soviet governments are also experimenting with a wide variety of anti-animal and anticrop agents, and there has been considerable interest in a recombinant DNA version of *Shigella dysenteriae,* a bacterial agent 300 times more toxic than dioxin, which was the active ingredient in Agent Orange, and 1.5 million times as toxic as Tabun, the gas used in the Nazi death camps.